WOLF'S CUT

BOOK FIVE OF THE NICK LUPO SERIES

W.D. GAGLIANI

Praise for *Wolf's Cut* and the Nick Lupo series

Dedication

As always, I'd like to dedicate this book to my Mom and Janis, and in memory of my Dad. In memory also of a little dog who had the heart of a Wolf, our Toby (2003-2012).

Acknowledgments

As always some thanks are in order, for no novel is ever written by one person alone. Therefore, great thanks to: co-conspirator and collaborator David Benton (the Alpha of Beta readers), Tony D'Amato of The Gun Store (Las Vegas), all my friends and colleagues (you know who you are), and Don D'Auria (whose patience is legendary). Also the hard-working crew of the Oak Creek Starbucks at 8880 South Howell.

I'd like to again acknowledge the stories my grandmother and parents told me of their childhood in Italy 1943-44, under German occupation and Allied bombing and the aftermath of the war. Some of those stories, experiences, and locations have made their way into this novel, as well as the previous one, *Wolf's Edge*.

This time around I would also like to acknowledge the work of composer Jerry Goldsmith for all his inspirational soundtrack music: *The Wind and the Lion*, *The Omen*, *Masada*, *QBVII*, and many more, but most especially for the musical scores of *Our Man Flint* and *In Like Flint*. It would be an understatement to say I listened to the *Flint* scores "a lot." I had them on Repeat. I've loved them since I was a teenager and now they often spur my writing sessions at least as much as my progressive rock stalwarts.

So many of our fellow writers have passed on recently...their untimely departures have left us poorer, sadder, and much emptier. Among them: Dr. Tom Bontly, Michael Louis Calvillo, David B. Silva, James Herbert, Rick Hautala, Richard Matheson, Gary Brandner, Philip Nutman... We will all miss them more than words can say.

One last thing: Please join Defenders of Wildlife... Because in reality true evil always originates with humans, not wolves.

Author's Note

The real Eagle River is located in Vilas County of northern Wisconsin. The real Milwaukee is located in the far southeast corner of the state on the shores of the great Lake Michigan. As always, I have altered these places as needed (geographically, socially, and with regard to local city and police department organization) in order to suit my purposes. All characters in these alternate versions of Eagle River and Milwaukee are either fictional or used fictitiously and in no way resemble their real-world counterparts. However, some things will always be true. If you drive up into the North Woods from Milwaukee, especially after dusk, you might notice lean shadows keeping pace with you just outside your view inside the tree line. And later, if you look up you might see the moon's silvery sheen filtering through the swaying treetops. Don't roll down your windows—and never, ever stop the car on a dark, lonely road…

Prologue

Rabbioso

Las Vegas

He chuckled as he drove out to the desert, straight out of town on the 15 and heading toward faraway Los Angeles, enjoying the way the city lights and the traffic thinned the farther he went from the Strip. Of course he wasn't going all the way to Los Angeles.

Soon he was leaving headlights behind and his eyes were no longer being stabbed by oncoming high beams.

This was where he realized how much he had come to love the desert, with its temperature swings of hot, dry days and cold nights. With its unusual flora and fauna that reminded him of how he was different, the desert seemed to have become the best decision he had ever made. He'd had good reason to make it, and his finances had vastly improved, too.

He'd thought about retiring when the leadership changed, sure, but the fact was that he liked his work and he wasn't sure he wanted to give it up yet. He'd been almost free to call his own assignments before, and whenever he took an assignment he'd mostly set his own hours. His schedule was so much his own that, except for the recent occasional problems of fealty and respect, he might as well have been retired. He sensed he'd have to revisit the idea soon, but not yet.

Driving in silence with only the occasional interruption, he nevertheless hummed a tune in his head he hadn't been able to chase away all day. He'd heard it in the back room at Paolo's, where they had discussed things with the idiot who had figured on holding out a portion of his week's take for the last five years. They always cranked the music way up back there while one of Paolo's specialists fired up the torch. Today it was just a length of rubber tubing, no torch necessary, and the guy had cracked after just a couple nicely delivered blows to the side of the head and one to the stomach. First he'd puked up his guts, then he had spilled them. They'd found a bagful of money inside a self-storage locker on Tropicana.

Joe Rabbioso flew, piloting the Lincoln another few miles into the desert, the song all the while stuck on infinite repeat in his head. "Start spreadin' the news…" He had developed a love of the Rat Pack's fifties and sixties output while out here. He could have played most of it from his iPod, but there were times it was just too nice to ruin a perfectly good silence with music, and now he wished he wasn't hearing the replay in his head. The occasional *thump* also broke his concentration…

He reached his usual turnoff and slowed, noting the lack of other lights in front of and behind him. The Lincoln turned smoothly onto the rutted track and he followed the rock markers that seemed randomly placed but weren't, until he reached the place.

There was another *thump* from the car's rear, a lot more audible now that the motor was ticking down.

Rabbioso smiled at the vast silence of the desert around him. He left the window powered down and inhaled the sweet smell of the night desert. His nose twitched. There really was nothing better.

He got out and stretched, cracking his spine with satisfaction. Then he stripped, first unbuttoning the baby-blue silk shirt and placing it on the driver's seat. He followed it with the vintage .45 Colt he always carried in the small of his back. Then he shucked off his jeans and his shoes (no socks), laying them all neatly on the seat. Naked now, his skin tingling in the night breeze, he plucked a sharp folder, thumbed it open, and went to the trunk. He reached it just as yet another *thump* echoed through the night air.

He opened it and grinned down at the figure curled around some random trunk debris. The guy couldn't complain, as his mouth was covered by a double strip of duct tape. The silvery tape also bound his hands and feet. His muffled voice shouted what sounded like pleas, but his eyes widened and he quieted when he realized that the man who had opened the trunk wasn't wearing a shirt. The sweat that had soaked his clothes (and stunk up the trunk, Rabbioso noted with distaste) now started to roll down his forehead and cheeks again.

The blade in Rabbioso's hand flashed and the man whimpered, but was surprised when the duct tape from his hands and feet fell away into the bottom of the trunk.

Before the guy could even react, Rabbioso had hauled him bodily out of the trunk and slammed him to the hard-packed dusty ground of the parking area. He stood over the guy, whose name he didn't know, and waited patiently with his arms crossed.

The guy wasn't sure whether to undo his gag or get up and run, first reaching for his face and then realizing that he could attempt to stand. His muscles were stiff and he probably ached from the beating, but the scent of freedom spurred him to his knees with a series of muffled groans. If he wondered why he'd been freed, he didn't make an effort to ask. He struggled to his feet, supporting his weight on the Lincoln's rear deck, breath wheezing from his flared nostrils, and then he turned to face his...*benefactor?*

Rabbioso always felt a stab of delicious enjoyment.

The guy's clothes were business casual, but they were soiled by blood and spilled liquor and sweat, and rumpled or torn beyond repair. He looked like a bum who'd hitched a ride, maybe stowed away in the trunk on purpose. His face was covered by patchy stubble, the result of having been on ice for a few days before they'd taken the tubing to him, but otherwise, except for probable bruising, he was none the worse for wear. He'd elected to keep his gag and collect himself before making a move, rushing the driver, or at least breaking into a run. Rabbioso could feel the guy's muscles start to coil for action, whatever shape it would take.

But then the guy squinted a little and his eyes adjusted to the brightness of the desert night after the pitch darkness of his trunk prison. His eyes seemed to focus all at once, and then they widened again.

Rabbioso could almost read his thoughts.

What was this guy doing, standing there naked?

And what the fuck, why was he...?

"Why am I sportin' wood, eh?" Rabbioso asked the guy, who clearly could not answer, but whose face was undergoing various transformations.

"Did you ever see the movie *Deliverance?*" Rabbioso chuckled when the guy started to sweat and tremble. He moved slightly, indicating he was about to bolt, knowing full well what the reference meant.

Rabbioso smiled. "A classic, wouldn't you agree?"

The guy couldn't help himself. He stared at Rabbioso's raging erection, which might have been impressive in other circumstances, but here and now was just...bizarre.

And very frightening.

"One of my favorites…" Rabbioso began.

The guy made a groaning kind of growl behind the gag and feinted left, then dashed away from the Lincoln, heading to the right. He shuffled at first, then picked up the pace as he caught his balance and started to find his way over the pebbly ground. He was ten yards away, the sound of Rabbioso's laugh in his ears.

He watched the guy run straight toward the rocky riverbed just beyond the flat area. When he'd almost reached it, he started a ragged zigzagging motion, probably thinking to avoid bullets. At this point, he was desperate without really knowing why.

Rabbioso let him reach the edge of the ravine, then he visualized himself transforming.

And in a second or two, he started to give chase. On four massive paws.

A short howl escaped his long snout.

Rabbioso loved this part.

He closed in on his prey.

It was over very quickly. And then the feeding began.

Part One

Chapter One

Lupo

Near Eagle River, WI

Nick Lupo fed the growing fire with another small log and watched as one edge blackened and caught. In a minute, it was snapping as the flame began to engulf the bark and reach for the meat inside. Soon the fire was tossing out a new wave of rippling heat, beating back the night's chill.

The flame licked upward and its flickering lit the pines that stooped over the tiny clearing.

Lupo gazed across the fire pit. The shadows there changed their shape and then he was looking at Sam.

Ghost Sam.

"Well, what do you expect?" the ghost said, with smiling querulousness that only he could pull off. "I'd rather not be a ghost, you know, but we all have to play the hand we're dealt."

"What, are you turning into DiSanto now? Leave the clichés to him, he's got you beat."

"Ah, he's a piker." The Indian's shape moved closer to the fire.

"I'll tell him to amp up his game." He flicked another short split log onto the fire and watched the sparks shoot up. "You cold? Can ghosts feel cold?"

"Man, we're *always* cold. I think that's the worst part."

"Worst part of being a ghost?"

"Of being dead, Nick. *Dead*, remember?"

"How can I forget? How many of us have our own ghosts?"

"You'd be surprised…"

"Look, are you here for a reason, or just giving me shit because of what happened?"

Ghost Sam raised a hand over the snapping fire. "Relax, relax, I'm just here for company. I start to worry when you're all alone. I don't like where your thoughts go, Nick. You're suited to solitude, but then again, when you're alone your thoughts turn dark. Scary."

"Now I'm getting scare lessons from a ghost?" Lupo watched the sparks fly off the snapping logs like lava out of a miniature volcano. He picked up the bottle he had resting against his boot, dug up a shot glass from one pocket, and poured a generous slug of golden liquid. The glass had a floating loon etched in it and the legend *Eagle River* below the regal bird.

He tilted the glass and let the strong, sweet taste of the B&B warm and slightly burn his tongue. It was one of his Up North traditions, the B&B. There was nothing like it to warm the gullet on a chilly night. Some people liked it on the rocks, but Lupo thought it was sacrilege. This was an elixir to be savored in small, grateful sips.

"Nah, you don't need my help to be scary. We both know that, don't we? So, no drink for me, eh? Cheapskate."

Lupo snorted. "I don't make the rules. You always get a charge out of what I eat and drink, right?"

"I'd rather have one of your Midtown Manhattans. I remember those fondly. I noticed you've changed the recipe."

"Just a little. Instead of the Angostura bitters, now I lay in a long splash of Campari. It's mellower and marries the Vermouth better."

"Nice." The shadow Indian nodded. "Sounds tasty. So you like the new therapist?"

Lupo barked a bitter laugh. "Subtle! Get me talking about booze and scaring and whatnot, then slip the knife in when I'm not looking. Good strategy."

"Thank you. I seem to have all the time in the world to come up with them." His face seemed to float through the fire for a second, coming out of the shadows. Sparks shot up suddenly from below as the newest log tilted down into the fire, but the Indian couldn't feel the heated embers. "So, what do you think of her?" he persisted.

Lupo sighed.

Marla Anders had taken over the vacated office of one Markowicz, the police department's attached psychiatrist, who had disappeared under mysterious circumstances about the same time as the head of Internal Affairs, Griff Killian.

Lupo shook his head. "I don't know what I think of her, but at least she seems to be willing to listen and not judge. Markowicz was a nitwit, a bumbler. But I can't say I've had much luck with therapists."

"No, Nick, you haven't," the ghost Indian chuckled. "But at least this one's attractive enough, if you like 'em a little on the brassy side. And she's still alive..." Two police psychiatrists Lupo had been forced to see later turned up dead. Well, the latest hadn't turned up, at least not yet. The new construction on Highway 45 would have to be dug up first. "Besides her looks, you think this one's better?"

"Barrett hated me, and I still think Marcowicz was blabbing to Killian. Unethical as hell, but Killian had a way of getting people to play his games. I'll never be able to prove it, though. At this point, I'd better not try."

"They weigh on you?"

"Well, yeah, having to get rid of the bodies does, but I didn't kill them, Sam. You know that."

In the shadows beyond the fire, the Indian's ghost made a solemn nod. "Indeed, but you disposed of the bodies."

"What the fuck else was I supposed to do?"

"You tell me."

Lupo snorted. "Apparently I'm seeing *two* shrinks!"

On one level, he knew he was just debating his own conscience, but then again, whenever he managed to convince himself of that fact, Ghost Sam would sway him with a quiet word whispered in Lupo's ear. Only this way had Lupo realized that Tom Arnow had allowed himself to be bitten by Heather Wilson so he could become one of *them*, a werewolf, in order to seek out revenge for the murder of his family.

Arnow's death—and the butchering of his family, for that matter—also weighed heavily on Lupo. He'd had nothing to do with the murder of his family, except that they'd wandered into the line of fire. But Lupo had been forced to kill Sheriff Arnow with his own hands, and he would forever feel the blood staining his skin.

"*No one knows what it's like to be the bad man,* eh, Nick?" Ghost Sam's sense of humor was particularly peevish this night. "Isn't that what one of your bands said?"

"Yeah, so I have a conscience! So what? Make all the jokes you want."

Ghost Sam spoke, sadness in his tone. "It's no time for joking. You're not done yet, Nick. There's more trouble headed your way."

Real or not, the old man's ghost was always right.

Heather

Somewhere in Nebraska

The flashing lights turned in behind her from total darkness. Seconds later she heard the siren bleating insistently on her bumper.

She'd been cruising along to the sound of The Cure, her speed constant and barely above the limit. The two-lane blacktop lay like a ruler through the endless bare cornfields and she'd long ago, about a thousand miles it seemed, given up the hope of finding a motel—any dump at all—for the night. Each remote crossroads consisted solely of two identical roads crossing at ninety degree angles, a few bullet-riddled road signs, and only occasionally an anemic streetlight making an alien cone of shimmering haze that hung overhead.

"Goddamn it," she muttered, letting up off the gas after regaining control from the cruise robot she rather capriciously called *Nick*.

She slowed gradually, then pulled over and glided toward the pitch-black gutter of a shoulder between the tall corn or wheat stalks, or whatever they were, and the road itself. The silver Lexus SUV crunched to a smooth halt and she powered down her window and waited. Behind her, the squad car kissed the rear bumper and she shot a glance into her mirror. She couldn't see much, only a shadow in the driver's seat.

Her engine ticked in the cool night air.

Finally the squad car door opened and a tall, gangly deputy unwound himself from the driver's seat. His boots crunched on the road's loose asphalt gravel. She watched him in the side mirror, until he filled it by standing slightly to the rear of her window.

"Hello, Officer," she said sweetly. She was a little dusty from the road, but she knew her hair was its usual lustrous honey-gold color, piled in waves around her classic face. She'd glossed her full lips in a favorite lilac shade, and she knew her eyes were large and limpid. She gave him a full-wattage smile before his face came at her out of the shadows.

Heather Wilson was well-versed in using her appearance, as well as the waves of sexuality she emanated, for her own advantage. It was the keystone of not only her career, but also her life. She hadn't been speeding, so there was a chance this trooper or deputy or whatever he was would just let her off once she batted her eyelashes at him. Maybe she'd blown a taillight.

The first thing she noted about the cop was that he had some sort of high-tech goggles hanging from a strap around his neck.

What's that about?

Then she noted that his craggy face was in the shadow cast by his tilted campaign hat.

A state trooper, then.

But...

She expected him to say something polite, to start his approach with the obligatory *Ma'am* greeting. *Ma'am, your taillight is out. Ma'am, you were going a little fast back there. Ma'am, your license plate is obscured.*

Instead he said, "My, my, my."

"Officer, what's the problem?" She squinted in order to see him. Actually she pretended to squint, because he was expecting her to have difficulty seeing him against the hazy overhead light. Hanging back aways also forced her to twist her body and crane her neck painfully.

She smiled tentatively. "Officer?"

He shifted his weight and his boots crunched on the shoulder. He made some sort of sound with his mouth. A half-whistle and hum. His face remained in the shadows.

She said again, "Officer, was I doing something wrong?"

Finally he spoke. "Please step out of the vehicle." His tone was flat.

"Officer?"

"Out of the vehicle. Now."

She sighed and released her seat belt. "Do you want my license and registration?"

"I want you out of the car." His hand hovered over an open holster, from what she could make out.

"Officer, you're scaring me. What's wrong? What's happening?" She twisted again, and heard him make the half-whistle.

"I'll explain after you step out of the vehicle. If you don't comply, I will place you under arrest. Do you understand?"

"Uh, sure, Officer, whatever you say."

She popped the door and stepped slowly out onto the blacktop. Her feet and legs seemed to disappear into inky blackness below. She edged away from the side of the car and it was like floating.

The road was quiet, dead. There was nothing, no oncoming traffic or anything to indicate they might not be the last two humans on earth, or at least in this quiet corner of Nebraska. There was just the slight rustle of dead stalks in the cool breeze that fluffed the golden hair off her face.

"My, my, my," the cop said again. His hand was still on his gun butt. "Lady, I'm placing you under arrest for aggravated DWG."

She had plenty of experience with police codes. But she shrugged. "DWG? I'm sorry, I don't know…"

"Lady, you were definitely Driving While Gorgeous. Now step over to the rear of your truck so I can check your credentials."

Now she got the goggles. He'd gotten a better look at her as she passed him, thanks to the night-vision gear. She almost chuckled. The freaks were always more inventive. "Officer? What...?"

He drew his weapon, a small-frame revolver. Nothing at all like what cops are currently issued. He aimed it at her. "I'm not going to ask you again."

She shivered. The air *was* chilly.

"Okay," she said, making her voice shaky. She stepped between the rear of her Lexus and the hood of his squad car, noting the rust spots she hadn't seen in the mirror.

"Now, I called in your plate and there's a flag on your jacket. You've been flagged as probably armed. I think we'd better have a strip search. Undo your clothes and drop them to the roadway." He gestured with the gun muzzle. "Hop to it. The sooner you comply, the sooner you can be on your way. If there is nothing...you can get dressed and get back in your truck and be on your way."

She nodded furiously and set about unbuttoning her blouse. She stopped halfway and looked at him, a question in her eyes. He waved the gun and nodded. *Get on with it.*

She whimpered a little and slipped off the silk, dropping it at her feet. Now she was standing in her lacy bra, her perfect breasts thrusting toward him, the nipples hardening despite herself. She knew they were visible through the sheer black material. She undid her belt and stepped out of the tight jeans, freeing her long, shapely legs. She kicked off her sneakers— expensive, though they didn't look like it—and dropped the jeans onto them. She glared at the guy, and her nostrils flared when she saw that he seemed to be panting through his open mouth, his tongue moving obscenely inside. He gestured with the gun muzzle.

This is getting tiresome.

She slipped two fingers into the waistband of her skimpy panties, not quite a thong but close, and peeled them down her thighs until they floated down to the ground and she stepped out of them. Her magnificent buttocks were bare now, and her shaved sex stared him in the face.

"Officer...?" she said, giving him one more chance.

He licked his dry lips and she heard a low groan coming from his throat. She knew what it meant. He was working himself up. His eyes fixed on her covered breasts.

She knew what he was thinking.

She shrugged out of the bra and it joined the rest of her clothes on the dusty, oily tar surface.

Completely naked now, she shivered convincingly. Her engorged nipples were dark peaks on her breasts and she knew when his breath caught in his throat that he was hers.

She'd decided to give up targeting innocent people for her own playful urges, but he wasn't *innocent*, was he?

"On your knees," he said, his voice hoarse. His breath was ragged. "Right here in front of me."

There was no doubt the revolver would go to her temple. He was that type. As much as the forced blow job would turn him on, as much as her lips wrapped around his cock would wind him up, it was the gun barrel pressing on her taut skin that would make him *really* hard.

"Sure," she said. "Anything you want. Just don't... I beg you, just don't taste too bad when I rip out your intestines."

"Uh, what?" The fake cop cocked his head, as if checking the recording to make sure he'd heard correctly. He took a half-step back, bringing up the gun. Still trying to process what she'd said, her meaning.

But she'd started to kneel, her hands reaching for the fly on his dusty pants and her lush lips opening, ready to pleasure him. And later to beg, no doubt. She noticed he hadn't even attempted to wear uniform trousers. *Idiot.*

Her submissive aggressiveness bewildered him, but he was hard now and nature was tough to deny. Despite himself, his sudden doubts, he stepped toward her again, his swelling dick reaching for her mouth.

And then Heather visualized herself making a smooth change, giving the DNA-realigning process a speed boost as she had learned from that other grand freak Siegfried, the evil CEO of Wolfpaw, and before the guy could react to the impossibility he saw, her face had become a long and graceful snout full of sharp fangs...

When her closing jaws clamped on his groin right through his trousers and tore from side to side, the fake cop's scream became a girlish shriek that echoed between the lines of shadowy stalks.

Blood puffed up around her altered face like a cloud and she spit out clothing material and the part of his genitals she had ripped from his body. The taste of his blood intoxicated her and called up her growl as she shook her head and then tore into his lower belly with her viselike jaws. *Sawing through ersatz uniform shirt, flesh, bone, and fat...*

His thoughts turned jagged, scattered snippets of all those extorted blow jobs he and his pals had enjoyed, but how this seemed like extreme payback.

Her eyes fixed on his as, panicked, he tried to bring the gun to bear...but the sight of his own blood splattering the impossible wolf the woman had become—not to mention his guts squirting out of the widening tear in his belly—made it impossible for his hand to work right. Still, the gun wavered in search of a target.

And then the wolf spit out more of his bloody entrails and clamped on to his wrist, tearing off both his hand and the gun it held.

His desperate shrieking took over the night.

One of his last sights was of the wolf's eyes rolling and changing color as it continued to devour him alive, its snout now buried again in his butchered stomach. The wolf's paws scrabbled in the gravelly tar for purchase as the animal's jaws ripped again and again into the soft and squishy flesh.

Heather ate her fill.

Chapter Two

Lupo

L upo had been looking up into the pine awning above, watching the smoke curl into the needles and disappear.

Now, when Ghost Sam said, "You're not done yet, Nick. There's more trouble headed your way," he dropped his gaze rapidly, staring across the flames at the hunched form of the Indian who had been his friend.

The Indian who both was and wasn't there. Who now seemed to fade into the dancing shadows cast by the flaring bonfire. Sparks burst outward and it was like a magician's trick—the ghost disappeared behind the hot cloud.

"What do you mean? Sam? What are you talking about?"

There was no answer. The spot where Sam had been was empty now.

Lupo raised his voice. He heard a desperate note in his tone. "What are you saying? What's coming my way? What—"

A warm hand touched the back of his neck.

He stiffened. Then slowly relaxed, wondering about his lack of awareness.

"Who are you talking to?"

Jessie Hawkins laid her other hand on his back and leaned over his shoulder, her hair falling like a chestnut curtain onto his flushed skin. When he tilted his head up to look at her, she met him halfway and their lips touched. She tasted of the woods.

"No one," he said. "Just venting."

"It sounded like you said *Sam*. You miss him, don't you?"

He looked into her eyes. She'd heard more, he would swear to it. There was worry in her look, and he had a sense that he was frightening her. As much as he considered himself a monster, he never wanted to frighten her, not Jessie.

Shit.

He sighed. "Sometimes it helps me to speak to him, to his *spirit*, I guess," he confessed.

Sometimes a version of the truth was the best thing to say. Sometimes it was less of a lie. Hell, he knew the truth would definitely frighten her more. The suspicion that he might be losing his mind, for instance. The worry that his tenuous hold on reality was slipping.

If she ever found out some of what he'd done. Of what he'd had no choice but to do…

No, it was better to go with a half-truth.

That made him only a half-liar, didn't it?

"I know what you mean. I talk to my dad sometimes, after all these years. It's comforting." She stepped around the rough-hewn bench and slid down next to him, her hands held out to the warmth of the fire. "I think it's fine. Whatever helps. We both have a lot of healing to do."

Lupo put his arm around her and drew her closer.

These last few days had been the best in a long time. For once they'd been able to step back from the cliff toward which they'd been heading.

He tried to ignore the bandages still partially covering one of her hands. It had almost healed.

"Want a slug?" He held out his shot glass.

She took some of the amber liquid, her eyes fixed on him over the glass rim. Then she put the glass down and it just happened, they melted together in a warm embrace that quickly heated up even faster.

The fire had nothing to do with it.

He slipped his hands into her open coat and drew her near. She laid her head on his shoulder, and then they moved and their lips met, and this time they did more than just touch. This time their tongues met and the kiss turned volcanic.

Lupo tasted the brandy on her tongue. It added a new element to the woodsy flavor of her lips. Even though she might easily have become a model—and she reminded people of a popular eighties supermodel with her looks—Jessie rarely bothered with makeup when she was relaxing at home, in her cottage on Circle Moon Drive, one of several she'd inherited. Lupo was still nominally her tenant, staying in one of her other cottages, but since they'd become a couple he spent most of his time Up North in hers, usually reclining in front of a roaring fire.

Now they were in front of a fire in the great outdoors, and the heat between them, added to that of the fire, was making them forget about the chilly northern air.

They made out like teenagers, their hands roaming on each other's bodies while their mouths connected them symbolically, making them into a single entity with rapidly warming needs.

Lupo pulled back for a second. "Too cold to, *uh*, go further here, isn't it?"

Jessie was almost breathless. "I'm game if you are." She swooped in for another lengthy kiss, giving him her tongue to suckle. A low moan erupted from down below in her throat, signaling her need. Their breathing turned rapid, almost desperate. They started to peel clothing layers, the bottle and the fire and the cold almost forgotten.

Lupo laid his coat on the pine-needle carpet that surrounded them, then added hers. He kissed her shoulders, bare now, and trailed his tongue toward her neck as she struggled out of her sweater and blouse, her bandages in the way until he lent a hand. They knelt on the rumpled coats.

She wasn't wearing a bra, and in a few moments he was cupping her breasts gently toward his mouth, his lips on her hardening nipples and alternating from one to the other while she ran her one good hand through his long hair.

She sighed as his tongue made circles around her nipples, his warmth chasing away her goose bumps.

He was always awed by her natural beauty and by her need, which matched his even though his was *enhanced* (as he put it) by the werewolf gene he'd carried ever since his teen years. Indeed, he had to force himself to hold back the Creature, who lurked beneath the veneer of civilization and always threatened to take control. Lupo had improved his abilities in that area, but when he lost control—in lust, as well as in anger—then the Creature began to push against the limits his human brain put upon it.

Now their needs were being met as he helped her shimmy out of her jeans and he took her hips between his large, scarred hands and gently maneuvered her back down on their flattened coats until she could kick her damp panties off and lay her legs on his shoulders. He kissed from her nipples, down the swell of her breasts, then laid a line of soft kisses down her flat stomach and stopped at her navel, licking around the tiny garnet stud she had recently added to her already perfect cleft, then wandered downward, his lips alternating with his tongue, heading down to the molten center of her heat.

She sighed contentedly under his hands, under his attentions, and he felt her muscles contract and loosen as he let his instincts take over, slowly working her up into a mild frenzy as she caressed his head.

He reached her thighs, leaving more kisses behind as he circled around and around, teasing, nearing the spot she wanted him to find. She groaned with frustration as he pulled back, his lips following the curve of her mound without touching her precisely where she wanted to be touched. Now he kissed the insides of her thighs as her breathing increased its rate, and as he abandoned himself to her pleasure, he had one last coherent thought before the animal needs took over.

He hoped Ghost Sam had gone wherever it was he went when he wasn't acidly critiquing Lupo's handling of his life.

Jessie's hands in his hair pulled him back to where he needed to be.

The fire snapped and crackled near them, sending tendrils of smoke up into the evening air.

Bastone

Las Vegas

The Don was enjoying his new television in the den, a sixty-inch Samsung about as thin as a cracker.

The room was decked out as a theater even though his was the only seat, a triple-wide black love seat crafted in the old country of the softest leather and specially imported. In fact, he thought it was the only one of its kind in the entire country, and the Don was pleased to be sitting on it now. It wasn't the only one of its kind in the whole country, but since he thought it was, not one of his guys dared break the news.

On the crystal-clear screen, two extremely comely and highly flexible women were pleasuring a well-hung stud with their mouths, taking frequent breaks to suck each other's tongue before getting back to business.

This had been the Don's favorite pastime since he'd turned fifty and put his father into the ground.

The new Don had immediately indulged his two main interests by uniting them. He had become a walking encyclopedia of both Mafia history and pornography.

You weren't supposed to say the word *Mafia*. But that was bullshit. Gus Bastone said the word all the time.

Gus had a theory. His old man was secretly embarrassed to be a gangster, a made man, a wise guy in the old tradition, and he liked to pretend none of that stuff existed. He wanted nothing more than to be considered a legit businessman. So whenever he'd had the chance to buy up some small chain of convenience stores or gas stations, even if he had to use some dirty money to seal the deal, he always maintained it would be clean money soon enough. He never called it laundering. He had funny ideas about his family enterprise.

Technically his father had been a straight-laced, old-country, old-school Mafia guy. One of the so-called *Mustache Petes*. A slightly younger one, but still firmly anchored in the older generation and most of their ways.

But then the old Don finally gave up the ghost and left the Bastone Family business to his only son to steer, and young Gus *liked* wrapping himself up in all the trappings of the Mafia and everything that came with it.

The Don was dead, all hail the Don.

But the new Don Bastone was *very* different from his father, and the little porn addiction was all his to enjoy. Hell, some of his father's colleagues collected shrunken heads, others pickled fingers and worse.

Porn had been a favorite of his before that, of course, but as the Don's son he had been obligated to hide his interests in the shadows. Only some of his best men knew how he spent his free time. That he had an entire room filled with a porn collection that might be the best in Vegas, if you didn't count the "sex museums". That he tended to let the porn run in the background even when he was in his office, taking care of business.

So this was not a quirk he was willing to share with all his soldiers, only a few of the captains—by and large those who were interested in the same things. The one captain who hadn't taken it seriously had disappeared. His family thought he had run away with a showgirl. There had been evidence to that effect. But actually Don Gus "The Stick" Bastone had personally put a bullet in the back of his head and then dropped the body in a vat of quick-drying cement, and the dumb bastard was now part of the foundation of an overpass on-ramp off US 15.

It wasn't the only killing Gus Bastone had done. Unlike his old man, he found he liked occasionally reinforcing his image. And he wasn't against getting his hands dirty.

Right now he wasn't soiling his hands, but the chick on her knees in front of him was definitely dirty. She was a showgirl at the Flamingo, so she was incredibly attractive, and she was a part-time escort, so she knew what she was doing. She was in the middle of showing him exactly why she commanded top dollar, her eyes locked on his while her mouth and tongue did the work.

There was a knock at the door. Don Gus, as he liked his most trusted men to call him, was not happy.

His attention slipped.

Kimberley Kandy fell out of rhythm and robbed him of his imminent orgasm. Since there was little that came close to the feeling of mouth-fucking a gorgeous showgirl who was on her knees while she happened to be in full costume and makeup, Don Gus became immediately irritated.

"Goddammit," he snarled, shoving Kimberly aside and knocking her to the floor. The door opened because he'd forgotten to turn the lock. She squealed when she hit the floor, smacking her head on a lamp base.

"Sorry to bother you, boss," said a thug named Tony as he pushed open the door right after the courtesy knock. He'd been on bodyguard detail only a week.

By then the Don had pulled his engorged flesh out of the girl's mouth and was halfway into hitching up his pants over the drooping member, but the damage was done.

Being caught with his pants down, literally, was not something the old Don's son took in stride.

Stuck with his hands in the folds of his skewed briefs and dress shirt, Don Bastone stopped struggling with his clothes and stood facing the door. He glared at Tony, who stopped abruptly as his eyes took in the view of his boss's embarrassment.

"Oh Jesus," he muttered. Then he soldiered on. "Boss, you wanna talk to—"

"Fuck you doin'?" Gus shouted, spittle flying. He was building up to a full blow of a temper, and all his oldest men knew to avoid it. But Tony was too new.

"It's Johnny, boss, he said it was urgent—"

"The fuck you doin'!" Gus shouted. "The fuckin' door was closed, you moron. I left word not to fuckin' disturb. You get it?"

Tony was slow, but he surveyed the scene again and his eyes widened. Don Bastone, pants wrapped around his ankles. Half-naked showgirl wriggling on the floor, crying and holding her nose. "Yeah, boss, but Johnny insisted you hadda be told he was on the phone from out east."

Bastone gathered himself and turned to help Kimberley to her feet. She was whimpering, still holding her nose. "I dink it's brogen," she mumbled between sobs.

"I'll get ya to a doc, my sweets," he said, surveying the damage. It didn't look like a break to him, but he tended to always be good to his women so he would follow through. "Just hang on a few minutes, and Tony here is gonna drive you to the doc's office. I'll make a phone call and you'll be all set."

"I'm supposed to work, Gussy."

He sighed. The day was pretty well ruined already. "I'll call your boss at the Flamingo. You'll be fine." He patted her shapely rear, regretful of his lost orgasm. "Tony is gonna tell me what the fuck Johnny wanted, then he's gonna run you over to Doc Shapiro's. Just wait outside, okay?"

She nodded. Her nose *did* look swollen, all of a sudden. He figured *that* line of sex was dried up for a while.

Fuck!

He waited for her to leave, then turned to the new kid. "Okay, now what?" Tony swallowed and repeated what he knew about the call. "Okay, put Johnny through to this phone here." The kid nodded. "And from now on, you interrupt me while I'm workin' and I'm gonna get Robb to have a *talk* with you. Know what I mean?"

The kid stammered, retreating. "Y-yes, boss."

"And don't call me *boss*."

Jessie

After the sweat had dried on their bodies and they started to feel the cold breeze, they still warmed each other's skin with their remaining heat.

Jessie nuzzled his chin and neck, feeling his gaze slide over the top of her head and into the trees around and over them.

Good thing we're both warm-blooded, she thought. They'd made outdoor sex part of their routine whenever they were apart longer than a week, although by nature it tended to happen near Eagle River and not in Milwaukee, where he was nervous about being caught.

"The MPD might have a word to say about one of their detectives cavorting in the buff in some city park," he'd said once, after just such a vigorous outing.

"Hm, I seem to recall some scandals of the sort back in the day," she'd responded, half-punching his shoulder.

"I was barely a patrol rookie then," he said, nodding. The eighties had been full of cop scandals in the city, but a series of improvements at the chief level had slowly eroded most of the bad-boy behavior, though it had become apparent that there were still some entrenched racism and corruption issues. This was why the MPD had brought in the attack dog Griff Killian. Now Lupo had good reason to try and forget the name, but he probably never would. He would forever remember the terrible task of covering up Killian's murder—which had been committed to inculpate *him.*

Jessie knew the situations he'd faced, the crimes he'd been forced to commit, were not his fault, but they weighed on him nonetheless.

She snuggled into his warm embrace, felt her nipples harden at the touch of his muscled torso. His hand behind her rubbed her back to generate some heat by friction, which she appreciated, but then snuck farther down to trace the lush curve of her buttocks.

"Mmmmm," she purred into his neck. "That's nice, mister. Can you spare a dime?"

Where the hell had *that* come from?

His response was to caress her firm butt even more sensually, his fingers slipping into the cleft between the globes of her ass until she was adding a deep growl to the purring. And reaching down for him, feeling his hardening desire.

"So soon, sir?" she said, chuckling, the long fingers of her unbandaged hand encircling him and making him pant.

He whispered, "The wolf gets what the wolf wants..."

"Let's help the wolf," Jessie said, sliding over his waiting body without letting go of his flesh, then positioning herself on top of him and slowly taking him, making him a part of her again.

"I love you, Nick Lupo," she muttered as he grew within her, and he started to rock her, reaching her best buttons with the ease of experience.

He didn't have to respond verbally, and she didn't expect it. His hands reached up between them and he tweaked her nipples in opposite directions as their lips met and they shared each other's essence despite the cool breeze that washed over them. They were making their own heat, and the snapping fire nearby didn't seem even nearly as warm as what they generated.

They increased the pace until she arched her back and screamed out in the throes of her orgasm, drawing him along with her until he also exploded, the two of them riding the widening ripples of their fulfilled lust and finally melting into the serenity of their rekindled love.

Jessie smiled then, because this time they shivered as they threw on clothes, tossed some sand on the fire, and ran for her cottage, their laughter following them until they were safely inside the cozy radius of another fire, this time in her stone fireplace.

Finally sated, they sat cuddled together on her sofa and he splashed B&B in their glasses. Jessie reached out hers and they clinked before sipping the warming nectar.

"I'm sorry you have to head back already," she said, swirling her glass. "These weekends always go by too fast."

She was the reservation doctor, and since the casino had taken off, she'd found herself on call a lot more often, dealing not only with the tribal emergencies but also with any that the many bused-in visitors might suffer. Now that the hotel portion of the complex was half-finished, there was always more work—construction sites being notoriously rife with accidental injuries from minor to fatal.

If being honest, she'd come to hate the responsibility of running the hospital, though it was a symbol of the tribe's increasing fortune, its coffers starting to swell again with the casino take. How could she argue with that?

Well, except for the therapy Nick had insisted she undergo. The therapy that turned the casino and its siren call into a sin for her.

Was she a gambling addict? Somehow it seemed she had become just that, though she had no idea how it had happened. Something buried deep in her psychology, triggered by the stress of Nick's situation and the evil that had come their way since they'd gotten together. Now that the sinister Wolfpaw Security Services had been vanquished, she hoped the therapy would take.

And Heather Wilson, what of her?

Jessie tried not to think of her often, and indeed she'd come close to killing the woman.

First of all, she was just too perfect a beauty. Heather elicited lust merely by being in the room, or within sight. Then she'd been turned into a werewolf, not by design, sure, but it had happened, and unlike Nick, she'd fallen in love with the shapeshifting. Whereas most people, like Nick, would have seen the condition as a curse, Heather took to it like...what would DiSanto have said?

Like a duck to water.

So besides being fifty shades of desirable in every way you could measure, plus intelligent and charismatic, she was *also just like Nick*...and that bond had jabbed Jessie in the heart more than she could possibly have imagined.

She still wasn't sure whether Nick had had a fling with the TV newswoman, but most days Jessie thought it was true, that *something* had happened between them. He'd more or less confessed, but to what? It was unclear.

Lying here in his arms, after two very nice sessions of what anyone would have called *great sex*, she still wasn't sure if she trusted him. Not with *her*.

Good thing Heather was far away, recovering from the wounds Jessie had inflicted. She'd been so angry that Nick had stopped her from doing what she had intended, but at the same time, she knew she was wrong to want revenge.

Nick would have said, *Revenge is what my people do. Hell, we invented the word vendetta.* But then he would have chuckled. Nick Lupo was the least vindictive man she knew.

She reached up and traced the line of his eyelids one at a time with her good hand. The other had been cut while he'd wrestled the Vatican blade from her grip. But she was lucky, it could have been worse...

She could have awakened from that encounter as a werewolf herself.

"Hmm," he sighed. "I could go for that all day."

She stroked him down below, playfully.

"And *that*."

They laughed. They'd been laughing more lately. Things were good. Or getting better, anyway.

"How soon?" she asked. Her hand was now nestled under his chin. His stubble tickled her.

"I think I'll go for one more run. The wolf's already feeling the confinement of being down in the city." He kissed the top of her head and they let the moment linger.

Then he was gone and she heard the door closing.

She remembered it all too well. Now that he'd left her, it replayed in her mind.

Long runs of light-colored fur started to sprout along Heather's back and shoulders and on her belly. Her manicured nails turned to claws. Her teeth became fangs. A growl erupted from her throat, and then another. Her eyes swirled and changed colors like a kaleidoscope.

Jessie was mesmerized, briefly.

But then she showed her other hand. It held one of the Longinus daggers from the wooden case taken from Mordred's car. Its blade seemed to glow as she slowly unsheathed it from the magically shielding wooden scabbard.

Heather's body blurred and she was now on four paws, a sleek giant gray wolf poised to pounce on the intruder and maul her.

The dagger's point cleared the end of the protecting scabbard. Jessie held it more expertly than Heather probably expected and approached the threatening wolf.

The wolf lunged.

Jessie's hand became a blur in motion, the bluish glow of the blade marking the arc of her attack.

They met in the middle of the room, human and wolf, both of them growling, protecting their territory.

Lupo

He felt *Her* call even though she was neither full, nor visible.

He had never understood the moon's influence. Heather accepted it without question, abandoned herself to it and made it sexual. Heather made *everything* sexual. Although there truly was a sexual angle because the werewolf gene amplified one's libido. It was just that Heather's was so highly charged to begin with, that the wolf had taken her over the edge.

And he'd never had a chance to ask, because every other werewolf he'd met was trying to kill him. Perhaps the late Geoff Simonson might have shared his knowledge, except his mind had essentially split into two halves and he had no idea he was also a wolf such as those he hunted so fervently.

Now it didn't matter; he was only interested in running.

And hunting.

Nick Lupo ran on four oversize paws, his black muscular body flitting through the forest's shadowy pockets. The carpet of needles and drying leaves crackled under him at first, until he began to stalk.

His nostrils were wide open and receptive to all the scents of the living forest. The wolf enjoyed the blast of stimulus, and Lupo himself had learned to enjoy it from the place his human side inhabited the Creature. It had taken years, but now he considered himself almost One with the wolf.

Slowing his racing pace, he began to search the air around him for dinner. The pine trunks were set farther apart in this area, making his stalking more difficult. His snout felt the cold breeze and tested the air. Finally there was less of the *human* element. But still too much for a hungry wolf.

He was ranging farther from home than usual because the tree zones were thinning. Or disappearing altogether.

More and more buildings—condos and small mansions and strip malls and professional centers—were going up in Eagle River's expanding outskirts. His territory was shrinking. Looking through the eyes of the Creature, Lupo saw only the beauty and majesty of the forest that was left. He directed the wolf's paws toward the rez, where he could count on finding both more trees and denser wooded areas, and therefore more wildlife. Tonight the wolf felt the hunger deep in its gut. Sex had that effect, cyclically, and he was on the prowl for an easy meal under the pine canopy.

After expelling a stream of steamy breath, his nose picked up the first promising scent, a plump rabbit who sensed he was being stalked and managed to evade the wolf's playful chase through the pines and firs. The exercise worked up the wolf's appetite even more, so when his nose caught the trace of deer, he went into serious stalking mode and was soon on the trail of a couple of very young does.

When the unsuspecting prey paused to drink from a narrow creek, the Creature crept ever closer from upwind. The does sensed danger, their fur bristling as they scanned their surroundings, but they seemed to miss the dark predator who was almost atop them but still hidden by the low shadows.

A leap, a brief scuffle, a flash of fangs and jaws, helpless squealing, and suddenly the Creature once again tasted hot blood on its tongue. One lucky survivor disappeared into the trees as the Creature took its time butchering the companion, ripping and tearing, then nosing into the hot carcass to feast on the delicacies within.

The wolf paused its buffet and sent up a self-satisfied howl.

Stay away, it said. *I'm still hungry.*

He fed leisurely, then bathed his bloody snout in the cold creek.

Then he shook off the cold droplets and ran. He ran as if the Wolfpaw mercenaries were chewing up the ground behind him. He ran as if he could escape everything that had happened to him since that terrible day when, as a teenager, he'd been cursed by the bite.

But then his human mind coughed up more recent events, more recent heartaches. He let the wolf run, tasting the chill night air, and let the memories wash over him even as his paws dug deep into the rich darkness of the forest floor.

He remembered.

The terrible stench of sizzling blood entered his nostrils as soon as he kicked down the door to Heather's condo.

He'd heard the grunts and growls from outside, and he knew what was happening. Jessie had intimated she would confront Heather soon, though he had no idea she'd taken one of the Vatican blades. Seeing the empty cradle in the ancient wooden box had sent him here, all the while praying to a god he didn't believe existed to let her be all right.

Jessie...

When he cleared the doorway, he saw he was too late. They'd danced around each other and now Heather's gray wolf had pounced, but Jessie had surprised her by unsheathing the magical blade and somehow she'd dragged its edge across the wolf's muscular chest, drawing black blood as her skin and flesh parted like roasted meat, the cloying smell of singed fur adding to the sickening blend of scents in the air.

Lupo instinctively tore off his clothes and kicked off his shoes, immediately visualizing himself going over. The transformation was quick as always, but seemed incredibly slow to him as he waited to be able to get his body between the two women. If Heather managed to bite Jessie, well...then he suspected Jessie would rather die than become a werewolf. Like another friend of theirs... If Jessie managed to kill Heather, she would be scarred for life—and she would either go to prison or cause Lupo's fall because there was only so much he could cover up. If he went down, then DiSanto would, too. They were inextricably bound.

The black wolf that had been Lupo snarled and leaped into the fray, his jaws reaching for and closing on one of Heather's front paws and yanking her body off balance, spraying her blood in the meantime.

Instead of backing off under Lupo's covering action, Jessie pressed her attack with the Vatican blade that might have been glowing, drawing it through Heather's lupine chest once again until the wolf's screeching yelp echoed through the high-ceilinged apartment. Once again a deep laceration opened in the gray wolf's chest and could not close due to the dagger's supernatural qualities. If Jessie had managed to hit Heather's belly with the same slicing motion, then her guts would have come tumbling out and it would have been over because wounds made with the daggers did not heal as quickly as those made with a normal blade. The silver blade was raised for another lunge, but this time Lupo's body managed to block Jessie's attack.

Forcing himself to keep his jaws away from her limbs, Lupo simply rolled over her.

Jessie's frustrated scream filled the space between them. Her lovely face was a mask of rage: teeth bared, her nostrils flared, and her eyes crazed with hate. In her hand, the dagger endangered Lupo's wolf as well as Heather's, but she seemed to have shed her own humanity. Right then she had become as much pure animal as they were...

It had seemed hopeless.

With Heather's wolf half-dead on the carpeting, and a crazed Jessie trying to get around Lupo's interfering body so she could deal the whimpering beast a final, killing blow, Lupo had willed himself back to human form, grasping for Jessie's hands while evading the blade. Finally he'd managed to trap Jessie by wrapping his muscular arms around her struggling body, eventually forcing the killing dagger from her grasp.

She'd collapsed, crying, into his arms.

He had checked her wounded hand then snatched her up — regretfully — and dragged her onto the balcony, where he had trapped her by locking the door.

Then he'd attended to Heather, whose wolf's body was a mess of scorched flesh lining long slices, many of which he hadn't even seen strike so accurately.

He'd tended to both of them. Jessie had wordlessly helped him with her own wounds.

Finally clothed again, with a dangerously wounded but slowly healing Heather tucked in her bed, Lupo had unlocked the balcony and taken Jessie home to his apartment. He had stood sentry over her as she worked the rage and shivering adrenaline spike out of her system, nearly reducing her to a comatose state.

Then the tears had begun.

Jessie

She waited for him to return from the forest.

She was wet, her juices running from the expectation. Going out to run and hunt as the wolf made Nick incredibly horny. Thirsty, too, but he'd put off drinking until after he'd crawled into bed with her and tamed the wild.

Jessie lay on the comforter, naked, her body glowing in the firelight. She stretched languidly. They'd already made slow, passionate love and she was sated. He was a romantic, attentive lover and their sex had always featured the kind of bond that transcended pure lust. But she knew his needs increased under the moon's influence, especially when it was full, and that sex with him after giving the wolf control for a while would be raw, almost desperate. It would be more physical, and she watched goose bumps grow along her arms.

Right from the first, she'd lusted for the dangerous side of Nick. Even before she'd known about the werewolf side of him, there had always been an air of danger about him—a sense that he was on the edge, not always quite in control. Now she knew why, and she understood how the wolf DNA or whatever it really was affected Nick the human.

She hadn't realized it until later but when she did, it surprised her that she wasn't afraid of this side of Nick anymore. And in fact that she enjoyed the nastier sex. They'd had the romantic, the sensitive, but soon it would be time for the forbidden lusts to be unleashed.

Jessie wished she could convince Nick that she no longer kept a stockpile of silver ammunition for *him*. Maybe she had, at first. Now she kept it because of the other werewolves.

She heard him at the door. Cool outside air muscled its way in with him, bringing with it the strong scent of musk that marked the wolf's passage through his body.

A shiver ran rippled along her muscles and nerves...never tired of seeing him come to her, his muscled, scarred body flushed from the hunt, his eyes still swirling like kaleidoscopes, his erection raging.

He approached the bed with the hunger and need flowing off his hot skin in waves.

Jessie understood that for some werewolves, this was the part they lived for. This and the killing and butchering of live meat. But Nick had conquered his needs in those areas. His problems he sometimes laid at the door of his heritage and his family history, some of which he had shared.

She saw him, stripes across his flesh from the open blinds. She'd left them open so the woods that stretched out from both walls of the corner room seemed to hover over them. She knew that right now, for a little while, Nick was straddling both worlds.

Silently he climbed into bed and her good hand reached out for his flesh again, fingers encircling its girth, feeling his excitement and the need. Her touch fed his need and then their bodies touched and they were kissing. He tasted of the wild in him, of the woods, and their tongues swirled around and then he licked her face and she shuddered.

She reached up and traced the long, straight scar in his scalp made by the Vatican blade when he'd fought Simonson.

Their breathing rate increased and fell into rhythm. His hands roved over her body's hot spots, knowing what to touch and how, working her up. First her neck, then nipples, then her smooth stomach, then her buttocks and thighs. She moved from the scar on his head downward, finding and caressing some of his other scars—his wounds healed quickly thanks to the werewolf DNA, but the worst injuries left scars that would never heal—and then she found his engorged penis again and drew him nearer. She rotated onto her belly and drew her knees up, offering herself, her own need now strumming her nerve-endings like taut piano strings.

He rose up behind her, his body between her thighs, and she felt him seeking out what she offered.

"Nick," she gasped, breathing hard, as he found her and slowly opened the passage and she helped him, her own flesh screaming with lust. She laid her face sideways and pleaded with him. "Fuck me, Nick, *fuck me there.*"

She was well aware that she had begun to talk dirty only after he had stopped her from killing Heather and she had recovered from the murderous haze that had overtaken her at the condo, perhaps to give him something of Heather's to conquer, she wasn't sure. Perhaps because she had come to the realization that she liked it.

Their skin scalding where they met, the tip of his engorged penis gently prying her open, his right hand snaked around beneath her and located the other center of her pleasure. His fingers sought her out and sent deep vibrations to her nipples and to her already stimulated brain. She hissed as he coordinated his two actions, encouraging him with the heat of her lust.

He entered her slowly, not letting the wolf's lusts override his own human ones, giving her time to adjust. She gasped as the invasive pain she first felt turned to pleasure when combined with his caress of her sensitive clitoris, and then he was in and thrusting and they were together for the rest of the ride, each feeding the lust they shared.

She lost track of time, feeling his body hunched over her back as his flesh reached deep within her, sweat pouring from him and landing on her skin where it seemed to sizzle...or so she could almost swear.

She wondered for the thousandth time what would happen if he lost control during this lustful act and went over. Hadn't that happened to Heather? She thought that's what Nick had told her. She wondered what would happen if Nick were to bite her. She knew he worried about it, too.

But then the orgasm rose up from twin directions and took her from inside out, wiping away the thoughts of danger and leaving only the swelling bliss as it shot like lightning fire through her veins and muscles, and she screamed out as he also reached his peak and pulsed his seed deep into her.

When the last vibrations were over she slipped forward onto her stomach and sighed contentedly as he collapsed onto her back. They lay like that seemingly forever, their bodies still linked. And, she hoped, their souls.

She fell asleep shortly afterwards, and when she awoke he had quietly dressed and slipped out of the cottage, but not before leaving a late wildflower on the pillow beside her.

She smiled, stretched. Curled up and squinted out the window into the woods. She forced the thoughts of danger from her mind and sought out the comfort of sleep.

Chapter Three

Jessie

When she awoke, the weather had turned gray and foggy, and the sky seemed ready to discharge a pelting rain. She really needed to get back to the hospital, but she was feeling lazy.

Well-screwed, m'lady, her mind provided for her.

She chuckled.

In the shower, where she indulged in a longer session of steaming-hot water than usual, her mind wandered again. She'd given Heather an ultimatum, and even now, having been claimed by Nick once again and knowing that he had chosen her, she felt a shiver down her spine that reminded her that none of this business was truly finished.

Besides almost killing Heather Wilson with one of Nick's Vatican blades, she had also threatened her with all the files she'd found on Heather's computer. The nosy, nasty reporter bitch had compiled files on them all and their activities, some of which were at the very least questionable if not actually crimes.

But many of them *were* crimes, and there was murder in there too, because fat chance a jury in a court of law would agree that killing people for lycanthropy was acceptable. They'd never see the outside of the insane asylum ever again.

No, Jessie had threatened Heather with exposing her to Nick. If the bitch wanted to turn them in, that was her problem—and she'd go down with them. But what Jessie wanted was to keep her away from Nick. The reporter had made little secret of the fact that she could take Nick from Jessie, and in fact she had bewitched him already and much too well.

First Jessie had copied all the files onto a flash drive, then she had deleted them all from the computer. But she was sure Heather was careful enough to have backups. She'd deleted the originals out of spite, just to make her point. In fact, she'd expected to drive that point home with the silver blade...but that hadn't happened thanks to Nick. However, he hadn't been able to stop Jessie from hurting the Amazon-like sex-starved bitch. The blade had made horrific wounds. Only Nick's intervention had given Heather the chance to survive them and, presumably, heal once again.

Jessie hoped the *cunt* had suffered plenty throughout the healing. She hoped it hurt enough to make Heather wish Jessie *had* killed her.

She hoped Heather felt the fires of hell melting her insides.

It was small enough consolation for being unable to finish the job she'd started.

By the time she was drying her hair, she'd let the anger wash away again. For one thing, Nick had been extremely attentive since those events. And Jessie had pledged to improve her life. She had taken control of her urges—she still had trouble calling it an addiction, even though her medical training told her she was lying to herself—and even though Heather Wilson knew better than to show up in Eagle River or Milwaukee ever again, she'd promised not to hunt down the bitch.

Jessie hummed an old Genesis song Nick loved. Somehow the lyrics of "Entangled" seemed weirdly appropriate.

She grabbed a quick bite from her microwave and was out the door fairly quickly.

Lupo

He drove the distance south in record time, letting his iPod playlists take him through the changing colors of the North Woods. He always felt some strange sadness leaving the north behind, especially when the trees turned from a majority of the coniferous variety to a majority of the deciduous. It was a tangible sign of leaving behind what he considered the idyllic for the pedestrian.

A selection of old New Age music by the likes of Tingstad & Rumble, William Ellwood, Will Ackerman, and David Lanz gave him respite from the harder sound of bands like Spock's Beard and Porcupine Tree he was listening to these days. The Alan Parsons Project and Eric Woolfson albums he often preferred on the way up. When heading south, he needed softer, more introspective music. Sometimes he threw in some Tangerine Dream to spice things up, or some middle period Marillion.

By the time he reached the city, he was ready to turn off the music and let the urban landscape leach the remaining peace and quiet from his system. The freeway traffic was dense and he couldn't select a proper accompaniment. Soon he was nosing into his building's first-floor garage space.

His eastside apartment, a spacious double condominium he'd had the opportunity to retrofit to his needs, seemed empty without Jessie. He tossed his duffel bag on the sofa and flipped on some lights. Her presence was palpable. The Creature within him could catch her scent, and Lupo remembered the time they'd spent together the last couple days.

And the lovemaking.

There had been a *lot* of lovemaking. Intense, raw, desperate, almost like a last-ditch effort.

But they were going through a rebirth of sorts, he realized. They'd set aside the mistrust—she of his connection to Heather Wilson and he of Jessie's unlikely gambling addiction, as well as Jessie's assault of Heather—and instead concentrated on healing both problems as well as their relationship.

The lovemaking had helped. It was communication at its most primal.

When Lupo was in her, it seemed to him nothing else mattered. There was nothing else, only the two of them, united in flesh. *Their flesh united.*

Sometimes it was okay if the flesh united first and the brain later.

He thought Jessie's gambling therapy was going well. It seemed the illogical urge to gamble had manifested due to her lack of control over what she thought was happening between Nick and Heather.

Maybe the bloody confrontation between Jessie and Heather, and how Lupo had been forced to break it up before it turned deadly—perhaps that had provided a catharsis of sorts. Sometimes he wished he still had Caroline Stewart, his first lover and a psychology professor, to help him navigate the subtexts of life. He sensed that *his* subtexts were more difficult than most.

Lupo threw his bulk into his chair behind his massive desk and flipped through his mail, distracted.

Those subtexts were grounded in the worst of his own dark tendencies.

To Lupo's shame, something *had* happened between him and Heather, but he didn't want more of it, despite the television journalist's many charms. Insatiable in bed (or *anywhere*, for that matter), adventurous, experimental, sensual, exciting, attractive beyond belief...Heather Wilson had it all.

But she was sex-crazy, what once would have been called a nymphomaniac.

And she was a werewolf, like Lupo.

Accidentally, unwillingly, a werewolf. But not tragically, because she had found almost immediately that she loved it. Loved the shape-changing, the power, the look of herself as a wolf, the incredible strength granted by some sort of science and magic blend. The prolonged life and the nearly endless youth. And the lust, the rampaging sexuality, the insatiable appetites carried by the werewolf gene.

Lupo found her irresistible.

Hell, he found Jessie Hawkins irresistible too, but Heather Wilson was...*different*.

Perhaps it was because she was like *him* now. Perhaps it was because she embraced it so completely, whereas he had spent most of his life denying it, fighting it, feeling guilty about it, right up to the suicide attempt that had been foiled at the last second by someone possibly even more fucked up than Lupo himself.

Jessie had snapped. After Lupo and Heather had joined forces to conduct a raid on the Washington, D.C., compound of Wolfpaw Security Services, the mercenary war contractor that traced its roots all the way back to World War II and the Nazis' last-resort *Werwolf* Brigade, Jessie had taken one of the two Vatican blades and attacked Heather with murderous intent.

She hadn't killed Heather (not for lack of trying), but she'd hurt the other woman badly. If Lupo hadn't caught up to her when he did, and stopped her, she would have been a murderer.

Thing was, he'd had little choice but to enlist Heather.

Wolfpaw had been more than just a mercenary army made up of werewolves. It had also continued the evil experiments first conducted by Nazi scientists in concentration camps, experiments the goal of which was to develop a better werewolf gene, one that would be nearly impervious to silver. They had almost succeeded, but part of what they needed was a chance to study Nick Lupo, for his "condition," as he referred to it, had come from different origins—and carried with it some inherent advantages.

And his family history contained more than was at first apparent, too. He learned his grandfather had been a young father caught up in the Italian partisan campaign during the last days of the war. The partisan brigade he had unwillingly joined had a pair of secret weapons—daggers that allowed humans to kill werewolves…but also allowed werewolves to kill others of their kind with less damage to themselves. The history of these daggers stretched farther back than anyone could have imagined, and it had been a Jesuit priest, Father Tranelli, who had obtained them from the secret Vatican vault next to the Archives, a chamber almost no one knew existed.

The Vatican blades had been separated after the war, and the tribe who occupied the reservation near Eagle River had obtained one of them thanks to a shaman named Joseph Badger.

Lupo shook his head.

As far as he knew.

Because there were still gaps in his knowledge. He expected Ghost Sam to show up and tell him the gaps were *large enough to drive a truck through*, but the clichés were more DiSanto's department.

It was too much, all of it was almost too much to process. He'd suffered so much since he'd been bitten by a neighbor boy as a teenager, never realizing that the universe had somehow placed him in this position. Never realizing that he was fulfilling some kind of destiny already laid out for his grandfather, who had succumbed to the bite of a werewolf even though he had become the partisans' best and most fanatic werewolf killer.

Giovanni Lupo's end had come at an unexpected hand, and Nick Lupo's own destiny had been set then, many years before he was born.

But Nick Lupo had never embraced his werewolf side, his *Creature*, the way Heather Wilson embraced hers.

Now he reshuffled the small pile of accumulated junk mail, circulars, political ads, and a few letters, dumping the disposable stuff in the trash. He flipped through the regular letters and spotted one that came from one of his mom's cousins.

This is weird, he thought.

His mother had recently succumbed to lung cancer, like his father several years before. In fact, it had happened in the middle of the Wolfpaw case, right when he was about to bring down the company and its board of trustees, and its CEO, the vile Schlosser. At the time, Lupo had been shocked to learn that the grandmother he had thought was his mom's mother had actually been his father's mother, the result of a long deception he had not quite understood. But a letter left for him and given to him by his mother on her deathbed had set him straight and informed him of events that, during the faraway war, had shaped his present situation — and indeed his entire life.

Over and over he flipped the envelope that had caught his eye, surprised by the return address. It was strange that his mind was turning over all these events, and here — at the same time—was a letter by his mother's estranged cousin, reaching him just now.

Somehow, Lupo felt he knew there was something of importance in his hand. He didn't know how he knew, but the *feeling* was there nonetheless. He'd always been susceptible to hunches.

In a sudden move, he tore the end of the envelope and tilted it. A key tumbled out and rattled onto the desktop. And then a folded sheet of paper fluttered out as well. He checked, but there was nothing else inside. He set the envelope aside, picked up the paper.

Your mother wanted you to have this.

It was signed with a single name. Not very forthcoming, his family. A duty fulfilled, perhaps, and nothing more.

He turned his attention to the key.

At first glance it was just a brass-tone key. It could have belonged anywhere. Maybe a padlock. It had a manufacturer's name on one side, and a number on the other in raised digits: J158. So, not a typical key at all—one with a specific purpose. Lupo thought, *airport or bus station locker.*

But why would his mother have had one of those? If she'd been a thief, or con artist, maybe. But he knew his mother had been none of those things. Now, his grandmother—the one who had pretended all his life to be another woman...well, that lady had secrets. Maybe this was *her* key? But that didn't feel right.

And it hit him.

Maybe this key belonged to his father.

He pulled out his iPad and started searching. Yes, he would try the airport and the bus terminal downtown. They'd added lockers now that the city had merged it with the Amtrak station.

But he had another, different hunch.

Google was helpful, but there were literally dozens of self-storage companies and locations.

This was going to take a little while.

Chapter Four

Franco Lupo

Genova, Italy
August 1945

The staircase was steeped in shadows, so he was forced to find a dark doorway that still allowed a full view of the rickety steps. The weak light at the top flickered with the inconsistent electricity, but it would be the only way to spot his quarry when he stepped out of the dingy second-floor apartment to go on his hunt.

Franco Lupo was now huddled in that deep doorway, a brick arch with a rounded door set in it that led to some sort of warehousing facility that had survived the Allied bombing runs. He hoped his slight figure wasn't visible from either the badly lit street or the staircase.

His quarry was careful.

He *had* to be.

As far as Franco could tell, his quarry had been a captain in the *Wehrmacht* but toward the end of the war he had been sucked into the *Werwolf* Brigade, and the story went that he'd found he liked it. This is what his source, an old guy wearing a greasy cap, had told Franco for a few hundred *lire* and a few glasses of red wine. Usually his information was solid enough.

Franco didn't care whether it was true, or where the old drunk had learned it. There were ex-German soldiers all over Europe in the days following the Liberation and many were left to live in peace. Some had formed family ties or cultivated important friendships while they were occupiers, and now they were protected.

Of course, some had been hunted down and outright executed, others prosecuted especially if they'd been either SS or Gestapo, or if their handprints had been connected in any way with any of the numerous atrocities committed even here, in relatively civilized Italy. The average German soldier who might have impregnated an Italian girl and later returned to claim his new family held no interest for Franco, even if some others might have been outraged enough to kill. In most cases, Italians lived and let live.

It had been only days since the second of two futuristic American bombs had brought the Japanese nation to its knees amidst the flare of a mushroom-shaped cloud of destruction. Even in Italy, the news had spread like a forest fire. People speculated how easily the Americans could have used such a devil's weapon against *them*, had not the Italian monarchy surrendered in September 1943.

Even for a people who had coined the word *vendetta*, the bombs seemed like too much.

But not to Franco, who understood.

Franco had smiled grimly when news of the death of the detested Adolf Hitler had been reported in April. Although, later, rumors indicated the possibility that a double had been used to fake a suicide and even now a diabolically resurrected *Führer* directed secret operations against an unsuspecting Allied invasion force. Franco could believe the murderous bastard had found a way to cheat death and continue to rain down destruction on his enemies. But the papers spoke of the reality of the bunker demise of the supreme dictator, and Franco turned his nose back to what he had been doing for over a year.

And his nose had been supremely successful indeed.

His nose was sensitive. His *heart* was not.

His heart hardened to an incredible degree, he now looked at the watch he had taken off a German corpse. The leather band was fraying, but the hands ticked their way around the steel dial with typical German efficiency. Clearly it was a watch produced in the early days of the war, when high-quality materials were plentiful to German industry. He rather enjoyed the irony.

It was almost time, if his information panned out.

A cool breeze off the Mediterranean ruffled his hair. The harbor, much of it still in ruins after numerous Allied bombing runs, was not far. This section of the city had been built up with factories and warehouses during the ill-fated alliance with Germany, the industry which later was usurped by the German war machine.

Franco stiffened at the sound of a single sharp *click*.

The door was nearly hidden on the landing and now it opened and a slice of yellow light stabbed out over the stairs.

He gripped the gnarled handle under his open wool coat and waited, his muscles tensing.

The steps were quiet, but Franco's ears had become sensitive. He knew his quarry was descending to street level, but slowly and with caution.

He faded back into the arched doorway, praying the shadow was large enough to cover him completely. He wasn't worried about scent, not yet: the footsteps were of the biped variety.

The steps reached the cobblestones and the man who made them headed directly for Franco's hiding place.

Franco started to pull the sheathed blade from under his coat.

The footsteps approached, coming closer, closer, and then Franco's quarry passed the arch and kept on the jaggedly uneven sidewalk slabs. Franco watched the matted hair but faded back into the shadows until the walker was well past, and then he slipped out and began to follow the ramrod-straight figure.

This one had to live.

For a brief while, anyway.

Chapter Five

Heather

As she drove away, she saw the glow of the burning car in her mirrors. She had driven the counterfeit cop's cruiser into the cornfield and debated whether to just leave it. Then, in a fit of anger, she'd torched it. There wasn't a town or village for twenty miles in any direction, so she'd be long gone by the time anyone came to investigate. They'd find blood traces of the ersatz officer, but probably not a whole lot of his body. She'd fed well and she'd covered her tracks, but didn't mind if they found the blood—that was the last they'd see of the guy.

And it tickled her sense of humor that they'd put the evidence together pointing to his creative sideline as a costumed performer…and that was it, everything else would be a dead end. The wolf had seen to it. They'd have to dig far into the corn and wheat fields to find anything at all. The irony of the predator finding a greater predator who turned the tables was right up her alley and she chuckled as she saw the dark smoke clouding the night sky.

An hour later she still hadn't passed any sort of rapid response to the burning vehicle. She knew from her own experience that the fire she'd set would burn out—possibly already had—and that the dew-dampened fields were not likely to catch fire.

Scanning through the buttons, she found some classic rock on the satellite and sang along to a Styx song in which she could lament having too much time on her hands.

She was heading east for a meeting and then farther east for a reunion of sorts.

And she'd used her time rather well, actually, even if some of it was painful enough for her to scream in anger and frustration into the night.

That bitch really sliced the hell out of me. If Lupo hadn't intruded, though, I might have taken her with me...

Her scars were finally starting to fade, though they still itched and burned like fuck and occasionally drove her crazy, mostly in the middle of the night when she was trying to sleep—or trying to play sex games with some anonymous new partner. The scars would never fully disappear she suspected, but they were almost invisible in subdued lighting, so she didn't get many questions...but she was definitely touchy about them. She had once almost lost her temper with a particularly cocky pseudo-cowboy from a roadhouse she'd taken home to her motel who kept tracing the lines that crossed her hard belly, not realizing that he was inciting not only her anger but pure burning pain. She'd almost crushed his head between her muscular thighs and broken his neck, a move she'd practiced with certain others until she could pull it off easily enough. She didn't even need to *wolf out* to end the guy's spin on the planet. He'd had no idea how lucky he was.

The anger could sneak up on her sometimes.

She set it aside until a Pink Floyd song reminded her of Nick Lupo. She did, indeed, *wish he were there*.

She was not really sure why she found him so damn intriguing. He'd been a werewolf long before she had, but he'd been so tortured about it, his life so fucked-up, that she was interested despite herself. He was damned good-looking, that was sure, but he hated being a *creature*, as he called it. Hell, she'd *loved* her new life as soon as she'd figured out the basics. She'd especially embraced the enhanced libido, the genetic multiplier of her already outsized sex drive. She'd taken the other stuff, like the eating of raw, live meat, as purely entertaining or at worst necessary.

An anchorwoman colleague of hers had once accused her of being a *Maneater*, like the song she'd said. Heather laughed aloud now at the memory. Hell, she'd proven her right!

In a certain weird way, running into Nick Lupo through the Wolfpaw and casino case, in which she'd been bitten by one of the mercenaries—the lovely Tef, whose body she had drilled with silver slugs before Lupo's inner *creature* had torn him apart—had brought her this new life and lifestyle. From what she now understood, besides expanding all her appetites, the werewolf gene also extended her life, and therefore her youth and beauty.

She had to admit, the slowing of her aging process wasn't anything to sneeze at. It was a gift only superheroes got. Not that she was anything like that. She was way too interested in herself.

But Nick Lupo was, in a roundabout way, the reason she was now a beautiful wolf whose ecstatic howls filled the night wherever she happened to be. And whose frequent sex partners benefited from the raw animal lust she now brought to everything she did.

She could still taste that fake cop. She licked her lips—no need to stop for a snack now. He'd been like a drive-through.

She chuckled deep down in her throat.

Things were looking up again.

Heather wasn't the type to let grass grow under her feet, as the old saw went. She'd had to take a break from television work, but she had great credentials and she gave great interview, and she wasn't averse to fucking a prospective boss.

No, she'd get back into television whenever she chose to. All she had to do was smile, maybe whistle...*put your lips together and blow*, as another blonde bombshell had once uttered in a different context.

Her book project was about to get an infusion of insider information. Her imminent meeting would add weight to her already scandalous history of Wolfpaw Security Services, one that she hoped would hit the bestseller lists given the company's very public implosion. Even though she couldn't tell the world the truth about Wolfpaw and its werewolf mercenaries, or for Christ's sake their origins, they'd been involved in so much everyday crime—as the congressional hearings had shown—that she didn't need to embellish, and the rest of it could stay buried for now.

She sensed that the world was better off not knowing about werewolves, but sometimes she was careless. She'd learned her lesson, but then again she had always tended to be carefree and she was likely to let the worrywarts like Lupo take care of things.

Right now, she was only interested in herself, her book project...*and Nick Lupo*.

The satellite DJ cued up Genesis, "*Tonight Tonight Tonight*."

She drove on into the night, reminiscing.

And looking ahead.

Chapter Six

Rabbioso

"You wanted to see me?"

He closed the study door and stepped inside his boss's inner sanctum. He had almost said *boss*, but just in time remembered that this particular boss insisted he never wanted to hear the word. Made him sound like a thug, he said on rare occasions when he was willing to share his thoughts.

Of course, all evidence pointed to the fact that he *was* a thug, but there were thoughts best left unexplored.

And right now he wasn't sharing any of his thoughts. Don Bastone's face was half-turned toward a wall-hugging flat television on which naked bodies entwined amidst groaning and moaning and the grunts of animal sex.

Rabbioso wasn't thrilled that the Don's tastes ran to the wall-to-wall porn he seemed to have on wherever he set up camp. He was happy, however, that both the Don's hands were in full view and not in his lap.

"Yeah, Robb. Sit, sit. Have a drink."

Rabbioso was also not happy he'd somehow become the vaguely distasteful *Robb*. He did stand at the cherry-wood side bar and pour himself a stiff straight Bacardi, though, swirling the gold liquid in the snifter. He'd developed a taste for rum when working in South America. Now he sat across from Don Bastone, who was finally driven to mute the action on the screen and reluctantly turn away.

The Don's current top lieutenant wondered what made a man need to wallpaper his world with carnality. As usual, he wondered but he didn't want to know. It was safer that way.

The rum warmed his insides after the cold desert run. The liquor masked the taste of blood still in his mouth. He waited for the boss to speak.

Bastone poured himself a white vermouth and added a generous slug of vodka, a poor man's martini in a water glass. He just liked it that way.

He was a handsome man with salt-and-pepper hair, but he was getting paunchy because he'd given up his previously active life when he succeeded to the family patriarchy. He was too young to be old-fashioned and he was too old to be a renegade, so he'd settled in as a sort of spoiled prince. His watery eyes reminded Rabbioso of those one might spot on a strait-jacketed inmate at some asylum. He always wanted to keep that in mind.

"That little problem, it's taken care of?" said the prince.

"Oh, yeah, definitely a done deal." Rabbioso swished some rum around. "No one will find him, don't worry."

The prince leaned forward over the desk. "I'm *not* worried. I expect success."

"Of course." Rabbioso nodded. He knew his place. *At least for a while...*

"How long you been with me, Robb? And how long you been back?"

Rabbioso thought, carefully. "With you twelve years. Took two, two and a half years off. Back two years now."

"How was the desert, Robb, when you were out there?"

He wanted to say, *It was dry, asshole*. But instead he said, "It was a fucked-up mess in more ways than I can count. But I made a lot of money and…served my country."

"And killed a buncha people, right?"

"I killed some." Keeping it vague was always best.

Bastone made a *there you go* gesture with one soft hand. "See, that's…what do they call it? *Street cred*. Am I right? Am I right?"

"Yeah, I guess that's what they call it." He sipped his rum, waiting to see where this was going. He could kill Bastone in about thirty seconds, but it wouldn't help him in the long run. The family would never stop seeking revenge. The Don had brothers, sisters, aunts and uncles, and several male children all chomping at the bit to make their bones. Revenge would look good on the resumé. Rabbioso would end up regretting it, even if getting his jaws into the bastard's guts would have felt fine indeed. For the moment, he preferred playing the fawning underling.

"*You* have it," the Don mused, continuing on his own path. He sipped his so-called martini. "My father had it. My uncles have it. Hell, my grandfather had it. Street cred." He looked at Rabbioso again over the rim of his glass, where the liquor touched his lips. "Do I have it, Robb?"

Fuck.

This was dangerous ground. Bastone was like an overgrown child. Petulant and self-involved, entitled, easily aggrieved. Not at all like his father and uncles, who were hard men and not soft at all. Their street cred came easily.

He wanted to tell his boss that if you had to ask if you had street cred, you didn't have it by a long shot.

But he didn't pause very long. To do so would have been no different than giving the wrong answer.

"Sure you got street cred. I've heard people mention your name in a whisper because they're afraid someone's gonna report to you. Your men know you've gotten your hands dirty." It was true, he had gotten his hands bloody on several occasions, but it hadn't gone well. Still, he'd proven he was perfectly capable of ordering the torture of men, and had. It wasn't really street cred, but if he thought it was, then who would have argued?

"Good." The prince sat back, apparently satisfied.

Rabbioso wondered what this was about, but he was willing to wait for the little prince to get around to telling him.

They drank in companionable silence for a few minutes. Rabbioso loved the golden color of the rum and savored the taste. Bastone sipped noisily, probably not even realizing he was making a face, not enjoying the taste at all. It was a grown-up drink, and the Don didn't qualify.

Part of having street cred was not making faces when you don't like something, Rabbioso thought. There were all sorts of things connected to having real street cred, and Bastone had very few of them.

The Don sipped again but didn't make a face. Getting used to it. "You know besides the Old Italy, I have interests in a couple other casinos here in Vegas, right?"

Trick question?

"Yeah, the Western Round-Up and the Patrician." Both were recent startups and doing well, if not spectacularly. In the constant reinvention of the Las Vegas skyline, one looked like an old-fashioned Rat Pack-era casino and the other was vying for some of the Wynn's clientele by aping its forward-looking architecture. Bastone was silent partner in both ventures, and had a small percentage of some other small off-Strip operations.

"But I don't have anything back home."

"Right," Rabbioso agreed, not sure where this was going.

"I would like to have something going back home, something to increase my street cred. You follow?" The Don stared at him across the desk.

Rabbioso knew the Bastone family had started out in Atlantic City before the old Don had spread out west. But in the sixties the old Don had resettled in the Midwest and made an effort to at least look legit, leaving behind the old-fashioned rackets—drugs and prostitution—for a full-on attack on the gambling world. With operations in both A.C. and Vegas, the family fortune had been made by the seventies. The problem was that the new Don, Prince Gus, apparently wanted to somehow increase his family's profile for the feds.

"Sure," he said. "I guess you have a new expansion picked out?"

"That's what I like about you, Robb," the Don said. "You get it right off the bat. Can't say the same for everybody who works for me."

Rabbioso sipped his rum. It was always best to let the prince do the talking.

"One area that's been untapped by those of *our thing*," the Don started, meaning the *cosa nostra*, a term few people used these days with the possible exception of feds in tiny puke-green offices, "is those fuckin' Indian casinos. That's like fruit ripe for pickin'."

"I think there've been some attempts to get in there, in the tribal casinos," Rabbioso said carefully. "But they got a Regulatory Act watching over them, and it's a bit tougher than just buying in."

"Who's talking about buyin' in? I'm thinking of musclin' in. And I got just the place in mind."

"Okay." Rabbioso figured the orders were coming now. He finished his rum, savoring the pleasant burn down his throat.

"Since my father built his house in Milwaukee, I kept a foot in that state. As you know…"

The Don had a mansion on Milwaukee's fashionable Lake Drive, where he spent half the spring and summer, most years. Behind the wall it was an armed compound, but from the street it looked like a woodsy lot with an oversize Tudor nestled among the trees. Circular drive, guest house. It was a fortress.

"I had contacts in the state lookin' out for an opportunity last couple months. And one has been brought to me, a new operation on a reservation next to Vilas County up north there. Not far from Eagle River, you know, where I go fishin' few times a year. Got a great muskie there once. Fought like a bastard."

Anyway…

Rabbioso said nothing. He wished he'd poured a bigger rum.

"Anyway, I'm actively lookin' to expand in that area, I have a contact on the ground, and a couple guys are there to get things off on the right foot. You know Johnny—" Rabbioso nodded "—and I'm sending you over to do some additional ground work."

"Huh, okay." Rabbioso thought fast. Eagle River, why was that familiar? He hadn't been fishing with the Don, maybe that was while he was…away. In the desert, as the boss put it. "Whatever you want."

"Have another drink," said the Don. He seemed to be in fine spirits.

Rabbioso did so, relieved he had something to do. He looked around the office, the inner sanctum, that few of the men got to see. That mounted fish up there, maybe that was the muskie the Don was talking about. It *was* a large fucker, shaped like a barracuda. There were bookcases full of books the boss probably didn't read. There were toys and gadgets lying around, like a telescope and a lighted globe. There was some tasteful art somebody else had probably picked out. It was an office like what the Don thought a rich guy's office should look, not so much one that reflected his tastes. Except for the TV and the 24/7 porn. *That* was the boss's taste. He got ready to hear the rest of his sentence, hoping he'd get off lightly.

He sat and took a long taste, and the Don continued.

"So I got somebody there and he found me a house. Sent me some pictures on the computer today." He flipped the flat monitor around a little so Rabbioso could see.

It was a huge two-story log cabin with two wings jutting out from the main house, a wide stone chimney rising from the middle, a pyramid-like center with wide-open glass panels right up to the green steel roof, a wraparound veranda and a basketball court-sized deck starting from the end of one of the wings and wrapping around the rear. Looked like a house-sized garage lurked out back on the left, too, with maybe an all-season pool enclosure. It was like a skiing chalet pumped up on hormones and steroids, a millionaire's fancy getaway in the mountains—except there were no mountains in northern Wisconsin, just some rolling hills and a lot of woods surrounding cold lakes shaped like fat fingers.

The damned assignment was looking better every second.

"Nice place," he said evenly.

"It's an oversize shack and they want two-and-a-half mil for it, the vultures." The Don smiled like a shark, all teeth and no lip. "But it was worth five and the dipshit actor who owned it had his career tank and now it's a fire sale. They'll take my lowball, don't worry. I'm movin' in, maybe about a month. You're going in early with a squad, lay some ground work, get some stuff done."

"What stuff?" Rabbioso's attention was slipping. He was trying to remember why he should know Eagle River, but he was also seriously loving the idea of letting the wolf run in those woods. You got tired of the desert, and he'd had plenty of that the last few years.

"There may be a spot of trouble with the tribe. Some people there will be all for our *partnership*, others will not. I need you to help smooth things with those who may not be in agreement. Pretty much up to you how you accomplish that. I pay you to troubleshoot, so troubleshoot. I want you to do pre-emptive troubleshooting."

Rabbioso was intrigued. "Give me the details and I'll pack a bag."

The Don smiled the lipless smile again. "I'm sending you and the muscle by car. Take longer, but you can bring your...*tools*. Pack two bags, one long and heavy. Figure on heading out tomorrow. Oh, and take this new kid Tony. After your stuff is done, leave him somewhere in the desert, okay?"

The Don laid out more details, and now Rabbioso's attention was focused.

He'd always been task-centered.

He saw the house photo still up on the monitor. Those woods were calling him.

Bastone had switched his attention back to the garish screen and unmuted the picture. Orgasmic groans and screams emanated from the action, which—as far as Rabbioso could figure—had never let up for the length of his stay. *How do those guys keep from popping?*

Suddenly he couldn't wait to get going, pack up the car and get out of the desert for a while. Away from Bastone and his weird ways. The little prince was acting more irrationally every month. Rabbioso almost made a face, but caught himself.

He wanted to hunt.

Two birds with one stone.

Jessie

The itch took her in the middle of her later shift.

The rez hospital was suffering an uncharacteristic lull at the moment. Bar fights were down, domestic battery was probably still level but no one was reporting any (not that *that* was unusual, really), and the flu epidemic had apparently peaked for the season. She had only a handful of patients and they were all comfortably tucked in and content.

She was just done with her second rounds this shift and had stopped for an iced tea in the cafeteria when she had a flashback.

A *flashback*?

What else could you call it?

The hospital was really an oversize clinic, though some rather impressive equipment like a GE MRI machine had been purchased recently with funds partly raised by the tribe's flourishing casino. But the cafeteria reminded her so much of the food court located in the heart of the casino, the lights of which she could see blinking erotically through the window...hell, she was almost certain the design of both spaces had been done by the same architecture firm, if you could call any food court space *design* of any kind. But as she sat with her tea and the lights caught her eye, the itch started in her fingertips and crawled up her hand, wrist, forearm, and suddenly she was scratching her shoulders, hugging herself as if she were cold.

Goddamn it, it *was* a kind of flashback.

The shivers started a few minutes later.

She hadn't told Nick about *this*, not about the fact that sometimes this happened to her despite the therapy, despite the meditation. Despite the willpower she'd been able to bring to bear so often to so many other things.

Jessie was strong. Nick always told her so. She'd always been able to do whatever needed to be done.

Whatever needed to be done.

Like using an axe on Nick's foot one very bad day.

Like using a crossbow or a shotgun to kill.

Like having sex with a lovely man who also happened to turn into a werewolf, sometimes not so intentionally.

Okay, it was *great* sex…but still, it was—like all those other things—something that required some kind of strength beyond the everyday.

She had that strength, in spades.

Well, then why was her skin itching and feeling as if ants were crawling all over it?

She scratched for all she was worth, hoping no one who passed through would notice.

She nodded at Sally, a nurse who may have given her a second look. She smiled at Doctor Gorgeous (no, his name was Gregorius, a new hire), hoping he wasn't frowning at her.

It seemed like a moment later she had dumped the drink in a trash can and was headed across the way to the casino's main entrance.

I'm just gonna go look for a while.

Her therapist had told her she could work her way up to walking into the casino and watching, like arachnophobes could benefit from seeing spiders up close or something, but she was jumping the gun.

Barely knowing how it had happened, suddenly she was sliding her player's card into a slot machine. Her ears were full of the C Major chord constantly playing, ringing, beeping, tinkling, throughout the cavernous space filled with aisles full of games.

She was at a game called *Wolf Run* (irony!) and watching the red credits drop as she pressed the Max Bet button over and over.

Nick had no idea she'd held on to the card. Nor did her therapist.

Jessie pressed Max Bet until she had lost a whole hundred whatever they were. Quarters? Dollars? She wasn't sure.

She wanted to cry.

Strong in every fucking thing in life, but this *thing*, this stupid habit, was beating her.

She cashed out, snatched her card from the slot when it reluctantly peeked out, and strode toward the door, thoroughly disgusted with herself.

Maybe it was good she'd come, and was now removing herself with determination. *Had to count for something, right?*

Then she spotted a *Wheel of Fortune* slot and granted herself a spin. *What the hell?* Maybe she could make up what she'd lost. *Then* she would leave. *Really, for sure.*

The tall machine towered over her, basically a typical three-panel slot married to a small wheel of fortune set directly above that was styled on the one on the syndicated TV game show, where a straight-across-the-screen win could be multiplied depending on the spin that was granted. It was one of a pod of four facing the compass directions.

She was vaguely aware that a two men were directly opposite her, one seated and the other hovering over his shoulder. They were smoking, which made her nostrils twitch, but even though she disapproved she'd become accustomed to the casino's smoking environment, which did not have to follow state indoor smoking laws. Besides, it was the price of doing business...as if losing cash to the House was somehow constructive.

Jessie wrestled with the urge, but slid her card into the slot anyway, getting an almost primal sexual thrill from it.

Her therapist said it might have something to do with the danger she'd faced so often, being with Nick, and she was reacting by finding a safer (but almost as unhealthy) outlet in the gambling.

Whatever!

She spun the cylinders and watched them until one after the other stopped. Three different icons. Without thinking, she spun again on Max Bet. This time all three cylinders stopped on the BAR-BAR icon and her credit total zoomed up. The wheel of fortune above came to life and played the theme music and she pressed the Spin button, which brought her a doubling of the credits, a win of probably seventy-five dollars.

She spun it again.

Winning held little thrills for her, though she was damned if she understood why.

The two guys on the other side had leaned over to look when the machine had signaled her win, then they'd ducked back behind their own machine. *Probably trying harder now that they know it can be done.*

She forced herself to stand, cash out and pull her card, then stepped over to a nearby slot machine island and circled it, looking for a specific model with which she'd had good luck. She spotted the quarter machine and settled into the seat. Idly she noticed that she was now directly behind the two guys at the *Wheel of Fortune*, but somewhat hidden by her machine and those next to it.

She slid in her card. Waiting as it totaled up, her ears picked up what one guy was telling the other.

"Look, dontcha think we should get back to the boss before it gets too late? Remember the time difference between here and Vegas?"

"Chill out, man. I need to make up for that last loser. You saw that chick win on these, right? I've heard they pay slightly better."

"Okay, Johnny, I'm just sayin' the boss is kinda impatient."

The machine made its sounds and Jessie was fascinated with seeing if the guy was going to win, so she ignored her own machine's blinking come-on and eavesdropped shamelessly.

The guy playing, Johnny, was a slightly too old pretty-boy type wearing a lightweight black blazer. He had longer-than-average dark hair slicked back so it stayed out of his way, but it emphasized his receding hairline. Though his features were sharp, he might have been considered a hunk maybe ten years ago.

Jessie felt guilty rating guys like this, but hell, didn't they do it with women all the time? She mentally compared him to Nick and found him wanting in every way, so that was something.

The other guy, the nervous one who wanted to call the boss like they were supposed to, was shorter and dumpier, and younger too, a sidekick type if ever there was one. He was wearing a distressed leather jacket over a red polo and black jeans. His features were soft, maybe too sedentary a life, and his skin was bad from childhood acne. His hair was short but shaggy and the kind of blond that was a bit too neon to be real. He looked around nervously as if he didn't want them spotted, but had apparently forgotten Jessie sneaking in behind them.

For some reason, call it a hunch, she found herself sliding her chair a little to the right so she could hide more of herself behind the slots, but could still peek around the corner and see them. Their voices weren't loud, but by a weird trick of the room she could hear them better than people on the other side of her island.

Johnny kept betting and his cylinders kept giving him losses. She saw him slide more cash into the slot.

"Christ, Johnny, you wanna lose that hundred? These games are rigged, man."

"Just—shut up, Marty, I'm gonna try a few spins."

"Hell, why not wait until the merger goes through? Then you'll be able to play every fuckin' day until you run outta money."

"Yeah, the *merger*," Johnny said contemptuously. He laughed. "When the cash starts leaking out of this joint it ain't gonna look much like a merger, just a huge drain guzzling right up into the boss's basement. We get a fat bonus, some folks here get their Cayman accounts fatted up, everybody's happy. The boss'll be a silent partner, see, and he's gonna suck this place dry. This tribe's not on federal land so they don't have to show their books and when the boss leans on people they do what he wants them to. No one's gonna know the money stream's going in a different direction, and no one can swoop down here and check. We're gonna be on staff to *facilitate operations*. I love this corporate bullshit."

Suddenly the overwhelming, perpetual C Major chord in all its bleating, blooping and bleeping jangle faded away in her ears and all she heard was the two nearby voices.

"Yeah, but we'll be stuck in this backwater. I'd rather be in Vegas any day, man."

"You seen the place we'll be living in? It's like a mansion. And the chicks here aren't half bad."

Jessie leaned back a little and tried to pretend she was playing her machine, but her eyes shifted to where the two lounged.

Her heart raced.

"Yeah, yeah, all you care about is the chicks. You seen any night life in fuckin' Eagle River? The place is a dump. Tourist trap, T-shirt shops, dive bars. Man, give me Vegas or the Big Apple, okay?"

"Well, you know the boss'll rotate us out in 'bout a year, when he's got his fingers in every pie here, so we'll have that much more cash to spend. You're gonna love this new joint I found in Vegas—and you're gonna need more money to have a good time there, believe me. The chicks there…let's just say the lap dances'll melt your balls. But it ain't cheap, and we can sock away a nice bundle here."

"So when does the muscle get here?" Marty said. He glanced around and Jessie leaned forward so she wouldn't seem like an eavesdropper.

"Any day now," Johnny said as he spun the machine. "Robb and the guys are driving. The house is almost ready, then we'll move in and the—"

The machine went nuts.

"Hey, lookit that!"

"Holy shit, you just won two hundred bucks!" Marty said, awed.

"Let's give the wheel a spin," Johnny said as the TV wheel theme played. There was canned clapping and cheering from the machine's speaker.

"Doubled!" said Marty. "You're a lucky fucker!"

"Drinks are on me. Let's blow this joint. There's a topless place just outside town. It ain't Vegas, but it'll do. They got two tits here just like home."

Jessie watched them as they collected Johnny's winning ticket from the slot, complete with annoying canned fanfare music. She stood up to try following them. But to her surprise they headed right for her, not the more logical other direction. *Probably lost, because casinos are intentionally made to confuse your sense of direction.*

She had to turn quickly to face her machine, half-huddled over it, then pressed the Bet button, because they were going to walk right past her from behind. She didn't want them to see her face.

Chuckling like hyenas, they sidled past the narrow aisle and she felt their gazes sizing her up. It was all she could do to avoid turning to stare right at them.

One of them—*Marty*, she thought—stage-whispered: "I'd eat at *that* buffet!"

And she *knew* he was staring at her ass.

She felt a flush creep across her face but pretended to be engrossed in her machine, which fortunately gave her a small win right at that moment, the red numbers climbing up until the counter stopped at sixty.

"See, you gave the little lady luck," Johnny said, clapping his buddy on the shoulder. "Let's roll, we got some work lined up after dinner."

"That's what I like to hear…"

Their voices faded into the background jingling and the noise seemed to increase in volume, roaring in her ears almost as loudly as the blood pumping through her heart.

Could it be?

Had the mob come to Eagle River?

Lupo

It was one of the older self-storage places, which made sense. Later Lupo could find out when it had been rented. He might need a warrant, but—looking at the manager's decrepit shack—a crumpled twenty might do the trick.

But first he wanted to see the contents.

He drove up to the gate, where a swipe box was mounted. There was also a keyhole with a covered switch. He felt eyes on him from the shack even though the window was covered by vertical shades. Leaving the car running, he stepped out and pushed the key into the keyhole. It turned freely a quarter turn. He flipped open the cover and pressed the button, then released the key so it could swing back to its initial position. The gate buzzed and started to open.

Lupo drove down one of the main streets between buildings full of separate units. Each block was lettered. He was hunting for J158, noticing he'd just driven past block F. He turned at the first crossroads and followed the letters. The blocks mostly looked the same from the outside. Finally he spotted block J and pulled up at the main door. He stared at it for a few minutes before walking up.

Once again, his key let him into the outside door. The corridor stretched out before him, dimly lit, with numbered, shuttered units on both sides. He found 158 quickly enough.

He stood at the door, heart pounding insistently.

Shaking his head, he held out the key. There was a sense, excited as he was, that once he opened the door he could never go back. He could never unlearn whatever waited for him in the long, narrow unit.

Did he want to know?

Did he want the responsibility?

This was where, in a movie, he'd learn that his father had been a serial killer or something equally disturbing. He barked a short laugh. He'd learned from his dying mother that his father *had* been a serial killer of sorts—a killer of werewolves. He'd been made one by circumstances beyond his control. He'd been turned into a murderer. He'd murdered Nick's grandfather, hadn't he?

His own father.

Lupo thought he understood his father's bitterness now. He wondered how much better their relationship would have been if Frank Lupo had shared his life's experiences with his son, instead of shutting him out.

But he hadn't, preferring to remain grim and silent.

He knew with certainty that his father would have killed him, had he realized his son had become a monster. He had that silver-loaded Beretta shotgun, and with it he had helped trap and kill Andy Corrazza, the neighbor boy who had been the innocent carrier between Sam Waters' son and Nick. Thankfully Frank Lupo'd never tried to take his son shooting, for Nick was sure he couldn't have hidden his painful aversion to the silver.

Lupo shrugged.

"Come on, Nick, what are you waiting for?" Ghost Sam's voice from behind his shoulder was somehow comforting rather than startling. "Let's see what your old man was up to. You've wondered for years what was up with him, so why wait now? Why put it off?"

Lupo nodded, steeling himself. Then he turned the key and opened the door.

Chapter Seven

Franco Lupo

August 1945

The ramrod-straight figure had passed his hiding place only a minute before. He followed from a distance.

The cobbled street was deserted and Franco stayed well back, using the sound of his quarry's boots on the bricks to orient himself. He tried to stick to the shadows but jumping from one dark spot to another would make him more visible, not less, so he hung back and let his ears do the work. The shuttered store fronts gave little shelter in any case, and he was afraid he would lose his only connection to a group of *them*.

Sometimes Franco couldn't even think of the word that described them, so he thought only of *them*, and of his hate. The all-consuming hate he felt for the monsters who had killed his father.

In the darkest part of the night, Franco knew *he* had killed his father. He knew what he had done, but he had convinced himself it had been his battle for his father's very soul, and therefore he would be forgiven.

But he might never forgive himself.

Now he hoped he could use this one to lead him to a nest of other monsters. Once he knew where they congregated, he would target them one by one and finish the job he had started during the war.

He came to a turn, not quite a corner, where the more modern street followed the slope of the land down toward the docks. There was a haze of light farther down the street, the first environs of the great sprawling port. It was probably a work area lit by floodlights.

Then Franco realized that he was alone on the sidewalk. He was still heading downhill, still on the way to the docks, but somehow his quarry had disappeared. He slowed and scanned the neighboring buildings. Several ancient block-like structures with few windows, one rebuilt since the end of the bombings, an empty lot where a warehouse once stood...and a number of shuttered doorways in the block he had just passed. The empty lot, however, was in shadows cast by the relatively low buildings around it, forming a sort of alley. He was even with it now, slowing his steps, and coming to a stop.

And just as he scanned the empty dark space he heard the growl, and in a flash his eyes captured the image of a white-skinned tall naked man, his penis erect and huge, blurring into that of a lean but muscular wolf in midair, a leap that would connect with Franco in a split second.

Its eyes blazing and wide-open jaws snapping, the wolf was already at the end of his trajectory when Franco's stunted reaction finally allowed him to finish drawing the blade from its wooden scabbard.

His sideways slash connected with the monster's matted fur as he shouldered the great head aside and the jaws snapped in midair. As the snout turned back toward him, the tip of the blade sank into the wolf's belly and Franco's arm followed through and the blade zipped the animal open. A great rush of hot blood spattered onto Franco even as he twisted away from the beast's flaying claws.

The monster squealed in surprise. *And terrible pain...*

Franco whirled so he could face the wolf when it landed, but the animal arrived off balance and its head smacked the pavement as its paws scrabbled for purchase on the smooth cobblestones.

Franco smiled grimly.

Here was a monster who wouldn't lead him to the others of its kind meeting nearby, but neither would it ever feed on a human again. Whenever he faced one of these monstrous visions of hell his faith should have been reinforced, but instead Franco's faith retreated further within the depths of his heart, what was left of it.

For who could accept the existence of heaven if creatures spawned from hell were allowed to walk the earth and feed on innocents?

The wounded wolf scrambled to face Franco, its slavering jaws trembling with the increasing pain. It continued squealing as the fiery burning spread through its veins and muscles and tendons.

Franco's weapon was doing its work.

He stepped back and watched.

Since he had begun using the dagger, he had seen wounds that should have been minor in nature fester and kill. This had been a serious wound—a straight slash across the beast's chest—and the nature of the dagger increased the damage exponentially. Sometimes the special silver set the monster's skin and blood to burning from the inside out. Franco never felt any pity.

The monster's eyes still blazed, but the light there was rapidly fading and the animal staggered sideways, its legs collapsing out from under its body but unevenly.

Its howl turned into a scream of unbelievable pain as the silvery poison shot through its flesh and organs. Its snout dug into the bricks as if it could burrow itself into the ground, and Franco quickly stepped up and drew the blade first across its neck and then into its belly. The flesh and muscle parted like lard and foul-smelling blood from above and entrails from below poured out onto the bricks.

The wolf's death throes fascinated Franco and he watched, dispassionately, as it died in agony. Its body twitched and shook and then finally lay still.

Then it blurred and it was the tall man again, gutted, his genitals shriveled, lying in a puddle of his own filth.

Franco spit on the body, then made the sign of the cross with the dagger before resheathing it.

Remembering that he was still standing in the street, he stepped toward the shadows and melted into the darkness.

There would be no surveillance of a meeting place tonight, but there would also be one less monster taking its victims from the city's outskirts, making meals out of poor farmers.

Tomorrow he would start watching again.

Franco figured there was no one else to do this job.

He slipped away before the *carabinieri* could find him standing over the ex-Nazi's corpse.

Chapter Eight

Shooter

The bus stop was one of the largest in the central downtown area. On the corner of Wisconsin Avenue and Water Street, near the sluggish river, it routinely pulled ten to twenty regular riders every twenty minutes who waited for one of the several routes that crossed at that corner: the Green Line, the 57, the newly redrawn 15, which had been returned to its Water Street roots, and most of the summer-only trolley lines that circled the more interesting portions of Milwaukee's stately old-fashioned downtown.

Unlike most other large city bus stops, this one did not have a Plexiglas and steel shelter structure, most likely because the bank building that dominated that corner left only a few feet to the edge of the sidewalk in both directions. A shelter would have impeded pedestrian flow as well as being an eyesore, if it was haphazardly connected to the building's limestone blocks.

Today was no different and for the twentieth time a dozen or so people had gathered to wait for the next Green Line bus, which was scheduled to arrive in the next three to five minutes. While the weather was not yet truly cold, the downtown breeze that blew in off Lake Michigan—which was almost visible just down the sloping Wisconsin Avenue—was frigid and the waiting riders huddled in their coats and hoods, accustomed to the lingering Midwestern winters even though of late they'd been milder. Milder but drawn out, most people agreed, was still better. Still, the riders perked up when they saw the bus making the slight turn as it came even with city hall and headed straight down Water Street.

Some of the riders noted that the bus seemed to be barreling toward the stop at a faster clip than was advisable, especially since in addition to the waiting group eagerly heading toward the curb, the light was also turning red. No driver should have been so lead-footed on their approach to a large stop and a busy intersection.

Nervous, one or two who were waiting took a few careful steps backward, away from the curb. Others paid little attention, stamping their feet in frustrated impatience.

Suddenly one woman screamed.

Two others looked up to see what was wrong and followed the screaming woman's stare and pointing finger, realizing much too late that the bus was not only still speeding, but had suddenly swerved toward the group.

People scattered as they became aware that the screaming bus was hurtling right at them, not slowing but increasing speed. Its front right tire slammed into the curb at an angle and blew, but the momentum and the racing engine caused it to jump the curb and continue on its way like the squared-off cylindrical cannonball it had become. The second front tire blew and collapsed but the bus was already gorging itself on the sidewalk full of slow-moving, confused victims, several of whom had simply stood staring in disbelief at its windshield and the great gout of blood that painted the inside crimson with splashes of grotesque pink.

Arms and legs were torn asunder as the huge vehicle ground up the riders it caught under its tremendous weight, ramming others and crushing a few more between its bulldozing front end and the bank's solid limestone blocks, leaving behind streaks of blood and entrails.

Screams and cries for help were smothered by the screeching created by the bus as its metal impacted the bank walls and its victims before continuing on toward the other major street, Wisconsin Avenue, where cross-traffic was caught in the runaway vehicle's sights. The bus engine screamed as it powered the vehicle across the corner, demolished the stoplight pole, and shed jagged parts like cheese passing across a grater, leaving behind broken and twisted bodies dabbed in red.

The bus continued into the cross street and smashed into a semi-trailer heading east on Wisconsin Avenue after crossing the near-side lane, the two of them spinning around and taking them all the way to the edge of the large bridge that spanned the river at that point, where despite the still-roaring engines they came to a halt because there were no wheels left to continue the forward motion.

The semi driver was crushed to death by the marauding bus, but could be credited with having stopped the killer vehicle's rampage.

Twenty-three people who had either been waiting for the bus or had been unlucky enough to be crossing one street or the other were killed or gravely injured.

The first uniform cop to arrive on the scene, a ten-year veteran named Voltanek, called for multiple ambulances, his voice cracking as he surveyed the devastation across the street corner and onto the avenue. His partner was able to set up a perimeter and start diverting traffic until the crime scene could be secured.

But when Voltanek finally boarded the bus to check on the driver and what might have happened there, what he found caused him to call dispatch again.

"I'm gonna need fuckin' Homicide here!" he squawked into his radio.

The call was routed to the Homicide squad room, where Detective DiSanto took it.

Chapter Nine

Heather

Madison, Wisconsin

A chilly breeze off Lake Mendota ruffled her hair through the car windows, which were lowered a crack.

She was meeting her source at one of the University of Wisconsin campus hangouts, a place known for its gigantic breakfasts on game day. The Camp Randall field house was visible just past the railroad tracks as she pulled into a space down the block on Regent, near Monroe. She was early, so she checked her face in the rearview mirror, fixed whatever looked wrong, which was never much, and kept an eye behind her. Traffic was light, and she wanted a chance to spot this guy if he decided to sneak up on her from behind.

She'd dumped her bags in a motel east of town on 94 and doubled back past the capitol building and straight down the spit of land between Lake Monona to the southeast and the larger Mendota, just north of the campus.

Not at all sure why this guy had picked this meeting spot, but she'd driven straight through since her little encounter in Nebraska.

She glanced at the mirror. Still nothing much behind her. She caught her reflection though, wondering if it was a mistake to have reverted to her honey-gold mane of hair. People were sure to remember her from her days as an anchor and investigative reporter in Wausau, and later Washington, D.C., though they might not be so clear how she'd been involved in the Wolfpaw takedown she and Nick Lupo had engineered.

Well, the two of them and that wacko Simonson, who'd turned out to have one foot in reality and the other in la-la land.

Now thinking of Lupo, the angled planes of his face, his long swept-back hair (against most MPD regulations), the compact muscular physique now crisscrossed by scars similar to hers...

She shifted in her seat. She was wet thinking about him.

She smiled at herself in the mirror, licked her lips, and remembered his body above her, thrusting, and beneath her with her legs astraddle as she rode him. And then: Her mouth on him, worshiping, licking, her eyes fixed on his, and the two of them watching each other's pupils spinning like multi-color kaleidoscopes.

And then this: On all fours with *him* behind her, his flesh reaching deep within her, finding her center, while their inner creatures connected, blending into one.

Screaming, grunting, growling with pleasure and finally collapsing spent and sweaty onto her stomach with him still buried inside her to the hilt, still hard and ready for more. And she, ready to take it.

The musky scent of her sex permeated the air and she shifted again.

Damn it, Nick, we were meant to be together.

Then again, there were issues—*obstacles*—to be overcome.

That bitch, Jessie.

Her newest scars still throbbed with aches she could barely stand, most days challenging her ability to appear unconcerned about anything. It had taken over two months to heal, and even then she really hadn't yet. She'd wondered if she would heal at all, this time. The Vatican blade wielded by *the bitch* had done its damage, had almost ended it all for her, and she still harbored a very real sense of hatred for the person who'd forced her to go on the run, literally to lick her wounds.

She'd screamed out incoherently as the silver poison had worked its way through her system, not at all sure it would. She'd managed to rent a remote cabin in the mountains and shrieked her way through the waves of pain that struck without scheme or pattern, wondering if she'd see the next full moon. She'd found that some pains were worse in her wolf form, while others were worse in her human form, making her walk like a damned cripple. Problem was, she never knew which pains would show up when. Her life had become a nightmare of scorching, slicing pain through her joints, veins, tendons, bones, and skin. No part of her seemed immune.

But she'd started to write whenever she could stand the pain. At first it was therapy. And then it became a mission. When she realized that she would survive, she had half a book about Wolfpaw Security Services written and the other half sketched out.

Of course, there were *things* she'd had to leave out. Details no one would want to see in a nonfiction work, that was for sure. But she still had plenty of material.

And today she would get some more.

Thankfully the image of Nick Lupo fucking her had receded and she could concentrate again on her meeting.

Which was just about now.

She entered the funky diner, found a place along a side wall, one of several angular high-backed booths. She ordered an iced tea from a bored waitress—business was down outside of game day, which was probably why her source had wanted to meet here. She drank the surprisingly good tea and waved the empty at the girl, instigating a refill.

A minute later she saw him approach, uncertainly standing outside looking around, until he seemed to think of looking through the large window that overlooked the street and saw her. She waved her cup at him, too, and he nodded and entered.

He was a good-looking guy who had let himself go. His body looked weary and out of shape, though it echoed what might have been a fine shape some years before. His face was lined beyond its age and his skin was sallow, his eyes rheumy. His hair was long but thinning to the point where his scalp showed through in patches.

What the fuck's happened to this guy?

She had some idea.

He caught her looking as he slid in across from her.

"Yeah, I look like shit. I was two tours in Iraq, one in the 'Stan, and then I signed up with the W gang."

She nodded. His name was James Wineacre and she wasn't sure how he'd found out about her interest in the *W gang*, as he put it—as if he didn't want to use their name lest they hear him. Although she had put feelers out in some quarters, looking for whistleblower types to come forward with more insider information.

"Depleted uranium ammunition," he said as if she'd asked, though she was thinking about it. "From the M242 25mm cannon mounted on the Bradley desert boats. I was a gunner, but it looks like I've become a statistic."

She summoned up some sympathy in her tone. "Sorry to hear it." She didn't do sympathy very well, but most people thought she could act.

"Yeah, shit happens," he said. "Hey, can I get some coffee, black, over here?" he called out. The bored waitress gave a bored nod and moved glacially to fulfill his request. He smirked at Heather. "You, on the other hand, look luscious." He grinned. He had sad dentures. His eyes took her in as if she were the latest Penthouse Pet or Hustler Honey, unabashed at the looking.

"Look, Wiseacre," she said cruelly, "you reached out to me. You got anything worth my time? There's some money attached if it pans out. But I don't have a lot of time."

I've got a Nick Lupo on my mind.

He waited for glacier-girl to bring him the chipped mug and a frown, but he ignored her.

"Okay, sweets, I get it. I'm not your kind of date." He slurped some coffee, impervious to the heat. "But I think you'll like what I got. See, I've followed some of your work. I was in D.C. when you were covering the hearings. I read some of your pieces, watched you melt the TV screens. You're on the right track with a lot of stuff, but you don't even know the half of it." *Slurp.* "There's a whole lot of shit on heaven and earth, my little Horatio, than you've dreamed of in your worst nightmare." *Slurp.*

Heather considered telling the asshole she knew all about the wolves that riddled the ranks of Wolfpaw, all the way up to the top. She considered telling him she knew about their plans to infiltrate the U.S. military to effect a sort of coup sometime in the future. She considered telling him she'd been there when Schlosser, the CEO, had blown his brains out (well, that was what Lupo *said*, anyway). But she shut up and waited to see if he broke some new ground. His phone calls had been somewhat intriguing.

Or I never would have come back this close to Lupo's territory.

Yes you would have.

Fuck you.

"I got a whole file with pictures that'll make your eyeballs burst, pretty lady, believe me." He slurped again.

"Oh, I do. There's a pretty good chance I know more than you think, but I'll take the chance and buy that file from you. We agreed on a price."

Wineacre grinned with barely repressed evil. "That was before. Now that we're here, I feel like *dickering*. The price went up a little. I've got another buyer lined up."

"You've got—"

Shit.

She looked past him through the window. Suddenly the people on the sidewalk were all suspect, and any who glanced inside at them made her spine tingle.

The idiot had invited someone else to the party? Didn't he understand what he was trying to sell was worth killing for?

She started again as if he were a child. "You've got another buyer and you invited him *here*?"

"I ain't stupid. Not *here*. It's another reporter type."

They might well have followed him. He wasn't the sharpest...

"Look, I was ready to go higher anyway. Tell me something that'll give me a hard-on and we've got a deal. Half now, half on delivery." She slid a fat envelope out of her bag. She had a compact Glock in there, too.

He snickered. "I like girls who talk like you. Bet you suck like a pro."

Heather felt the fur start to run up her forearms and a growl worked its way up her throat. She was close to going over just to show him a thing or two. She swallowed the urges down and the hair retreated. He never noticed.

She gave him the eyebrows instead. Maybe he got the message.

"Okay look, there's *a lot* in this file. A lot you won't even believe, but the pictures I got will convince you. Here's another tidbit though. You and everybody thinks the W gang got taken down when that CEO blew out his brains. The board of directors disbanded, some of 'em are under indictment, some flew the coop. But this is better than all that."

He leaned forward, tipped the rest of the coffee into his mouth, then whispered, "That future coup you speculated about, it's already in progress..." He set down the mug with a satisfied *smack*.

Heather processed the information. If it wasn't bullshit, then maybe it was worth buying. Her breath suddenly hitched. If the coup was still on, that meant... Her eyes widened.

Wineacre was looking at her. "Yup, you got it. There's a group behind the W gang. Sure, there was a visible chain of command flowin' downward from that CEO all through the W organization, includin' some military higher-ups. But there's a super-secret group of generals and their plans haven't changed all that much because of the investigation and the grand jury indictments."

"Names?"

"Lady, do we have a deal on the file?" He waved the slow waitress away. "I got to get the file if you're buyin', and then I cancel the meet with the other buyer."

Heather hissed in frustration. "Okay, the envelope has the full amount you were asking, but we'll call it half. I'll give you the same amount again when you hand me the file. Is it a stack of paper?"

"Nah, I ain't an idiot. Flash drive."

Another fucking flash drive?

"All right, let's go." She eyed the window. Was someone standing there, staring inside?

"Hold your titties," he said, snatching the envelope and flipping it open. He counted, damnably slow and in no hurry. "Okay." He tilted his head in the direction of the door. Heather tossed a ten on the table and stared down the waitress, who seemed too bored to handle the cash register anyway.

They stepped out onto the sidewalk and immediately Heather felt eyes on her skin, a creeping goose-bumpy feeling that once again raised her hackles. Was it her or the wolf? She had no idea, but every person she could see seemed suspicious suddenly.

She followed Wineacre down the sidewalk, keeping an eye on other people passing by, but no one seemed the least bit interested in them. He was chattering nervously about something or other she had no trouble ignoring as she watched his feet and hands and occasionally scanned all around them. A few minutes later they reached a tired old Volvo station wagon that might have once been green but now seemed gray, and he made a motion. *Wait here.*

Standing still some yards away, she saw him dip his body near the rear of the car and reach into the wheel well, hunting around above it until he took out a magnetic key box.

"I told ya—" he started to say.

And then the air around them was shredded by machine gun fire that sounded like a bunch of weed-whackers in action. *Suppressors!* her mind supplied, as if she had time to care.

Wineacre whirled around as if to flee, but suddenly she realized he was merely being torn apart by the slugs which were zipping through him and smacking into the car behind him. Blood was spurting from several entry points in his torso, and then his head burst apart when a new batch of slugs caught him there as he sprawled back against the Volvo. He was just flapping to the ground like an empty sheet when the key box in his hand flipped toward Heather.

Her wolf's instincts had been active in the meantime, and she was barely aware of the fact that she had immediately dropped to the grimy sidewalk, rolled a yard or so out of the line of fire, and initiated a change. She struggled for a second with her slacks, but then slid out of them lithely and turned to see the key box heading straight for her.

She snatched it out of the air and kept rolling until she'd slipped off the curb and onto the street, behind a neighboring parked Explorer. A burst of slugs sought her out and chipped the sidewalk concrete in her direction as she continued rolling, feeling the sharp chips dig into her skin even as the fur began to grow in patches and she was visualizing herself as the slender, muscular wolf and hiding behind the SUV. She had just enough time to slide the key box under the SUV and hearing the *click* as it adhered, then her DNA did its realignment thing and she was over in a flash...she had managed to shed the ripped clothing and now she ducked under the Explorer and dumped her bag into the shadows.

Unlike Nick Lupo, as she well knew, she'd been a natural at this whole wolf-thing, and she'd learned to control her Creature faster and better than Lupo ever did. He'd been too busy fighting it all his life, whereas she'd embraced it and the powers it granted her, and she'd never had a problem maintaining both awareness and control while her body was the wolf's.

Now she stayed down and out of sight, almost supernaturally convinced the shadows had hidden what had happened to her. Her view was hampered by the large SUV's bulk, but she was low enough she could see underneath it, and her eyes found Wineacre's dull, staring gaze. The top of his head was gone and the rest of his torso looked like hamburger extruded through a grinder. Whoever they were, they hadn't much cared about her—they'd been after *him*.

In fact, Heather thought it was possible *they* had gotten there late and didn't know he had already met her, or that she was the person he was meeting. She remembered that she'd been more than a few steps behind him when he'd gone for the key box. There'd been no other people nearby on the sidewalk.

In her mind, completely in control within the wolf's body, it seemed the shooters were interested only in killing the ex-soldier. *And whistleblower.*

And they'd done so. Now what?

Jessie

The night shift in the casino was quieter tonight and she didn't spot any of the security guys she knew. Not that she would have told them what she'd heard. For one thing, she couldn't verify anything the two thugs had said.

And they *were* thugs. They looked like thugs and talked like thugs—well, at least they talked like TV versions of New York thugs. Maybe they were bullshitters. Maybe they were acting like *Sopranos* guys just for fun. But Jessie had developed a damn good radar for trouble, first as a rez doctor who had pretty much seen it all on both sides of the reservation boundary, and second as someone who'd been through hell and back with Nick Lupo. After what she'd seen—*and done*, she reminded herself—her radar was honed to a razor-sharp edge. And these guys had definitely set off her radar's alarm bells. Something about their confidence, their mocking tone, told her they weren't kidding.

There was trouble brewing, and she wasn't at all sure what to do about it.

But here was a start.

She waved at Donna, the eternal secretary, as she walked into the rear of the casino, hoping to see the tribe's newest elder and, by extension, head of the council and CEO of the growing casino enterprise.

"Hey, Donna, is he in tonight?"

Bill Grey Hawk had ascended to the head of the tribal council mostly by virtue of attrition—the Wolfpaw mercenaries had decimated the membership and once Davison was gone, murdered, there wasn't much of the old guard left. Grey Hawk and his family had been taken hostage by the freelancing Wolfpaw killers and they'd seen "things" on Cranberry Island. Grey Hawk himself had seen Nick Lupo and that mercenary Tef turn into wolves and fight to the death. His wife might have seen too, but she and her kids were so traumatized that these days they barely ever stuck their noses off the rez.

"Yeah, Jessie, I'll announce you."

"No need," Jessie said, approaching the office door before Donna could make the call. She wanted to catch him relatively unawares.

Grey Hawk was tall and gangly, almost gaunt, with unevenly silvering hair tied in a long ponytail that stretched down his back. Even in his sixties he still favored jeans, leather and buckskin vests, cowboy boots, and string ties. He looked more at home in the Southwest, Jessie had always thought, than near the Great Lakes. But then people affect all types of behaviors. Hell, some of the Indians who claimed to have come home to the rez were of questionable tribal integrity. In theory such legacy and tribal claims were checked and verified, but the process was slow and lagged and—truth be told—was sometimes amenable to the occasional nudge in either direction. Some previous members of the council had been lured back to stack the *Yes* votes for the casino project, for instance, although they'd been murdered by the Wolfpaw mercenaries at the behest of the mysterious Mr. XYZ, who'd had his own reasons to halt the project.

Grey Hawk smiled tightly when she walked in, and stood behind the massive desk Davison had commissioned from an Indian artist friend. It looked like driftwood-supported glass and aluminum and it was supposed to symbolize the tribe's past and its promising future.

Not for Davison, she couldn't help thinking.

"Dr. Hawkins, what a pleasant surprise," he said.

She thought his eyes didn't agree.

She smiled. "It's nice to see you, Bill. Please, everyone calls me Jessie."

They shook hands and he waved her to his leather guest chair. She sat on its edge, fidgety. He followed suit, sitting in his own chair behind the decadent desk.

"Jessie, what can I do for you?"

She considered.

How much to tell him? Blurt out all of it?

She really had no proof, just an overheard conversation and a gut feeling.

Nick would have agreed—he knew her gut feelings were usually accurate.

On the money, as DiSanto might have pointed out with his usual profound approach.

She decided to go all in, without dancing around it. "Okay, I know this sounds like it's out of the blue," she began, "but I heard a couple thuggy-looking guys talking down in the casino earlier, and frankly I'm a little concerned."

His face reflected concern. He reached for his phone. "Is this something for Security to handle? I can have them here or on the floor in about two minutes." The phone hovered in his hand.

"It's serious, Bill, but I don't think it's a case where Security can help, at least not yet. Maybe later." She deliberated again, then spoke bluntly. "Bill, I think the Mafia may be interested in grabbing a piece of the casino. They sounded like shady advance guys from some group out East, by way of Las Vegas. They had no idea I could hear them, so they chatted openly about it. Said their boss is in Vegas and moving here to suck the casino dry."

Grey Hawk set down the receiver. "Jessie, these are serious issues. Do you have anything concrete I can use?" His eyes shone at her, grateful. He was alert now.

"No, no solid evidence, just a few lines of conversations. Wait, though, I remember their names. One guy's name is Johnny—he seems to be in charge. The other guy's name is Marty. They look like...well, they look like mobsters on TV and in the movies. Hard faces, mean, smartass mouths."

"Sure they weren't actors rehearsing? We've had some theater groups coming is as part of the usual tours..."

Jessie almost made a dismissive face. *What? Actors? Are you kidding?*

But she held back out of respect.

"I can just describe them, I guess, but they definitely seemed like serious people to me, Bill. They weren't bullshitting. I thought about it, but they sounded very much like people who'd work for some drug kingpin."

"Well, Jessie, let me call in my new security head," Grey Hawk said as he dialed. "You can give him the information." There was a tinny squawk from the phone and Grey Hawk simply asked whoever had answered to stop into the main office.

They made small talk, which seemed surreal to her. A few minutes later a tall, linebacker-wide man wearing a black suit and a short black ponytail appeared on Grey Hawk's doorstep.

"Charlie, come in," he said.

He looks familiar, she thought. And his eyes widened in recognition of her, as well.

"Charlie Black Bear," he said, extending a large hand. "You're Dr. Hawkins. We met awhile back, when I was working down in Milwaukee. You were involved in that Archer case with Detective Lupo."

"Yes, I thought I remembered you." First she thought about how many of the newer generations of Indians were carrying their tribal names with them into the white world. With a lot more pride than previous generations. Then she remembered that things hadn't ended well for him. Hadn't something terrible happened to his family?

They shook hands.

"I'm sorry," she said, smiling tentatively, "but I remember you had some bad times right after that case. Nick told me a little about it. I'm very sorry."

His eyes hardened, withdrawing. "Thank you. Things happened that couldn't be helped. I'm moving forward now, getting my life back together."

Nick said it was very bad, and none of it might have happened if they hadn't worked together that one time.

It was yet another reason Nick often felt cursed—people around him ended up suffering.

Suddenly she was very nervous about being here.

Bill Grey Hawk repeated what Jessie had reported, and Jessie filled in the details. To his credit, Charlie Bear ("I usually leave out the middle part.") listened intently, his expression serious.

"I don't like shit like this going down in my casino," he said when she was finished. "I'll keep my eyes open, and so will the crew. If you can describe them as much as possible, whatever you remember..."

"Definitely," she said. As a doctor, she tended to be attentive and observant.

Meanwhile she noted that Grey Hawk had made a sour face when Charlie's referred to the casino as his. But that was how all security people thought—they took things personally.

She described Johnny and Marty, and Charlie took careful notes on his iPhone, while Grey Hawk sat with a thoughtful look. When they were finished, Charlie said, "Bill, I'm going to write this up and send it to my team leaders to disseminate."

Grey Hawk nodded. "Good, good."

They shook hands all around and Charlie left, and then Jessie was following but Grey Hawk stopped her.

"If this is really going on," he said, "we'll stop it, don't worry. I'm on it."

"Good, Bill, thanks."

Jessie left, wondering whether she should call Nick. Would it be best to leave him out of it, or would he want to know?

But if she told him, she'd have to admit having broken her promise and her therapy. If she hadn't been in the casino, she wouldn't have heard the conversation.

I'll tell him only if I have to.

She noted that her taste for the mindless gambling seemed tainted for tonight, and she left the cavernous building behind without a second look.

Treewalker

He was just arriving home when his phone buzzed.

He pulled into his driveway and stepped on the brake, then reached for the phone. Coverage was spotty this far from the center of town, so he wanted to take the call even though he was tired and rather unwilling to get involved in any more arguments. He was already on the outs with the majority of the council and this was bound to be another one of those contentious calls questioning his intelligence and his motives.

Questioning why he would want to oppose every measure that could bring the tribe more revenue.

Oh, I don't know, because this one's real trouble...

He recognized the caller's number, so he flicked the screen and answered. "Yeah, what now?" He'd apologize some other time. It was late, he was exhausted, and he'd spent half the day dancing with the same issue. He wanted a drink, a comfortable seat, maybe a little weed, and a movie, not necessarily in that order.

"Yes, I was there, remember? I don't care what they say, it's clear to me that some of you are either too naïve or you've convinced yourselves—lied to yourselves—that your way is what's best for the tribe. I get it. But you aren't—"

The voice squawked on the other end, not letting him finish. He sighed.

"True, I'm too young to remember when we didn't—"

He waited for the caller to slow down so he could interject a word or two.

"Look, I really just want to get home right now," he said, interrupting. "Can't we discuss this at the next meeting?"

He waited again. Then: "I didn't plan on becoming an *obstacle*, okay?"

In fact it had happened completely against his will. He'd been halfway through a tour in Afghanistan when shrapnel from an IED had taken out a chunk of his arm. By daily standards, he'd been lucky—the painful wound was not life-threatening, and he'd been rotated home. He had moved back to the rez when his last surviving relative, his grandfather, had passed away and left the new condominium to him. The building was one of the renovations begun after the casino had finally opened, doing well almost immediately. Before he knew it, he'd gone from almost prodigal son to tribal council member, mostly due to the fact that his grandfather had been a revered member to his dying day.

Now he waited for the perturbed voice to slow down again, but it was no use. Days like this, he wished he hadn't returned at all. But the place had been his home, growing up, and now he felt some sort of obligation to try and improve it. The casino, against the odds, had begun to improve things. Conditions were improving noticeably, including Jessie Hawkins's new hospital, new housing, new sewer facilities, a new power plant breaking ground soon...

William finally gave up. He clicked the call *Off* and slid the phone into his pocket. There, let him rant on to a dial tone. Did they have dial tones anymore?

He stopped at the door. It was slightly ajar.

William stopped to think. He'd closed and locked the door, hadn't he, all those hours ago?

A tingling in the back of his neck reminded him of Kandahar, where it seemed he'd learned to live with the feeling that something was about to happen.

He pushed open the door silently.

Nothing.

The lights were off, as he had left them.

Cautiously now, and as silently as he could manage, he crept inside and left the door open. Slats of blue light made patterns across his carpeting and minimalistic furniture, some from the cathedral-high ceiling skylights and some from the tall triangular windows that reached all the way up to the peak of the building's façade.

No sounds.

William waited a minute, then two, waiting to see if an intruder would show himself. He had a .40 Glock in a drawer, inaccessible to him right then. His eyes adjusted to the silvery gloom and he scanned the great room, checking the pockets of shadow created by the hutch, the dining room table and the narrow mission-style chairs huddled around it, the sofa...

He'd learned patience in the desert.

He stood, still as death, waiting. As he had done many long nights.

Nothing.

He started to relax. Surely someone who had broken in would have been flushed like quail by now. He turned, his hand reaching out for the light switch,

Two simultaneous things happened.

One, someone clamped his hand in a vise and pulled him off balance *from outside the door.*

Two, a bright beam of light blinded him.

They'd been hiding in the bushes outside.

There were two of them, and they slammed him against the wall hard and closed the door simultaneously. Pictures fell off their hooks and shattered on the foyer's tile floor. William's wound had weakened his arm and he found he had no strength to defend himself, because as soon as the back of his head cracked the plaster, the other thug placed a solid fist in his gut that stole his air in a *whoosh*. He couldn't even raise his other fist, because the same guy who punched him did it again, so hard the blow lifted him off the floor. They let go simultaneously and he collapsed in a heap, gasping for air.

Then they took turns kicking him in the ribs, breaking him in half with each well-placed foot. They'd clearly done this often enough to have developed a system and a rhythm.

He felt a rib crack under the onslaught, then another. The jabbing pain inside his chest almost overwhelmed that which his booted feet caused on his skin and bones externally. All he could do was cover his face and head. They didn't seem to be interested in either.

This is a message. They don't want visible damage.

His brain was in slow-motion mode, so he tried to use it to get a good look at them.

Their faces were covered by some sort of hoods. One was wearing an old-looking leather jacket, the other a blazer or suit. They looked like small-timers, hired muscle. They grunted with each blow. When they stopped, they were panting.

Every nerve ending in his body was afire, it seemed, but he had all his teeth and they hadn't broken skin anywhere that would be visible even though he knew they'd actually kicked him at least a dozen times. He'd piss blood for a few days, if they didn't start again.

The bigger of the two, the one in the suit, grabbed William's lapels and yanked him into a sitting position.

The two stood over him and he realized they hadn't spoken yet.

"Chair," the larger one said. The other one, in the leather, went to the dining nook and returned with a kitchen chair which he set between them.

William blinked as he watched them. He wanted to ask *Why?* but it was pointless—he was certain he was about to find out. And he was certain he already knew.

"All right, Mr. Tree Walker," the one in the suit said. He'd caught his breath after the exertions of kicking a man in the ribs repeatedly. "Or is that *Treewalker*, one word?" He turned toward his companion, Leather, who was standing by like a loyal assistant. "Interesting name. I wonder where it comes from."

Leather shrugged his uncaring.

"It's just so...native. So where does it come from, Treewalker?"

William pondered very briefly. Not playing would get him beaten again. Playing might not. He played.

If I can get to that Glock, though...

He swallowed the sharp pains throughout his torso. "One word. My family worked in the logging industry as far back as anyone remembers." He paused to catch his breath. Talking hurt more than he would have imagined. "They used to run the logs down the rivers to the mills. Guys would walk on the logs when they jammed up and the name stuck." His voice hitched as something sharp jabbed something soft inside him.

Fuck.

"That so?" Suit said. He turned toward his assistant. "Hear that? They walked on trees. Precious. That's one of the things I like about this area. You know what another one is?"

William said nothing.

Suit lashed out with his foot and caught him in the very same place something was grinding into something else and he couldn't help it. He screamed.

"You know what another one is?" Suit repeated.

"No," William said, his voice a croaking whisper. "What is it?"

"That's better." Suit smiled without humor of any kind, and wrestled a strand of oily hair back over his skull. "The other is that there's a place to gamble up here in the middle of Fuck-All Wisconsin, and it's run by this pissy little band of fuckin' Indians, taking money from poor people on food stamps and getting' rich enough to live in places like this." He waved at their environment. "But see, I *like* that. I like it and I want it to continue. My boss, he wants it to continue. It's set to continue, except some people want to stand in the way. I hear when that happens, places mysteriously burn to the ground. So people shouldn't stand in the way."

He kicked William again, enough to drive that jabbing right through his brain. Or so it seemed. He curled up like a poisoned insect and hoped they'd stop with the kicking. He was sweating furiously now even though all his extremities felt cold, wondering where this was going. He didn't like the chair.

Every breath was like fire in his chest, his liver, his gut.

Suit swept back his hair again. "Another reason they shouldn't stand in the way is that..."

He snapped his fingers. Leather went around them and outside, returning with an aluminum briefcase, which he set on the chair.

He *really* didn't like the chair.

"Another reason is that when people stand in the way of progress, they stand to lose somethin', know what I mean?"

Suit opened the briefcase with two snaps of the locks, then took out a blue metal cylinder with a brass nozzle and set it standing on the chair seat.

Propane torch.

Fuck, no.

Suit's eyes widened. "Ah, you recognize it? Good." He took out a hacksaw and set it on the chair next to the torch.

William was measuring the distance to that damned drawer. His Glock might as well have been on another planet. He was so wrecked up that he'd never get up and make it past them to get to the damn drawer.

Suit took the hacksaw in one hand. "Are you right-handed?"

A red haze flowed down from William's forehead and covered his eyes like a veil.

"Are you right-handed?" Suit asked again. "Tell me or I'll assume it doesn't matter to you."

"Left!" William croaked out.

"Good. Take his right hand."

Leather jumped to it.

"Noooo," William groaned through the pain. He'd assumed the guy would be mean enough to go for the dominant hand

and lied, but it had backfired. The guy *was* mean enough, and he hadn't bought it.

Leather stretched out his right arm and knelt on it, starting another line of pain. His hand lay helpless on the floor, curling uselessly as if it could run and hide.

Suit took the hacksaw and bent down. When he lay the metal blade onto William's squirming wrist, William screamed long and loud, and they let him. Waited him out. When he ran out of voice, the stabs all over his insides doing their own screaming, he was reduced to sniffling and snorting, words tumbling out of his mouth with saliva and snot mixing and running down his chin.

Suit made one cut and William's skin parted like pork fat, blood bubbling into the wound and running out in a hard trickle that started to pool on the tiles.

William struggled, but Leather's weight on his arm, plus the damage they'd done to his insides sapped what was left of his strength.

He prepared for the next cut.

He'd seen plenty of torture in his time, and he knew what would happen next.

Suit leaned in low and whispered in William's ear. "Do you remember what I said about standing in the way of progress? Do you?"

William's eyes streamed tears. "Yes," he said, his voice cracking.

"What?" Suit said, leaning onto the hacksaw so it bit into William's wrist again, drawing more blood.

"Don't," he whispered, desperate. "Don't. Stand in the. Way."

"Right. That means don't make a fuss about the merger, see?"

"Uh-huh."

"The merger. Stop messing with things you don't understand or appreciate. Okay?"

"Uh...yes. Yes!"

"Break a finger," Suit said, and Leather grabbed William's pinky and bent it back until they all heard the snap of bone like a twig.

William screamed.

"Okay, let him go," Suit said. Leather stood, removing his weight from William's arm so that the blood went rushing back in. Of course, so did the broken finger's pain.

"Consider that a down-payment on the real event."

Suit collected the torch and the hacksaw and snapped closed the briefcase.

"I want you to know," he said, leaning close to William's head, "that I was all for making this a real message. But I was told to give you a chance to rethink your position. If you don't, my friend and I will be back. And my briefcase."

He stood and kicked the chair across the room, where it crashed into the flat television and knocked it off its stand.

"Get some pressure on that wrist. Have a nice night."

Suit and Leather stalked out, leaving the door open.

William lay on his floor, bleeding, for a long time before he tried to stand. When he did, he passed out.

Chapter Ten

Heather

The bursts of suppressed gunfire still rang in her ears, but now they were the wolf's ears, too, and every tiny sound was magnified. She heard the approaching shuffles and slid as far as possible into the SUV's shadow.

She held the wolf ready, her muscles rippling and a low growl gurgling from deep down in the throat.

Sure enough, three masked men dressed entirely in black approached the Volvo, bulbous submachine guns held at the ready. She figured they'd probably take out any passersby who chanced upon them. They didn't seem prepared to talk their way out of anything—it would be death they dealt. Two of them flipped Wineacre over like a broken doll and patted him down while the third stood guard. They shook their heads and one of them swore. Then one of them scanned Wineacre's Volvo with some sort of device, perhaps an advanced metal detector that could tell the difference between the auto metal and a foreign body. Again, a shake of the head and a curse.

Heather had figured she could hide here in the shadows until they left, but they seemed bent on locating whatever Wineacre had held. They must have seen her duck away, figuring they'd shot her. *And they didn't even care to check on her.* They were damned sure of themselves. What they weren't sure of was whether he'd had the flash drive on him or not, and whether he'd managed to get rid of it.

Which meant they *had* to make a quick search of the nearby parked cars, perhaps finding the keybox she'd attached to the Explorer.

She made the wolf wait patiently, but its muscles thrummed under the skin and fur as it eagerly awaited liberation. Drool dripped from its fangs.

Two of the gunmen started to check between parked cars in each direction while the third stood guard.

The one heading right for her would reach her in seconds. She gathered the wolf beneath her for a lunge.

When the gunman poked his head and gun muzzle just behind the Explorer's rear bumper, the wolf leaped out with a long growl and knocked him onto his back, its paws smashing into his chest. Before the guy could get off a scream, Heather's lupine jaws ripped out his throat and voice box, and he died with a gurgle in a shower of blood.

Only seconds later, the wolf was swallowing up the few yards between it and the sentry, who was only then whirling around.

Time slowed to a crawl, but the wolf darted like a flash of light through the molasses of the background.

The sentry brought the MP5's suppressed muzzle up, slugs already exploding out in a deadly stream, but the wolf was both quick and impervious to lead.

Heather felt slugs tearing into and through the wolf's body, splattering cars and buildings alike, but whatever magic made her heal in minutes also masked the pain, and when the wolf's crimson-dappled jaws reached the gunman its fangs first tore his face off and then, even as he screamed while trying to bring the gun to bear, ripped out his throat as well.

The third gunman started sprinting toward them and raised his own gun, but then put on the brakes as if he'd had second thoughts and reversed his course, heading for a break in the row of parked cars.

Unfortunately for him, Heather's wolf had had much practice bringing down running prey—in an early phase of her new life she'd arranged to make an occasional hunt and meal of a homeless vagrant—and now the wolf's four paws ate up the distance and caught the last gunman before he could dive into a waiting car...

The wolf snapped its jaws around the guy's right leg as he ran and tossed him aside easily, his head smacking the side of a parked car with a sickening crunch. His body came to rest against the curb in a heap, his head dangling loosely off the broken neck.

Despite the guy's obviously terminal state, the raging wolf leaned in and bit through the guy's throat, swallowing as much hot blood as possible in the gush from his torn jugular.

In doing so, Heather was surprised to see that the guy was a woman when her long hair came undone...but the wolf was hungry and, the three killers now dead, it ate a quick snack of hot flesh before heading back to the Explorer.

Heather visualized herself back in human form and seconds later she was groaning with the sudden sharp pain of the several bullet wounds that stitched across her torso.

She fell to her knees, scraping them on the cracked sidewalk, and nearly fell over.

Fuck!

She'd been hit more effectively than she'd realized.

Her body screamed as her human form suddenly absorbed the trauma of the damaged tissue and bone.

And now she saw that a few shocked passersby were beginning to cautiously approach the scene, their eyes focused on the naked woman groaning amidst the carnage.

With a cry of frustrated rage—*and excruciating pain!*—Heather snatched up Wineacre's keybox from below the SUV, the remains of her clothing and bag, and staggered to her feet, bashing into the Explorer's side and reaching out to break her fall before regaining her balance and running for the alley that opened up nearby.

Shouts followed her and then sirens approaching quickly from the east.

She stashed most of her things in a doorway two blocks away, then changed into wolf form and bounded toward a wooded lot behind a row of well-kept Tudor houses. Immediately the pain lessened as the healing process began to work on her wolf's body. She would heal in human form, too, but the wolf was optimized for healing and after stumbling a few steps, she disappeared into the small urban grove and found hiding shadows.

Heather hid there as her wounds healed, grateful the shooters hadn't been armed with silver slugs. Clearly, they hadn't been expecting any werewolves. Just a ruined human being as a whistleblower, an easy target for the hit team.

She'd had enough of silver eating her up from the inside. Lead was like pellets from a kid's gun by comparison.

Screaming sirens seemingly by the dozen approached the neighborhood, heading for the crime scene. Though the guns were suppressed, they'd caused plenty enough loud mayhem. The place would be swarming with uniforms and detectives in short order.

She had to get back to her car before cops started logging plates, looking for witnesses or perps.

And she hoped to hell she'd killed the bastards.

She was starting to believe the world had enough werewolves.

Heather ordered her wolf alter ego to bide its time. But her heart was racing, and she wondered just what she would find on that flash drive, once she got back to her laptop.

For now, the magnetic key box was safe in the wolf's jaws.

Lupo

It was a large space, about equal to a medium-size room, and it had a light switch. Lupo flicked it and a caged light bulb in the near corner lit up and threw a shadowy cone of light over the room's contents.

He sensed Ghost Sam's presence behind him but the elderly Indian didn't say anything at all.

Lupo closed the door so any visitors wouldn't notice the light.

The walls were lined with cheap, battered file cabinets. Tucked between a dozen tall cabinets was an ancient government-style desk, a gray hulk that jokers always compared to Communist-era office furniture. Stacks of cardboard boxes, some of them water damaged, teetered here and there throughout the open floor space, making a maze of the room. More boxes were piled atop the file cabinets and leaned over, threatening to spill their contents.

"Jesus Christ on a stick," Lupo muttered. The place was cluttered and dusty, musty-smelling and somehow gave off what he might have called *bad vibes*.

"It's almost like an office," Ghost Sam pointed out unnecessarily. "Did you know your father came here?"

"No," he said absently. "No, I had no idea."

Lupo stepped up to the nearest file cabinet and pulled open a squeaky drawer. It was stuffed to bursting with old stained manila folders with a fine layer of dust coating their top edges. He plucked one out at random with a range of dates, labeled *Giuliano, M., Comm.*, blew the dust off, and saw what appeared to be a set of diary pages on ancient lined paper. Handwritten notes in Italian seemed to be a sort of activities record, in chronological order. The dates at the top of the page were August 1962. He shuffled through the loose pages. There were entries for 1959 to 1962 in this folder, far as he could tell.

He squinted in the weak light. And scanned the last sheet in the folder, also dated August 1962.

Arrivato 21:09, cenato con Martinelli, T., nido protetto, att. 23:35. Successo.

Apparently Mister Giuliano had arrived at 9:09, dined with someone named Martinelli at a protected nest, and something had happened at 11:35—something *successful*.

Lupo tapped the paper as he thought.

Given the date, the abbreviation *Comm.* Probably not *committee*. No, Lupo thought it more likely it referred to *communism*. So who was a *communist*? Not his father—he'd hated communists almost as much as he hated Nazis.

The abbreviation *Att.* could refer to *attention*, but if this was what he thought it was, then it could also refer to *attentato*, an *attempt*—an *assassination attempt*, perhaps? If so, then it had been successful.

Lupo navigated between stacks of boxes and crossed the storage room, chose another file cabinet and pulled out its lowest drawer. Kneeling, he blew some dust off the folders and picked one at random from the middle.

The date stamped on the cover was 1946. Inside, three sheets of yellowing paper with tiny fountain pen notes. This one bore an Italian name, *Rosso, F.* But in parentheses there was *Franz Rosch, Ausch.* noted nearby. Lupo felt a shiver. *Auschwitz*, most likely. This guy was a German soldier. He flipped through the pages. *SS* stood out in a short paragraph with which he had difficulty. The writing was neat and cramped. It was a young version of his father's hand, he was certain. Locations, times.

He set the folder down on the open drawer and took a long breath.

"You thinking what I'm thinking?"

He'd forgotten Ghost Sam, who seemed to be looking over his shoulder even though he was too far away.

"This guy was in the SS, stationed at the concentration camp. Changed his name and stayed on in Italy after the war. Probably would have got away with it. But... Looks like my father hunted German werewolves after the war." He pursed his lips. "Maybe later he switched to communists."

"Communist werewolves?" said Ghost Sam.

"Well, why not? At this point, who's to say how many there might be everywhere?"

"There is one other possibility, Nick..."

"What?" Lupo thought he knew what his own personal haunt would say.

"Maybe at this point your father could no longer distinguish between real shapeshifters and the ones in his mind."

Chapter Eleven

Franco Lupo

August 1945

He was watching the tenement from the rear, a gravel- and glass-strewn alley that stretched across a wide chasm to the rear of another pre-war building that bore the bullet pockmarks of battles fought with partisans. The tip had come from the same wine-soaked old sailor, who told him with a yellow grin that he hadn't asked about the subject's frequent destinations. For a few hundred more *lire* Franco had an address, though he was now out of money.

Business came first, then his own financial situation. He wasn't proud of the way the old drunkard, his source, had played him out of the last of his money, but he'd deal with that tomorrow. Right now he wanted to determine how many werewolves met in the walk-up apartment, and then he wanted to figure out how best to wade in and kill them all.

The shutters were down but he knew that the fourth window from the left corner on the fifth floor was the one, the meeting place.

He was trembling with frustrated anticipation, considering crossing the no-man's land of the alley even though it was wide-open and he could be spotted by a lookout. He was here, the meeting was going on there. The anger made him seethe. Who knew what the bastards were discussing, planning? Who knew whether they had a captive with them on which to feed? He'd seen that once in the past year, werewolves who survived the war getting together and feeding on a prisoner. The screams still haunted him at night, the few hours' sleep he allowed himself, or that his conscience allowed him.

He fingered the gnarled grip of the dagger tucked in his belt. He was inclined to ignore danger and forge ahead. His feet danced in place as the evening's chill started to seep into his bones. His collar was up, but the Mediterranean breeze was turning unseasonably cold.

Franco stared at the window with an intensity that made his eyes burn. They started to water and he blinked away the tears, not sure whether he was angry, sad, terrified, or determined. He touched the bump in his coat made by the dagger and made up his mind. Reaching under the flap of the threadbare pea coat and slowly drawing the dagger, he stepped out of the shadows, his feet already taking him to whatever awaited in that shuttered apartment.

Whatever happens, I will be free of this sense of uselessness...

One step, two, and then strong hands grabbed his shoulders and held him in place.

Startled, he struggled hard against the restraint but found that he was unable to move, his arms pinned to his sides. His hand could feel the dagger, but couldn't move to draw its blade.

His mouth was open, but he knew screaming wouldn't help. His struggling turned violent, but now other hands grasped him and pulled him back into the darkness.

His very flesh preparing to be torn and rent by iron jaws full of sharp fangs, he saw himself as a dead man. *Young man, never to age. Man with a mission, never completed.*

He twisted his head around to try and see his attackers, but the hands on him kept him facing the building he'd been watching. The rough bricks scraped his face raw.

"Damn you, finish it!" he snarled, wriggling against the powerful hands grasping him.

"Hold your piss, shithead."

"*Porca Madonna!* If I get free—" His entire body shook with the effort of struggling against the restraints, trying to turn and see his attackers' faces. Blood oozed from the cuts on his face.

Then the concussion of an explosion flattened Franco and whoever held him against that same wall.

The *boom!* that rolled across the alley was like a slap on his ears, the slow-motion flash seared his eyes and the heat singed his eyebrows.

Across the way, the shutter at which he'd been staring disappeared in a spectacular ball of flame that blew out a section of the brick wall. Debris rained like shrapnel all around and several sharp chips stung his exposed skin as his body was squashed against the wall behind him and the hands loosened and he tried to belatedly cover his face from further injury by chunks of jagged masonry and glass still in the air like projectiles.

His ears first roared, and then his hearing was suddenly gone and intense pain lanced through his eardrums and into his brain pan.

When Franco managed to reopen his eyes painfully and try to comprehend what had happened, he was able to make out one of his attackers.

Corrado!

Chapter Twelve

Heather

She galloped down a claustrophobic alley on four paws, keeping to the shadows and trying to get her body healed while she thought through the problem.

She knew she needed to heal before changing back to human form just for the pragmatic reason that the pain would be almost unbearable. But she had to stay away from her car and her clothes. And either one or the other could be found by the crime scene investigators after the scene was secured, complicating her problem in various ways.

Of course, securing the scene would take some time. There were dead people all over the sidewalk, there was a lot of spent brass lying in coagulating pools of blood, and there was no way for the cops to know whether the situation was over. The tactical squad would be the first logical arrival as they secured the area and made sure there were no more shooters.

But they wouldn't shoot a dog, would they? No reason to. And to most people, especially in poor light and at a glance, she would look like a dog.

She decided to make a large circuit and sneak her way back into the crime scene, write off the clothing, reach her car and change—and pull out hopefully before being spotted as a naked female.

She set off, determined to make her plan (such as it was) work.

But by the time she felt healed enough to force a change and return to her own lovely human form, the tactical squad had fanned out to cover most of the block.

And her car was located within the police perimeter.

Fuck their efficiency!

Heather rethought her plan.

She'd never felt bound by morality or the drive to do the right thing. She'd read Alistair Crowley and, even if she wasn't one of those who supposedly *followed* the occult magician, she could relate to his basic tenet: *Do what thou wilt shall be the whole of the law.*

And so she angled around until she had mapped out a roundabout path and followed it, keeping to the shadows. The wolf's body looked sufficiently like that of a dog that the armored cops who spotted it, after flinching at the motion, simply watched it pass as she had expected. She kept to the outer edge of their perimeter, switching from sidewalk to street and back, darting between parked cars, occasionally passing right before the hard gaze of men and at least one woman whose hands held submachine guns up to their shoulders ready to fire.

When the wolf had reached the farthest point of the perimeter and passed the final armored officer, she noted that he simply turned his back on her, keeping his eyes fixed on the inside of the perimeter. Presumably he was in contact with the rest of the team through the tiny microphone angled in front of his lips, but he appeared to be listening to orders rather than issuing them.

She doubled back behind him, stalking him as if he were a deer, and stealthily reached a spot just a yard or two from his armored back. Tall yellow letters stood out on the black of his uniform jumpsuit and vest, and Heather made the wolf concentrate on that as a target. She crouched and tightened like a spring.

Waiting...

With a single low snarl, the wolf lunged.

The cop was taken completely by surprise as the wolf's near two hundred pounds of muscle and bone landed on the back of his neck, the impact instantly fracturing both left and right clavicles with a loud *snap!* that echoed across the street.

Dropping forward, his submachine gun rattling out of his grasp and clattering out of reach on the sidewalk, the cop managed only a loud grunt and, before he could gather his voice for the automatic pain-triggered scream, Heather's wolf jaws had closed around the exposed area of his neck and torn first in one direction and then the other.

Her strength as an oversize wolf was tremendous, and the cop was dead literally seconds after the incredible shattering pain from his ruined flesh reached his brain. His ruptured jugular gushed like a pressure hose and the metallic tang of his blood invaded her nose.

She lapped up a tongue-full, but then exerted enough control to pull the wolf away despite its immediate bloodlust.

His comm unit squawked in loud distress as the team leader shouted questions, questions the cop would never have a chance to answer.

Heather forced a change and she was *over* in a split second, her naked human form as lithe and graceful as the wolf's.

She leaped over the twitching corpse and snatched up the MP5. As a journalist and adventuress (as she referred to herself) she'd made sure to learn the ins and outs of a wide variety of firearms. Finger on the trigger, she aimed at a row of windows on the second floor of a storefront across the street. Her first short burst ripped through a section of wall, but her second shattered a window, then a second as she held and raked the gun sideways. Hot brass splattered out of the breech and clattered all around her as she emptied the magazine.

The cop's comm unit came to life with the tinny sounds of excited, inquisitive voices.

But by then Heather had ditched the MP5. She forced another change, went *over*, and then the wolf was running full tilt away from the dead cop and back into the shadows, heading first for the Explorer and then for where her car was parked.

As she'd expected, the rest of the tactical team rushed to the aid of their fellow cop, following the sound of the gunfire and shattering glass—as well as his sudden radio silence.

In her wolf form she slinked past the converging cops and used the shadowy areas of the street to reach her car without being seen—or, having been glimpsed, most likely ignored.

She visualized herself human again, and the DNA realignment happened instantaneously. It never failed to thrill her, and the chemicals released by the transition tingled through her system as they always did, leaving her parched and...*horny*.

She laughed quietly as she dived into the car, scrabbled in her bag for her keys and turning over the ignition, barely waiting for the engine to start and then doing a no lights slow-motion U-turn out of the space and heading away from the crime scene.

Heather felt a slight tug of sorrow at having killed the cop, but there was little she hadn't already done or contemplated doing while seeking her own survival, and she'd just chalk it up to one of those end-justifies-the-means rationalizations of which she was queen. He had to be sacrificed to ensure her survival, especially given what her source had to tell her. What he had given her.

She drove slowly, avoiding the urge to floor the accelerator and get the hell out of there. Sirens were beginning to converge from all directions, it seemed, and tearing away in the opposite direction was one sure way to be noticed. Surprised at how easy her escape had been, she started to obsess.

If they'd been more on top of things, she imagined the cops would have tried riddling her car with slugs, but probably her surprise maneuver had worked so well they'd simply not had time to process the diversion.

Her vision blurred and she swerved a little toward the center line before she corrected and tried to blink the blur from her eyes. The windshield was like water in a fish tank, distorting everything and making her very uncomfortable.

The sudden carnage had amped up her blood, but maybe now she was coming down and it was a little like standing straight up from a crouch, blood rushing away from the head, making her almost dizzy.

The spell lasted a few seconds, long enough to keep her speed under the limit. A police cruiser, siren screaming, tore around a corner up ahead and careened toward her and fishtailed back into its lane as it hurtled past, its grim-faced passengers scanning her in the few seconds they had. She was low in her seat, in shadows, and they would have had to be using night-vision goggles to see she was naked.

As Heather's vision cleared, and the cruiser full of cops disappeared in her mirror, she realized that if that first tactical squad had managed to record a few license plates at the scene, her safe car was no longer safe.

"Fuck!"

Time to find alternate transportation.

Heather's blood sang in her veins.

Sometimes she really loved her life.

She was still clutching the flash drive her source had died to get her.

Now to see what was on it.

Lupo

An hour's digging resulted in more of the same, folders containing information that seemed to reflect surveillance records stretching back to after the end of the war in Italy, which was nevertheless still during the war for most of Europe.

Lupo stood in the center of the storage space, hands on hips and gazing at the file cabinets, and tried to visualize his father standing where he now stood. Perhaps seeking out certain information. Perhaps adding to it. Or maybe simply reliving days that up until now his son had never suspected existed, even though he knew his father had traveled while still a young man. He'd become a cabin boy on ships immediately after the war and had spent twenty years at sea in various capacities. But now there appeared to be a new narrative he had to apply to his father's life story.

There was something nagging him, though, something he had noticed in a fleeting moment that had dissipated all too quickly.

What the hell had he seen?

Lupo turned and there was Ghost Sam, leaning on a nearby file cabinet. Of course he wasn't really leaning, but his image seemed to be. Whenever he manifested (or Lupo's brain conjured him), he seemed to do typical things, act in ways anyone could relate to.

"What?" Lupo said, annoyed. Ghost Sam popped in and out and occasionally Lupo was just tired of the whole thing. He wondered if his brain was splitting into two personalities. Was *he* Ghost Sam?

"Nah, you're not me," the ghost said, apparently reading Lupo's thoughts. "You only wish."

Lupo snorted. "I sure wish my haunt would stop fucking insulting me."

"Then there wouldn't be any reason for me to keep showing up and saving your ass."

"Just get on with it," Lupo muttered. "You came back, so you must have something to say. Or maybe I have something to say and my brain needs to hear it coming from you, even though you're dead. I get it. So let's move on."

"All right, all right," Sam's ghost said, waving a placating hand. "I did have something to add. You figure this stuff's been here for years, right?"

"Uh, yeah. I mean, look at how much there is. I remember seeing this storage company years ago, and if I could get a court order, I'd bet this space has been rented for years. I'm gonna talk to the manager."

"Okay, but unless this material was just brought here recently, you'd expect it to be covered with dust, right?"

Lupo groaned. *Of course!* That was it. He smacked himself in the head. *That* was what he had noticed, but only subconsciously. The tops of the files were dusty. But the rest of the storage space was not, really. There was a thin layer of dust he could see on top of the file cabinets and other flat areas, like the top boxes on some of the stacks.

But it was not a lot of dust.

"Shit, can't believe I missed it," Lupo said.

"That's why I hang around," Ghost Sam pointed out smugly. "Told you."

Frank Lupo had been dead a couple years now.

So who had been dusting the place?

Chapter Thirteen

Franco Lupo

August 1945

The explosion had muffled his hearing. A pile of cotton had somehow grown between his ears.

He shook his throbbing head, trying to clear it. Trying to get back his hearing. His ear drums screamed and he wondered if there was blood dribbling out of them. He couldn't tell—his skin had lost its sensitivity. Pain lanced through a dozen scrapes on his face and chin. A curtain of gauze also made sight blurry.

He tried to think through the haze.

Then he remembered.

Corrado had done this.

The last time he had seen Corrado…had been around the time of his father's death.

Around the time you killed your own father.

His father had become a werewolf. He had to be killed, to restore his human soul.

His head spun as well as throbbed.

The explosion.

He blinked his eyes rapidly. Images began to sharpen again.

Across the way, the building he'd been watching now had a huge black hole in its side, and tall flames licked through the jagged opening, blackening the stonework around it. Windows up and down the block had been blown out and now looked like empty eye cavities. A bloody face was visible here and there, cautiously peering from behind the damage. People on the street were picking themselves up slowly, painfully.

He looked for and found Corrado, unchanged from when he'd known him. Someone else was with him.

The three of them wiped droplets of blood from countless tiny cuts out of their eyes. Moving sluggishly, they slid back behind the cover of the building corner and another set of hands helped them stagger away from the alley.

Next building over, still across the way from the building that had housed the meeting place, a door popped open and Corrado pulled Franco inside and down a hallway to another anonymous doorway. Inside a huge mostly empty apartment, a small group of ex-partisans huddled around a lopsided table. The ceilings were high and the floors made of marble despite the building's tenement status. Most old buildings were built to last no matter how rich or poor their tenants.

"Che cazzo...?" What the fuck?

Franco should have been glad to see his old partisan comrade and brigade leader Corrado, but instead his hands snatched Corrado's lapels and he snapped the older man's body against the wall.

"What did you do? You fool, you probably didn't kill anyone. They are wolves, Corrado, you fuck, and their wounds heal, so they all survived—"

The seated men leaped up, their chairs toppling.

But Corrado ripped Franco's hands off his clothes and their blood mingled. "Shut up and listen, *idiota!*"

His eyes bulged and Franco fleetingly thought the older partisan had gone insane in the few short years since they had last met. "*Stupido*, you were going to dance in there and, what, wave your dagger around? Slice off some *cazzi*? They would have eaten you and spit your bones out into the hall. There were too many in there for you to deal with…"

He waved his men away and they sat, grumbling.

But Franco wasn't finished. He leaned forward and stuck his face into Corrado's. "And you, you know blowing them up doesn't work. Their fucking wounds heal!"

"We are not so stupid, eh, *bambino mio*."

The goatee Corrado had always worn had filled out into a gray-flecked beard now and that, combined with his military greatcoat, gave him the look of a wild-eyed Bolshevik. Talon-like fingers gripped his chin and forced Franco to face the ex-partisan as he snarled, spittle flying.

"We had two kilos of silver shrapnel in the bomb, you fool," he said. "I know very well how effective that is in a roomful of werewolves. But you, you could have been killed by them if you'd stuck your nose in the door, or worse yet, you could have chased them off and now they would still be alive. Our bomb eliminated four—maybe five wolves. We can't tell yet. The silver will make sure they'll stay dead. None of those wounds are healing anytime soon. *Capisci*, Franchino? You would have made them chase you, all just to have your stupid revenge, eh?"

Franco's eyes shifted downward. He couldn't take Corrado's flaming gaze, the intensity of his hate for the wolves was so great. It seemed even greater than Franco's own hate, but likely for completely different reasons.

"Then why did you not try to stop me with reason? You must have been following me to find me just in time to keep me from botching your assassination attempt."

"Listen to me, you young fool," Corrado spat out. "We would have talked to you if it would have done any good, but you were about to rush in there without any recon. Probably they would have torn you apart, but maybe there would have been enough time for you to get caught in our explosion—you would have been reduced to bits and pieces now being collected with a broom and dustpan..."

The rest of the men in the room stayed out of the confrontation but remained wary. Franco knew he gave off hate and rage in waves. As hardened as they looked, he doubted they could have done what he had done since the war. But he didn't know them and they were clearly loyal to the old partisan.

He backed away from Corrado, his eyes still locked on the older man's.

"So you knew they met there, in that apartment?" he asked, his voice quieter, more under control now.

"We knew. You killed one we were counting on getting alive, but I guess it doesn't matter how they reach hell, or at whose hands. We could not have let him live very long, even though he had been useful to us before." He paused wistfully.

"Useful? You mean he collaborated with you?"

Corrado smirked, then spat, "Don't be ridiculous. He knew we would have killed him either way. No, this one had been useful without knowing it. We know whom to follow and when. If we didn't follow some of the wolves with great care, we would have lost the lot of them. Sometimes infinite patience is the best virtue even if we would rather act in the moment. Anger and hate can be useful, but without some self-control they'll get you killed. And then the fuckers win, no?"

Franco nodded reluctantly. He chafed at lectures. He always had.

"Let me join you," Franco said.

"No."

"I've proven myself!"

"You can kill a wolf, sure, but you're a lone wolf yourself. You don't like rules, you don't like to work with others."

"How many of you are there?"

Corrado winked. "Sorry, Franchino, there is a point at which you can know too much. You have seen our faces, so you are almost there." He winked at someone behind Franco's shoulder.

Franco started to whirl, his fists rising, but it was too late.

He felt a pain in the back of the head, saw an explosion of fractured white light, then saw nothing but blackness as his head reached for the marble floor. And found it much too quickly.

Chapter Fourteen

Heather

She had driven straight through to the southern outskirts of Milwaukee, right to a strip of crumbling independent no-tell motels she knew very well indeed. She'd sought anonymous safety here before. A quick cash transaction and she was barricaded in a second-floor room with hardly any floor space and a long streak of dark stains on the carpeting. She didn't care, as long as she could power up her Macbook and take a look at Wineacre's flash drive.

She'd made a quick stop at a liquor depot—they were all over the place in the Milwaukee area, veritable warehouses of booze, and she was now indulging in a Scotch rocks, something for which she'd developed a taste after her initial werewolf bite. It took the sting out the butcher shop taste of human blood and gristle that lingered in her mouth after one of her wolfing experiences, as she thought of them. She didn't need it now, but enjoyed the minor buzz it brought.

Standing tall in her jeans and tight cotton top that played up her cleavage, she resembled nothing other than a gazelle in the wild.

No, more of a predator than prey, she thought. Cheetah. Always on the move, always fast. Always looking good.

She popped the drive into the laptop and double-clicked on the icon. It was an installer, and it did its thing and suddenly she had a no-nonsense directory up and started to click in, here and there, watching as windows popped up, reading some here, skimming there. She enlarged some document facsimiles so she could read signatures. There was a lot to read and look at, but she was getting the gist of it, when some kind of errant sound from the window made her paranoid's sixth sense kick in and, despite figuring she had to be safe here, she took her Scotch to the window and peered through the rubber curtain.

Across the wide parking lot, at the far end of the property, she saw two black SUVs with tinted windows pulling in and pausing just inside. Moments later they separated.

Fuck!

How, how did they track her here, and so quickly?

Shit, after the glimpse she'd had of the Wineacre material, she had a good guess.

She took the time to shut down the software, pulled the flash drive and stuck it in her pocket, then ran a program a hacker friend of hers had created for her. *It's guaranteed to destroy every fuckin' byte on your hard drive and turn the computer's insides into slag,* he'd said. She'd commissioned it in case she ever had to make a quick exit and couldn't be burdened with carrying any hardware.

She peeked through the curtain and ascertained that a group of men in black was now starting to fan out at the far end of the lot.

Taking only her leather jacket, her wallet, and the flash drive, Heather listened at her door for a moment, then slipped out into the deserted hall and was heading away from the commando group, down the stairs and out the back. There was a smaller parking lot back there, probably for staff, and then a narrow strip of scruffy bushes and trees struggling to survive among the fuel fumes, and she pushed her way through the greenery and found herself where she'd planned, at the farthest reaches of a truck stop crowded with resting semis and peopled with the bright-eyed clientele that usually signified artificial means of maintaining wakefulness. The heavy scent of bacon grease and fried chicken was a thick, noxious cloud. She ducked low and ran toward the parked trucks, some of them with lights on inside their sleeper cabs.

As she ran, she unbuttoned the top three buttons of her top, making sure her chest was able to make a statement.

Fifteen minutes later, after some quick and thoroughly enjoyable negotiations, she was headed out onto the interstate, seated next to a tall mountain of a man who smiled every time his eyes roved past her cleavage.

She'd told him she needed to get to downtown Milwaukee. She had always been heading there, of course she knew that even if she'd denied it, but now she had no choice.

Far behind, Heather's room was penetrated and her laptop hastily checked. Then it was skittered like a rock across a pond, cracking open its useless husk against the wall.

DiSanto

He shut down his phone a bit more abruptly than he'd planned and looked around to see if anyone had noticed.

Louise, giving him hell again about missing a family event. It wasn't his fault he'd drawn the double duty, but he supposed if Lupo had been back he might have been able to beg off early and make it to whatever it was—an in-law birthday? he'd forgotten—about which his wife was hassling him.

So here he was, in essence covering Lupo's ass again.

DiSanto hated down time because it always led to dangerous, disturbing thoughts...

His relationship with Nick Lupo had always been excellent, but he had to admit it had become complicated when he had been shown proof that monsters do exist after all.

Nick Lupo was a werewolf.

A fucking werewolf.

He told himself that, once in a while, ever since the recent events that had led to the Washington, D.C., raid on a war contractor he'd seen on the news at contentious congressional hearings. He considered himself an open-minded individual, and he'd often bragged that he accepted the supernatural, but when it came down to it, he probably had been a complete skeptic.

Until he'd watched a naked Lupo run toward the trees, then suddenly blur and come down running on four paws instead of two legs. Somehow, in some fucking bit of supernatural *something* DiSanto couldn't possibly understand he'd turned into a large black wolf, and he'd looked over his shoulder at DiSanto and the others and *fucking* howled...

DiSanto snickered. Wasn't it funny how he'd run out of clichés to use that day, at least for a short while.

He'd come to terms with it since then. He rarely referred to it, Lupo's *wolfing out,* and certainly not where they could be overheard. He hadn't confided in Louise, his wife. She was already on edge about the job and how it had become more complicated since he'd been partnered with Lupo. She wasn't a big Nick Lupo fan, not Louise, *nossir...*

Matter of fact, she'd disliked him almost from the first.

Which reminded him about something. DiSanto had often wondered why Lupo's two police psychologists had come to such strange ends. Julia Barrett—well, she had hated Lupo and tried to catch him red-handed, but had run smack into a serial killer. That was at least explainable, if fucking bizarre.

But what about Marcowicz? *What was his first name?* DiSanto hadn't liked the weaselly guy all that much, and he knew Lupo had suspected him of betraying his confidence to Internal Affairs. And then he'd disappeared, just up and vanished. *Presto!*

Which was bad enough, but Marcowicz had disappeared at exactly the same time as the department's top IA cop, Griff Killian, a dogged ex-New Yorker who had also seemed to have it in for one Nick Lupo.

DiSanto had these thoughts often these days.

Those guys hated Lupo. They got in his way, or caused him grief. Then they...disappeared.

Sure, department scuttlebutt went all over the map.

They're a gay couple and eloped to get married!

One killed the other and then took off.

And other highly unlikely scenarios.

But then there was: *They were offed by a dirty cop and buried somewhere.*

DiSanto couldn't be sure about Marcowicz. He was a wimpy therapist no one had really liked and who had raised few eyebrows with his going missing. People just figured he'd snapped, or dropped out. Run away from someone or something.

But you couldn't say that about Killian.

That guy was a pit bull if ever there was one. He should have had denim scraps hanging from his snout from all the bad cops he'd chased and caught and convicted. He had been convinced Lupo was dirty and had gotten in his face, when he wasn't busy stuffing it with those disgusting frozen burrito gut-bombs he used to stockpile in his office.

He'd been after Lupo. And then *he* had disappeared.

DiSanto glanced around the near-empty squad room. He put his feet up on his desk and leaned back, wishing he didn't have these thoughts.

Nick Lupo was a friend. Hell, a *good* friend. As well as his partner. And a fucking hero cop with a buttload of commendations who had helped more folks than DiSanto could count.

But why did people who crossed him just…disappear?

Or what about that gangbanger who'd been shot down in his car? Why did that also cause him the occasional paranoid episode?

DiSanto wasn't sure what had happened to that Wolfpaw CEO, either. Suicide, they had ruled. And it made sense. But only he, DiSanto, knew that just before the fatal gunshot Lupo and someone else he wondered about—that hot television reporter—had confronted Schlosser.

He didn't want to have these thoughts, but he did have them.

Too many big coincidences?

What had they said on *Seinfeld*, that infinite source of quotable lines?

There are no big coincidences and small coincidences, there are only coincidences.

And Ian Fleming had written of coincidental meetings that "the third time is enemy action."

And, for the record, DiSanto believed that there *are* big coincidences. And those were the ones that worried him.

DiSanto shook his head. He was veering away from the focus of his worries.

He knew damn well that Lupo was a good guy, but his life was undoubtedly complicated by the whole wolf thing, and DiSanto wasn't sure his friend and partner was always in control. Both Lupo and Jessie Hawkins had alluded to these difficulties, and DiSanto remembered well that on the day they'd shared the secret with him she'd held a silver-loaded shotgun at the ready.

Just in case, she'd said.

Every month or so DiSanto fell prey to some of these thoughts and he wondered why.

The squad phone bleated the annoying tone. Lupo kept changing it to the one he knew DiSanto hated the most. Despite his guilt-inducing thoughts, DiSanto grinned as he picked up the call.

His grin faded as he listened.

"Holy fuck," he muttered.

Other phones were starting to ring, the few nearby hands plucking up receivers, then grunts and curses following as other units heard the news.

A minute later he dropped the phone and looked for Lupo in the squad room. Nope, not back yet. So now what? Roll without his partner, or try to track him down?

He'd have to check with the lieutenant. He grabbed his coat.

Not much reason to hurry, from what he'd been told.

It was going to be a long night, and he might well end up handling it alone.

Sometimes Nick Lupo seemed to be willing to juggle way too many balls. Or were they *grenades*?

When he got into his car, he belted in and then dialed Lupo. *Where the fuck was he?*

Lupo

He was in the Maxima, Ghost Sam seeming to float in the seat beside him, when his phone played the theme he'd given DiSanto's number: the red phone from *Our Man Flint*.

"Yeah, Dee," he said after he scooped his iPhone off the passenger seat, killing the comically annoying, insistent bleat.

"Nick, I know you're probably still too far away, but, man, we got a bad one. Remember that bus shooting?"

Lupo didn't bother to tell his partner he'd already gotten back. He hadn't planned on going to work at all. "Yeah, I remember. That was, uh, Bilick's case, right?"

"Was. Man, this one's so bad there's already word Ryeland's gonna put together a task force. I just had a call about that. Remember, they had dick since that shooting went down, what, about a month ago? Six weeks? But today the shit really blew up. Looks like a half-dozen dead on a downtown bus and a shitload more killed and hurt when the bus went out of control and crashed the bus stop."

"Ah, fuck. You figure it's the same guy?"

DiSanto hissed through his teeth. "Seems likely, doesn't it? I guess it could be a copycat. Either way, it's an escalation. This is all-hands-on-deck stuff."

"Okay, I'm heading in." Lupo started to edge to the next exit. "Meet you at the scene?"

"I'm rolling now. It's Water and Wisconsin, so I'm almost there already. Uniforms closed both streets down for about a half-mile. EMTs are starting to clean up the wounded. Just heard the TACs guys finished their sweep without findin' anything, and forensics is on their way. It's just us now, the ghouls."

"All right, see you there."

"Yeah. Sorry to ruin your afterglow, man…"

"Yeah, later," Lupo growled.

You don't know the half of it.

DiSanto wasn't as annoying as he had been back when they first partnered up on the gang task force, but now and again, even though he had graduated to homicide full-time, he went back to his early ways. But despite all that, Rich DiSanto was a good partner, a good sport for covering up some of Lupo's problem areas, and a dead-eye with his Glock and most other weapons.

All in all, even though Lupo gave him hell *just because*, he respected the hell out of his partner for having handled the knowledge of what he called his *condition* with some kind of grace and open-minded acceptance.

Sometimes he could see in DiSanto's eyes a kind of veil, as if suddenly he was reminded that this thing called a werewolf existed in his once-completely science-based world. When that happened, Lupo felt a little like an insect pinned to a board.

But he'd been forced to share his secret with two men in recent times, and while Tom Arnow was gone, DiSanto was very much around and Lupo had no idea how he could manage without the younger man watching his back on occasion. DiSanto was a lot of things, but unreliable wasn't one of them— in fact, he was the opposite, reliable to a fault. Lupo realized one of his greatest challenges would be to get Dee to see that occasionally they'd be forced to do some things off the books.

Lupo worried about the day he needed DiSanto to forget something he saw, and the younger cop refused. Then what?

He had to put the worry aside.

Worry... Sometimes it seemed that was all he ever did. At times, protecting Jessie was the only thing on his mind, despite the challenges of protecting someone who insisted on living six hours away. If the tribe had never built that damn new hospital, he might have convinced her to move down south with him. As it was, he had to make the best of it. As they had just done once again.

He tried to clear his mind, but echoes of what he had found in the storage space lingered. All those files, from so long ago. They were from another world, not only another time. They were a link to a man who hadn't been his father, not that he could recognize. There was research to be done and gaps to fill in. Maybe it had to be done in a hurry. Maybe somebody else had a stake in that space, in all those files.

Focus!

DiSanto's call. Another bus shooting. He forced himself to return to the mindset he used when on a case.

The bus thing was just too strange. It was getting out of hand, wasn't it? Random crimes happened all the time on county buses, which was why there were cameras, and private security guards riding some of the routes at certain times of day, mostly coinciding with the school day.

But this, this was different. Had all the markings of a guy clearly working out some sort of issue, a gripe he held against someone or...an institution? But he'd graduated from random shootings to mass murder now?

Why?

Lupo shook his head.

There might be some evidence left on the bus, some sort of lead as to what the perp was trying to do, or what he thought he was doing, and then they'd have a direction to go in rather than barking up all the wrong trees and waiting for the bastard to strike again. Goddamn, there was so much of that, waiting for something terrible to happen, that you almost started to wish it would just so you might have a shot at some evidence or clue that would lead you right to the asshole doing the shooting.

On the other hand, a big case might be just what he needed right now.

It might take some of the heat off him, some heat off the mystery of the missing cop and psychologist, so it might actually be helpful to have all hands on deck with this. Though...nobody wanted to see innocents gunned down—or run down—for some whack-job's own DIY therapy.

Which reminded him, he had an appointment with Anders tomorrow.

Maybe he could get out of it.

Maybe there'd be more bus shootings.

He became aware of Ghost Sam again, the gauze-like presence in the passenger seat, who was looking at him with what might have been a cross between disgust and pity.

"Sure, easy for you to pass judgment, Sam. I bet you get extra credit."

Ghost Sam said nothing, but when Lupo looked over his shoulder the apparition was gone. Or his mind had turned out the light. He wondered often if he really saw the ghost of Sam Waters, or if he conjured up the image in some perverted self-destructive maneuver.

He chuckled and shrugged. If he was going crazy, then so be it.

He pointed his car onto the ramp and gave himself over to the music, the new Steve Hackett disc he'd been carrying around but hadn't put on his iPod yet.

He lost himself in the swirling acoustic guitar opening and tried to put everything else out of his mind until he reached the scene. It was the closest he could come to a Zen approach to the complexities.

He waited for Ghost Sam to show up again and mock him, but he didn't.

Chapter Fifteen

Lupo

"Christ on a crutch," Lupo said when he got there.

Two police choppers and a local station's bird were circling above the tall buildings. The TAC Squad was still piling equipment into their black van.

Probably dejected they didn't get to hunt anyone down.

Uniforms armed with semi-auto rifles had been posted on street corners for a half mile in every direction. DiSanto was nearby, coordinating another group of uniforms before starting a canvass of witnesses. He waved, then got on with it. It was Homicide's turn.

He waited for the fire department guys to finish with their cutting equipment. He figured it was the Jaws of Life, or something like it. They'd used whatever it was to saw through the jagged metal crap that was blocking most of the bus's front door. The cop Voltanek had been able to stick his head and half his body inside, enough to take a look around and realize he needed to call in, but not much more than that. He was standing off to the side now, shaken.

Lupo approached him, nodding a greeting. They'd previously met at several crime scenes, but nothing like this.

Voltanek was a veteran who'd been around, but Lupo noted that his hands shook a little now.

"Lew…"

"Hey, Detective Lupo. Hell of a thing here. Fucking crazy." He looked like he wanted a drink.

Lupo sympathized, but he'd seen so much since the Wolfpaw mercenaries had invaded his life that he doubted this one would be so shocking.

He squeezed through the jacked door and came face-to-face with the driver, who'd been shot in the head from behind. He'd died in the driver's seat, most of his brain and face splattered all over the windshield. His lifeless body sprawled over the steering wheel, his foot locked on the accelerator, the dead driver had turned the bus into a huge battering ram and his dead hands on the tiller guided it right through the corner where the doomed riders waited.

Standing inside the wrecked door, his eyes roved backward from the driver's seat. There were several more victims on the bus, he realized. At least four people, maybe five, were sprawled in various grotesque poses of death, their arms and legs bent at unnatural angles. The smell of feces was strong, wrestling with the metallic tang of drying blood. There were gummy splatters throughout the inside, some covering the seats and side windows.

No one was alive, obviously, and now the crime scene techs would have to take over.

From what he could tell, the damage indicated a large caliber weapon, like a .44 Magnum. No brass was visible from where he stood, supporting the likelihood of a large-frame revolver. The shooter had probably walked up the aisle and shot passengers one at a time, reaching the driver and then shooting him, too. Then the bus had gone out of control and barreled down the street, swerving to the right and finally sweeping over that last bus stop and continuing on into the intersection until the semi stopped it.

Lupo could see it happening, a rider way in back drawing the gun from a holster or bag and, before anyone could become aware of it, shot the next passenger forward of where he was.

Or *her*. But that wasn't likely. Most mass murderers, statistically, have been male.

Then he made his way forward, shooting as he went, the driver probably trying to figure out what was happening in his mirror, until he became the last victim.

Had to have happened just blocks away, already in the downtown area.

He turned and stepped down off the bus.

DiSanto was still talking to uniforms near the wrecked semi. Other cops were holding gawkers as far away as possible with hastily erected barricades. TV news vans were starting to line up down both streets. Nearby medical personnel had given up on the semi driver and were waiting to hear from Lupo regarding the bus. He shook his head and they went off to join the other EMTs who were dealing with the victims on the sidewalk, where things didn't look all that much better.

The crime scene guys had arrived and Lupo waved them on in. It was like a crowd surrounding the vehicle, approaching from all sides. Wearing their suits over their regular clothing, and latex gloves, they descended on the bus and started squeezing into the doorway. It looked like the set of a science fiction movie about weird viruses taking over the world.

"Hell of a mess in there."

Ghost Sam was back, hovering near the bus entrance, as always unseen by any of the people who went to work on the crime scene.

Lupo nodded brusquely. He had become aware of his tendency to respond to Sam and how others looked at him when he did. He had to be careful. Cops who talked to themselves in public made people nervous.

"Wasn't there a shooting on a county bus last month?" Sam persisted.

Lupo nodded again. The shooter had dived out the back door and disappeared, leaving a passenger dead and a group of witnesses traumatized.

The driver had testified that the shooter had picked a quarrel with him regarding the fare, then had screamed and shouted at the passengers until a well-dressed office worker had braced him in an effort to shove him off the bus—an effort in which the driver had not helped—and that was when the shooter had pulled a gun and killed the office worker. The perp had worn some sort of mask under a hoodie. His screams had been reported as *ravings, incoherent,* and *crazy.* Two functional on-board cameras had caught a fuzzy image of the guy, but he'd been careful to avoid facing them and the third camera was damaged, so all they really had was his back.

"These might be related," Ghost Sam said, "but not in the way you think."

Lupo thought Ghost Sam was *plugged into* whatever plane it was that afforded him a look beyond what normals saw, but he tended toward riddles.

Since he wasn't real, Lupo figured, he had to interpret what the ghost meant whenever he made pronouncements.

DiSanto was now working his way through the crowd of onlookers along with a dozen uniforms. Lupo surveyed the people's faces, too. He'd had experience with the perp hanging around to gloat or get a charge out of the cops' work, but what were the odds of that happening again?

With the canvassers and the techs going about their work, Lupo stood by and lent them the weight of his thinking. His eyes roved over the outside of the bus, examining the shattered glass windows, the blood splatters in and out of the bus itself. The three blue bubble camera housings were all shot to hell, he noticed. *Have to find out about those.* He was almost certain the recorded video could be viewed remotely via wi-fi, but he wasn't sure if it was buffered on board or streamed directly off the bus. There would be nothing after the slugs took out the housings and lenses, but before that? *Maybe.*

Something told him it wouldn't be that simple. Probably the shooter had a way to remain anonymous, even on camera.

He became aware that someone was still standing near him. "What do you think, Sam?" he muttered. "What about those connections? Why keep this shit to yourself? Is that what you call help wherever you are?"

Suddenly he spotted Sam's image at the other end of the bus, his arms akimbo.

Shit.

He turned and it was Voltanek who was standing near him.

Voltanek stared at him, his eyes still shocked—but was it from the horror of the scene, or because Lupo was talking to himself?

"What?" he barked. "You got something, Vol?"

"Uh, no, I was just lookin' at the mess and you were obviously busy…"

Busy being crazy, I get it.

Lupo started to speak, to defend his babbling, then stopped. The thought hit him like a blast of cold air.

What the hell had happened to the shooter?

If he'd shot everybody, including the driver, how had he gotten off the fuckin' bus?

"Vol, what if the guy was still aboard? Did you look at every vic's body?"

"Uh, no… I—I couldn't get in, and it was such a mess, I didn't want to contaminate…"

Fuck!

"What if he was still aboard, blood on him, and somehow got off with the techs?" They had been traipsing in and out of the bus.

"Jesus, Lupo!"

"Do we know all the techs? Do they all know each other?"

"I dunno."

"Start checking. Wait, did you let in any EMTs before I got in there?"

Voltanek shook his head. His neck was like a bull's. "No...but there were a couple hanging around the door. I sent them to check on people in the street since they couldn't get through the fucked-up door."

"Yeah, unless one or both of them had just come off the bus."

"Shit, I never thought of that..."

"Don't worry, it's a long shot. Check into whether you can spot this couple you saw, they might still be hanging around."

"I think they got into an ambulance and left, Lupo."

Shit. It would have taken some amazing timing, but maybe they'd pulled it off.

"Okay, here's what you do. Check on that, make sure they did leave. Also, get a bunch of uniforms and hit all the businesses on Water Street from here and heading north. Start checking security cameras for anything at all. If anyone won't cooperate, make a list and we'll get warrants. Then... Well, start with that."

"Sure, Lupo." He stalked off, giving Lupo a respite and allowing him to spot Ghost Sam a few yards away.

Lupo started a list in his head.

DiSanto

He couldn't shake the feeling that the shooter was standing nearby, watching the aftermath of his handiwork.

For one thing, God knew it had happened before, to both him and Lupo, not realizing that the perp they were looking for was hanging around, getting his jollies from the chaos and death and destruction. Pyromaniacs worked that way standard, but psychopaths were too complex. Some of them did it, while others liked being safely away from the action.

What kind was this one?

DiSanto worked the crowd along with the extra uniforms, taking statements, jotting down names and addresses.

Occasionally he watched Lupo as he worked the bus and the fringes of the bus area, where the metal monster had come to rest.

He'd bet a kidney Lupo would get the task force. He was senior, sure, but he was experienced and decorated—a freaking hero—and possessed a cross enough personality that would translate well on camera, always looking annoyed at the questions. He always looked a little harried, a little under-shaved, a bit too sleep-deprived. He was a natural.

DiSanto had learned to cover for Lupo quite a bit, and Lupo took advantage altogether too often.

"Can you tell me anything more?" he asked a woman who was bundled in a coat much too heavy for the coolness. What if she had an explosive vest under that…?

Nah.

She was shaking her head, taking his card, shuffling away.

He was a little bitter right then.

Hell, I've earned the right to a little bitterness.

Lupo

The new head of the homicide squad, Lieutenant Antoine Ryeland, made his way to the center of the crime scene, wading through the crowd.

He was impossible to miss.

Over six and a half feet tall, African-American, of such impossibly wide shoulders that he was forced to wear custom suits, all of them luxurious. On the day he had taken command Lupo had privately compared him to Shaq. The guy was that big. He towered over DiSanto and most of the other detectives, and though Lupo was himself a large man, Ryeland still had him by probably sixty pounds. All muscle, from what Lupo could tell.

As soon as he'd arrived, he had immediately given the veteran homicide cops latitude, backing, funding, and most important, his attention. For the most part, the detectives had quickly realized that he was less likely to bend under political pressure than a long series of previous captains and lieutenants. So far Ryeland had lived up to that expectation, but if there was a case in which pressure would be brought to bear quickly and ruthlessly, this would be it. Anything that scared the public was considered toxic in the department—you had to contain it or lose favor so fast the blood would rush to your head while sitting in your chair.

Ryeland found Lupo and stalked up. He was wearing a raincoat and an old-fashioned fedora, an affectation that looked so right no one had griped about it.

"This is worse than the last one," he said without preamble. "We're gonna hear about it."

"Yeah," said Lupo.

"I don't imagine you've got anything like a lead yet, do you?" He squinted sideways at Lupo.

"We got the lab techs in the bus now, but it's a mess. Probably like DNA soup. Never be able to tell much about any one specific person, unless they can separate all the samples and a long shot gets us a match. I'm not very confident."

"No. I would guess not."

"But I do have a cop who thinks two EMTs who were near the bus early on may have left. I figure it *could* be that one or both was disguised, but dressed as an EMT and just faded off the bus. Only thing, the bus door was a mess. They might have had a hard time getting on, or off. If they were legit, they had to wait. And if so, why leave so soon?"

Ryeland nodded. "Follow it up."

"Voltanek's on it. Also, I need some muscle behind a canvass of private security cameras all around this intersection, and I figure going back a mile, mile and a half on Water."

"All of them?" Ryeland blew out a puff of breath. "That's a lot of people to approach."

"Not all of them have cameras anyway. And if you just show them a picture of the crime scene, they'll forget all about stone-walling."

"Anything else?" Ryeland seemed to be all business. Lupo imagined there would be no problem getting camera footage from anyone who had any.

Lupo combed his long hair with one hand. "One more thing." He pointed at the TV trucks that had been pulling out just outside the cordon, on-air talent handing microphones around as they began interviewing witnesses. "When you make a statement, ask that anyone with cell or personal camera footage of the incident or anywhere on the bus route come forward and let us take a look."

"Good, that's worth a try. Not really tourist season, so I doubt it will help, but..."

"You never know," Lupo finished. "If we had some of that facial recognition software handy, maybe—"

"I've requested it as part of a system-wide upgrade. If we need it, we can get the Feds to lend a hand."

Usually local law enforcement resented FBI interference, but Ryeland was trying to shake the old-school image of rivalry among agencies and Lupo agreed. If it could help, then there was no reason to refuse it.

"This guy never made any sort of statement after the first shooting. If we find out there's some political motive, they'd swoop in anyway, them and DHS, calling it terrorism."

Ryeland made a face. "Well, I can stand the usual Feds, but I don't know anyone who likes Homeland."

"Yeah, that seems to be the consensus."

They contemplated in silence for a half-minute.

"If he follows the pattern, there won't be another shooting for a month or five weeks."

Ryeland said, "Unless he's of a mind to start escalating. Frequency. Method—hope he doesn't graduate to explosives. If he does, then it'll get flagged and we'll have Homeland shoved way down our throats."

"I think he *likes* the shooting, you know? It's...old school. Kinda gets your attention, but in a different way."

"Sure fuckin' does." Ryeland inclined his head at the early television truck arrivals. "All right, Lupo, you got this in hand..." The big man took another long, panoramic look around the scene.

Bus and light pole debris was strewn everywhere, and techs were sweeping it all up carefully, documenting locations. Taking photographs, video. Black vans waited to take it all away to be sorted at the police warehouse facility and labs. White-suited lab personnel crawled over everything like huge maggots, eating, digesting. They'd be at it all night and part of the next day.

Ryeland nodded, satisfied. He needed a series of bullet points to shoot back at the mayor when the inevitable questions were asked.

What are you doing to catch this asshole? Is this terrorism? And What are you doing to prevent another shooting?

"I'm expanding the task force," Ryeland added.

Lupo grimaced. "Sir, I have, uh, some personal time coming, and Dr. Anders has insisted that I take it." This was true. He'd resisted taking more than the couple days he'd spent up north with Jessie, but she had insisted. Now he wanted to try and deal with his father's storage space contents. He thought he could convince the Doc to make the request official, if he needed to.

"Shit, Lupo, this is the worst time. I need someone good on this case. You're experienced, and…"

"Dr. Anders—"

"I'll deal with Anders," Ryeland snapped. "Leave her to me. I need you to lend your experience to Detective DiSanto on this. I'm making him head of the task force. His file looks good and I think it's time he stepped up. He's ready to head a major task force."

Lupo was left with his mouth hanging open, with nothing to say. He'd expected to be given the task force.

Ryeland squinted at him suspiciously from his slightly higher gaze level. "Why did you want off this thing?"

Lupo tried to recover from the surprise. "Not *off*, Lieutenant, just not heading. I will definitely still lend DiSanto my full support."

"I'll talk to DiSanto. Meanwhile get out of here and dig up something else I can tell the cameras."

Lupo grinned without humor. "How about 'The investigation is ongoing and we're following up several promising leads we can't comment on yet.'"

"Son of a bitch, they warned me about you."

"Yeah?"

"Yeah, that you're mostly off the reservation. That you'll say anything."

"Sir, those words have served cops well for decades."

Ryeland nodded. "So they have, Lupo. That doesn't mean I'm gonna like saying them. I'll get crucified in the media tomorrow."

"Pretty much happen no matter what you say."

"The sad part of that is surely the fact that it's true." Ryeland spotted the closest media truck, which was raising its satellite gear while still vibrating from its abrupt stop. "Okay, you win for now. But you help DiSanto get me something soon, so I can make good on those leads we're claiming we have."

Lupo nodded and watched the lieutenant stalk off to talk to DiSanto, interrupting a witness interview. Then he headed for the TV trucks to hand his head on a plate to whoever wanted it.

Lupo set a course for DiSanto, who appeared shell-shocked.

Welcome to the big time, my friend.

Chapter Sixteen

Rabbioso

They pulled into the Best Western late, after a quick drive-by at the casino to get the lay of the land. The place was hopping, so it was easy to see why Bastone was so hot to get his hands in the tribe's pants.

Rabbioso had Tony driving. The guy was a moron, but he was a good driver and he seemed eager to please.

He watched the younger thug surreptitiously from the passenger seat.

It displeased him to know he was required to dispose of the newbie after the deal was done, so he rather hoped the kid pulled a huge boner, the blame for which would justify the punishment.

The guy in back of the SUV insisted on being called Deuce, a name that everyone twisted into *Douche* when he wasn't in the room. You'd think he would be aware, but no, as far as Rabbioso could see, Douche was oblivious. He was a slab of muscle, though, most likely steroid-enhanced—his biceps were the size of Rabbioso's thighs. Both wore their hair buzzed in the new way, with lots of man-jewelry calling attention to them.

Rabbioso would have to put the kibosh on the chains. Good thing neither went in for silver, he thought.

Piled behind them were bags of personal gear and several high-impact plastic carrying cases for long guns and a stash of H&K MP5 submachine guns. Each of them carried a personal piece, and Rabbioso wore a backup, a compact Sig in an ankle rig. He figured this would be sufficient—they weren't starting a war, they were merely *massaging a merger* that had already been set in motion, according to the Don. They were meeting Johnny, who'd been the point man. But now he was meeting a little last-minute resistance, some changing of the mind.

Well, Rabbioso was there to change minds back to their original point of view.

"It's early enough," he said to Tony. "Let's check in, drop off our shit, get a bite to eat, and meet Johnny so we know what's up. I'll call him when we get to our rooms."

"Okay, boss."

"Don't call me boss," Rabbioso said.

Tony shrugged.

Thanks to their GPS unit, a half hour later they were checked in and pulling around the typical Best Western building to their entry. Their rooms were scattered along the second floor, overlooking a mostly empty parking lot. The motel was on the outskirts of Eagle River, and it would take a little while to reach the rez casino. They carried up their bags and gear, and Rabbioso had Johnny on the phone ten minutes later.

"We're here," he said without preamble. "What's going on?"

Johnny was silent for a few seconds. "Nothing too bad, but I warned the boss that some elements who signed off on the deal are now having second thoughts. Not all elements, just some."

"Are we talking taking out some of these elements? Or just breaking some arms and legs?"

"A few fractures will do the trick. I had to have a talk with some fuckin' Indian, name of Treewalker. Stopped short this time, but I'm ready to go medieval the minute the boss says so."

"Well, I'm the boss on the ground here," Rabbioso said, "so you can wait for the word from me. Got it?"

There was a pause at the other end. "Yeah, sure. Whatever you want."

"Don't worry, if it needs doin', we'll do it. I don't wanna go too far and give them reason to get the cops involved. I don't think it'll happen."

Johnny said, relieved, "Okay. I'll keep Marty on a leash."

"Same leash as you, Johnny. I know what you like."

Johnny only chuckled.

"Believe me, if we have to, we'll go there."

They set a meeting place, and Rabbioso went to scoop up Tony and the Douche. They'd pick up some dinner at the casino. According to Johnny, they'd find the place was better than expected in the food department.

Rabbioso didn't much care. A rare steak would go down well, but not as well as a live bleeder, some four-footed mammal from the woods squirting hot blood directly into his gullet until he died. Robb would have preferred human, but he should probably play it cool at first.

He was sure the woods would be full of campers and hikers when spring rolled around, but for now he had to make do. The occasional snowmobiler could disappear without too much fuss, especially if a banged-up machine turned up at the bottom of a lake or stream.

Then again…

All good things in time.

Bastone

Las Vegas

He was distracted by the phone.

Damn it.

He put out a hand to hit pause on the remote, stopping the action right in the middle of some particularly nasty backdoor sex.

"Gotta get this, dear," he said, smiling down at the showgirl who was gobbling him down her throat. She blinked at him, intent on what she was doing. She didn't care, really, as long as the checks cleared. Well, by *checks* he meant cash. He made a motion to allow her to continue. Hell, she was too talented to interrupt. *Trudy?* Was that her name?

"Yeah?" he barked into the phone.

"I'm patching through a call from Wisconsin," one of his men said. "You said if anyone from—"

"Yeah, yeah, go ahead." He smiled down at the slowing mouth. "You too, dear."

There was a click and then he heard a familiar voice. It was perturbed and rattled off a few sentences before Bastone interrupted.

"Look, I said you could call me, but that don't mean all the time. I got things to do, too. Now, what's got your panties in an uproar?"

He listened briefly until the voice was finished.

"Okay, well, they didn't cut off his hand, right?"

Trudy was bobbing up and down faster now, and he started to lose focus on the call.

"It was a courtesy call, that's the way I see it. If I say they should, they're gonna go back and take that hand. I'll add it to my collection. And maybe I have them take yours, too, you don't stop the whining. You see what I'm sayin'?"

Trudy was getting hard to ignore.

He listened some more.

"Look, let me put you on hold." His finger stabbed the right button and it was just in time. He felt the orgasm build quickly, his penis swelled, and then he was finishing. Trudy stayed with him, then cleaned him with a tongue bath.

Nasty. Instant stress relief, he thought. And damn if prostate cancer was gonna get him, as it had his father and grandfather.

He patted her on the head, then she got to her feet, her long and lean body hunched over him, and they kissed passionately for a few seconds. He loved tasting himself on their lips. It was one of his little secrets. He thought the girls liked it, but they liked the cool thousand he'd slip into their accounts even better.

"Bye bye," she said, smiling, and he waved as she went off to get ready for her show.

"Later, Trudy."

"*Trina*," she corrected.

"Whatever."

He brought back his caller, who was audibly stewing on the line.

"I got some muscle in town right down the street from you. That's right, I promised to send some backup, right? You just keep doin' what you been paid to do. They'll take care of anyone who makes too much noise, okay? So what's her name?"

He listened.

"A doctor, huh? Hawkins? Name's familiar. All right, calm down, I'm not gonna have her whacked or anything like that. I get it, she's important. Sure, sure, I know. You can trust me, right? Haven't I been right all along? Man of my word."

He picked up the remote and unpaused the action on the screen, then fidgeted with a solid gold pen on his blotter.

"I'm not gonna have her *removed!*" he said. "Sure, I said I give you my word. Okay?"

He tuned out the voice. He watched the sweaty, oily sex on the television, rolling his eyes.

"Yeah, yeah, I'll be in touch. Stop worryin'."

He hung up.

"Fuck this shit. If I want her head, I'll have it." He checked his contacts list and quick-dialed.

Fuckin' voice mail.

"Robb," he said into the handset, "we may have a problem. Fortunately, you're in a position to take care of it. I want you to take *good* care of it. So call me back and I'll give you specifics."

He watched the screen for a while, but he couldn't get into it anymore.

Time to move into his new colony.

The New World is so full of treasure, he thought, chuckling. *It's just like before. The Indians are in the way, but not for long.*

He knew enough history to understand how that had turned out for the people who were the obstacles.

And beyond that, what was to stop him from opening a "competing" casino? He had to have his people check the laws for the exact wording. There were a half-dozen major Indian casinos in Wisconsin, and they could *all* use a silent partner. Of course partnering even with only one was illegal, but all he had to do was play it cool, keep the transactions mostly in cash, and make sure his contacts all did well. Very, very well. The Cayman banks still welcomed his referrals, even kicked back a small but not insubstantial percentage. And then when he pulled the strings, he could occasionally allow the tribe to build something sparkly, something they could hold up as proof they were cashing in on their own gaming. It would be nice and flashy, but there would be the cutting of corners—with his connections in construction and the inherent kickbacks. Making this kind of generosity a rare occurrence would keep the cost low.

He could see a chain of Indian-themed casinos bearing *his* mark.

Maybe use Columbus as a focal point. He could see a *Nina, Pinta* and *Santa Maria* ride, an Indian attack, maybe a musical based on the queen—what was her name?—sending old Chris out to sea, or whatever the fuck. He could get that Italian singer, the one the ladies loved even though he was blind, to write the music. Or sing it.

Don Gus Bastone had a plethora of ideas. And no one was going to get in his way.

He went to pack.

Rabbioso

The damp evening air felt good in his open snout after years of the dry desert. He was running through the densely packed trunks of a grove near their motel. His long tongue lolled sideways like that of a domesticated canine, but he was anything but that.

He followed a tasty scent and when the rabbit panicked and broke cover, Rabbioso was all over it, chasing him through trees in the zigzag pattern the tiny mammal hoped would allow him to escape the feared predator.

But Rabbioso was an experienced hunter and he was in no mood to play. The rare steak had only whetted his appetite for warm blood flowing from a living artery. Since the meet was set for later, he'd gone for a walk—leaving the motel and heading for the nearby tree line. It wasn't the middle of nowhere, only the outskirts of town, but the wildlife was half-tame and didn't know any better than to hang around nearby. If they didn't die squashed on state highways and county roads, then they'd be handy for snacking.

Rabbioso brought down the fleeing hare, broke his neck with a twisting jerk of his long snout, then bathed in the hot blood that flowed like nectar down his throat.

He trotted away, deeper into the grove, feeling rather unsatisfied.

He'd been restrained when stationed in Iraq and later Afghanistan, because his status as on duty military—several different below-radar assignments that took him to some of the worst fighting—had kept him within sight of comrades and commanders around the clock with very little exception.

But when he'd mustered out and accepted a gig with Wolfpaw...well, then he'd watched how the wolves in their special units followed their noses and hunted down insurgents and innocents alike, feasting on both the sun-dried flesh of the elderly and the young and tender flesh of boys and girls. For a while, gone was the restraint he'd worked so hard to maintain while in uniform with a flag on his shoulder—the reason the Wolfpaw wolves called the regular troops *flags*. The mercenaries wore a stylized wolf's paw flash on their shoulders and wolf's head collar insignia on their black BDUs. A closer look would have shown other, more interesting symbols, but Rabbioso was all about the opportunity to wolf out. He didn't believe in ideology or nationalism. There was food, and there was non-food. Friends were non-food—usually. Everyone else was on the bubble. Rabbioso enjoyed his liberated feelings toward his nocturnal lunar habits, as he sometimes referred to what he did.

So while he'd promised himself restraint here in Eagle River, he found that he was wobbly on the concept. The rabbit had been an appetizer, barely quenching his thirst for living blood and still-warm flesh. It was like an egg roll before the meal, or in Bastone's world, a plate of *antipasto* before the main course.

He continued to run on his large pads, his weight seeming to barely make a dent in the needle-covered ground. This was so much more refreshing than a run in the desert, especially in the Middle East!

When he caught the scent of a human nearby, and a group of deer too, he stopped and melted behind a tight grouping of pines, swaying in the delicious wafting of fresh flesh and the blood that flowed beneath it.

He caught the bright blue-white light of a spotlight through the trees, like an alien craft landing site. On hearing the crushing of leaves underfoot he estimated one human, booted, attempting silence as he awkwardly maneuvered outside the perimeter of a small clearing recently vacated by four-foot mammals. Shining deer with the spotlight made them freeze before bolting, which allowed the illegal hunter to take a much better shot. Illegal during hunting season, or if done with a weapon in hand, shining was usually legal until late September to a certain time of night, if the purpose was simply to observe the deer in their habitat. In this case, however, Rabbioso caught the scent of gun oil carried on the wind along with the human's blood smell.

So Rabbioso gave in to his gurgling stomach and stalked the petty criminal whose intent was to shoot a deer against state law.

Of course, Rabbioso would have brought down the deer himself if hungry enough, but doing so with his legs and jaws alone he did not consider the same as using a weapon such as the rifle this hick probably carried.

There.

Trying to cross a thicket without snagging his clothes or making too many sounds.

Rabbioso's night vision was sharp, his wolf was still hungry, and the human was carrying a rifle and a spotlight. He'd just flicked it on seconds ago, but had apparently spooked the group of deer before he could freeze them in the light. He was mumbling curses under his breath, making sure that no other nearby deer would stumble on him.

Clearly a high-IQ scholar.

Rabbioso stalked him, knowing his own slight sounds would never reach the human's ears.

In minutes, Rabbioso was in position. When the human crashed his way through scraggly autumn underbrush, his light flicking on and off—either as a signal or as pure stupidity—the wolf was in the nearby shadows, his black coat hidden within.

The human half-tripped, stopped, looked up...and froze.

The wolf growled a warning out of pure enjoyment.

The human gasped, dropped the spotlight—which broke with a tinkling of glass—and attempted to deploy his rifle. Unfortunately the full body weight of the giant wolf was just about to reach him, and when it did the snarling animal planted its paws on the chest and flipped the human's body onto its back.

The single scream was a gurgle.

Rabbioso tore out the bearded man's throat and let the blood gush in an arc, from which he drank like a fountain, his fanged jaws curled up in a sort of smile.

Later, when his thirst was quenched, the wolf nosed through the dead man's clothes and his fangs tore into the stomach, releasing the main course.

The wolf slurped through the rest of his dinner.

When he was sated, he howled and enjoyed the echo of his melancholy call.

He listened, but there was no response.

New wolf in town.

He ate more, just because.

By the time he left the body, it was barely recognizable as human.

Chapter Seventeen

Jessie

The downtown section of the rez wasn't very large, but several new buildings including her hospital and the casino gave the two-block stretch the look of a bigger, wealthier community. Work had begun on a small central square, a park and meeting area, and a sort of commons. Only a couple blocks away the homes and apartments were still dilapidated and rundown, but here one could almost imagine that the tribe's luck had really turned. She was sure it was turning, but it would take time to really help everyone.

And certainly not if the mob was horning in. She shook her head. She might well be wrong and the whole thing was a misunderstanding. *Like the song.*

Bored with the cafeteria offerings, she left the hospital for a quick meal at a diner located in a new building nearby. The casino lights tempted her, however, and she stopped at the midway point and hesitated.

Casino food or diner?

She shrugged. As she started toward the casino, she saw someone she recognized. It was the thug with the slicked-back hair. He almost hadn't popped out at her, as she was seeing him for the first time in sunlight, but it was definitely him. He sauntered past her in the opposite direction, clearly not recognizing her.

He really only looked at my ass.

She waited for him to pass, ignoring him, then stuck her nose in a souvenir shop window until he was farther away.

She knew Nick would have a fit if he knew, but she had to find out what mission this guy was on. She followed him as unobtrusively as she could. He seemed arrogant and unused to watching his back, so she had no trouble.

He walked to the Main Street General Store, where he bought cigarettes and stood around a few minutes until he was joined by another guy who approached from the parking lot. She hadn't noticed him pull in, but he came out of some SUV. The new guy was wearing a canvas safari-style jacket and it looked good on him, not a fake but like one he'd actually taken to Africa or somewhere exotic. His hair was sandy and surfer-long, and he wore one of those attractive three-day stubbles on a face that was cut right out of a teenage heartthrob magazine, albeit one ten or fifteen years old.

Hell, he looks like a young Bruce Campbell.

She watched a fair amount of movies and television with Nick when they weren't rolling around in bed, so she knew the actor Bruce Campbell's look very well. So in her mind, he was now *not-Bruce*.

She couldn't hear him, but he stood close to the slick-hair guy and they chatted while Slick smoked. The new guy waved his arms a lot, reminding her of Nick.

Italian?

Sure, it was a stereotype. But Nick always made her laugh by pointing out all the usual stereotypes he himself, and his family, had fit in neatly. *Just because it's a stereotype,* he would say as he waved his arms over his head, *doesn't mean it isn't at least based in truth.*

The two thugs—and she couldn't help herself, she was thinking of them both as thugs now—kept talking long enough that she entered the souvenir shop, said hello to the owner, then hung out near the front so she could keep an eye on them. The slick-hair guy was pointing down one street and then another, definitely giving not-Bruce directions. So, not-Bruce was new in town.

They broke up about ten minutes later, their conversation having gotten heated a few times, but resolved on friendly enough terms. Slick-hair guy went off in one direction and not-Bruce in the other, but not back to his car.

Jessie waved at the shop owner again and rushed out, trying to decide which one to follow.

Based on the way he'd controlled the conversation, she went with not-Bruce. He walked without care, having no reason to suspect she was following. There weren't many shops to browse, but she didn't have to worry as he seemed to have a clear-cut destination in the direction opposite of the casino.

She shadowed him but tried to appear aimless, while keeping an eye on him at all times.

Jessie was surprised when he entered the new library, a long building with a high-peaked corrugated roof. She made her way inside and hovered close enough to the information desk to hear the librarian direct him to the microfilm machines across the large room. She knew the librarian so she hovered out of sight, ducking into a section of magazine stacks and hiding in the shadows as the not-Bruce guy turned on the charm and got help with the machinery. The librarian brought him several reels in boxes, and he set about scrolling through and reading.

Not typical, she thought. *Mobsters don't read, do they?* Or was she profiling?

Impatiently, Jessie paged through every magazine on the racks as she waited for the guy to finish whatever he was doing. He was methodical and quick, very competent. There was an air of capable menace about him, bottled up and suppressed but crouched there, in the background. He scared her, though she wasn't sure why. When he finished, he left the reels and waved at the librarian as he left. The woman was busy with a patron, so Jessie took the opportunity to quick-step over and check what he'd been so occupied reading. He'd left a reel on the machine, so she switched it on and saw the Madison newspaper account of the "crime spree" recently perpetrated by the three unemployed Wolfpaw mercenaries.

Shit.

The other reels were the local papers as well as the *Milwaukee Journal Sentinel* from the same time period.

The guy was researching *them*.

Now she *had* to tell Nick.

Chapter Eighteen

Franco Lupo

December 1945

The cafés under the huge arched *portici* of the storied Via XX Settembre in the center of Genova's old town, near the harbor, had stacked their outdoor furniture when the weather turned chilly and the rain tended to spit out of a gray sky almost every night, but their interiors were busy with pre-Christmas traffic.

Franco sipped an espresso while standing at a ledge in a café that seated twenty but whose clientele this evening probably numbered a hundred. Bodies were jammed close together and Franco had to keep shifting slightly on his heels to see his quarry.

The tall blond Aryan should have stood out, but as there were numerous large ships in harbor, some of them Scandinavian, anyone would assume the tall man in the pea coat was one of the sailors off his freighter while the holds were filled. Franco had been tipped to this particular man by one of his informants, the few who were left who would talk to him. In recent months his information stream had dried up, and he suspected that Corrado and his thugs had something to do with it.

After they'd so ignominiously smashed him on the back of the head and dumped him in an empty portside warehouse, he had considered tracking them down and smashing a few heads himself, but he hadn't been able to find them. They'd gone to ground very effectively, though he knew Corrado's group still stalked werewolves—the occasional newspaper report of a strange murder never failed to set off bells in his head, especially when they occurred near the harbor or in the *caruggi* sector of the Old Town. The narrow twisting lanes, paved with ancient cobblestones, were perfect for ambushes...Franco had done the same himself.

The Aryan was mostly ignored by the bustling clientele that included several uniformed officers of the Allied occupation troops remaining in the garrisons, but Franco kept one eye on the man himself and another on anyone nearby who might also have been interested. The tall sailor drank an espresso laced with lemon and *grappa* and munched a slice of street *focaccia*, the local salty flatbread. Franco snickered. As a werewolf, surely the Aryan would have preferred fresh meat. The fact that he was lying so low indicated there was a purpose to his circuitous route this evening. Now he tilted the tiny cup all the way up, slurped the last of the strong coffee, laid it on its saucer and pushed it back toward the barman. He dropped a bill on the counter and made his way to the door, squeezing between oblivious customers.

Franco bristled when the Aryan brushed past him. He imagined he could catch the wolf's scent on the man, but in reality he just smelled of stale sweat and bad ship's cookery featuring the more plentiful onions and potatoes. Still, his informant was rarely wrong, and Franco had developed a knack, a seventh sense—as he thought of it—that told him there went a shapeshifter. Maybe it was because the man's features were vaguely lupine.

He slugged down the still hot coffee and rattled the cup as he abandoned his post and hastened toward the door so he wouldn't lose the man in the evening foot traffic.

Though rain still slickened the streets, strollers stayed dry under the high romanesque arches of the venerable shopping district which was only just then beginning to reawaken after years of neglect and austerity. The Italian people were resilient and their innate lust for life forced memories of its war-torn cities to begin fading under an umbrella of hope.

Franco followed the Aryan down a length of the Via XX Settembre toward the Piazza De Ferrari. Perhaps he was attending a meeting—Franco decided to see where he went, before drawing the dagger and exacting his brand of revenge.

Sure enough, the Aryan was proceeding along a zigzag route that took him ever closer to the *porto antico*, the old harbor, and then he slid into a rain-washed *vicolo* of the *caruggi* and stuck close to the shadows afforded by the narrow lanes.

Franco clutched the sheathed Vatican blade under his coat. It seemed to give off a sort of heat that made his fingers tingle, but he knew it was his imagination. Perhaps a werewolf in human form would feel the tingling while the dagger was sheathed, the tingling being much preferable to the scorching, skin-melting agony the presumably holy silver-plated blade could bring both user and victim.

The Aryan strode through the thinning evening crowd ahead, oblivious to his tail. Franco had become adept at blending in, and as a teenager still, it was not so difficult to appear aimless and harmless despite everything that had changed him. He bobbed and weaved through the few legitimate strollers who were left, noticing that the composition of those walking the streets was now changing to include prostitutes in search of johns and johns in search of company for the night, or an hour. Ladies called out to Franco upon catching sight of him, a strapping lad with wild hair and such a serious face, but he ignored them. He hoped their calls didn't alert his quarry, but the tall Aryan continued on his way — apparently well-acquainted with the twisting lanes. Wherever the guy was going, Franco now wondered if he himself would be able to find his way back out of the old city sector. Fortunately, the cold winter evening breeze off the Mediterranean was impossible to miss. If nothing else, he would reverse his steps and then keep the wind on his right instead of left. Unless the winds shifted, of course.

Franco shook his head in frustration. *Pay attention. Don't lose the man.*

Passing shuttered shops and the occasional bullet-riddled wall, Franco finally saw the man knock on a door set under a brick arch. Someone let in the Aryan after a few moments' questioning, and Franco knew he would have to wait. There was no good way for him to pass whatever test might be thrown at him by the bouncer, whoever he was.

He looked around. There was a dingy *trattoria* across the way and he spied a few tables inside the window. He entered and saw that there was no other clientele. He scraped the bottom of his pocket and ordered a slice of *focaccia* with onions and a glass of cheap wine. Then he took up vigil in the window, waiting to see when the Aryan would leave.

Of course, he realized that the man might have given him the slip by leaving from a rear stairway, but Franco was confident he hadn't been spotted.

He chewed the barely passable, almost stale flat bread. *No wonder there was no clientele,* he thought. This place was a dive.

Waiting, he cast his mind back.

Franco had changed after his father, Giovanni, had succumbed to a German werewolf's bite and had been banished by Corrado's partisan brigade. It seemed only old Father Tranelli, the drunk Jesuit who had acquired the Vatican blades, had felt some sympathy for the young family now left fatherless. Of course, he didn't know Franco had been the one to put his own father out of his misery.

Now Franco wondered whether he was wasting time chasing an innocent man. Well, innocence was relative.

He'd investigated a dozen such cases and had simply faded into the shadows when he had established that these former German enemies were now harmless. Though he might have craved revenge for other reasons, he now had limited his life's work to only those straggler Germans who fit the profile.

Those who were more monstrous than even the evil SS and Gestapo troops. For even those dreaded uniformed troops wouldn't *eat* their human prey.

Suddenly the door opened and the Aryan exited, carrying under one arm a thick packet.

Franco swallowed the last of his bread and weak wine, thinking of it as a sort of communion, and quickly followed his quarry.

Apparently they were still headed for the harbor, and Franco remained invisible but doggedly on the trail. When the Aryan selected one of the narrower slips, bordered on either side by a cracked cement pier and dilapidated warehouses, Franco instinctively followed. There was little work or traffic on the pier, but plenty of cover existed and he was able to keep to the shadows. Shortly, they reached the rearmost of three medium-tonnage freighters docked end to end. Only one had smoke swirling up from its funnel, signaling its likely imminent departure. Its strung lighting burned bright in the winter haze, delineating the ship's railings and its gangplank.

The Aryan climbed the angled gangplank after a quick check of his surroundings. Franco slipped into the shadows and watched as the German, satisfied, climbed up to the deck.

As the tall one crossed the cluttered deck, Franco took his short opportunity and scampered up the rusty gangplank until he was aboard. He saw the Aryan disappear into a doorway hatch set into the rear of the superstructure.

Porca fortuna!

If he didn't follow, he'd never be able to find the bastard again.

He ducked to lower his profile, but he needn't have worried. The deck's clutter cast plenty of shadows he was able to exploit as he moved from crate to bale to stack of chains and finally reached the same hatch as his quarry.

He twisted the heavy latch, dreading the sound, but it was freshly oiled. He slipped inside, where the continuous throb of the ship's engines finally caught up to him. A long passageway stretched out in front of him, its paint peeling and half its lights burned out. Closed hatches lined both sides of the corridor.

Now, where the hell...?

Suddenly he was grabbed and pulled into an interior companionway he hadn't spotted behind him. He twisted, fighting for his life, and broke free momentarily, and then both he and his attacker slid down the sharp-edged metal stairs.

Pain erupted from a dozen spots all over his body, jabbing cruelly, and then with almost no chance for time to register, he ended up bunched at the side of the rail. Below him the stairs continued.

He shook his head to clear it, but the pain intensified. But when he looked, he knew that if he'd rolled farther he might well have broken his neck.

There was a groan, coming from nearby.

His attacker!

Franco rallied his screaming muscles and tried to stand. Then he came up with the blade, ready to fight.

But…*the voice was familiar.*

Franco felt an almost brain-crippling sense of surprise, and for a second he forgot the already bruising pain.

Chapter Nineteen

Jessie

His voice was immediately comforting, even if it was only on the phone. Truth be told, she still tingled at the way they'd tangled themselves together—and apart—so much in the time they'd had together. So at first, she just keyed in on how safe the sound of his voice made her feel, even if he was now hours away.

"Hey, sexy," was what he said when he picked up.

And she hadn't even sexted him anything yet. She'd been known to do that occasionally, a woman most likely too old to be messing around with selfies, sure, but what was wrong with having a little fun, even at her age? When she no longer looked good enough, she'd quit. In the meantime, when the mood struck—so did she. And Nick had always appreciated the special touch.

But this time she hadn't sexted, she had merely called, and even though his response had spread a loving and very lust-filled warmth throughout her system, she felt nothing but regret at having to change the mood immediately.

Well, maybe not quite yet.

"Hello, sailor," she whispered throatily into her iPhone. "I'm hoping your ship, uh, slips into port again soon. The port misses your big ol' vessel."

He chuckled. "That just might get me through the next few days, Jess. Thanks! On the other hand, it's too bad there isn't a shot of the harbor for me to look at…"

"I can remedy that," she said mysteriously. "Maybe later."

"Deal. Anticipation, you know. It's great to look forward to…docking."

Jessie laughed. "I think we've dragged the metaphor through the mill enough!"

"Ooh, a mixed metaphor. Very sexy!"

Damn good thing there's no one around to listen, she thought. This could just be pathetic on our part. And it was so much nicer than when they fought like the proverbial canines and felines. She winced. It was nice to talk to Nick and feel *connected* again. But then she brought down the mood by asking, "What's with the next few days?"

"Ach, we've had another bus shooting. A really bad one. Let's just say if this had been a bomb, we'd be all over the news as a terrorist attack."

"My God," she said, unconsciously touching her cheek. "I'm so sorry. Is there anything I can do?"

"Nah, thanks. We'll sort it out, I think. But Ryeland's starting a task force. And get this, he's tapping Dee to run it."

"That's great! Your partner's very reliable. I'm happy for him. You?"

He sighed. "I should be upset, I outrank him every which way. But I'm tired, Jess. I don't mind taking the second slot on this one. It's gonna be bad if we don't get this crazy fucker. We think we already have a pattern, so we may have some time before he hits *repeat*, but it's…let's say puzzling."

"Listen, I don't want to—"

He didn't hear her. "Plus there's this thing about my father..."

"What?" Her spine went a little cold. She knew most of what he'd recently learned about his stern father, but he kept tripping over new angles—new dead ends.

"You know, let's talk about it another time. What did you need?"

"Nick, I hate to unload anything else on you..." She had second thoughts now. "Shit, now I wish I hadn't called."

"You kidding? You...gave the vessel a very rigid keel."

"L.O.L., Nick," she spelled out deliberately, knowing it annoyed him.

"All right, O.M.G., can we get to the good stuff?" He chuckled.

She loved that they'd gotten back on track after what she sometimes called *The Incident*. That damned night she'd gone to Heather Wilson's place with murder in her heart and a deadly werewolf-killing blade in her hand.

"Okay, listen, this might all be a big bunch of nothing, but..."

She tabled her fears and plunged ahead. She told him what she'd overheard. She told him *most* of what she'd overheard. She left out what she had learned at the library, but she wasn't sure why. There would be time to mention that later.

Still, Nick made a long *hiss* at the other end.

Lupo

Christ, can it get any worse?

Ghost Sam had issued his cryptic warning, but he hadn't clarified. The ghost, or Lupo's own prophetic ability pretending to be ghostly, seemed to be consistently right. But who knew it was going to be this much crap to deal with?

The bus shooter escalating. His father's secrets slowly unpeeling like a damned onion. And now, what? The fucking Mafia? Could it be true?

Lupo trusted Jessie with his life. She'd saved him enough to sure prove it. And as he thought about it now, he trusted her ears and her perception.

If she heard thugs referring to a completely illegal tribal casino grab, then that was what she'd heard. Her only flaw ever had revealed itself to be her sudden and incomprehensible gambling addiction, and...

Shit...

In the excitement of their little game of innuendos and then the hard info, he'd completely overlooked the fact that she'd been *in the casino* when she heard them talking. He was pretty sure her therapy discouraged return visits.

But he knew they had a good food court and she'd eaten there before.

I'm not going to judge.

Hell, Anders would have frowned at him if she heard him judging another's problem.

He was trying. There was more to worry about than some harmless gambling, if the tribal rez—and damned Eagle River itself, although the town was outside the boundaries—was about to be overrun by thugs.

He walked through the graveyard squad room. It seemed almost every single cop, uniform or not, was doing something related to the shooting, or filling in somewhere else to make up for those who were. What he needed was an expert, someone to run this intel past. He knew just who, and he bet she'd be around right now. Her section was made up of her, all by herself, and she was famously a late arrival and late-night lurker.

He headed for an office at the far corner of the cavernous room.

There was a soft glow from her desk lamp shining through an open door.

Colgrave

Damn it!

Why did they have to do that?

She held up the coffeepot. It was empty again. The last guy to help himself to the toxic sludge they often dared call coffee hadn't bothered to put any on. But as punishment he had to be lying dead in a cube somewhere—no one could survive this stuff hitting the bottom of the stomach. On some damned television show somebody would have brought in an expensive espresso and cappuccino maker. But this wasn't a damned show, and everybody was a cheapskate.

Including her. Much easier to complain than to actually do something about the problem.

Sergeant Danni Colgrave gave up on the coffee, figuring the Starbucks around the corner was good enough. The steady line of police customers was probably what kept the place in business.

She stepped back toward her office and spotted a tall, muscular detective leaning against the doorway.

"How ya doin', Colgrave?"

"Nick Lupo, what brings Homicide to my door? You guys never come around." She smiled, softening the rebuke, and sidled past his bulk to enter her tiny office. Overstuffed file cabinets, a desk, a couple chairs bearing stacks of papers, a Cold War-era coat rack with her leather jacket bunched on one of its hooks, and some institutional style artwork, made up the office décor. Her computer monitor, a laptop, and a phone were the only modern things in there. Everything else was paper, stacks of file folders presumably arranged in some kind of order.

She snatched a smaller stack off one guest chair, dropped it on top of another stack on her desk, then squeezed behind the desk. She waved Lupo into the empty chair, noting that today he was limping. He lowered himself into the seat.

Either his injury was inconsistently painful or he sometimes forgot to limp. She didn't care, it wasn't her business. Rumors on Lupo ran the gamut. Hero all the way to crooked cop, even killer. His temper was well-known. The way IA's Killian and Lupo had wrangled was epic, and then Killian had vanished. Some had wanted Lupo investigated, but there was no indication the disappearance had had anything to do with the homicide detective, and Killian had been hated by almost everyone in the Department. Hell, she had one encounter with the bastard herself, and she wasn't terribly unhappy he was no longer stalking the hallways like the Reaper.

"So, what can I do for you?"

She felt almost naked under his gaze. Not *that* way, but laid bare emotionally. She'd noticed he seemed to carry burdens, and sometimes his intensity was off the charts.

He looked that way today.

Before he could answer, she added, "I heard about the bus shooter. Any leads?" She was far removed from that duty, though on call if somebody requested her. Maybe this was what he wanted?

Lupo sighed. "That motherfucker's not done, I can just tell. We just don't have anything. He's neutralizing the bus cameras, and then he's just…disappearing. I just got some prelims from the crime scene techs…because it's a bus, there's DNA everywhere, dripping off every damn corner of the thing. Could take them months to try and separate all the different lines, if they even can. Ryeland's getting pressure already, and there's a task force..."

"Of course, that's what the politicians always want," she said.

"Sure, otherwise it looks like we're not doing anything. But anyway, we have to try to predict what he's going to do. If there's just one more shooting before we get a solid lead..."

"And you think there will be."

"He's escalating. Traditionally that means we'll be playing catch-up forever. Only way to get this guy is to get lucky. These days there's a decided lack of luck floating around."

"So how can I help?" Colgrave said. She'd always believed in cutting to the chase.

Suddenly Lupo seemed embarrassed. His hands fidgeted in midair.

What's this? she thought.

"Uh, it's not about the bus shooter. It's, uh, something else. Just dropped into my lap. You're the head of OC, and I need your expertise in that area."

She enjoyed his embarrassment a little. Like he was sorry he didn't need her help for the bus shooter. But that wasn't her area, anyway, so she was not likely to get sucked into it. Which suited her just fine.

"Sure," she said. "Like what?"

"I think it may be old-school mob."

"We don't get much old school. In fact, we've had so little organized crime intervention to do, I'm not sure how I can help." She looked up at her ceiling, thinking. "You know the one legitimate local mob family from around here was busted up in the seventies and eighties, right?"

He nodded. He remembered the DeLucas well.

"There hasn't been much action since then. We do keep eyes and ears on the up-and-comers, the Russians and Serbs. And now I hear about Albanians. Occasionally there's a blip in what might be tong activity, but it's usually related to geography because Chicago's Chinatown is so close by. Otherwise we tend to get skipped. Though I figure one day they'll discover us and our relatively open port."

Lupo looked over her head as he formulated his explanation. Colgrave stopped talking, so maybe he'd just spit it out.

"Well, this is very unofficial, but I have a source who says a group out of Vegas and out East is about to muscle in on the tribal casino up near Eagle River."

Colgrave sat back in her chair, stunned. "Shit! Tell me more."

"Not much to tell. Appears some guys are in town to make sure no one gets cold feet. The interest will be as a silent partner, but that's still in violation of the tribe's treaty rights. They can't accept such a partnership, even a legit one."

"You're right, this wouldn't be acceptable from any point of view. For one thing, the Indian Gaming Regulatory Act requires that tribes receive at least seventy percent of their casino revenue, and any kind of partnership would likely be a crime after payroll was met. And that's for a legit partner. Clearly, a mob interest would be off the books. They'd use it to launder money, for one thing. Plus it would be a stream of clean cash coming out, probably heading straight for numbered bank accounts." She paused, letting it all sink in. "You sure about the source?"

"Yeah," he sighed, "the source is good."

"Anything more specific?"

"No, but there's zero chance there's a mistake in what was overheard... The chatterboxes are enforcer types, sent in to smooth the way."

"Wait, Lupo, this is based on something somebody just *overheard*?" She couldn't help making a face.

He leaned forward. "I know, I know. This is why I'm coming to you in stealth mode. I don't wanna get the big heads all aflutter. Yet. But I believe this is real. There's something else. The current chief elder on the council, who's automatically the CEO of the casino, seemed to be clueless about it, so—"

"So you're saying maybe they'll fend it off? That it's not a sure thing?"

He smiled with a grimace. "What the fuck's a sure thing, these days?"

"I hear ya. But…"

"Look," he said, using his hands to punctuate, "I just figured I'd give you a heads-up, maybe the chance to stick your finger up in the wind, see where it's blowing from. If it's nothing, no harm done. But if it is something…"

Colgrave sighed. "Okay, what outfit is this supposed to be?"

Lupo grinned more sardonically this time. "Gonna have to work for it. I only have the names of two torpedoes, Johnny and Marty. Don't know anything else, not yet."

Colgrave gave him an awed stare. "My compliments, I haven't heard the term *torpedoes* with regard to organized crime in…like, four decades."

"Come on, Colgrave, you weren't around four decades ago."

"I might have been." *Okay, I was about three, but still…*

Lupo stood up. "I'd better go, I don't want to raise any flags by being here." He looked down and met her eyes, and she noticed how great his were for the first time. *Dark and haunted.* Just her type. "I really believe my source. If this is what they heard, this is what they heard."

His intensity convinced her.

"I'll...make a few calls, reach out to some of my sources. How's that?" Her hand hovered over the phone, as if she would do so immediately.

"It's a start." He smiled. "Thanks, Danni. We don't get to work together much. Ever. Maybe this is our chance."

"You predicting homicides?"

"The way my life's been, I have to say it's definitely possible."

"You realize it's out of our jurisdiction, right?"

"You're just doing me a favor right now. We'll cross that other bridge if have to."

Or something like that, she thought as he left her office. She stared at her phone, thinking.

Lupo

There's something about that Colgrave, he thought as he navigated through the squad room cubes to the oversize one he shared with DiSanto.

Their desks were no longer the old-fashioned battered corporate workhorses they used to be. The modern cubes encompassed a single long desk on which both their computers sat, back-to-back, facing their own walls. File cabinets lined most of the space below the desktop. Stacks of paper and folders leaned in every direction on the desktop, because like cops all over they still wanted to see paper whenever they could. Smart phones and iPads were making inroads, but Lupo was old enough to have a foot still firmly planted in the old world of paper forms, even though every form was now available online and stored on servers. The department even had an IT division designing police apps in order to disseminate mug shots, rap sheets, and typically paper-oriented forms that once littered the squad room like confetti after a parade.

But though Lupo appreciated the app idea, some of the other so-called improvements had proven less than reliable, if not outright buggy.

He was privately snorting his distaste of the newer systems—not because they were *new*, but because they often simply did not work the way he wanted them to!—when he turned the corner ready to drop into his chair and...

Heather. Heather Wilson.

Damn it.

She was sitting in his chair, her long legs stretched out so her feet could rest on a small square of desk not covered in Cousins Sub Shop, Chinese restaurant, or National Avenue Mexican joint menus, or the ubiquitous old-school manila police files. She was paging through one of the files.

What the fuck?

The last he'd seen of her, she was leaving for good. After the takedown of Wolfpaw, Heather and Jessie had almost killed each other. In any other world he might have been flattered, they'd almost killed each other over *him*.

But instead it just pissed him off.

He felt the rage boiling through his system now.

"What the hell are you doing here?" he blurted out, snatching the file out of her hands.

But down below the surface of his skin, the Creature felt something completely different.

She turned those eyes on him, eyes that had probably doomed lesser men to slavery at her feet.

She had that effect on men.

Hell, she'd even worked as a dominatrix. Sure, supposedly in pursuit of the story (and the Wolfpaw CEO), but he bet she'd liked it. Liked it a lot. She would have been perfect for the part.

Heather Wilson was the closest thing to a sex machine he'd ever seen, and he'd seen plenty of deviancy in his days working his way up the ranks.

Jesus, she was gorgeous. He immediately felt her impact on him when she turned her smile on him, her lush lips curling upward with genuine *flirty* delight.

Probably not only at seeing him, but more likely also at his reaction. She was too perceptive, a quality that had served her well in her career as an investigative journalist and television anchor.

Sure, she worked a story like a bull in a china shop, but made such a lovely bull that no one noticed or cared about the damage.

"Nick, is that any way to greet an old friend?" She batted perfect eyelashes at him playfully.

He was lost. Her eyes captured you even when they weren't doing their werewolf kaleidoscope trick. She was just like that. He'd almost fallen for her the day he'd met her, as had good old Tom Arnow, then the sheriff of Vilas County. Those *animal attacks* had turned out to be anything but, and Heather had come out of that fiasco as a werewolf ...something that should have been traumatic, as it had been for Lupo, but she had taken to it like a duck to water, as people in Eagle River—or DiSanto—would say.

"What the hell are you doing here?" he repeated. There was no reason to be polite, as she'd caused him a fair amount of trouble ever since she'd been bitten.

Part of the problem was that she enjoyed causing trouble, and she truly enjoyed being a werewolf.

The combination was lethal. He was sure she'd murdered a number of innocent people in her time.

She pouted at him. He could understand why that pout on your television night after night raised temperatures and ratings. She would have gone far in that field, but he figured she'd been knocked off-track by the events since they'd met.

For some reason he couldn't feel any sympathy.

He'd had a hard time adjusting to his condition, and yet he was able to keep himself from causing havoc for everyone he knew. Mostly.

He sighed.

Fuck.

There was no getting rid of her. Maybe he didn't really want to. The thought stung a little.

He sank into his own guest chair.

"What do you want, Heather? Why are you here?"

She held up a hand with something in it. Her fingernails were long and violet, her trademark. The item was a flash drive.

"Long story short, Nick. I need to take a look at what's on here. Somebody—a fucking team of commandos or something—just tried to kill me to get it back. Well, actually they killed the guy who gave it to me. Other people were collateral damage and I would have been, too, if I hadn't..."

He sat up. "Where? When did this happen?"

"Madison. Check your wire—is that what they call it still?"

She told him what had happened in reporter's verbal shorthand, and he bet she left out some parts. Whenever she went out of her way to paint herself innocent, he'd learned, she was covering up something.

"Why did you meet this guy? What's it about?" He made a face. Not very likely he would get the entire story, but he had to try. There was no one around the squad room at the time, everyone most likely busy on the bus shooting. Ryeland was pulling out all the stops.

She told him about the book she had started writing, about Wolfpaw and their crimes.

"It's gold, you know. A true crime book with government and military conspiracies, money misspent, innocents killed and tortured. It can't lose. Best seller for sure. This guy Wineacre had inside info from his time overseas. He convinced me he knew stuff no one else alive knows."

"You can't say anything about...I mean, the wolves..."

She chuckled from down in her throat. "Well, of course not, silly. No one would believe me. Except other wolves, anyway. No, Wolfpaw was involved in enough mayhem even without the lycanthropy that the book will have no lack of exciting, stimulating—"

"Look," Lupo said, cutting off her sales pitch, "I don't care what you do, can't you just leave me out of it?" He felt anger rising up like an acid tide. Hoping he could control himself.

"Aren't you the least bit curious why a team of fucking hitters would want to kill a guy who had inside knowledge of Wolfpaw? Nick, they were like Rangers. Reminded me of those Alpha teams of Schlosser's."

"Werewolves?"

She thought about it. "I don't think so. I think they were human, maybe because Wineacre was human. Or maybe they didn't think they needed to wolf out..."

"And maybe because there are no Alpha teams left."

Heather nodded uncertainly. "So we thought. But you know, we never hunted them all down. When Wolfpaw went up in flames it was the board and Schlosser and some of the major players, but the rank and file, they just faded away. Who knows where they went, what they're up to."

"You just said you didn't think they were wolves."

"Right, I don't. But then we've got both, right? The wolves who disappeared, and now a team of killers. Middle of Madison, Nick. A hail of gunfire like at the OK Corral. You're gonna hear about it any minute."

He sighed.

Why did she always bring trouble with her?

"Give me the drive." He sighed as she handed it to him, her fingers brushing his longer than they needed to.

A *lot* longer.

Chapter Twenty

Colgrave

After Lupo left her office, she sat staring at her computer monitor, as if an answer would pop up there if she just waited long enough.

With a sigh, she rubbed her eyes.

How often would this kind of off-the-books shit land on her lap?

She'd risked her career once, for Rich Brant and his niece, and though *that* had ended well for them, she'd suffered for it.

But she was an empath, she'd decided, and she couldn't stay out of other people's quests. For justice, rescue, a good pizza. *Whatever*. It was who she was, and she knew she couldn't live with herself if she didn't help someone with a crisis and when the crap blew up in the person's face.

Sometimes too much empathy gets you in trouble.

She reached into the locked bottom drawer of her desk, where she kept some things not completely endorsed by the department. She had a safe at home for such gear, but occasionally needed one of them here at work, and in short order.

She plucked out one of a half-dozen burners, pre-paid cell phones that made tracing the owner highly unlikely. Always a terrorist's best friend, they could also be useful to a cop who sometimes skirted the tight line of the law. She sometimes wondered why the pit bull Killian hadn't come after her, certain she would come up on his radar someday. The fact that he had mysteriously disappeared hadn't bothered her all that much— the guy was hated by just about everyone.

Had to wonder about that, though.

Maybe the guy had run back to New York for a woman.

Yeah, right.

The flip phone was a low-end LG and she powered it up, then scrolled through the several contacts that made it useful to have the untraceable phone in the first place.

She dialed one of the numbers and got nothing but a leave-the-message beep without the message.

You know what to do and when to do it, as they said.

"It's Colgrave," she said, speaking softly into the voice mail. "That favor I did for you last year? I need payment on it." She paused, wondering how to phrase the question without giving too much away. *Should have thought of that earlier.* "Got two names. Some kind of muscle. I just need to know who they work for and what they do for him. Johnny and Marty. That's all I've got, and I don't know anything else. Consider us square after this."

She shut down the phone and popped it into her pocket so she could catch the voice mail or text.

Then she went to work on some outstanding files that needed updating, the whole time thinking of Nick Lupo hanging over her desk. He had that Italian tragic look she'd seen before. His dark look wasn't just the hair, the eyes, and the complexion—he himself was dark. She wondered how deep it went.

It wasn't that she was interested in him, exactly. Only that he was…intriguing.

Secrets.

She could sense them clinging to him like phantoms in an Old World cautionary tale.

Of course, she had some of her own.

Around here, it seemed everybody did.

Lupo

The damn flash drive was full of things to give them all nightmares.

Folders upon folders of photographs obviously taken on the sly, documents stolen from God knew whose offices, most marked with official stamps of this government agency and that. Wineacre, whoever the hell he'd been, had done an incredible amount of digging, most of it dangerous. He'd stolen the files, but many of them had to have been stolen from someone even before that.

Specifically, Wineacre had identified a small group of generals who had been part of the Wolfpaw plot to infiltrate the services with werewolves, who could then be used to execute a future coup from the inside. Wineacre's material was explosive. But completely impossible to corroborate.

Lupo had assumed that when Wolfpaw went down in flames, mostly on their own criminal activities, their plans had crashed too. But he hadn't figured they had already infiltrated at the higher ranks.

The Pentagon was lousy with werewolves.

He could kick himself. He *should* have figured.

"We should've thought they wouldn't just be looking to get werewolves into uniform," he said now, as he stretched back in his chair. "Why work bottom up when you can work top down?

Looks like they've had wolves in place for decades, slowly working their way up the ladder of command. All Wolfpaw was doing was spreading more wolves across the ranks."

"And most of these fuckers trace their roots all the way back to the Nazis, so you know they're not patriots in the usual sense of the word."

"Whenever anyone talks to me about patriotism," Lupo said, "I always want to remind them that Nazis were patriots too. Usually takes some wind out of their sails. Nothing is simple, no matter how much people want it to be. You can be a patriot and be wrong, goddamnit."

They scrolled through folders full of photographs, many of which they couldn't show anyone. Who would believe? Other than people already in the know, there was hardly a chance someone being hit with this stuff cold would just tap themselves on the head and say, *Of course! Why didn't I think of that? Werewolves!*

"There's too much here to look at in a week, let alone one night." Lupo yawned. "What do you think is their endgame? I mean, Wolfpaw wanted to infiltrate the services. Who knows how far they got in terms of the rank and file. According to this information your friend Wineacre was able to steal, collect and collate, it looks as though they've already succeeded. But it takes more than a few generals and even a couple brigades or battalions of werewolves to create a coup."

"Does it?" Heather's rather lovely right eyebrow arched upward. "Are you sure?"

"What do you mean?"

"The fact that no one would believe they were facing monsters would make it harder to help them, wouldn't it? Unless you could manufacture silver ammunition in bulk and somehow substitute it for their regular rounds. So it might not take more than a few of each. And you've seen the folder with the tech specs—these guys have been developing technology on their own, funneling money from Pentagon appropriations like they were mobsters skimming from a casino…"

"Funny you should say that," Lupo said, laughing without humor.

"Why?"

In a few bold strokes, he mentioned what Jessie had told him. He knew Heather wouldn't care much about Jessie's stake or any danger she might be in, but he was right that the information caught her ear.

"Wow, you've got your hands full, don't you? This bus crap, and now the Mafia wants to horn in on the casino? What's next, the hellmouth opens up under the precinct?"

"Hmm," he said. People already figured the hellmouth was wherever Heather Wilson happened to be.

"So should we go on reading? We have to figure out what to do, don't we? I mean, there's nobody else standing between these assholes and a free country, is there?"

Lupo squinted at her. Whatever the lighting, Heather was a sight to behold. Even bedraggled and half shot-up, nails chipped, makeup smeared, she looked great. *But…*

"What's in it for *you*, Heather? You mentioned patriotism, but you've never struck me as much of a patriot."

There it was. A challenge.

She smiled and once again he could see why men fell in love with their televisions whenever she was on the screen.

"There are different types of patriots, Lupo." She paused, thinking. "I'm not a flag-waver, but I like to have the option. These Wolfpaw bastards want to take away our options. I'll never be for that. I'll never agree to it."

A nice speech, Lupo thought, concise and believable. But he knew damn well that Heather would always be out for herself first, and if some good came of it, that was fine too.

"What about your book?"

Her eyes flared in sudden anger. "So what? Sure, this will all make a killer book. Doesn't mean I want their plot to succeed. It'll be great to be able to write that a small group of true patriots crushed the fake ones, won't it? Don't we like to see the little guy and gal win?"

"Sounds like a country song in the making…"

"Yeah, right, that's one area I'm not looking to make inroads into."

They went back to reading. Lupo selected documents and photos to print, making a kind of "hits" version he could show someone else. He was already thinking about having to take care of this off the books. Soon he had a thick paper file that was still only a fraction of the complete picture.

"Not for Ryeland," he explained as the printer spit out sheet after sheet. "But maybe for DiSanto."

"Your cute little partner?" She beamed.

"You stay away from him, Heather! Dee's married. Got kids. He's a straight-up guy. I had to share the wolf thing with him, I had no choice, and that makes him special. Hell, he hasn't yet put a silver bullet up my ass, but I'm sure he's thought about it." He stared at her, his forehead furrowed with seriousness. "Leave him alone. No sex games."

That was asking a lot. Heather was all about sex games.

"I promise," she said, but she was smiling that damned smile of hers, and he wasn't at all sure he could trust her.

"Listen, I have to get some sleep. Lots to do in the morning. We'll be doing the task force thing. Reports will be starting to flow. I need sleep."

She turned doe eyes on him. "Where will I go?"

"Shit, there's plenty of motels. You got GPS, find one." Cruel perhaps, he thought, but she really had caused him a lot of trouble in the past.

"I was hoping to bunk in with you," she said, pouting.

"What? Are you crazy?" He looked away. Or the pout would get him.

She leaned forward, all intensity. "Didn't you hear what I said? I was in a fucking random motel and they found me—they found me without even knowing who I was or what car I was driving. Doesn't that make you wonder?"

"Maybe they're tracking the flash drive?"

"Doubt it. Wouldn't they have taken out Wineacre before he could hand it to me? No, they're using their technology, and what it is...is buried in there, somewhere. I'd bet my wolfiness on it. And you know how much I love my wolf side..."

"Well, fuck, Heather, if you're right, then aren't you dragging me into their sights too?" Lupo was worried about Jessie, and here was the sexiest woman he knew offering to throw herself—and possibly a hit squad or two—at him, when all he wanted was some sleep.

She batted her eyelashes at him until he couldn't help but laugh.

"Christ, you're a piece of work."

"Yes, but can I come over? I promise I'll keep my hands to myself."

"I'm gonna regret this," he said. "I just know it."

"Is that a yes?"

"Grab your stuff. And the drive. I'll show that file to Dee tomorrow. Let's go." He clicked off the light in his cubicle.

As they left, the squad room was starting to fill up with the night shift and those who were already working on the bus case. And Lupo thought he saw a shadow behind the shades in Colgrave's office.

Lupo shrugged. There was a time you could get to be *too* damn paranoid.

Couldn't you?

DiSanto

He ran into Lupo and his *friend* Heather Wilson outside the precinct. He was going in to prepare some paperwork, some copies, for the task force. He'd work about an hour, then head home to tell Louise she should probably not expect him home for the next few days.

On the other hand, running the task force was like a promotion and she'd sure like that. He'd be able to parlay it into some kind of better karma at home, too, where his stock had decidedly fallen since Lupo and Jessie had shared Lupo's secret with him.

His secret identity.

That was how DiSanto sometimes thought about the whole werewolf thing, unbelievable as it was. Like a superpower.

Now running into Lupo and that Amazonian warrior, Heather, the same chick who'd given him secret boners when watching the news from Wausau. He never explained why he liked to watch those newscasts, but he figured his wife had figured it out. Why the fuck else?

Anyway, they were leaving and Lupo gave him a bullshit story about some research they needed to do. Hell, he didn't think Heather was welcome to come back. Not as far as Jessie Hawkins was concerned, anyway.

Lupo waved a file folder between them. "Dee, I've got some stuff to show you, but it's gonna require a long backstory. And it's dangerous, and we'll be in it up to our necks. And it'll be off the books..."

"What?" DiSanto's smile was pasted on. Not at all sure he wanted to hear this. He had a task force to run, he didn't have time to mess around with Lupo's secret life.

Christ!

Lupo reiterated briefly, and DiSanto nodded dutifully. When they walked away he couldn't help wondering where they were heading together.

It all added up to a bad scene coming.

Chapter Twenty-One

Lupo

He wasn't sure how it had come about, but they were in her hotel room.

It was one of those residence-type motels, better than average, with a room-wide window overlooking one of the airport's newer runways. There was an arched nook with a cherry wood desk and dresser at one side, and a sofa/armchair conversation pod arranged around a flat television at the other. In the center, a king-sized bed piled high with pillows.

Neither of them were availing themselves of the furniture now.

Heather's long, lean model's body leaned against the window.

Her blouse was unbuttoned and her black lace brassiere was visible, but as she slowly slipped her arms out of the material the blouse slid to the carpet. She kicked it away. Her breasts heaved against the sheer lace, the nipples thrusting through it. His fingers brushed her there, one side and then the other, and she sighed, shivering.

He took a nipple between thumb and index finger and twirled it like a marble, feeling it stiffen at his touch.

She moaned and reached out to stroke his hair, her buttocks planted against the windowsill.

She posed like that, a living pulp novel cover, her golden hair cascading around her lust-filled features. He switched from one nipple to the other, then he took the nipple his hand was now neglecting between his lips, his tongue bathing all around its tip. His hands roved down over her taut belly and undid the button on her waistband.

She leaned her head back against the window glass as he licked and nibbled her breasts, his hands slowly undoing and peeling her jeans down her thighs. She groaned softly as he exposed her tiny panties, which barely covered her mound. Impatiently she helped him strip off her jeans until she could step out of them.

He moved his mouth—and his tongue—down from her breasts to her belly, down to where the material was stretched tightly across her most intimate, responsive spot. He sank to his knees and her hands came to rest on his head, fingers combing through his hair as he gently nuzzled aside the silk triangle and exposed her bare mons. She leaned into him forcefully and he smelled her excitement.

His tongue now gently circled down from her pierced navel, closer and closer to the center of her need, and she curled backward so she could thrust herself at him, at his face. He could see her labia now, blooming like a flower as she parted her thighs, and when his lips approached that delicate array of petals she gasped with pleasure. A tiny red jewel glinted there, another piercing. Her hands tightened on his head as his breath brushed across the secret folds she was now opening to him and him alone.

But then he backed off and she groaned in frustration, hands working against him when she thought he was planning to abandon her after all the teasing.

He wasn't.

Forcefully his hands began to turn her around to face the glass, her reflection in the window like that of a goddess imprisoned in a black mirror.

Fighting him for a brief moment, then letting him have his way, she now leaned on the window, her hands spread out to both sides. He was still on his knees, but now his view had changed and the globes of her perfect buttocks had come under his searing touch. The thin strip of black fabric that barely protruded from between her buttocks was just inches away from his face. He stuck a finger under the material and started to slide the rear of the thong out of his way, even as he began to drag his tongue across her hot skin. The shape of her toned ass further excited him as he pulled her back toward him and parted her legs at the same time so she leaned forward into the window, spread-eagled. He spread her rounded globes apart so he could see her dark-tipped pussy lips, dappled with the dew of her excitement, hanging open wantonly beneath her. The piercing and jewel glittered in the bright light, a metaphor for what she was revealing to him, what she would grant him.

He kissed and licked her buttocks in tiny, widening circles, then straight up and down where they met.

She hissed softly as he pleasured her, his mouth seeming to burn her soft skin as he centered on her most secret of places. Her hiss turned into a groan at what he was doing.

After a few minutes, he rose and undid his belt, dropping his trousers and briefs with altogether too much ease. Then he hunched over her shapely back, reaching forward and around her to fondle her breasts and nipples as his erection prodded her from behind. She gasped and reached back with one hand to take his length in her violet-tipped fingers and guide him toward her. She rubbed the tip of his swelling penis on her moist, sensitive skin. He pulled her hair firmly and turned her face around, and their mouths and tongues met above as their flesh united below, and then he thrust into her and she gasped again, her lips hungrily devouring his.

As the speed of his thrusts increased, sweat pouring off both of them, he sensed the Creature beneath the veneer of his humanity beginning to claw its way to the surface. Tufts of dark hair began to bloom on his hands and arms, and he felt them blooming across his back as the wolf inside him demanded his release.

He thrust more rapidly now, their skin slapping together more violently. Their slick bodies united, rocking against the window harder and harder, their flesh screaming in unison, he felt the always tenuous control he held over the Creature slipping away, and...

In the throes of his passion he threw off the mantle of his human skin and visualized himself going over—*could no longer help himself, really*—and then he was *Over*.

The usual feeling, the *it's a fact, Jack!* he'd felt since the earliest days of his curse, boiled through his system, made his blood scream.

He was no longer human.

Heather's eyes opened wide in shock, but then she screamed in the throes of her own orgasm, and her body blurred as she, too, gave herself over to the needs of the monster within, and he saw the glowing silver disk of the moon high up in the corner of the window, and he howled—

Lupo awoke in a sudden rush that tore the blood from his veins and left him dizzy and disoriented, covered in a sour sweat that clung to his nostrils, and with a raging headache that squeezed his temples mercilessly.

Jesus.

He blinked repeatedly, checking his surroundings. He was home, in his bed, and Heather wasn't there. Neither was Jessie.

He was alone, but his body ached as if he'd run miles over a jagged landscape and, to his shame, he realized he was also painfully aroused.

And tufts of black hair on his arms and hands were only just starting to retreat.

Chapter Twenty-Two

Heather

It had been all she could do to sleep in his guest bed and not head down the hall, slip under his king-size sheets and put her lips on the erection she knew he'd probably secretly harbored ever since he'd seen her.

She loved pleasuring men with her lips and tongue and she did it well. She'd used the skill many a time to turn a man into an ally. She was pragmatic about it. No different than bringing someone a favorite coffee or pastry, no different than offering a nice meal and a drink. It was a payment, sometimes a down payment, and it could be its own reward. She was all about their reciprocal offerings, too, never you mind, but she'd truly learned to get her way in this way, of all ways. Heather was all about the goals she set for herself, and getting to them was just part of the game.

Which was why it annoyed the hell out of her that Nick Lupo not only ignored her once he'd given her the guest basics, but that he'd also locked his door loudly enough that she could hear it. She'd figured she was the one with the power here.

Of course, she could have ripped the knob off the door, but she wasn't sure that ploy would work on this particular subject.

No, he'd been felled by an acute case of *the Jessies* again, and after she'd done so much to break them up. Hell, she thought the bitch's gambling addiction—where the fuck had that come from?—would have done it, in the end, but it hadn't. It had soured things, sure, but they'd gotten past it somehow and now they were all cuddly again.

Well, Heather was here now, and the Jessie-bitch wasn't.

Heather loved a challenge.

She was sure he'd looked rough this morning, and she'd driven her point home by eating her breakfast while wearing one of his robes, one she left nice and loose, her nipples poking through like the *Twin Peaks* sign. She chuckled at that. Then she'd taken her time and put on her makeup where he could hardly avoid her, taking over the kitchen table as he tried to eat and drink coffee which he'd almost spilled.

Yes, she smiled, he'd looked rough indeed.

She'd introduced a deadly strain of Heather into his veins, she was sure of it.

Marla Anders

She looked around her office and shuddered.

Two people who had sat in this chair, leaned on this desk, had died while on the job.

She still felt freakish about occupying an office belonging to two murder victims. One victim, Julia Barrett, had most definitely been found. The other one, Marcowicz, was technically missing, but Marla had no doubt he was dead.

It was just a matter of time until they found his body, she was sure of it.

She didn't like to advertise it, but the dead sometimes spoke to her.

Not in a movie sense, showing up like ghosts clad in white, or rattling chains like bad imitations of old Jacob Marley.

Nor in a dreaming sense, where they spoke to her or whispered in her ears while she slept.

No, the dead gave her messages in other ways. They left items arranged in a specific order, or left notes made up of highlighted words from different sources. Sometimes she would pull three random books from her shelves, turn to a random page from each, find an underlined passage and, when she put the three passages in the right order, they formed a perfectly correct sentence. A sentence which was relevant to something she was doing, or which would prove somehow prophetic or explanatory.

She'd become used to this sort of personal Ouija board situation, once famously freaking out a dinner party until the gathered friends all decided she'd been putting them on with a prepared bit of theater. She had reduced the whole thing to the level of a parlor trick, which made her uncomfortable, but doing so had allowed her to face it. And then she'd become accustomed to the strange messages.

Used to them, that is, until she accepted this position with the MPD and learned about her office's previous occupants and their fates. She'd peered at the perimeter of her office and wondered whether she'd have reason to regret taking the job.

And then the messages started coming, messages that seemed to be from the two previous therapists and no one else. It was as if Marla's ghost river had dried up, except for two small trickles that kept her on her toes. Indeed, the Marcowicz and Barrett notes had become the stuff of nightmare for her. For once started, they seemed to want nothing more than to send her cryptic notes. Most of which she tried to ignore.

Less than a month after arriving, she'd stumbled upon a notebook stuck in a drawer of her desk and it turned out to be some of Marcowicz's notes. Since then, she'd met with Detective Nick Lupo a half-dozen times for mandated therapy sessions, and she'd been immediately intrigued. She watched and listened more carefully than with any other patient in a long time.

Marcowicz had written long, rambling notes and observations on something Lupo had discussed. While Marla knew she wasn't meant to have seen the notes, she had and there was no unseeing them. And what Lupo had confessed to David Marcowicz had given her a strange sense of déjà vu she could not shake. Coupled with the notes directed at her, she both feared and looked forward to her meetings with Lupo.

And at today's meeting she planned to ask him a serious question.

DiSanto

He was driving when he caught himself picturing Lupo's friend, Heather Wilson.

Pretty much out of the blue, too.

Just like the way she'd shown up again.

The woman was a goddess. He had only met her a couple times before, but she had made an impression that popped up in his mind at the most inopportune times.

She was amazing. Picturing her *fuck-me* body topped off by her *suck-you* lips caused him an instant physical reaction, and he felt a guilty flush rising on his cheeks.

Plus there was the very good chance she was also one of Lupo's kind. He wasn't quite sure, because no one—not Lupo, or Jessie, of Heather herself—had ever confirmed anything either way. But DiSanto sure remembered the day of the Wolfpaw compound raid, knowing she was supposed to be present. He had seen Lupo bounding away from the compound in his wolf form, accompanied by another wolf. A smaller one.

Was it Heather?

He was almost sure it had to be her. The animal's lithe grace had reminded him of the reporter's, as if her inner beast reflected the way she looked in her everyday form.

So much was wrong with that day, the day of the raid, besides the political and military hoops they'd had to jump over. Fortunately Wolfpaw's bad behavior and nasty hearings had predisposed everyone to the possibility their actions were criminal rather than mere "bad apples," as they'd first been painted. But even so, the sense of utter wrongness that he still felt was like an annoying itch on the portion of his back he couldn't reach.

He had provided the cavalry once again, sure, but he knew damn well some bad stuff had gone down in there. The fact that he was on Lupo's side didn't mean he wasn't uncomfortable with what might have happened.

Might have, my ass.

He knew something had happened. That CEO, Schlosser, had shot himself.

Or had he?

He shook his head, wishing he could unthink these thoughts.

The shooting had happened while DiSanto and a caravan of state and federal law enforcement vehicles wended its way down the private drive, arresting sentries along the way. They'd laid down their guns without firing a shot, which was fortuitous because there would have been mass casualties.

And *then* he had seen the wolves.

Well, anyway, that second wolf…was it Heather? He was in a betting mood, and he bet himself a million dollars it had been her.

How many of these creatures existed?

He bet another million he didn't have that there were more than they, including Lupo himself, knew or expected. According to Lupo, the ranks of the Wolfpaw corporation had been rife with werewolves.

Shit, he got goose bumps just saying the words in his head.

And it was so weird that Lupo's name meant wolf, and he was one. DiSanto had grown up in a very superstitious household, a very patrilineal, repressed, stuck-in-the-past kind of family, and although he had disappointed his parents tremendously by not becoming a priest, or for that matter sticking with the church-going, it was hard for him to dismiss all those years of indoctrination.

Was Lupo a monster, a creature of the devil? Was he evil?

And if werewolves existed, what else might exist? Were vampires and witches that far off the realm of the possible?

And...

And what did Heather Wilson look like naked? She was fresh in his mind, so he could picture her quite clearly and it was something to behold. What would it be like to have sex with her? *With a werewolf?* Would she change—*turn*—while having sex?

Hell, he didn't know, but if the bulge in his pants was any indication, he'd like to find out.

He turned into the precinct's underground parking, wishing he could take his mind off the Amazonian beauty and focus on his task force. There would be lab reports to read, meetings to officiate, assignments to hand out. He'd worked late, caught hell from his wife yet again for barely coming home to sleep a few hours, then he'd left again.

Nick, I wish you were the guy. Not me.

Still he wondered how much he could trust his partner. Nick had been distracted lately, and why not? Two beautiful women after him, a fuckin' werewolf army gunning for him, his mother dying—and something strange going on there, with his father...

Just based on all the distractions, he had to wonder.

Would Nick be there when good old Rich DiSanto needed his partner?

Chapter Twenty-Three

Lupo

He was heading for the precinct after not enough sleep. He was still trying to shake the nightmare—well, most of it had been very pleasant indeed, but that was why it was also a nightmare—when Colgrave called.

"I've had a hit on your names," she said, speaking softly so he knew she was already at work.

"That was fast."

"I had enough favors to call in," she said. "My contact had to make some calls himself, but he tells me there's a pretty good chance this Johnny and Marty are goons who work for a mob guy who works out of Vegas."

"Crap."

"Yeah, I thought you wouldn't like to hear it. His name is Gus Bastone. They call him *The Stick*."

He barked a laugh. "Cute. His last name actually means *stick* or *rod* in Italian. What else?"

"His father died recently and he took over the family business, started calling himself a Don, like the old days. He's young, but old enough to remember the old days. *Godfather* stuff, you know? He owns a casino in Vegas, the Old Italy—it's new and not doing great, but it could start doing better. He's hired some pretty famous chefs for his two restaurants, gets in some old-time Italian acts. He ripped off the New York New York idea, and since somebody beat him to Venice he has a Streets of Palermo, a fake Coliseum, the Naples harbor complete with fake ships...more like that." She paused.

"I'm guessing there's more than just what's in his crappy little casino."

"Yeah, word is that he's a little nuts. Wants to be like the old man, longs for the old ways. Has some thugs working for him who go further than the usual leg-breaking..."

"Like what?"

"Well, one guy is known for making people disappear. Like, they are never found again. Your friends Johnny and Marty— one of them, or both I suppose—seem to enjoy using a bone saw and hand torch combo on guys who're getting a message."

"Jesus!" He felt his stomach dropping through the floor of his Maxima.

"Yeah, there's a little more."

"Okay?"

Colgrave was being cagey. Lupo heard a tapping sound, like a pencil hitting her teeth in rhythm. A weird nervous tic. He'd noticed it before. It had grabbed his attention when he was in the room at some department meeting or other, partly because it was so unconsciously phallic.

He pictured her, that glossy auburn hair—or would you call it chestnut?—which reminded him of Jessie. Her long, straight nose separated dark, smoky eyes beneath untweezed eyebrows. Her mouth was wide, generous and sensual, yet he'd thought it seemed made for laughing, if the curl at its corners was any indication. When she smiled, strong straight teeth glinted between her full lips. Her figure was lithe, but mature. She'd always reminded him of a slightly older version of Jessie. He had to admit he'd always liked her and wished he had had the chance to work with her more.

His attention was wandering. He forced it back on track.

After a pause, she said, "Word has it he's bought a large house in Eagle River. It's a log cabin mansion with a guest house and a compound of about two acres. There's been activity there, like they're getting ready for the boss to visit." She paused. "Or move in."

"So this is all confirmed?"

"Far as I can tell, yes," Colgrave said.

"Hmm…" On top of picturing her, he was also trying to clear his mind of the Heather aftereffect. But the thought of an eccentric mob boss moving in on the tribal casino and having a reason to pay Jessie a visit caused his stomach acids to feel extra toxic.

"You know, I'm interested in this too, now," she went on over his silence. "The Organized Crime unit's been fairly quiet—once they made gangs their own thing we haven't had anything to speak of. The local mob was busted up in the eighties. But if they've got hard-ons for tribal casinos, for one thing, you'll need help. This Bastone guy sounds like a character out of a Puzo book, but maybe that's just his shtick. He's not faking the dangerous part."

"Tell me about the thug who disappears people."

Colgrave sighed. "My source didn't have a name, but apparently he's been with the family some years, except for a few tours in the Middle East."

Lupo's ears pricked up. "Yeah? Soldier boy, huh?"

"Yeah, and also a contractor after he mustered out. He's definitely a killer, but no one can ever find any evidence."

Lupo had heard enough.

He ran a nervous hand through his hair. He was suddenly very glad Ryeland hadn't put him in charge of the bus case.

Now he and DiSanto could cut loose and hardly anyone would notice.

"Thanks, Danni, I owe you."

"Noted."

"Seriously, if you need anything..."

"Lupo, this guy's trouble. If *you* need anything, just call. Or you know where I hide out."

"Okay." He did have a sense that she was sometimes on the edge. On the *borderline*. She had that rep among the detectives, anyway. She had some dark secrets, that was for sure. And he was more curious than he had any right to be.

But there was more important shit to worry about...

He clicked off and dark thoughts rolled through his head like an up-north thunderstorm in midsummer.

Why did shit like this always happen in threes?

Chapter Twenty-Four

Lupo

For the first time since he'd started the mandated therapy sessions with the police psychologist, he could almost say he *liked* the therapist.

Marla Anders was forthright, serious, discreet from what he could tell, and she really seemed to listen. And it didn't hurt that she was a beautiful woman unlike that crone Barrett, who'd had it in for Lupo. It had been her undoing, though, and then the new psychologist who had replaced her was Marcowicz and he'd been almost worse, selling him out to that vulture Killian.

Now they were both resting together in eternity, thanks to a couple favors he'd called in.

Not their murders, only their disposal.

Lupo'd been set up to look like a murderer, but he'd played his hand faster and his connections had given him an out. He was all out of favors there, he figured.

No, it didn't hurt that Marla Anders had flawless olive skin, her oval face crowned by lustrous black hair that she wore cascading down one side of her head onto her shoulders. She looked as if she should have had a bright tropical flower woven through its silky strands. He figured she probably traced her heritage to some interesting confluence of African-American and Latino bloodlines, and as far as he was concerned she was more or less the most attractive woman to be found in the MPD's central precinct on any given day, with the only possible exception being Danni Colgrave.

He grinned. Sometimes he enjoyed being that chauvinist cop everybody hated. It was just part of being a male cop—the locker room was never far away.

He'd suggested postponing his session, but Ryeland was adamant that there was no reason.

"Besides, DiSanto's picking the rest of his team today, the lab results won't be in, we've heard nothing from anyone, and the mayor called with his full support. For today, anyway." Ryeland chuckled wryly. "Keep your appointment. I want everyone on the team to have a clear record, and if you start skipping sessions, that's gonna look bad. And everybody's gonna try following your lead. My system will collapse."

"Well, you know where I'll be then..." Lupo had said, hiding the sinking feeling that his star was starting to fall.

Now he was sitting in Anders' office, across her neatly arrayed desktop. Marcowicz had been something of a slob, but Anders was almost OCD. There wasn't much on the smooth surface and everything was lined up with perfection.

She had been watching him grinning. "What's funny?" She smiled to show that she wasn't offended by his private musing.

She had a nice smile, he realized.

"Just thinking about some of my previous sessions in here." Well, it was true.

"You didn't feel they were very helpful?" She raised an eyebrow.

"You could say that. They seemed to be more interested in what I thought about the weather on any given day." *That* wasn't true. They'd been interested in pinning some of the strange happenings on him.

"I'm sorry about that," she said and sounded sincere. "I'm just interested in giving you a forum to get anything off your chest you feel might help you. We can talk about anything. Since your injury—" she glanced down his leg at his prosthetic "—you've been through a lot."

If you only knew, he thought. At least he'd remembered to limp a little when he'd come in.

He nodded, and told her about the cases he'd worked. He had to lie about some of it, of course, but if he sat there without talking it would just infuriate her into disliking him, too, so it was best to play the game.

He went on at length, as she nodded encouragingly.

She'd encouraged him to share, and for once he'd found someone he instinctively believed really wanted him to.

She was startled by his losses. He talked about his longtime partner, Ben Sabatini, who had been murdered by the serial killer Martin Stewart. Then he'd lost a good friend in Sam Waters, casualty of the first encounter with Wolfpaw mercenaries. He'd lost another friend in Tom Arnow, briefly sheriff of Vilas County—and his guilt there would forever remain. There was no end to the list of heartaches he'd suffered since those days. It was good to talk about them, even if in oblique terms.

Anders seemed genuinely touched. "You must have a lot of ghosts."

He started to nod, then said, "What?"

"You know, I believe that some of us experience our ghosts more than others..." She looked up suddenly to find him staring at her. "I mean, I—I'm just sharing a thought I've had. Recently..."

"Yes?" Lupo said, leaning forward. *This is strange.*

She seemed to realize that somehow her session had been reversed. "Excuse me, I've been working on a series of articles — a book, really—and sometimes I get off on a tangent."

"Sounds like an intriguing subject," he said. She was embarrassed, as if he'd caught her at something. "What you said about ghosts, though, I'm really interested in that."

She looked up suddenly, her eyes catching his, trying to draw him out.

And then he had the thought that maybe she was acting, that she was setting him up, as if she knew...could she have read Marcowicz's files? It was one of his many missteps with the previous psychologist, telling him too much, believing it would truly remain between them.

Was she trying to get him to talk about Ghost Sam?

Chapter Twenty-Five

DiSanto

He was planning his day of taking command of the task force. He'd made a list of detectives he wanted to grab from other units, and he'd sketched out how they would proceed.

Of course he would take his partner into the task force. Nick was better suited for working alone, true, but DiSanto knew he could set him loose on his own tangent and he'd grab on to it like a pit bull.

It would take several days for forensics to give them a complete picture of what had happened exactly. Beyond knowing that an unknown shooter had taken out passengers and then the driver—and then disappeared—they needed to know the order of things. They needed to catalog and watch camera feeds from every public and private camera along the route of the entire incident, all the way to where it had ended tragically in death for so many.

For a small, *contained* incident, it had caused a shitload of casualties.

His mind buzzing with possibilities, ideas, tactics, and more points to add to his list, he finally entered the squad room before 8:00 a.m., and it was already a hub of activity.

In the glassed-in corner, detectives were sitting around the long conference table, holding coffee mugs. A smartboard was on, with tables and charts scrolling across it. Three strangers in suits stood positioned around the table, one of them with the remote.

"Sonofabitch," DiSanto muttered. He was standing there, just staring, trying to process what he was seeing. That was *his* meeting, going on without him.

"Yeah, it's the feds." Ryeland had sidled up without a sound. For his size, that was impressive. "Didn't give me any fucking choice."

"They're taking over?"

"Yeah. You can be part of the team, but it's their ballgame. Which begs the question, what does Homeland want with our shooter? He doesn't fit the terrorist label."

"They're not FBI?" DiSanto asked, stifling his anger. He thought Ryeland had changed his mind about him and called in the dreaded feds.

"Nope, I never called 'em. These are DHS, so they're ten times worse." Ryeland lowered his voice. "Tread carefully, especially with the tall guy wrangling that remote. Name's Hart, or Bart. Anyway, something's going on we don't know about, and we're in the middle with no clue."

"Thanks. What about Lupo?"

"He's on the team too, but he's in with Anders I think. He seems distracted, your partner."

"I don't think so."

"'Cause I know he gets himself pulled around—he's had more strange stuff happen to him than any ten guys. Yet he always comes out clean. Just from reading his cases and personnel file, I mean." Ryeland turned and fixed DiSanto with a harsh stare. "You know anything you can share?"

"No, sir. That is, I'm not aware of anything improper. If that's what you mean…"

"I'm easy, DiSanto. As long as bad guys go away for a long time, I don't question much. But I don't want too much off the reservation poaching. *Capisce*?"

DiSanto nodded. "Got it."

"Now you'd better get to that meeting before they have you transferred to traffic control, or parking patrol." When DiSanto's eyes widened, Ryeland added. "Kidding!" Then: "I think. That Hart-Bart guy is an asshole."

DiSanto shrugged and made his way to the table behind the glass while the guy with the remote droned on, squeezing in because no one had left him any space.

"Jesus," he muttered.

"Sorry, Dee," muttered an older detective named Mosher. "They herded us in here and took over. Seems like we're in the middle of some deep, dark conspiracy—but they're not tellin' us what it is."

"Hey, sorry to be bothering you over there in the corner." The gravelly voice belonged to the agent Hart-Bart, who'd stopped his monologue to glare at DiSanto's interruption.

"Carry on," DiSanto said. Always a slave to his own wise mouth. He made a florid gesture.

Hart-Bart frowned, stared at him two beats longer, then continued.

"As I was saying, there have been several shootings in the Chicago area that we think are perpetrated by the same individual. This is why we were able to latch on to yours and offer our help. There doesn't seem to be a motive, but we're putting together an extensive file."

"How is that any help?" DiSanto whispered to his coconspirator, who waved him away.

"Well, they haven't figured out a motive, haven't caught the guy, don't know squat." DiSanto's voice carried, and Hart-Bart stopped again and glared at him.

"Detective…"

"Yeah, yeah," DiSanto said, gesturing again. "All ears."

His fellow detectives grinned, but Hart-Bart's eyes turned dagger-like. He chose to ignore, however, and continued with team assignments.

DiSanto looked around the squad room. Still no Lupo.

He stalked off in search of Ryeland, shaking his head.

"This is bullshit…"

So much for the task force. He and Lupo could work the case better on their own.

Lupo

His call found her while she was on break.

"Nick!" Her voice was breathy. He loved that sound.

"Listen," he said, without much preamble. There would be time for some tenderness later.

"Yeah?" She picked up on his intensity.

"I got the word and it's not good." He went on to give Jessie an abbreviated, slightly edited version of what Colgrave had told him.

"This is terrible! I have to tell Bill."

He thought about it. "Okay, tell him what I told you, but that's it. No investigating on your own. No hunting for Mafia guys. Listen, I grew up on the Hardy Boys and Nancy Drew, and The Three Investigators and Brains Benton—okay? I was into the whole kid detective thing. Maybe that's why I wanted to be a cop. But that stuff is for kids and when they get caught sticking their noses into some criminal's plan nothin' happens to them. You see? This is real life. These guys play rough. They might not really like you sounding the warning to everybody you know."

"Well, I have to do *something*, Nick. You remember Charlie Bear, from that Archer thing down in Milwaukee?"

"Yeah?"

"He's working casino security here now. Isn't that what he did down there?"

Lupo winced. He was glad they weren't on FaceTime so she could see his look. He remembered what had happened to Charlie because he hadn't played ball with some very bad people, people they'd had time to get to know later on. Charlie's family had paid the price.

"Yeah, he did do that kind of work. And he helped me out, but it got his family—uh, it was a bad thing that happened." He didn't really want to get into the details, not with what Jessie was facing now.

"I did remember. I told him I was sorry."

Like that would help. His family was exterminated.

But she didn't know everything. He'd never told her.

"Jess, I'm serious, you have got to hang back on this until I figure out what to do. It's not like you're tattling on the class clown here. These guys are really outside our world when it comes to legal and illegal."

"Can they be any worse than Wolfpaw werewolves, Nick?"

"That's not fair. That's two different things. But yeah, I think they might be worse. At least Wolfpaw hid most of their crimes. These mob guys like to hurt folks publicly, to leave clear messages to other people who might cross them."

He almost told her about the guy with the saw and blow torch, but decided she'd think he was being melodramatic.

"Nick?"

He heard something in her voice. Something more. Something *else*.

She knew something she hadn't told him yet.

"Yeah?" Cautiously.

"I followed one of them. He's a new one, looks like they squashed together a safari guide and a surfer, reminded me of Bruce Campbell. Not Bruce from *Bubba Ho-Tep*, more from *Army of Darkness*..."

"Great, you're following thugs because they look like movie stars?"

"No," she dragged the word out patiently. "I followed him because he looked like he was on a mission. He was."

She told him about the research the guy had done.

"Shit! Jess, you've got to back off. Even more so now. It's like worlds colliding..."

"What are you talking about?"

He sighed. This wasn't a good time, or a good place. Nor was it advisable. But if he didn't, he'd hear about it later. And he'd suffer for it, maybe in a trivial way. But maybe not. Maybe he'd suffer for not having been honest and open. Maybe he'd suffer because when the worlds collided *they'd blow up*.

"Jess, I'm not sure whether what you saw is connected to what I've got going on here—"

"The bus shooting?"

"Uh, no." He paused and breathed, hoping the extra oxygen would keep him from fainting. Well, not fainting, but being zapped from afar wasn't out of the question. "Uh, no," he repeated. "There's something else going down. Something happened in Madison..."

"Oh, yeah, I saw a headline about it online, but I didn't have time to read it."

"It was some kind of commando action against civilians, apparently trying to get hold of some very sensitive information that was being, uh, transferred from a whistleblower to…"

Fuck!

He was on his cell. So was Jessie. It was like broadcasting out to the universe. He'd just gotten so used to yakking on the phone that he'd forgotten even the most basic safeguards. Other people didn't have to worry about their paranoia panning out. But if Heather was right, then they'd tracked her. Somehow, even though they shouldn't have been able to.

Could they have tracked her right to him?

Thanks, Heather.

But no, that was too much paranoia, wasn't it?

Jess was talking in his ear. "Yeah, you were saying? Transferred from a whistleblower to…who?"

"A reporter. A certain reporter. In this case, our old friend Heather."

First there was silence on the line.

He didn't dare breathe.

Then there was a *gasp-inhale-growl* so vivid that he wondered if Jessie hadn't been bitten by a wolf. It sounded as if she were transforming into a raging creature over there.

Damn it.

"Heather's back?" Jessie's voice seemed to have gained a few octaves. She seemed to have become someone else. Her voice was more of a deep croak. *"That fucking whore-bitch Heather is back?"* She breathed loudly. "Please tell me I misheard that."

"I can't. You heard it right. She had nowhere else to go. She brought me the drive with the info because they were willing to kill to get it. They *did* kill for it."

"Jesus, Nick!"

"I know…"

"You don't know! You don't get it. That woman has been a thorn in our side since she first stepped out of her stupid Lexus. I wish we'd never seen her. I wish...I wish she'd never gotten out of that goddamn lake, Nick. I wish I'd killed her. I wish she was *dead*."

Lupo was shaken by the level of vitriol. And he decided this was no time to tell Jessie he'd let Heather crash at his place.

"We can talk about this later," he started.

"No, there's nothing to say."

"Yes, Jess, there is. This crap she brought me would have found me eventually. I— My name was in the material, Jessie. And yours. They were thorough. I had to read carefully, line by line, to find it. But they'd have dragged us into it eventually. Take my word for it."

"Well, that's the problem, Nick. *I always do*."

And she hung up.

Chapter Twenty-Six

Bastone

They'd landed at Madison's small airport and had driven two rented SUVs, Ford Expeditions, up to Vilas County. The GPS had led them to the town, and through it, then up US45 and down a long stretch of 17 heading east, and then finally through narrow blacktopped county roads that dipped and circled around lakes and over channels. Finally they'd nosed onto a deceptively overgrown turnout and circled around a rutted driveway a half-mile up to the house he'd seen in the photographs, which looked like a mansion except it had been fashioned of logs and glass and stone.

Bastone heaved a sigh of relief when he realized that it was a damn sight better than what the driveway had concealed. Maybe it was left that way on purpose, to discourage visitors. His driver had almost missed it.

He had four guys with him, minor muscle, but he'd wanted to have two vehicles on hand. Plus Johnny's and Rabbioso's crew—this way they'd have enough fucking cars to get around and spread out if needed. He'd buy some vehicles later on, once he'd cemented his ties with several state dealers. His name still meant something in Wisconsin, but he'd have to jog some memories in order to get some deals on the rolling stock.

Now he stepped out of the Expedition and stood behind the open door, inhaling the pure scent of fresh air and pine or whatever the fuck it was. He just knew it smelled good after the heat stench of Vegas, with its sweaty showgirls and pretty boys.

Although about now he could go for a showgirl or two. Well, they hadda have chicks here, too. Meantime, he had his collection…no, scratch that, he'd have some of it when the box he'd shipped arrived in a day or two. He was told it wouldn't be smart to put the smut in his checked bags or carry-ons, so he'd had no choice but to ship some over.

"Bruno, get my bags."

"Yes, sir," the driver said and went to it.

"Manny, open up the doors and get the cars in the garage. And get in the kitchen—I think we're gonna need some comfort food. This is home now."

"Sure thing, boss."

"Don't call me that."

"Uh, sure. Pasta okay?"

"Fuck you think I am, Tony Soprano? I want some corn-fed steaks. Fridge should be stocked, if that nut Johnny knows what's good for 'im."

Bruno and Manny hopped to their tasks.

"Jingo, get freshened up then head into town and track down Robb and Johnny. Tell 'em to bring the hardware, we're naked out here." *What the hell kinda name was Jingo?*

"Sure," said the mountain whose name was Jingo. "Get Marty too?"

"Fuck do I care about Marty? It's Johnny and Robb I want, they're my lieutenants. Marty's a lowlife like you."

Jingo slinked away and Don Bastone felt a little guilty, treating him like that. But shit, that's what his father would have said. *You hadda fill the role, or they'd fill a hole with you.* That's another thing his father had said.

That left Joey without a job to do. "You," he snapped, "help Bruno with the bags."

The young Don felt like draping his overcoat over his shoulders like his father would have done, before entering his new castle, but shit, it was almost too hot here even though he'd been told it got cold. Some of the trees around them had shed leaves, but most of the woods looked still green and impenetrable.

So he made do with folding the leather coat over his arm and heading up the cobblestone walk to the main door, which Manny had left wide open. Once inside he took a tour and had to admit it reminded him of one of those luxury condos dotted around the high-roller casinos, except here the atmosphere was more real because the woods came right up to the back end of the house. The drive wound around the house and ended at the double-height garage. The great room was like a hotel lobby except comfortable, with a three-story stone fireplace on one wall and a balcony above, glass facing out.

And at an angle from the rear of the house, a new wooden pier stuck out like a middle finger into one of the elongated lakes that everybody raved about here. He stared out over the water that lapped gently on the pilings.

Fuck, I'm gonna have to get a boat. Hell, two boats. A fast one and one of those floating living rooms.

Bastone grunted with pleasure. He picked a double bedroom—that was a master with its own den off to the side and a bath about the size of another bedroom. The Jacuzzi looked ready for action, and he wondered who he could trust to get him some girls. The goddamn casino he was buying into hadda have some showgirls, right? He'd ask Rabbioso. That fucker would know.

He threw his stuff on a huge desk in his bedroom, loosened his tie, and wished he had some blow. The champagne he'd asked to be placed in the fridge would have to do.

Then later he would decide just how to make sure the fuckin' Indians down the road knew just who was the new boss.

He figured he'd enjoy that part.

Jessie

Still seething, she entered the casino and was immediately assailed by a giant headache. For once, the constant C Major chord symphony didn't attract her or make her hands itch. She didn't feel her player's card scratching the skin of her thigh through her jeans. She didn't want to see the red numbers climb or fall with each button push and roll of the cylinders. She wasn't interested in seeing single, double, or triple BAR BAR BAR flags roll together across the middle of the screen.

She headed straight back, past the theater entrance, past a bank of ATMs, past a caged cashier and a free soft drinks and coffee bar, and then past the back Security counter. She waved at one of the newer guards who knew her but not well, and opened the double doors into the tech office area as if she belonged there, and he let her. She stalked down the hall and reached the main administrative area, with offices and still sparkling-new conference rooms behind glass walls, leather chairs arranged around dark wood slabs with gold highlights and tech hook-ups for laptops and phones and high-tech projectors.

For the first time she wondered how much all this had cost. She wondered how much the tribe made daily. And she wondered how much, once the Mafia stuck their greedy fucking hands in the flow, the tribe would still be able to have.

And Nick had told her to take it easy!

Damn him, and Heather too.

She blew past Donna and entered Bill Grey Hawk's office.

"Dr. Hawkins!" He'd been huddled over his phone. He hung up and turned toward her.

She stalked up to his desk, which had also cost a pretty penny.

"Bill, Nick tells me to be careful, but you have to realize that there are mobsters in town, and they're here to take over the casino. Nick is looking into it, and then he's going to drive up here and we're going to meet with you and the council, and we'll—"

"Doctor," Grey Hawk interrupted, his eyes widening, "Please meet Mr. Rabbioso—" His head indicated a guest she hadn't seen.

"Mr. Robb will do," said not-Bruce, who stood from where he'd been sitting on the leather sofa in the corner and held out his hand. He looked very dashing in his safari outfit.

"Oh, I'm sorry," she said, her voice fading. She touched the thug's hand and it gripped hers nicely, and she stared in his eyes and saw the darkness there, the cold, and it was a mismatch from what his skin felt like, and suddenly she was afraid.

"It's all right, I was just leaving. Doctor? It's very nice to meet you."

"Uh, likewise." They touched hands briefly and she felt it again.

But what was it?

He took his safari jacket and his not-Bruce looks out of there and she saw that Bill was visibly shaken.

"What's wrong, Bill?"

"Nothing. Mr. Robb was...nothing, Jessie. We were finished. What can I do for you?"

He turned to face her and she thought he was literally shaking.

Strange that he'd been on the phone while the guy sat on his sofa.

"I just came to tell you that I told Nick about what's happening. I assume you know this Mr. Robb here is part of the group—more like conspiracy—to take over the casino and hotel. I just want you to know, we're going to find a way to help."

She looked around. "Where's your man, Charlie? He should be in on this."

"I've sent him on an errand down in Wausau," Grey Hawk said. "Jessie, we're already starting to draft a response."

"What the hell, Bill? A *response*?"

He recoiled from her anger.

"This isn't a corporate takeover! They might use the same language, but they're on a whole different level of predator. And you've seen what real predators look like, haven't you, Bill?"

She was referring to what he'd seen on that beach, when Nick and the Wolfpaw soldier turned into wolves and fought almost to the death. That was when Heather, the bitch, had put several silver slugs into her lover's body. And then she'd become one of them.

But Bill Grey Hawk had seen enough. Though he'd never spoken of it since, his return to the council had been a fragile one, *because he didn't want to know.*

And Jessie suddenly figured out what she'd seen in Mr. Robb's eyes. It wasn't cold or darkness. She'd seen an amused look, but even more she'd seen a sort of kaleidoscope effect that he attempted to hide by making his eyes twinkle at her.

She had seen a wolf below the skin, crouched there— waiting to spring.

Wolfclaw

Somewhere in Northern Minnesota

Spotlights blazing, the McDonnell Douglas 902 VIP circled the helipad once before settling down. Its quiet twin Pratt and Whitney engines were slowing almost as soon as its wheels touched the concrete.

General Walt Lansing popped the large cabin door, grabbed his leather duffel and a thin briefcase from one of the empty seats, and hopped out with a wave at the pilot.

The general was a ramrod-straight, silver-haired buzzcut cliché of a military man, his uniform fitting the image down to the last colorful campaign ribbon on his chest. Arms swinging, he made his way past the perimeter guards to the main lodge and disappeared inside.

After following a long hallway paneled in knotty pine, he reached his apartment and closed the door, then stashed the briefcase on the desk, the duffel on the bed, and ran the shower. A half hour later he reemerged wearing a khaki jumpsuit, combat boots, and a black beret. Only two insignia, a death's head on his collar and a stylized red claw on a shoulder patch. A few minutes later, he joined the rest of the assembled group in the two-story library.

A crackling fire blazed in a huge fieldstone fireplace set in the center of the inner wall. Around it, six others clad in similar attire lounged on rich maroon leather club chairs. Satellite butler's tables held decanters and glasses of golden and clear liquids. Cigar smoke swirled in the center of the room, reaching toward the two walls of stuffed floor-to-ceiling bookcases that faced each other. The room's outside wall was made of glass and framed the night-washed woods over which the cantilevered section of the house was perched. This portion of

234 / W.D. Gagliani

the log house was the only nod to modernism — the rest was purely frontier ski lodge in style.

When Lansing entered, the others looked up. No one leaped to attention, for this was a gathering of equals. Their salutes were informal affairs, more like casual waves, and he returned them with a wave of his own.

Across from the fireplace were generals Eammons and LaPorte, both Army. Closer to the bookcases and facing the others were generals Heissen and Johnston, both of the Marines. The other two, huddled over a chessboard table, were generals Pedersen and Torre of the Air Force.

"Gentlemen, welcome," Lansing said, even though he was the late arrival. He crossed to the well-appointed bar and poured a generous single-malt. "Let us toast our continued good fortune."

He held up his glass, waiting for the others to follow suit.

"Wolfclaw lives on," he said. He waited for the others to respond, then drank and enjoyed the smoky flavor of the Scotch.

"Wolfclaw," they intoned, though a mite weakly.

They drank and he waited.

General Johnston was the first to speak up outside of the toast. Lansing had expected it. "Walt, the board was dissolved, Schlosser is dead, the main compound was raided. Wolfpaw no longer exists. What are we toasting, really?"

Lansing looked around, a cold smile stretched across his face. "We should be toasting the fact that our firewall held, my friend. We should be toasting that no one has broken through. We were to be toasting that no outsider knows the nature of our group, no one knows that the work of Wolfpaw continues without pause. That no one knows we still exist as an entity. And that no one knows we are all gathered here in this place. These would all be good reasons for a toast. But as you know, we have had a leak and we cannot toast our continuing mission—that is, until we take care of our problem. I believe we can still contain it, and then we shall be able to toast the fact that our main goal is still within sight. Does anyone doubt me?" He glanced at each of his colleagues, in turn.

Heads shook, some more convincingly than others. He chose to look on the positive side of things, for now.

"That's good, very good. We have much to discuss over this weekend, and I appreciate that you've all dropped everything to be here. Of course it's an annual tradition, but we could have gotten that part out of the way tonight and tomorrow. I'm glad we'll spend Sunday and Monday focused on our business. And in the meantime, our forces will meet their first test by removing our enemies before they can strike out at us. But there is time for everything to be explained and demonstrated. Tonight, however, first we play."

They drank again.

Lansing added, "And then we feast." He winked. "Then play again."

Part Two

Chapter Twenty-Seven

Wolfclaw

Somewhere in Northern Minnesota

General Lansing had changed into his black Wolfclaw jumpsuit. A closer look would have shown that his collar insignia on one side was a stylized death's head similar to the traditional SS uniform, and on the other a stylized wolf's head. The red shoulder flash was a set of claws with his general's stars arrayed in a semi-circle below.

The others had changed into jumpsuits as well, and now all stood casually in the specially appointed bunker below the rear of the lodge house. There were three sublevels, with only the uppermost appearing to be a normal basement. A well-hidden elevator shaft was the secret entrance to the sublevels, and this was a portion of the deepest. The lavish room was accented by fieldstone columns, walnut paneling, and art of a certain type. Indeed, much of the art—which included wall-hanging tapestries, paintings, photographs, and sculptures—depicted sex acts of every description and permutation. Greek and Roman erotica, some of it museum-quality, inhabited sconces set in the walls at regular intervals.

Lansing opened an engraved double door at one end of the chamber, revealing a small anteroom about the size of a walk-in closet. Inside, two cages faced each other across a slightly tilted stainless steel slab about six feet across. Blood channels set in the sides and lowest edge led to a drain set in the concrete below.

The cages held two animals, a medium-size dog of indeterminate mix on the right and a small goat on the left.

Lansing turned to face his fellow officers. His fellow *celebrants*.

"Gentlemen, it's my pleasure to call this annual tradition to order. Let the Lupercalia begin!"

The others intoned a hearty, "Hear, hear!"

With that, General Johnston stepped forward and took the goat, bleating and struggling, from its cage. Meanwhile Lansing reached into the right-hand cage and removed the slightly sedated dog, whose jaws tried to grab its tormentor's arms but couldn't. Both men elevated the animals briefly in front of the others, then swung them onto the steel table, which for this purpose served as the chamber's altar and secured them there with short chains.

The prescribed sacrifice was ready.

Everyone knew what to do, because they had done this every fifteenth of February since they had ascended to their positions.

With little ceremony beyond a quick flourish, both men brandished ceremonial daggers and in a synchronized motion slit the animals' throats, holding down the thrashing, struggling bodies as they bled out into the stainless-steel channels. Heissen and LaPorte stepped forward, golden grails in their hands, and let a stream of each animal's blood enter the jeweled cups.

The bleating, whimpering animals died quickly, their blood first gushing, then trickling, and finally dripping down into the drain.

Lansing and Johnston left the drained carcasses where they lay still chained to the altar and turned to take the grails, which they held for the others to behold.

Then they took turns anointing each other's foreheads with a dab of each creature's blood, as had been done since time immemorial during this ritual.

The blood drying on their skin, excitement rolling off them in waves, they all rode the walnut-and brass-accented elevator car to the first floor and exited the rear of the building beneath the cantilever extension, where guards had assembled the thirteen.

Dressed in light olive drab fatigues, the thirteen men huddled together, shivering, nervously eyeing the muzzles of the dozen H&K MP5 submachine guns aimed their way. Their eyes were wide at the thought of their situation, which they could barely comprehend. Twenty-four hours earlier they'd been on the street in various urban centers, living out of Dumpsters or in and out of shelters, some eking out a bare living by "canning," collecting cans in huge trash bags for the tiny cash return. Suddenly chloroformed and bagged like carcasses, renditioned in their own country, they had awakened here in a tiny cell, naked in a cold climate, supplied with thin fatigues and cheap sneakers. Then they'd been forced to bathe, dress in the generic clothes, and had been assembled under this roof as snowflakes floated in on the breeze and melted on their heads and hands.

Now they had become the main attraction for the ritual.

Lansing and his group spread out in front of the thirteen, staring at them with grins spreading across their faces. The general nodded at his guards, and every single one took a step forward and snapped their gun muzzles upward.

The captive men, startled, groaned and started to chatter, question their fate, complain. Some began to pray. One shouted obscenities. Fear and anger swept over the group, and there was a ripple of movement, as if they might rush their captors in a last-ditch attempt to escape whatever fate awaited them.

But then their voices faded and went silent. Their muscles may have tightened, but not in readiness. No, their muscles tightened in a classic fight-or-flight dilemma as they tried to process what they were witnessing.

Lansing had said, "The Lupercalia continues, gentlemen. All hail."

"All hail!"

The generals spoke in unison.

They had started to strip out of their jumpsuits, first unzipping and dropping them to the ground, then stepping out of them, naked, their penises tumescent and bursting blue in the cold air. As they stood, their erections facing the thirteen confused and frightened men. Eyes were wide in shock. But disgust was written in their faces as well as the shock. And yet, they seemed fascinated by the sight of these naked men approaching.

Perhaps not so much fascinated as hypnotized, they watched as the men and their erections advanced.

Close, closer…

Still fascinated, but now by the men's eyes, the pupils of which seemed to change colors and swirl like kaleidoscopes.

Fascinated…until they spotted coarse hair beginning to sprout up and down arms, backs, and across chests. Hands sprouting fur and wicked claws. Heads blurring and re-coalescing as pointed snouts filled with fangs, and long, lolling tongues.

The thirteen men screamed and bellowed, shrinking away from the impossible sight. Their bodies collided in the panic of trying to put something between themselves and these monsters that were manifesting before them.

At this point, the guards fired long bursts into the air, over the men's heads, herding them out from under the cantilever roof. They needed no spur, however, as the half-man, half-wolf creatures lunged for them on hind legs tipped with wolf paws, their fearsome growls filling the space and echoing through the nearby woods.

The men—who had become *prey*, pure and simple—broke ranks and made for the tree line.

All except one who was brought down almost immediately by two of the fanged monsters. The victors of that encounter began to tear into their victim even as he shrieked in excruciating pain, their claws and fangs making short work of his thin clothes and grinding through bone and sinew, releasing a gush of blood and, soon, intestines and organs.

The wolf-men feasted, their snouts dappled in crimson. Growls and drool escaping, their jaws sawed through limbs and sought out the tastiest bits as the human expired under them.

Of the others, two thirds reached the trees. Four were snagged by snarling wolf-men and batted to the ground, where the fangs went to work amidst screams that were cut off, one by one, as the humans died.

One lone wolf gave chase past the tree line and into the forest, his howls marking his progress as he tracked the homeless men who fled, crashing through the evergreen trunks in a headlong rush that lacked control... Lacked control and any hope of survival, for soon the only partially sated wolf-men had rejoined the chase and howled their joy at racing through the frigid woods, the scent of terrified human like a fine aroma in their nostrils and adrenaline like wine in their veins. And the moon above spreading her arms to encompass them all.

Soon all the prey had been felled, and all the wolves had fed to near-bursting.

Lansing alone knew about an experiment that was taking place, but he would share that news when the time came.

They returned to the lodge on four paws, their brown, black, and gray fur spattered with blood and brains, their tongues still tingling with the taste of live prey.

The generals of the Wolfclaw group forced a change despite the moon's loving call to continue romping. Their stomachs sated, the next phase of the festival was upon them. They showered then rode the elevator back up, reconvening a while later in a special lounge, where an even dozen long-limbed women of luscious curves and movie-star looks waited, their bodies draped over leather armchairs and sofas in various stages of undress. Sheer fabric barely covered ample assets as strategic strip-lighting highlighted glossy hair in a multitude of shades.

The generals entered the lounge, their erections raging.

The werewolf gene amplified natural libido, and these men had achieved their ranks through sheer ego, guts, and ruthlessness—their libido was already heightened. The realigned DNA of the change channeled all their qualities into their bloodstream, and granted them an insatiable stamina and desire most Viagra users would have found enviable.

"Enjoy the final phase of the Lupercalia, gentlemen," Lansing said, though it was unnecessary. His colleagues were already pairing up, doubling, tripling, with their dates of the moment, slender scarlet-tipped female hands reaching out for swollen male members, faces and tongues meeting, limbs beginning to intertwine already, the groupings blurring into tableaus of sighs, groans, and grunts.

Before long the room had become a series of bacchanalian chains as bodies lay end to end and every other possible way, their mouths and genitalia joined in seemingly countless permutations. Soon the various rhythms of the fluid couplings filled the air along with the heady scents of musk and sweat, sex and testosterone. Every so often orgasmic screams erupted from complex mountains of flesh. Here and there blood flowed—in this company, no bodily fluid was off-limits.

The wolves fed their other appetite in this way, a secret update of the long tradition of the Lupercalia which had evolved soon after Roman popes had begun to decry the original.

Tomorrow the generals would meet for important Wolfclaw business, for show and tell, and for entertainment.

But tonight—*tonight they would fuck like rutting animals.*

Bastone

"Okay, Billy-Grey, okay," he said into the phone.

The Don rolled his eyes. The large screen across from his bed showed three chicks in some sort of lezzie threesome that he'd just decided he should see more often. Tongues and twats and asses, the occasional boob, and some dildos. It was easier to place yourself in the action if there wasn't some tattooed hung asshole to ruin the beauty of the staging.

One of his boys had got this shit from a local rental shop (they still had them here?) and the stuff would have to do until his own collection arrived.

"Yeah, I get it. You're all nervous now because this doctor chick knows too much. What did she do?" He chuckled. "She really is a busybody, eh? Fuck's my guy doin' in the library, huh?" He'd have to ask Robb about that. Still, this *puttana* had no right to insert her nose into his business.

One of the chicks was wielding a monster pink dildo up there. *Jeez.*

He listened to the pencil-pushin' Indian a little more.

"Okay, man, I'm gonna send one of my guys to give you a little bit more protection, in case the chick's cop friends come callin', all right? You okay with that, chief?"

He nodded along with the acceptance and gratitude as if the fucker could see him.

"Yeah, sure, I gotta protect my investment, yeah? No worries on your end. Your worries are just about over, believe me. When I take over, I take *care* of stuff, know what I mean?"

"Okay. Yup, gonna send him now." *Fuck off, Injun Joe.*

The Don watched raptly as the pink dildo appeared and disappeared, doing its thing on one chick while the other licked the dildo wielder. Note to self: *get more of this lezzie shit.*

When it was over and all three women had loudly proclaimed their happy endings, he shut off the screen and dialed his phone. He'd expected to find no signal up here, but no, they had plenty of towers. Maybe this wasn't middle of Fuckville, after all.

"Hey, Johnny? Lissen. When you got a free moment, take Marty with you and visit the Tree guy. Yeah, make it like we discussed. Then make that second trip, also like we discussed. Yeah, I'll give Robb the word." He shut down the phone.

Just like the old days.

Well, the days of his father and grandfather.

He wondered what else he could find locally. Sure, this stuff was hot, but he was in the mood for something nastier. He was looking for something more intense. Maybe he should have asked Johnny to bring a camera.

He shrugged, then turned his girl-porn on again. *It would do, for now...*

Chapter Twenty-Eight

Wolfclaw

Somewhere in Northern Minnesota

General Lansing entered the conference room with his assistant in tow.

The other members of the Wolfclaw Group had taken their places around the custom mahogany conference table. The paneled room was lit by way of natural light provided by a row of electronically controlled skylights above and a narrow strip of stained glass panels just below ceiling level, another nod to the lodge's Frank Lloyd Wright-inspired design.

Careful scrutiny would have discovered the stained glass panels depicted various werewolf scenarios. Hunting and devouring human prey was a repetitive theme. Red glass fragments abounded, their color adding blood to the scenes.

Lansing had commissioned the conference room stained glass himself, and then the artist had disappeared. He'd become the lodge's first hunt subject. Lansing had been careful in his dealings with outsiders, and the lodge's true purpose had been carefully protected. As far as the outside world was concerned, the lodge was a private sporting club.

Which was true in so many ways, Lansing reflected.

He addressed the group. "Gentlemen, thank you for being punctual. We have had a very relaxing few days, and we still have one night of festivities. New women are being shuttled in as we speak, so we can all look forward to more stimulating relaxation, but today we have some business to discuss."

A paneled screen slid open on the wall behind him. A metal-lined door behind the panels rose with a smooth hydraulic hiss, and the others could see a large chamber behind it.

"I'd like to welcome you to our future control center," Lansing said, pointing.

The others mumbled their approval. They couldn't see much yet, but at first glance the chamber's contents appeared impressive.

"Follow me, gentlemen," he said.

They entered the Control Room and fanned out in both directions after the door hissed closed behind them. Four long tables holding banks of electronics in rackmounts alternated with cockpit-like cocoons that held sleek padded leather chairs. In front of each station was a trio of flat screens, a keyboard, and a joystick mounted on an adjustable swivel-arm. Comm gear lay on the table next to each keyboard.

"Gentlemen, as you all know, the United States Air Force maintains drone control centers at bases in Nevada and Florida. From those remote areas, human operators pilot Predator, Reaper and Global Hawk drones—or Remotely Piloted Aircraft, as we now refer to them—from relative safety and comfort. Such control facilities have allowed us to strike at our enemies in more countries than I care to name, a list you all are quite well aware of. RPAs have rather quickly taken over much of our air war against terrorist factions dedicated to killing Americans, and we all laud the efforts of these units."

He looked at each member of his loyal group in turn.

His eyes hardened.

"However," he continued, "on one day the date of which is still undetermined, pilots seated at the controls in front of you will capture command of this country's drone squadrons and, together with a special squadron built to our specifications, the drone program will become the center of Wolfclaw's coup, and the government will be ours."

The assembled generals mumbled in gleeful agreement as Lansing pointed with pride at the high-tech command module. Then they broke into a rousing round of applause.

"Gentlemen, we have left the country in the hands of politicians much too long. Once under our control we can begin to return it to its former greatness. Once under our control, the world will again fear our nation and come to us on bended knee for the right to exist, to survive, for we will hold the key to survival, and we will be ruthless with its use."

The assembled generals clapped again.

Lansing wondered if they'd clap so enthusiastically if he were to go on to reveal how he planned to bring to fruition the long-term Wolfpaw plan to institute a Fourth Reich, the same plan created in the final days of the Second World War. A plan that reached back even farther in time, but which had borne its first fruit at the very end of the Third Reich's existence.

As the Axis fell, the Werwolf Division had been charged ostensibly with harassing the advancing Allies, but it had also been the spearhead of a global conspiracy to infiltrate the armed forces—and eventually the governments—of those allied against the Reich. Wolfpaw had simply been a convenient vessel for the late twentieth century version of the plan. They'd done well, lasting into the twenty-first century, but now they had stepped aside as an entity and given way to their backing entity, which was Lansing's baby—a coalition of werewolf generals who not only admired the Roman and Germanic way, but who also thought their way of ruling would be best for their country.

Lansing smiled as they finished applauding.

Schlosser had been a misguided fool. A useful fool, to be sure, but a fool nonetheless. His experiments to increase a werewolf's tolerance to silver had yielded good results, as had those of his ancestor who'd been funded by the Nazi war machine. But the younger Schlosser had been a warped sexual deviant who'd preferred sex to the true glory offered by the werewolf gene.

And he'd not really understood that the true improvement of the lycan gene wasn't the mere tolerance of silver, but the strange and thus far misunderstood magic achieved by one Joseph Badger, an unlikely scientist-alchemist awash in a sea of foolish beliefs and practices who had, despite his lower than low origins as a so-called *Native* American, somehow still managed to concoct a ritual with historic implications, a ritual which somehow blended two previously divergent types of *magick*.

A ritual that no one had so far been able to duplicate.

Lansing hoped to correct the situation.

"Yes, gentlemen," Lansing continued as the applause died down, "we have a holy mission to complete. You see before you some of the tools we will use, but as you know there are more twists and turns to our game than the obvious." He scanned the room, meeting their eyes one by one. "Any questions?"

"One here," said Heissen, the Marine general. "An update on the unfortunate leak discovered just a few days ago?"

Lansing's expression resembled that of someone who had swallowed a whole lemon.

"Heissen, I was getting to that." He glared at them all, irritated by the fact that they chose to focus on the irrelevant negatives rather than the glorious positives. "We've located the individual responsible for passing the information to the whistleblower. Realize, we have layers of involvement at each level. One bad apple, as you know, sours the bushel. We have him. Our team should be dealing with the whistleblower any time now, a low-life by the name of Wineacre, though at first he managed unfortunately to escape our cordon. You can be certain those responsible for allowing that to happen have paid for their incompetence."

He started to herd the group back out of the as yet unused control room.

"Since you asked, I have a surprise for you. Follow me to the discipline room, and you'll have a chance to meet the leak himself. I recommend you bring a bib. It will be messy."

He walked behind them as they chuckled and exited, and the metal door closed behind them, then the screen.

Lansing heaved a sigh of relief. Having a scapegoat handy had been a stroke of genius, allowing him to avoid challenges to his command ability and agenda. And he did not want ay challenges.

As the group headed for the elevator, he licked his dry lips. Soon they would be awash in hot blood.

Chapter Twenty-Nine

Franco Lupo

December 1945
Father Tranelli!

F ranco had always thought the priest had been killed. By a
wolf, a bullet, or drink.

The priest was not wearing his collar. And he didn't look as
drunk as Franco remembered.

"Are you trying to get yourself killed, boy?" The priest was
livid, as well as in obvious pain. "What in God's name are you
doing here?"

Franco bristled. "I should be asking you the same. Why are
you here? I thought you were dead. What's going on?" His
wine-soaked voice echoed along the steel bulkheads.

"Lower your voice! *Sei matto?*"

"I'm not crazy, I am angry." He didn't lower his voice.

Too late, he heard a low growl from the top of the staircase.

"Behind you!" Tranelli's eyes were wide, but he was quick
enough to draw a Vatican blade. *The other blade.*

Franco whirled, his body still screaming in pain from the
fall, and looked up just in time to see the silver-streaked wolf
pounce on him from above. Snarling jaws and sharp claws all

reached out for him. The wolf's eyes glowed red like the demon he was, a demon straight from the pit of hell.

The Jesuit now behind Franco uttered both a prayer and a curse, and by the time the wolf was hurtling through the air, there were two targets. Momentarily confused by the quick movement, the werewolf's focus slipped and threw off his aim. Franco expertly sidestepped him, keeping the snapping jaws away from himself in the process, then his body slammed sideways into the beast's and his blade bit deep, tearing a long gash in its side from chest to haunches.

The wolf let out a hideous scream as the silver-edged weapon burned and sliced into its unholy flesh, releasing a hissing steam and a gush of corrupted blood onto the metal stairs.

Next to him, Tranelli's blade also flashed and its point pierced below the monster's snout and punched up, through its throat and into its brain.

The beast squealed and dropped to the stairs, convulsions wracking its body as the touch of the holy silver destroyed its internal organs and essentially burned it from the inside out.

The stench of scorched fur and blood was overtaken by something worse as the beast continued to sizzle, but now it was the mangled, disfigured corpse of a disemboweled human.

The same human Franco had followed aboard.

The body was half-melted, rivers of liquid fat and flesh congealing in revolting pools around its splayed-out limbs. They stood over it for a moment, and Franco thought the priest would pray, but he did not.

"You fool!" the priest hissed. "Now what? We've been following this *pezzo di merda* in order to find out who he's delivering to, and now look at him."

The Aryan was naked and very dead, his body a mass of still-crackling roast meat.

Tranelli lurched past Franco and up the steps. He picked up the package the courier had been carrying, abandoned in his piled clothes. He opened it carefully and pulled out a banded wad of notes. Franco looked up—he was young, but he'd seen American cash before.

"Thousands," said the priest. "We wanted to know who he'd deliver to. We only know some of the transaction." He was defeated.

Franco felt his face flush.

"Do they know him?"

"We're not sure. He meets different ships."

"I can take his place, deliver the money. If they don't know him, I might pass."

Tranelli laughed, but it was cold. "Do you speak German? No, I didn't think so."

"Well, when I am discovered we can turn the tables on the other one and kill him too."

"You think too small, *bambino*. We don't want to kill one termite here and one there. We want to find the whole treeful of insects and chop it down, then burn it to the ground."

"Why haven't the others heard any of this?"

Tranelli smiled. "The crew are still on liberty. Only the captain and a few motormen are on duty. But the engines are turning over, which means they'll weigh anchor tonight."

"Are any of the others wolves here, on board?"

"Child, we don't know! It's why we watch. And wait. It's called gathering intelligence. You seem to be losing yours, whatever intelligence God has granted you."

Franco talked fast. He had learned much in his stunted childhood. "He must have been coming to see the captain. Let's assume that is the case. So I make the delivery, see what he says, then play it by ear from there. You are with Corrado?"

Tranelli nodded, uncertain.

"You tell him to get here before the ship sails and we can get the information out of the captain. I can be persuasive."

Tranelli shivered visibly at the look that crossed Franco's face.

Chapter Thirty

Wolfclaw

Somewhere in Northern Minnesota

The *discipline* room was misnamed.

It wasn't a room for people to be punished.

It was a room where those who were being punished could be tortured and killed, then disposed of, all in one convenient space that incorporated a compact incinerator—ostensibly for trash—as well as drains to wash away blood set directly into the ground beneath the sub-basement. It was soundproof.

Now the room was occupied.

The man on the gurney had stopped thrashing due to fatigue. He'd been strapped to the rolling deathbed for over forty-eight hours and all his attempts to slip out of the restraints had failed, leading only to the loss of his strength and the incredible pain he now felt in all his muscles and extremities. His voice had become a croak from all the screaming.

Useless fucking screaming, because no one could hear him.

And they wouldn't have helped him if they could.

He was clean-shaven except for stubble grown while in captivity. He was of medium-height and build, and he had infiltrated Wolfpaw Security Services two years earlier. Then he had been sucked into the slimmer, super-secret inner-sanctum group due to his willingness to engage in sex with a general of the armed forces.

That general did not know this lovely young man had been a plant. The general would be here today, too. And likely he would pay for his indiscretion almost as brutally as the man on the gurney.

Of course, the man on the gurney was past caring what happened to his lover, the general. He had been planning to talk plenty. He thought he'd drag the general down with him, if he could.

He doubted this would save him, but at least he could die knowing he'd exacted some payback.

He snorted, recapturing for a second his sense of counter-culture cynicism.

Hell, he'd been recruited and had taken up with the general specifically so he could help bring down that new symbol of the military-industrial complex, a man in uniform whose secrets were mind-blowing even to one as well-schooled as he had been. He had wormed his way into the inner command structure based purely on his abilities to give head and give and take anal sex as required by his *lover*, and not always within the group of two.

With another snort, he realized that now he was leaking streams of tears out of the corners of his eyes, and it burned and made his cheeks and facial hair tickle almost like its own form of torture. And he could do nothing about it.

He wondered what they would do to him.

He'd seen enough to know what they *could* do.

He struggled again, briefly, then lay back down to rest. If they loosened his restraints, he would take whatever opportunity presented itself.

But time itself was against him, loosening his hold on ambition.

It might have been hours later, he wasn't sure, when the metal door was unlocked and the generals filed inside. *His* general was one of them, but there was no eye contact between them.

The big gun, Lansing, took up position at the head of the gurney, so he appeared to be upside down. He waited for the others to encircle the bound man, who suddenly realized his opportunity had come and gone.

He was a dead man. Of this he was certain.

He prayed for quickness, but he was sober enough to know his prayer would not be answered.

Perhaps his general would intervene, he thought, however illogical it would be. He grasped this small bit of hope and clung to it like a man floating in the ocean might grasp a floating corpse.

"Gentlemen, behold our whistleblower. His name is irrelevant, but what he has done is not. You see, this miserable piece of human trash has endangered our entire operation by creating a file on our activities, a rather extensive file, and then disseminating it to another thorn in our side. You'll be happy to note that particular loose end has been tightened, leaving us only this one."

Suddenly Lansing's hands shot out and grabbed both sides of the prisoner's head, turning it aside so they all could see the throbbing artery.

"Tell us who among us has helped you," Lansing said as he lowered his head to stare into the man's upside-down eyes. "Tell us and you'll be spared."

The prisoner knew he was finished, but now he hoped if he didn't point the finger, his lover would take pity and find a way to rescue him. If he spoke out against the general, he would die anyway. If he stayed silent, however…

The warring emotions wracked his weakened brain.

He stared back at his tormentor now, feeling Lansing's large hands squeezing his skull.

"One last chance," Lansing said. "We can make things easier for you. It doesn't have to end this way."

The prisoner remained silent.

"Very well. General Johnston, it's your move."

The prisoner's pupils dilated. *They had the wrong man! There was hope after all…*

But Johnston nodded once, then in a blur drew a Sig semi-auto with a bandaged hand and shot General Heissen once in the head.

The silver-plated 9mm slug blew up the general's cranium and splattered everyone nearby, though no one moved. The dead general's almost headless body crumpled to the tile floor with nary a twitch. Rivulets of tainted blood sought out the slope toward the drain.

"The Corps looks after its own in good times and bad," Lansing said. He nodded at Johnston, whose hand was smoking, the stench of burning flesh strong in the close room. "Thank you, General."

Lansing turned back to the prisoner.

"He will not be helping you, despite your hopes. I don't know how you corrupted him and secured his cooperation, but you have cost us a good ally. Your actions will now cost you."

At his nod, the remaining generals blurred and the prisoner had enough time to see their heads turn into monstrous wolves' heads, complete with snapping jaws full of wicked fangs and coloration that resembled their human faces not at all.

And then they took turns ripping into his chest and belly, tearing out his organs and feasting on his entrails as he watched, screaming incoherently, until his eyes glazed and he was just meat to them.

As he had always been.

Prey

He was running, and he had been since the monsters had released him along with the others.

The others, the *game* they would hunt like deer or gazelles.

He'd heard the guards laughing about what would happen to them, and he had seen and heard what happened when the monstrous humans became true monsters and chased down his fellow prisoners.

His fellow *game*.

They were both food and also a game, a pastime for the fat-cat generals and their minions to play with until they bored of them, after which they would kill and devour them. If they were lucky, they'd be killed first.

He had seen some of his fellows devoured while still living.

It was a sight he would never forget, not if he lived to the age of one hundred. Of course, he knew he was not likely to live through the week. That he had survived this long, evading the two- and four-footed wolves who hunted them, was almost a miracle.

He wondered if his DNA had kindly left him with some sort of scent inhibitor. Or maybe he simply smelled less than his friends from the cages. It didn't matter why, all he could do was keep running, hoping to cross some major road or freeway through this godforsaken landscape that might as well have been on the moon. He might once have enjoyed this portion of Minnesota, but frankly now it was just an alien landscape of impenetrable forest, rushing river, freezing lakes, and bare-topped hills.

He was just cresting a hill now.

The view brought home to him with a painful rush that this *game preserve,* as they referred to it, was hundreds of square miles. Not the kind of place you could walk out of without clothing and equipment. And food. Just the thought of the word made his stomach rumble, then flip with a sudden onset of nausea that bent him over with dry heaves so violent he hacked up blood.

When he was finished heaving the acid contents of his guts and blood from his raw throat, he leaned up against a tree trunk—*another goddamn pine, there was nothing but pines*—and tried to think straight.

He'd been held prisoner so long he had forgotten about choices, decisions.

Should he climb over the hills, or around them? They were gentle, glacial in origins—not that he cared—and normally they would have been hardly impossible obstacles.

But again the thought hit him that without good boots, a warm coat, hat and gloves, and food, and water…then it might as well have been the surface of Mars. And he wouldn't last that long, while his hunters would have all the time in the world. He'd seen guards driving ATVs, so they didn't even have to run him down on foot.

Or on four paws.

He made his decision and crawled up and over the small hill's crest, suddenly aware that there was no cover.

And suddenly aware of a buzzing noise rising up behind him.

A high-pitched, insect-like buzzing that rose in volume until it was almost deafening.

Chapter Thirty-One

Prey

He was on the bare hilltop when a pair of round black helicopter-like flying devices crested behind him, their motors screaming like angry wasps. They hovered over him as he whirled, staring at the machines that seemed to be watching him.

They were watching him.

He had no time to feel fear, but his guts heaved and he knew his destiny was playing out.

He threw himself to the side, scrabbling for the opposite slope, steep as it was, hoping to outmaneuver whatever the hell the things were.

But they followed him, swinging sideways in unison so they were still overhead as he rolled partway down the rocky slope, scraping arms and legs on jagged rock outcrops. His right knee shattered and he screamed at the sudden pain, but he kept rolling, and then he heard his left forearm snap, and by then he was whimpering and rolling, heading for the nearest trees and knowing that crashing into any of the trunks would break his spine or shatter his skull.

And still the two flying devices followed, maybe fifty feet above him, keeping to a simple formation—one flying slightly higher than the other.

He screamed.

Wolfclaw

Camera lenses followed the rolling, falling body.

They "saw" his face, bracketed the features in a square reticle the image of which was immediately transmitted to the distant control room, where the Wolfclaw group was assembled in real time.

"At this point recognition has taken place," Lansing pointed out as if he were leading a museum tour. "All it took was a good clear look at his face, and the software did the rest."

The generals looked at each other and nodded.

"Engage targeting," Lansing ordered, and one of the remote pilots repeated the order, flipping a switch on his console. His monitor display changed to a set of red pulsating crosshairs like might be employed in a video game. "Reapers armed," reported the pilot.

"Reaper is our own design of miniature missile," Lansing explained, though most of his group had read the literature. "Each UAV, or Unmanned Aerial Vehicle, deploys one missile. At present."

The unfortunate target, designated an expendable, was attempting to stand on a sprained or broken limb, his face turned toward the UAVs, his mouth open in a soundless scream.

"Once locked on target," Lansing explained clinically, "there is no kill-switch other than a self-destruct sequence both pilots must initiate. The drone is armed, the target is acquired, and the preprogrammed countdown begins. If the target seeks shelter, the UAVs hover until the target is acquired again. Their batteries last eleven hours, allowing them to outlast most targets."

They watched intently as their targeted human raised an arm as if to protect himself from the hovering, screaming vehicles.

Lansing turned toward his compatriots. "The countdown sequence has begun due to its near-Artificial Intelligence brain, which makes decisions faster than we can without the hesitation."

"Ten seconds," said the pilot. "Five. Three. Zero."

As they watched on the screen, the image blurred when the camera shuddered, and then a silent contrail was briefly visible until the Reaper missile exploded and nearly vaporized the struggling human target on the hillside.

There was spontaneous applause in the control room. Bits and pieces of what had been a man rained down silently and covered the hillside.

"Pilot, hold the second Reaper." Lansing smiled at his audience. "No need to waste a second weapon, as one was most obviously sufficient. Had he managed to somehow evade, which is unlikely, the second Reaper would have finished the job."

On the screen, the bloody remains of their experimental prey smoldered in neutral black-and-white.

"Return the UAVs to base," Lansing ordered.

"Sir."

The feature demonstration was over.

A handheld device was handed to Lansing. He stared at some lines of text, then swore.

"Gentlemen, it appears our containment team was unexpectedly outwitted by a werewolf. Not one of ours, I might add. We've taken losses, and we do not have the flash drive."

In a rage, Lansing swept half the modules of an unoccupied control pod across the room and into a wall, where they shattered.

The others filed out of the control room, leaving him alone to fret in any way he preferred.

He brought up the data and information he'd been given by the Wolfpaw inner circle, and ordered one of the technicians to feed it into the UAV control software's blank fields.

Lansing frowned.

There was danger of all their plans going to hell, and he was not going to let that happen. The fools in Wolfpaw had done enough damage. And now there were these thorns in his side, these annoying human obstacles. Led by that obstinate cop, they'd become a tight little group of obstacles. Lansing was still interested in the cop because his origins were different—he was different—though not many understood why. Lansing knew it was due to what that one shaman, Joseph Badger, had been able to accomplish, which had made Lupo a stronger, more resistant strain of werewolf. Others had been genetically engineered by Nazi scientists using soldiers as guinea pigs and slaves as experimental prey. But somehow Badger had succeeded in nearly replicating the Nazi successes without the genetics. If only they could take Lupo apart in a lab…

But there was time for that later. First Lansing had to try and fend off Lupo's little bunch. There was always the cop's lady love. Lansing smirked. Snatch her and Lupo would come to them. It was in the works, but frankly they had other paths to follow first. When the time was right, he would turn to the pathetic resistance of Lupo's group of loyalists.

If he had to kill them all, then so be it.

Chapter Thirty-Two

Bill Grey Hawk

The first clue he had that things were going bad was when he heard a scream outside his office.

His door exploded open, rattling its hinges and slamming into the wall.

The thug named Johnny was the first inside, followed by his trained monkey, Marty.

"Don't even think about it," Johnny said. In his hand was an ugly black pistol.

Grey Hawk's hand stopped short of the drawer where his father's World War II trophy, a Walther P-38 sat, oiled and ready. He knew he'd lose the race. He looked at them and he knew he'd lost the fight.

He knew he'd run out of time.

"Your lady out here's gone home. Marty has some papers for you to sign, then you can go *home*, too." The way Johnny smirked, Grey Hawk knew *home* was some sort of euphemism. He thought briefly about going down fighting, but he'd lost the chance.

Marty was reaching into the drawer and plucking out the Walther.

"Lookie here!" He held it up loosely, then tossed it to Johnny. "Fuckin' museum piece."

"Too bad. Tends to make me think our friend here wasn't gonna be very friendly." He dumped the confiscated gun into the trash can in the corner.

Marty slid a three-sheet document on the desk in front of him.

Grey Hawk looked at Johnny, questioning.

"It's all legal," said the thug. "It's your resignation."

Nearby, Marty giggled.

"Get my briefcase," said Johnny. He still pointed the pistol.

Marty nodded and left the office, returning a moment later still giggling.

"Thanks," said Johnny, his face flushed. He took the case and in a flash Marty held the gun.

Bill Grey Hawk suddenly knew that he was dead if he didn't sign the document.

And he was dead after he signed it.

He felt the reality all the way down in the bottom of his gut.

He tried to conjure up a picture of his wife and kids, who had been through so much.

But he couldn't. Their faces were fuzzy, blurred.

"Sign the documents."

Grey Hawk found his voice. "Why? Your people can't legally take control of the casino. This does you no good."

Johnny laughed. "It has nothing to do with the casino. It's just for your, uh, your people. It's a—whattya call it? A *formality*. It's the boss's way to make sure your folks will understand when you disappear…"

Grey Hawk leaped up and made a break for the door, but the desk was too massive, too large, and Marty beat him to the corner, grabbing his shirt and hauling him back. He forced the older man back down in his chair and shoved it up against the desk. The pistol went to his temple.

"Not friendly at all," said Johnny.

He stepped up and laid his briefcase on the desk, opening it so the contents were visible.

"Sign the papers, old man."

"No." Grey Hawk's voice was a croak.

Johnny took out a hacksaw.

"Sign the papers."

"No."

"Are you left-handed?"

He tried to out-think the thug, but he got confused.

"You're a rightie." Johnny said with a nod. "And if you're not, oh well." He took out a blue bottle with a nozzle.

They stared at each other. Then: "Hold down his left hand."

Marty did.

"Sign?"

Grey Hawk's mouth was pasty and dry and completely useless. His only leverage was to not sign, but the pain would cripple him and then he'd sign. And then they'd kill him.

Johnny laid the saw's blade on Grey Hawk's wrist. Apparently he knew just where to place it. Like a man about to slice a baguette, he moved the blade up and down and again, drawing blood with shallow slices. Grey Hawk was resolute.

"Here's good," said Johnny, smiling.

Grey Hawk saw that the thug's forehead was shiny and his upper lip was slick. The thug licked his lips.

Marty held Grey Hawk's hand down like a steel clamp.

Johnny drew his arm back and the first downward cut went all the way to the bone.

Grey Hawk screamed. Blood ran over the desktop and onto the carpeting.

"Sign?"

Grey Hawk was going into shock already.

"Fuck! Put the pen in his hand." Marty complied, squeezing the gnarled fingers until they grasped the implement loosely.

Johnny struck a match, turned the nozzle on the torch, and adjusted the blue-red flame to a pinprick tip. Then he took the hacksaw and went to work.

The screaming began and didn't end until long after Grey Hawk had scrawled a signature on the sheet and it was whisked away before any blood could get on it.

By the time Johnny switched to the torch, Bill Grey Hawk's curled-up hand lay on the carpet like a sun-dried crab.

And he was slumped on the desk, his gore-flecked cauterized stump tucked under his head. His heart hadn't survived the trauma, and Johnny hadn't intended to stop in time anyway.

"Bring in our new friend," Johnny said, wiping down his face and hands. His eyes were glazed, as if he'd injected heroin.

Marty fetched William Treewalker, who had been sitting in the outer office, hands covering his ears. At least he had his hands. Trembling, his knees weak, he stared at Bill Grey Hawk's body.

Johnny was putting things back in his briefcase. He gestured at the desk.

"Your office now. Clean up this mess."

Lupo

They'd tiptoed around each other ever since she'd walked past him, gloriously naked, on her way to the shower. She had one of his towels wrapped around the back of her neck, but her perfect breasts thrust out at him completely unencumbered, and her wide mouth had curled up in pleasure at his discomfort—and at his long glance.

"Christ, put some clothes on!" Her mocking laughter from the bathroom followed him all the way to the opposite side of the apartment, where he sought refuge from her as far away as he could get.

The woman was toxic to relationships. She knew it, and she loved it. He'd end up taking a lot of crap for having put her up in his place, but on the other hand he firmly believed she was in danger.

He waited until she sounded occupied in the bathroom, then sat in what he'd designated his music den, a leather sofa facing the bay window and a wall of compact disks that made up his prized collection. He flipped through a stack of recent purchases. He'd been dragged screaming into the iPod universe and enjoyed it, but he was still an album man who preferred scanning through liner notes even if they required a magnifier to read. There was a new Marillion he hadn't listened to yet, and a recent Wakeman disk that promised a return to the old style.

I'll be the judge of that.

It would be best to distract himself and keep his mind from reminding him what Heather looked like naked. She was a goddess.

He reached for his headphones and saw Ghost Sam standing in the corner, fading in and out. Great, now *he* was hanging around to catch a glimpse of Heather naked. *I didn't think ghosts would care about naked chicks, but what do I know?*

Ghost Sam made a gesture with one disembodied hand, but Lupo wasn't sure what it meant.

A strange, insistent buzzing made him look up and a shadow crossed the window.

He thought, *bird.*

But he immediately knew it wasn't a bird.

Another sound, this time at his front door.

A light shuffle, a very soft *clink*.

He knew that sound. It was a gear *clink*, something metallic on a belt *clinking* against something else.

He dove for an extra-wide bookcase a few feet away, his hands scrabbling under one of the shelves, flicking a tiny latch and coming back with the MP5 submachine gun he kept clipped on a hinged flap cradled in his hands.

He was too late.

His door imploded and a flash-bang grenade went off with its tell-tale *crump!*

He'd anticipated it by a second or two and had squeezed his eyes shut.

Now he opened fire with the suppressed MP5 and sprayed the doorway, where two sets of black-clad assassins had followed the grenade and fanned out in search of the flat's occupants, their gun muzzles searching for targets.

Lupo beat them.

His first short burst took down two, making a mess because he'd held the muzzle up to go for their heads. The bolt was not completely silent, reloading rounds with the usual metallic *clack-clack-clack-clack* and loud reports, part of the result of suppression.

Sure enough, the commandos were armored-up and he'd have barely hindered them had he aimed for their torsos first.

He was already swinging the bulbous muzzle sideways while the first two fell in a heap, squeezing out another long burst that took down two more before they could bring their guns to bear. One of them let loose a burst that stitched a pattern on the brick wall behind Lupo, spraying him with jagged stone chips. The third commando dove through the arch that separated one flat from the one next door he had bought to make a larger living space.

A growl erupted across the flat and the oversized silver-gray wolf that lunged out of the white bathroom door disappeared through the same arch in pursuit of the armored assassin who'd escaped Lupo's gunfire.

Heather!

Lupo leaped behind the sofa and aimed for the door—five, was that a standard team? An Alpha team? But if so, they'd have come in as wolves. He waited for a few seconds, and was rewarded with a delayed-effect assassin who had hovered outside to catch defenders unawares.

Lupo raked the last killer with another burst, zipping him across the legs so he could try to interrogate him. But before Lupo could reach the guy, a pistol appeared in his hand.

Feeling the Creature's reflexes overriding his own, Lupo dropped and rolled while rounds whizzed by over his head, then he finished the job by squeezing the trigger on the MP5 and emptying the magazine into the wounded survivor. The last commando slammed back to the floor with a wet *splat* from the back of his head.

The werewolf in the other room was tearing the commando apart, ripping out his throat and then shredding his clothing and armor, digging into his belly with ravenous jaws. When Lupo approached, the wolf dug in her front paws and stared into his eyes, growling a warning. Heather was not in the mood to share. She tore muscle and tendon, and her fangs made short work of the unfortunate commando's organs and intestines. Her snout was covered with gore and her eyes smiled at him.

Jesus, thought Lupo, who wasn't so used to watching it happen.

And not on his goddamn floor, which was slick with spilled and splattered blood.

Six of the fuckers.

One of those he had shot groaned, but before Lupo could reach him Heather leaped from one body to the other and tore out the survivor's throat. He died with a cut-off scream and a gurgle as he bled out.

Damn it, I would have liked to get some answers from the asshole first.

He left Heather alone with her second unexpected meal, and checked out the doorway.

Fortunately by now his neighbors were likely to be all at work, and all the guns had been suppressed if not exactly silenced. The door was barely hanging on one hinge and he was able to wrestle it into place then lock it. His flat was a mess of death and gore, and once again he was left holding the bag.

Jesus.

Maybe he should just lay down plastic tarps permanently instead of carpeting.

He figured he might still squeeze one favor out of a certain somebody who'd taken care of a surplus corpse situation for him recently. Would they accommodate him, and what would he owe *them*?

He turned and saw Heather back in human form, still naked, her face streaked with the two commandos' blood. She was smiling orgasmically and her nipples were engorged. Hell, she was glowing and the musk came off of her in waves, so strong that Lupo almost jumped her right there. And she was ready for him, willing him to do it, her eyes on fire and her cheeks flushed and muscular thighs apart just enough that he could see her labia prominent as she posed for him, showing him how awesome a creature she was.

The werewolf gene had turned Heather into some sort of sexual tornado, capable of sweeping up everything in its path.

It was all he could do to stay away.

"Get dressed," he growled. "There's probably more of them."

She pouted. "But, Nick, you know you want me—"

"Fuck, Heather! Wake up! We've got a mess here and there may be more of these assholes waiting outside. There's more to life than fucking…"

"If you say so. Your little bitch muzzling you, sweetie?"

He rounded on her. "Get the fuck dressed. We've got to get out. And I have some calls to make."

She eyed the other corpses, still in no hurry. "What a shame to let these perfectly good snacks go to waste. You sure you don't want a bite? Hey! *Ouch!*"

He'd snagged her arm and manhandled her back into the bathroom. "Get dressed!"

She finally snapped to it.

He found a phone clipped to another flap, a little trick he'd learned from a past association, and called a number that was listed in very few places. It was a burner phone and contained a few contacts only. He explained to the voice who responded what his needs were and promised a return favor, in essence selling his soul. He didn't even want to consider what they'd want in return for their help.

But what choice did he have?

He could never explain to Ryeland what was happening, and now Hart-Bart and his crew were running things.

He was promised a call back later, and he had no choice but to accept that response for now.

Heather was ready, hair still damp from a quick shower, all the blood gone, wearing painted-on jeans and a knit top that showed her still-hard nipples. She threw on her leather jacket.

"Lead on."

Chapter Thirty-Three

Colgrave

She was hovering around the edges of the task force encampment, wondering whether Ryeland would snag her and throw her into the mix. She normally didn't care, but ever since Lupo had whetted her appetite for some good old-fashioned intrigue, she thought she'd like a taste of this mysterious bus shooter. Organized Crime had been dull lately.

But as she watched and listened, she became convinced that the feds had tied up Ryeland beyond all possible hope. He'd provided the cogs, but they had brought in the machine—and they considered *everybody* cogs.

She went to their coffee table because, let's face it, it was better than what her side of the squad room was making available. Colgrave knew she could still turn heads, and sometimes that quality plus a clear-cut mission (as in an occasional coffee run) could get you acceptance where furtive lurking simply got you chased off. So she waited for a new batch of coffee to brew and kept her ears open.

Not far from where she stood, she caught a bit of something that made her ears perk up.

Hart-Bart, the nickname that had made the rounds for the DHS fed nobody liked and whose real name people were intentionally forgetting, snapped his fingers at Ryeland, who frowned but answered the call anyway.

"I need you to get me some background on a couple of your homicide cops," Hart-Bart said without preamble.

"Whatever you need," Ryeland muttered. "Who?"

"Dominic Lupo and, uh, Richard DiSanto."

Colgrave almost looked up, but caught herself. She poured coffee and pretended to be occupied with the creamer, then slowly stirred the mix while staring at a folder she'd carried for cover.

"They're no longer on the task force," Ryeland reminded him. "You must mean two other cops. Let me look at the list—"

"No, Lupo and DiSanto," Hart-Bart said. "I want their personnel files brought to me. I'll be right over there." He pointed at a corner PC station, dismissively. "Make it snappy."

Ryeland looked like he was going to argue or complain, but he visibly swallowed his retort, turned and walked away.

Colgrave also stepped away, but she could have sworn she felt Hart-Bart's laser-like eyes on her back all the way across the room to her office. When she turned just before hiding again, she noted that Hart-Bart was whispering in the ear of one of his minions, who nodded. Then he looked right at her.

She ignored him and closed her door.

Then she dug out one of her burner phones.

Lupo

They were in the park near his place. So far, they hadn't seen or heard anything suspicious. Life seemed to have rolled on despite the death that wrapped its arms around Lupo's flat.

The call was from an unknown number, but he took it and it was Colgrave, telling him all about Hart-Bart's request.

"He's not even interested in newer info—he wants to see the old paper files. What the hell did you do? I mean, he's here to investigate the bus shootings, isn't he?"

Lupo was at a loss and said so. "Man, I don't have a clue, Danni. I was just raided at home by a team of commandos—"

"What?"

"Yeah, long fuckin' story. This is something to do with the Wolfpaw thing, except I thought it was over. My friend Heather Wilson was with me, and we just about got whacked."

There was a short silence. "Uh, should you be telling me this? What about Ryeland?"

"Danni, you have to keep this under your hat. This Hart guy, Bart whatever, if he wasn't interested in me and Dee, I'd say we're coming in. But now I have to wonder if the whole fucking mess is connected."

"Keep it under my hat? What happened to the commando squad?" Her voice was suddenly high-strung, humming with released adrenaline. At least, that was what Lupo thought.

"We killed 'em, Danni. These guys play for keeps. I keep enough firepower around to do the job."

"Shit! And now what? Is your place shot up?"

"Shot up and bloody as hell," he said, sighing. "I have, uh, some friends who trade favors."

"Friends I would know?"

"I imagine if you tossed out a few names, one of 'em would ring a bell, yeah."

"You sound like you've...done this before."

"Danni, I know you don't have to trust me, but believe me, people are in danger and I'm trying to keep them safe..."

She was silent a long half-minute. "Lupo, for some reason I believe you. I've heard stuff about you, I'll admit some of it's pretty bad, but I always got a different vibe. I sensed there's a whole outlier thing going on and...I can relate to it." She laughed. "Maybe I need to make an appointment with Anders."

He winced.

"I'm a little out of sorts, Danni," he said finally. "I've got that problem brewing up north with someone I care about square in the way. And now this, right here. And I don't think I can take it to Ryeland, not with DHS all over him. And me."

He heard a tapping. She was doing the pencil thing with her teeth again.

"How can I help?" she said.

Lupo let his eyes rove up and down the street, looking for anything out of place, anything that signaled danger. They'd located the hit squad's parked SUV and were watching it from the park. Leaves whipped around them in the cool breeze. It all felt so surreal, again.

"You mean it?" he said.

Heather

She'd seen a side of him that was relatively new to her.

A bloodthirsty, almost out-of-control side.

He hadn't wolfed out, no, but he'd hesitated not at all in splattering the commandos' guts and brains all over his own place. And he'd explained that he would trade favors with some shady group — maybe the mob? — who would clean up the premises for him. He wasn't completely sure some neighbor hadn't actually been home and called the cops on him, but Lupo had taken charge with a cold-bloodedness she found refreshing (*for him!*) and completely alluring.

Now *that* was the Nick Lupo that melted her thighs. *And pussy.*

But now that they'd been blown, he was all business. She couldn't help it, she felt like pouting.

"Nick, what are your plans now? I know what these guys are like and they never stop coming. They'll just send more teams after us. The next one will probably be armed with silver ammo. After that, they'll send wolves. I mean, I think they were caught flat-footed by what happened in Madison, when I was in the middle of it."

Lupo was hugging a tree, peering around it. They had a perfect view down his street, and so far nothing much had happened. She supposed soon a van would roll up and several barrel-chested men would take some loose carpeting upstairs and remove some slightly heavier carpeting later. Or something like that.

"Look, Heather, I'm not sure I have any plans now. What I have is that I'm pissed off. They fucked up my house."

"Well, they were after *me*. Doesn't that bother you? Not even a little?"

"I'd *give* you to them if I thought it would keep them the fuck away from me," he said bitterly. "But I figure it's too late for that. Now they want me too, and they know where I live."

"You don't mean that, do you?" She made a face.

"I do. You've been nothing but trouble, and frankly I've got enough of it without you. What would you have me do? We're not exactly in the position of calling on the Pentagon for help, are we? According to those files your guy gave you, the Pentagon's rotten with these fuckers. They've got all the time in the world. We don't."

Heather snarled. "Well, we've got to do something. We can't just wait for them. Why don't we head west and raid that house? Looks like they're running things out of there. Wineacre has plans, directions, layout. We did it to Wolfpaw's D.C. headquarters, what's to keep us from a repeat performance?"

Lupo was leaning out from the tree. "I don't—" he began, but then he ducked back, quickly. "Get down!"

She dropped flat like a panther, her wolf itching to get out and do what it did best.

"What is it?"

"Not sure," he said. "I heard a buzzing just now. And I remember hearing it just before they broke down my door."

"Okay," she said, unsure. She was half-wolfing, her eyes rolling and changing color, hair growing and retreating in long tufts on her arms and legs. She stifled a growl. The park was empty, but she wasn't sure letting out her wolf here was a good idea.

"Look, I'm gonna get the car and we're leaving."

Before she could argue he was heading back toward his building.

She smiled a wolf's smile. He was mad because she excited him, and he couldn't stand it. He was weakening. All she had to do was keep up the heat. Eventually he'd choose *her* over the Jessie-bitch.

A few minutes later Lupo's venerable black Maxima squealed to a halt across the sidewalk. Lupo leaned over and waved her across.

She straightened and started to walk toward the open door.

The high-pitched buzzing Lupo had mentioned suddenly drowned out every other sound, and suddenly Lupo was screaming *"Back, back, behind the trees, get down!"* and he was diving out of the car and rolling, and then there was an explosion that seemed to squash her head and rupture her eardrums, and the Maxima left the ground in a ball of fire. A second explosion rocked the sidewalk and tossed a nearby parked SUV into the air, ripping it apart when the gas tank ignited.

"Down, get down, it's looking for you!"

She had no idea what was going on, but Lupo shouted once more, "*Facedown, facedown! On the ground!*"

And she did it, and the buzzing increased its pitch until it sounded like a monstrous wasp and seemed to hover back and forth, and Lupo was rolling toward her, shouting for her to stay down.

Not far away, the two demolished cars raged like an inferno.

The buzzing increased, then retreated.

"*Jesus, what was that?*"

"*Drones!*" Lupo called out, grimacing. Debris was still raining around them. "*I think they've got facial recognition.*"

And that's not all, he thought.

Chapter Thirty-Four

Lupo

When he took the phone call from Charlie Bear, something told him it was more bad news.

"Lupo, things are going to shit over here."

"Thanks for confirming my fears," said Lupo. "Here, too."

"We just were told we have a new head of the council and casino CEO. The board read Grey Hawk's resignation and had a special vote about an hour ago. They voted in this guy who came back not that long ago, Bill Treewalker."

"What does Grey Hawk say about it?"

"That's the thing. See, no one can find him. It's like he signed this long resignation, named a successor, and disappeared."

"Jesus." This did not sound good, not at all. "What about his family?"

"Haven't seen 'im. Car's gone, he's gone. They're going crazy. Treewalker says he doesn't know anything except Bill had asked him if he was willing to take over the position. He'd said yes, and that was it until he got the call."

"Any chance it's true?"

"Given what Dr. Hawkins told us about the takeover? I doubt it."

"Yeah, I thought not. Shit."

"And, Lupo," Charlie said after a long pause, "I saw that Treewalker had a carpet-cleaning service into the office. They wouldn't talk to me, Lupo. He wouldn't look me in the eye."

"Paid off?"

"And threatened. I heard Treewalker tell Bill he'd had some kind of run-in. He sounded scared. And now the office cleaning worries me. I think Grey Hawk was in the way of the takeover and got himself killed. Messy."

"How long before they come after you?"

"Don't worry, I'm very suddenly on leave of absence. I'm not showing my face at the casino until we can sort this out, and I'm packing extra hardware. I might be on their list."

"You might at that. I'll call Jessie, see what she says."

Charlie was silent.

"Charlie?"

There was a pause. "I was hoping you'd know where she is. I called her, Lupo. Got voice mail. She's, uh, not at the hospital. No one's seen her."

Jessie

Earlier, she had driven past the house's driveway after following not-Bruce's SUV. She'd spotted him pulling over and talking to the two thugs from the casino, in fact right near the casino.

She was miffed at Nick, and it didn't take long for her to make a decision. He'd told her to not play Nancy Drew.

Damn him.

Talking down to her. She could take care of herself, goddamn it. She had a Remington shotgun in the back of her old Pathfinder. She had proven she knew how to use it. Her run-ins with a serial killer and two bunches of Wolfpaw werewolves should have made that clear to him. But Nick was an old-time chauvinist, convinced not that he was better, but that she was weaker and needed help. She'd pulled his butt out of the fire more than once, didn't he remember?

Fuck it!

She turned the Pathfinder and followed not-Bruce, wondering where the hell he was staying. Wondering if the mob had staked out some sort of headquarters. Made sense, didn't it? She'd follow him, find the nest, and *then* she'd tell Nick where it was, wrap it up in a neat little package.

Nancy Drew my ass.

She drove, her anger fueled less by Nick and what he'd said than by the knowledge that the slut Heather was back in their lives—back in *Nick's* life—and that meant trouble was sure to follow. Whatever she'd brought for Nick to look at was bound to cause them a shitstorm, of that she was convinced.

She slammed her hands on the wheel.

Damn you, Nick Lupo.

You're supposed to love me. Why is it that whenever the she-devil bats her eyelashes you drop everything to help her?

It occurred to Jessie that she was overreacting, but really, she told herself, have you *seen* that sexpot? Could *anything* about her really be an overreaction?

She followed not-Bruce's taillights from as far as she could, because traffic was thin between the rez and Eagle River, except for the occasional buses full of gambling old folks.

Heading for the cathedral, as the song said.

When he disappeared she almost drove past the overgrown turnoff, but she caught a glimpse of red as he hit his brakes somewhere in the thicket, and she pulled off the road onto a sloping shoulder.

She weighed her options. Shotgun or no?

Damn it, Nick was right about one thing. These guys were dangerous.

She took the Remington and a pocketful of 12-gauge shells.

And she headed up the long and twisty rutted driveway.

Colgrave

Lupo and DiSanto met her in a diner a few blocks from the downtown precinct, where they all ordered coffee and burgers. When they were alone in an isolated booth, Colgrave asked Lupo for details about his *situation* up north.

Lupo was fidgety and out of sorts, nearly out of his mind with worry because he hadn't been able to get hold of Jessie. Her phone went straight to voice mail, which he said wasn't like her.

"I'm sure she didn't listen to me," he said. DiSanto nodded—he seemed to agree that Lupo's lady friend was headstrong.

Not to say *stubborn*.

"So you think she poked around and got scooped up?"

Lupo nodded. "Yeah, at least I hope that's as far as it went. Think about it. If news about the planned casino takeover gets out, they'll have feds crawling up their asses. So the best thing to do is take her out. I hope they're too smart to actually kill her, but they may be deciding what to do. Frankly, I'm not sure these guys respect too many boundaries."

"And what they probably did to Bill Grey Hawk," DiSanto added, "we can't even figure right now, but it doesn't look good."

They explained about the call Lupo had gotten from the casino security guy, and the strong possibility they'd tortured and killed Bill. Colgrave was a little shocked, but not surprised.

Back in the day, this stuff was standard practice. Bastone was just the kind of wise guy to bring it back.

"They installed their own puppet," Lupo said. "A guy named Treewalker they apparently threatened earlier and who must have seen the light. The elders' council held a special vote. They must figure they can control this new guy better. I just hope Jessie didn't walk in on something."

Colgrave waited for the awkward college-age server to bring their food before answering. They waited impatiently as plates were juggled and dropped off.

"So what's your plan?" she said afterwards, taking a bite of her burger. She watched Lupo rip his rare cheeseburger off the bun, slather it with standard mustard, then wolf it down not so much with hunger but with a sort of controlled rage. She realized he wasn't eating for enjoyment, he was fueling up for a fight.

DiSanto was more delicate, taking a careful bite of his turkey burger. Health conscious? He kept sneaking looks at his large silver-and-black chronograph.

"My plan," said Lupo after swallowing, "is to go up there and look for Jessie. It's a six-hour drive and I'd be going already if this other thing hadn't happened. If she's nowhere to be found, then I'm going to fuckin' raid this Bastone's place." He smiled bitterly. "Call it a black op, Danni, because there's no other way. Too much red tape, too much procedure, and too many untrustworthy bastards around. Ryeland might go for it, he's just that kind of guy, but his hands are tied now."

She noticed for the first time that he had numerous tiny scabs and scars on his face. Recent trouble with sharp fragments? She also noticed his hands were scarred up as if he'd had his skin melted somehow and then healed, but not very well cosmetically.

DiSanto said, "From what you said, it looks like the DHS guys have some sort of hard-on for Nick, too. We're running out of time, and we have to go off the books."

"A rescue mission? Hell, I'm in." Colgrave had a soft spot for long odds and black ops. She had a friend, a Vietnam vet named Rich Brant, who had taught her much, and she'd helped him out of a few jams, one especially hairy one over which she still had nightmares. Her police career was always hanging by a thread, so why treat this any differently?

Lupo nodded, chewing the last of his bunless burger. Blood had pooled on his plate and he sopped it up with the last forkful of meat. "Good. But actually I have *two* situations..."

"What?" She stared at him. "What are you talking—you mean this other thing you just mentioned?"

He nodded. Plucked a thick manila folder off the seat next to him and slid it over to her.

"What's this?"

DiSanto took over. Apparently they'd discussed their approach.

"Nick's gonna take care of Jessie. Her disappearance. But that's not all, there's something else going on...something with this asshole Hart-Bart and his minions. But we don't know what or what game they're playing."

She sighed. "All right..." She ate some of her fries, but she'd lost interest.

They took turns giving her a basic rundown of the information contained in the Wineacre file, as well as what had just happened to Lupo and Heather Wilson.

The whistleblower had assembled a treasure trove of information and names that would have made her hair curl, if it wasn't already. She shivered as she listened to what they had to say and scanned grainy photographs.

Lupo was winding it up.

"I think they've managed to marry facial recognition software with drone missile guidance. The fucking drones homed in on Heather's facial features. That's just my theory, but I read something online recently that had been leaked by a software engineer, who later turned up dead in an *accident*. Imagine linking facial recognition with surveillance camera feeds from anywhere in the world... and maybe even tying in to spy satellites' routine sweeps. They could target anyone, anywhere. Program their drones to become kamikaze killers. Sounds crazy, but it seems like a pattern in their methodology. Anyway, I'm guessing all they need is clear enough photos of me—*anyone*—and they'll do the same."

She struggled with it all. It was too much to digest. "But if it's true, how has all this been kept secret?"

"Killings and disappearances, Danni," Lupo said. "This is why I don't trust DHS. They've put the lid on things. I haven't tried to go public, but they've shut down any other avenue anyway. Those explosions at my place didn't make it onto local news, at least not yet. It'll be a sanitized *neighborhood gas leak* kind of story when they're done with the spin cycle, bet on it. Maybe the bad guys have hijacked technology that's supposed to stay secret. Pretty embarrassing, right? They're scrambling to contain and cover up now."

Colgrave pushed her unfinished burger and fries aside. She felt a mix of disbelief and yet...acceptance. She knew *things* went on all the time. She'd been behind the scenes, had seen the sausage being made, as it were. Plus she had connections, and *they* had connections. She was savvier than most. She'd walked the line, many times. She'd teetered on that edge. Now she looked from Lupo to DiSanto. They didn't seem to be scamming her. She could tell.

She tapped the file. "I should read this? Now?"

They nodded grimly.

Lupo reached for her cold burger. "You gonna eat that?"

Chapter Thirty-Five

DiSanto

He had no idea why she wanted to meet with him, but he found himself doing it anyway.

Heather Wilson was in a booth in a Third Ward bistro in which he could barely afford the water and lemon slice. She was munching on breadsticks and as he walked up, seeing her like that, a thick breadstick in her mouth, he was frankly relieved he could sit immediately.

"Glad you could make it," she said, sliding the breadstick out from between her lips, giving him a sexy grin. They shook hands and she held his longer than necessary.

Such an old trick, he thought, but he couldn't help but enjoy the electric touch.

"Uh, I have to meet Nick again in a little while. What did you want to see me about?"

Heather rolled her eyes. "Right to the point, eh?" She made a tight little smile and handed him a breadstick. "They're very good."

He hadn't meant to, but he took it, hoping to brush skin again and they did.

"You've been Nick's partner for a while now, haven't you?"

He nodded, still holding the breadstick like a sword.

"You know he's a little...different. Right?"

"He's very dedicated," he said, enjoying her awkward fishing. He was supposed to ask *how* different?

"Yeah, well, he's obstinate and obsessive," she said. "You can call it dedication if you want." She picked up another breadstick from a large mug where they grew like petal-less flowers, but she played with this one. "What do you know about his private life?"

DiSanto watched her manipulate the breadstick in about as phallic a way as anyone could.

"I know enough," he said. "I know about the—"

She was mouthing the breadstick, smiling around it, her eyes seeming to swirl like kaleidoscopes and...

Wait, were her eyes changing color?

"Do you know what Nick and I share, Richard?"

He couldn't stop staring. He nodded and shook his head at the same time.

"We share *lifestyle*, that's what we share."

He felt one of her feet climbing up his calves under the booth.

Why?

What did she want?

"Is Nick planning to do something about the information I gave him?" Her tone was that of a particularly sly interrogator.

Her foot was parting his thighs, her toes reaching, reaching...

"I, uh, I think he's prioritizing. Jessie may be in trouble—"

"Damn it!" she said vehemently. "That fucking bitch, she's always in the way."

DiSanto thought Heather would stand up and stalk out, but she didn't.

Her foot pried even farther between his thighs, toes finding and caressing his growing manhood even as he tried to back away. But he couldn't, the booth was bolted down and her hands had grasped his across the table and held on, her eyes fixed on his, as her foot massaged his groin until his head spun with insane lust and desire.

Later, he had no idea how they'd made their way to his car where it was parked behind the old converted warehouse that housed the bistro, but she was straddling him back to front, guiding his length inside her as she rocked up and down and wickedly sideways. His hands reached around her torso and cupped her firm breasts, pinching her bloated nipples. She moaned with unabated desire, leaning back on him in the limited headroom, turning her head so she could seek out his hungry mouth with hers and lock lips.

Her tongue was a living thing probing inside his mouth and he thought he would faint if she didn't stop soon.

But, damn me to hell, I don't want to stop...

Heather

She'd had a thing for DiSanto since she'd met him, truth be told, and just about the best way she could think of to screw — *really* screw with Lupo right now — was to screw his *saintly* partner, he of the wife and kids and the wholesome parochial school vibe he gave off.

She loved corrupting people, especially when she could use it to mess with someone else.

As it turned out, she didn't have to work hard to corrupt this one.

He was thrusting up into her even as she pumped up and down on his solid erection, and the pleasure was almost enough to send her over. She felt tufts of coarse hair popping out on her arms and legs and back, knowing he couldn't tell, and almost wishing she would just let it happen, turn into a werewolf right there, taking his pleasure and lust and then devouring him like a black widow spider after mating.

Their rhythm increased and they grunted like animals as the car rocked unevenly backward and forward, and when she sensed he was swelling within her she unstraddled him and flipped acrobatically around so she could lower her head to his sweaty lap and take him in her mouth as he reached his moment.

She drank from him almost desperately, then reached up and forced his mouth to hers, kissing him with ruthless abandon.

His eyes widened as he stared into hers and she knew he was entranced by the swirling of her pupils and the changing of colors he saw there, and when she finally released him he recoiled—spent, humiliated, but somehow ensnared by her although she was already straightening her clothes and climbing out of his car.

"Tell Lupo I'm doing what needs to be done. I'm heading out, and he can go and rescue his whiny little bitch. You tell him he's an asshole."

As she stalked away, she turned and saw him putting his face in his hands.

She smiled.

Now she knew what Lupo thought was happening, and his plans.

She had copies of the flash drive data, of course, and had already plotted a route. She would have preferred heading out with Lupo and maybe even his trained little monkey partner, a raid like they'd done with the Wolfpaw headquarters in Washington. *That was magnificent.*

Figuring she had little time before those killer drones found her again, assuming Lupo was right about it all, she collected her rental car and set out to drive back across the state, through Madison, and finally over the Mississippi and into the northern woods of Minnesota. Along the way, she wondered how many cameras and eyes in the sky tracked her.

She would do this herself.

Fuck Lupo.

Chapter Thirty-Six

Lupo

H e was in a rental car. He couldn't afford to get caught at
the precinct, not with the possibly crooked feds looking
for him. He'd taken DiSanto's advice and rented a late-model
Mustang. But now he was missing his old Maxima. They'd
grown up together.

Still, this isn't all that bad, he thought, gazing at the retro
rounded gauges. The engine purred better than it had a right to.

She caught him on his unofficial line, the number of which
he had given her earlier when she'd agreed to think about it.

"Yeah, Danni?"

Beside him, Ghost Sam nodded as if he knew what she was
going to say, and agreed it was good.

On the line, Colgrave made a long sigh. "I may be killing
my career. I want you to know… Ah, fuck it. I'm in. All the way
in."

Jessie

The place was huge, like an Up-North dream house made of
logs and glass. She could see the lake behind it, with a private

beach and pier. No boats. Woods all around. Not-Bruce's SUV was parked out front.

This was good enough, wasn't it?

She'd back out of the driveway, keep her head down, and call Nick. This had to be the Vegas mobster's little compound, didn't it? Made sense, it was an upscale place but on the remote side, and it was close enough to both the rez and Eagle River to give them the feel of having whatever they needed. It wasn't Vegas, but that wasn't why they were here, was it? The rez casino, and hotel that was almost finished, was making a bundle. It was an untapped stream. Of course a Vegas guy would see this as a boon.

Okay, she thought, *just a little closer. Maybe I can figure out how many goons he brought with him besides not-Bruce. Robb, or whatever his actual name is.*

She hugged the driveway's shoulder but from the side of the woods. The pines came right up to the gravel and she was able to navigate the undergrowth and keep an eye on the house at the same time. She wasn't one of those who grew up learning woodcraft, not really, but she was awful silent for a half-city type.

She approached the monster cabin, a sort of expanded Cape Cod with side wings, a wraparound deck, and a huge garage, while keeping an ear tuned to the doors and windows. The glass was reflective, so she'd never be able to tell whether anyone was watching. But why would anyone watch the woods?

They were probably playing billiards or xBox, or whatever mobsters did when there weren't strippers and poles around. Maybe they were eating pasta. She grinned. Nick would love her stereotyping. He'd make a crack about *her people,* the Indians, sure enough.

She straightened a little to step over a narrow gully, and when she had landed on the other side she took a few steps and then something hard poked her in the side.

A voice whispered in her ear, so close she felt the heat of his breath.

"Well, well. What do we have here?"

Chapter Thirty-Seven

Lupo

"**D**amn it, Dee! Didn't she say anything else?"

DiSanto shrugged. He had just told his partner cryptically that Heather had indicated she was going to survey the Minnesota house herself. It was identified on Wineacre's satellite photos, and somehow he'd also managed to obtain a schematic of the Frank Lloyd Wright-inspired structure.

"She's pissed, Nick. Said to tell you you're an *asshole*. Nothing you haven't heard before! She expected us to raid the place, but you're distracted by Jessie. She's...uh, possessive. I think she has a thing for you. Sounds like she hates Jessie."

Lupo snorted. He'd never described for his partner exactly what had happened when the two women had gone for each other with murder in their hearts.

Yeah, she hates Jessie, all right.

Lupo was pissed too. Heather was a selfish, spoiled, raging narcissist and opportunist, and the fact that she was heading into the jaws of hell or something like it was her way to draw his attention away from Jessie. He guessed she hoped he would take his team and follow her, leaving Jessie to deal with the mobsters on her own.

Well, fuck that.

Lupo made up his mind quickly.

"We have no choice, we're gonna have to split up. You and Colgrave follow Heather. Hopefully you'll catch up to her before she does something stupid. Maybe she'll just keep the place under surveillance. Fat chance, though."

"What about you?"

"I'll meet up with Charlie and try to find Jessie. If she's in the hands of this Bastone character, we'll bust her out. Assuming we're not too late."

"Not much of a raiding party—two people."

"No, definitely not. We may go down in history as the dumbest rescuers ever."

DiSanto looked sheepish, as if he were hiding something. Lupo wasn't sure what it was, but it had drained Dee of much of his boundless energy and enthusiasm. He figured Heather and her body had something to do with it.

Not my problem. He had enough of them.

He looked at his watch. It was time to call Colgrave and see how quickly her connections could come through. They'd need some gear she had announced she could borrow.

She had some fuckin' *strange* connections.

Heather

It was a gigantic fucking house, yet it would have been impossible to find without the satellite view she had matched to a map. The roads in and out were more like overgrown rutted tracks, and the nearest freeway was miles away.

Northern Minnesota looked just like Northern Wisconsin— same vegetation, same lakes and streams and channels, and same innumerable lake cottages and resorts. This place was large enough to be a fancy-ass resort, but it was so out of the way one could only stumble on it or zero in as she had done. It was more like some reclusive celebrity's crib.

But the human remains spread out over the forest that wrapped around the installation reminded her these folks didn't play nice.

Well, neither do I.

She left her car several miles away, stripped, and went in after a particularly enjoyable change. She'd always felt orgasmic when changing, and loved the feeling. She figured Lupo never felt that way, which explained why he was such a whiny boy. Well, he'd met his whiny girl match, hadn't he?

Here's Heather, doing your job for you.

She had no real moral stake in this fight, but she loved a good story, loved an adventure, and loved devouring human prey. Sometimes these things aligned and she did something that was less than evil.

But evil suited her just fine.

She literally stumbled on a patrol of two armed humans, surprised them, and had one's stomach slit open and the other's throat ripped out with her jaws before they could even raise their rifles. As it turned out, one had silver loads and she had to keep her distance, but the sentries were both dead.

She moved on, the house looming up over the trees.

It did look like some sort of alien craft, but it had human-style antenna and radar pods sticking out of it.

Overconfident.

This Wolfclaw group—couldn't they come up with some *original* monikers?—was clearly decadent and self-important. They'd left humans to guard the place, and humans were no match for *her.*

She dispatched two more patrols, the blood singing in her throat, happy when her fangs could tear some tidbit from each corpse. And soon she was close enough to spot the rear door.

There was a single bored-looking sentry, and she was upon him long before he could raise an alarm.

She changed back to her human form, never worried about her nakedness, and used a key card she found in the dead guy's possession to open the door.

As soon as the door swung open, she changed and leaped in on all fours...

And found herself in a cage with silver-lined bars.

She screamed a half-howl and collapsed, flashing back and forth from wolf to human as her body fought against the effects of the silver all around her.

She felt as if a hundred needle-point flames had been turned on her skin, burning through layers of fat and muscle and boiling the blood in her veins. Then a sharp object pierced her skin and in seconds the pain was joined by something else.

She howled again, long and loud, knowing beyond a shadow of a doubt that *this* was the most pain she had ever felt. She regained her human form.

Then she blacked out.

Chapter Thirty-Eight

Bastone

He paced the den, which was almost like a library because there was a wall of bookshelves. They were bare, of course, but he would do something about that. Eventually.

Right now, he paced because he wasn't really sure what to do.

Deuce was holding a nickel-plated Beretta 92F on their visitor, and she was something else.

He admired her from behind a hard-eyed squint.

She was magnificent. Sure, she was a bit older than the showgirls he usually preferred, but she looked like a showgirl who had taken great care of herself and moved to the woods. She wasn't wearing much makeup, but he saw a lot of potential there. She had a model's face and body. Her features were magazine quality.

What the fuck was she doing here, in Fuckville?

And what the fuck was she doing here, at his house—*his fucking house!*—with a loaded shotgun?

Rabbioso was leaning against a wall, a relaxed pose, watching.

"So what's her story?" Bastone asked him.

"She's the reservation doctor, boss. I mean Gus."

Bastone glared at him.

"She's more than what she appears. She was in Grey Hawk's office telling him she knew about us coming in."

"She's the one?"

"Yeah, I guess she overheard Johnny and Marty shooting off their mouths in the casino…"

"The fuck, what are the odds?"

"Truth is stranger than fiction," Deuce interjected.

"Shut the fuck up," Bastone said. "Just hold the fuckin' gun."

"You'll have to let me go, you know," said the doctor. She didn't seem afraid at all. "There are people who know where I am, and if I'm missing too long, they'll come looking. And I'm guessing you don't have much in the way of a plan yet, and you can't afford to call attention to yourself."

"Keep talkin', Red, I *really* like your voice. You got some mouth on you." He leered.

Now she did shudder visibly.

Don Bastone did not like the implied disrespect. Not at all.

He licked his lips obscenely.

"I like your voice and your mouth, but I absolutely love your ass," the Don said, just to needle her. He figured she'd cower and break down and start spouting all the information he thought he needed.

But she didn't.

Instead she laughed.

Big mistake.

Heather

She awoke, her limbs feeling leaden, and her stomach turned suddenly and she retched up globs of bloody meat. Her throat was on fire and her chest throbbed, and the pit of her stomach felt like an acid bomb had been detonated inside its walls.

"Oh, *fuck!*" she gasped when she could formulate a word. Blood dribbled from the corner of her mouth. *Her* blood.

She felt the healing starting, but slowly—very slowly indeed.

She forced herself to her knees, unsteadily, and let her head hang like that until she was more or less certain it wouldn't fall off.

"You don't know what happened to you, do you?" The voice was electronically enhanced and unrecognizable. The tone was monotonous, robotic.

She flipped out a middle-finger salute. Then gargled up more blood.

The voice chuckled. The sound was chilling.

"Wolfsbane, my dear. First I dosed you with a dart, and then I force-fed you our own concoction of two strains of *Aconitum*. Your guts should feel like shit for quite a while, until you manage to pass or vomit it all out of your system. But by then you'll have other problems."

"*Fuck you,*" Heather croaked through her ruined throat. "Fucking fuck."

"Oh my, I'd have thought an accomplished television personality such as you could do better than that."

Her head was spinning, but she felt the effects of the poison herb lessening. Her family had always bragged of an ironclad stomach—maybe she'd continued the trait into her werewolf-hood.

She made a huge effort and managed to get to her feet, though unsteadily. She tottered, but slowly straightened.

"I *am* impressed," said the voice. "You are tougher than some of my male wolves. Too bad it won't help you."

Jessie

She hadn't meant to laugh. It was more of a nervous laugh, not a mocking one. But the self-styled Don was clearly sensitive to mockery. He was so dapper, even here in the woods, he just had to have an inferiority complex of some sort.

So when she laughed, he rushed up to her and cuffed her across the face.

Hard.

She thought she felt something snap in her nose, and a dribble of hot blood touched her upper lip and crossed it, heading downward.

"No one laughs at me," he said with a growl, getting into her face. "No one. I don't care if you're curing cancer up here in the fuckin' wilderness. Got it?" He drew a small but more than adequate pistol and pointed it at her.

She nodded, holding her nose and checking for damage and more blood.

She was lucky.

For now.

But she suddenly realized that Nick had been right.

Damn him.

He'd been right that these guys were dangerous. Big money was involved. They didn't take kindly to being thwarted. *Or to being mocked.*

She felt his eyes rove over her entire body.

He raised an eyebrow. "You can make it up to me right now. It's all up to you what happens next."

She tried to keep herself from trembling, but a shudder worked through her anyway. She was cold suddenly and hugged herself.

The Don paced. "Robb, get Johnny and his briefcase, would you? I think we may need to convince her to talk to us about just what she said to who. *Whom.* Whatever." Rabbioso gave her a brief apologetic glance, nodded and left the room.

"Hey, Deuce, you get out too. I want some privacy for the lady." The thug looked surprised. Bastone waved the gun. "I got this. Go check the doors or something. Take a half hour." The thug obeyed, and then it was just the two of them.

Jessie had some idea what he was planning, and she pledged to herself that she would make a run for it if she had the chance.

Maybe all she needed was to stall. She'd been out of touch long enough to worry a few people, at the hospital and elsewhere.

Was Nick on his way?

She had counted seven or eight goons. If Nick was coming, would he spring a trap being set for him?

Not if she could help it.

While they waited for the apparent torturer, Jessie observed this Bastone character carefully.

And she just knew, instinctively, that he would turn to sexual violence. What *he* didn't know was that she had learned to defend herself out of necessity, because her association with Nick Lupo had led an assortment of monstrous humans right to her.

She fell to her knees.

Bastone stood over her, surprise splashed across his face which changed to delight.

She gave him ideas.

Chapter Thirty-Nine

Lansing

He was one of the super-wolves, as they referred to themselves, those who had been genetically engineered to reduce silver's effect on them. The Nazi experimenters had done the majority of the work, and the idiot Schlosser, the CEO of Wolfpaw, had surrounded himself with a team that had finished it.

Silver affected Lansing less.

Much less.

Which was why he was able to lie above the captured female werewolf—the reporter, wasn't she? The one who had received the stolen data?—while she was chained across a Roman-style ritual settee on her stomach, her hands and feet restrained by silver-lined bracelets that had to be scorching her and hurting like hell, without actually feeling all that much discomfort himself. Nothing more than a pinching-tingling, anyway.

The woman called Heather came out of her blackout right when he forced his engorged flesh between her buttocks.

She screamed and he pushed harder, expecting the pain to become intolerable as he tore into her nether regions with the abandon he usually reserved for a hunt, or a battlefield action.

His thrusts should have had her damn near fainting, but suddenly he realized that her screaming had started to change in tone.

She was enjoying *his brutal invasion.*

Clearly she was still in pain from the silver bracelets, and the skin all over her body bore the scorch marks of the silver restraints and cage she had occupied for hours.

But as far as he was concerned, what he was doing to her should have hurt and humiliated her beyond belief, yet here she was, moving under him like a willing participant.

He was momentarily grateful none of his fellow generals were in attendance. He had dispatched them to the other facility, after leaving a skeleton crew here. His anger flared and he increased his pace, slamming violently against her back, forcing her submission—

He paused, flabbergasted.

She was laughing.

She was laughing at his futile effort to torture her. A tortured captive, suffering unbearable pain, and yet she could laugh.

She was laughing at *him*.

"You're pathetic," she said, her tone mocking even though her voice was cracked and breaking up because she *had* to be suffering.

Lansing lost his head. He forced a change and his DNA realigned in that split-second and suddenly a black wolf was where he had been moments before, sharp fangs going for her neck even as he continued brutally mounting her with his radically altered anatomy.

And in the next moment—while her torturer was engaged in his own hate—she also forced a change, which altered her shape sufficiently and allowed her to tear through portions of her own wrists, which had now become forepaws, so she could slip out of the upper bracelets.

Lansing, or the wolf that had been Lansing, was crazed with hate and lust and did not fully realize what she had done until she managed to perform a half-flip underneath his rutting body, surprising him by going for his eyes.

Her fangs ripped through the top of his lupine head and tore out his eyeballs in a double shower of gore.

Heather

The general's screeches were cut short as Heather's snapping snout grasped the older wolf's throat and first crushed, then demolished it, causing a great gush of arterial blood to wash over them both.

Though still chained by the rear paws, Heather's mutilated wolf body continued to bite and tear until Lansing's lay still.

The pain was immeasurable, but Heather Wilson had already suffered the worst the Vatican blade could do—*thanks to the Jessie-bitch*—and she had survived.

She damned well could survive *this*.

She knew Lansing would start healing if she didn't finish the gruesome task she had set herself.

So she scrabbled from underneath his dying body and rapidly gnawed through her own hind legs, enough to also slip those bonds. The silver in the bracelets burned her snout like hellfire, but she was determined to survive this motherfucker. Her brain was overloaded with pain messages from all those mutilated spots on her body, but she was stubborn and willing to do anything to cling to life.

There was always the magical healing. Once again, she was counting on the healing.

With a mental scream, she ripped into her own body and chewed her own flesh. She hoped she wouldn't pass out.

The inhuman screeching of her bones, skin, and muscle united to cloud her thinking.

But once free, though nearly fatally wounded herself, she was able to drag her body off the settee and away from the blasted silver, where she could begin healing. She dragged her attacker closer, then buried her grotesquely wounded snout into his belly and ripped through his flesh until she was nearly drowning in his bloody entrails.

When he barely resembled a once-living being, she crawled away from him and gathered herself in a corner, mewling from the pain that lanced at her brain from a thousand wounds, each worse than the other. She curled into a bloody ball and forced her body to begin healing, wondering whether she'd manage to recover enough to find her way out of this hellhole.

"Fuck you," she spat, but it was a hallucination because she was still in wolf form, and her snout could barely have formed a whimper let alone words.

Heather's consciousness blinked in and out. And then just *out.*

Chapter Forty

Lupo

"Goddamn it, Dee, what the fuck are you doing?"

His earpiece was silent except for a continuous hissing. What had happened to DiSanto and Colgrave?

"What's going on there?"

Hisssssssss.

"Maybe they're being jammed. That place looked like a techie's wet dream in those photos."

Charlie was nearly invisible beside him in the evergreen undergrowth that spread across the rear of the Bastone house. The red and white pine trunks that dotted the area around them and a stand of black spruce created a natural camouflage into which their black BDUs effectively disappeared. Their faces were covered by night-vision goggles.

They'd driven at speed in Lupo's rented Mustang. He'd armed the car with a portable lightbar and used it extravagantly. He'd also called a connection at State Police headquarters who had agreed to alert patrols his friend Lupo was on the job and to let him pass unhindered. Yeah, this would come back to bite him. He imagined the DHS guy, Hart-Bart or whatever, getting a call next. Lupo was used to working on the edge, but this was ridiculous even for him. Who did he think he was, Lucas Davenport?

Ghost Sam had hovered in the backseat, a grim expression on his permanently lined face. Lupo saw him in his mirror but said nothing. And by then Charlie was squeezed and folded into the passenger seat after being picked up. He'd helped by checking local realtors and had made a list of several large mansions sold recently. They'd crossed off three and the fourth had been the obvious one.

He checked his watch. Time was running out. Had they cut things too close?

Still nothing but a hiss in his ears.

Lupo grunted. It was possible DiSanto and Colgrave were trying to get out a signal from across the western Wisconsin border, but couldn't. He was almost shaking with rage. Things were getting out of control—no, had been out of control almost from the start. Right from when Heather had shared the contents of that drive, damn her to hell. Now he didn't even know where she was.

But he knew where Jessie was, and there wasn't all that much time to get her back safe.

He thought about what they'd likely done to Bill Grey Hawk. Inquiries had come up empty. Who knew how many body parts had been dispersed?

No, they were too serious to have deemed her involvement as anything but dangerous.

Maybe it's already too late.

Shut the fuck up.

He tried to keep tears out of his eyes. Like the song said, he made a stone of his heart.

There was work to do.

Jessie

She knew she presented too much temptation for Bastone while on her knees. Her eyes were closed but she sensed he was stalking closer.

She felt the gun muzzle on her forehead, a cold circle that chilled her blood.

"Just like that," he said, his voice cracking. "*Stay just like that.*"

Jessie didn't know much about him, but waves of undiagnosed sexual addiction seemed to wash off him like liquid grease.

She shuddered.

She heard his clothes rustle. She could smell him. His breath ruffled her hair.

No, he isn't really!

She squinted and saw enough.

His pistol in one hand, he was struggling to loosen his pants with the other.

So much for that romantic, dashing look he affected in his clothing. Somehow she knew that even his henchman, the safari-dressing not-Bruce, wasn't *this* crass.

But she'd had enough of men at the moment, and instead of being frightened she sensed she'd been emboldened.

Riding a wave of surging adrenaline, Jessie went for his open fly and his gun hand simultaneously, reaching in for his groin and grabbing whatever she could with strength and authority.

As Bastone squealed in hurt surprise, her other hand wrestled his pistol away, and she was up and still squeezing him with all her strength and shoving him into the wall of empty bookshelves. The back of his head smacked loudly into the edge of a pine shelf and he went down in a heap. She released his mushy genitals as he fell and ended up with the gun.

The door opened and the slick-haired thug, Johnny, entered with his briefcase in hand, and dropped his jaw as he faced the steady muzzle of Bastone's gun which Jessie now held.

"Stop right there," she said, her voice quavering more than she wanted it to.

The catch in her voice must have given him the wrong impression, because he smiled widely...

And went for a shoulder holster under his jacket.

"No!" she shouted, but it was too late. She saw his hand come back out with some kind of black handgun and he was bringing it up when she fired.

Bastone's gun was a hammerless snubnose 5-shot .357 Magnum, small but powerful, and Jessie was a crack shot. The bullet took the thug high in the chest and flipped him into the wall, where he slid on exit-wound blood and lay still. Blood also seeped through his clothing with amazing speed.

Jessie's first reaction was the urge to cry. Really, as a doctor she wanted to help people.

But he'd gone for his weapon and she'd seen and been through too much to let some two-bit thug get the drop on her. She realized, a little sadly, that Nick had rubbed off on her.

Bastone was groaning in the corner, blood streaming from his head wound, rolling around and holding his groin.

The gunshot had been a *bad thing*.

There was a commotion out in the hall. Not knowing how many thugs were out there, rushing toward the den, Jessie only had one option. She unlocked the French doors and found herself on the sprawling deck, from which a staircase led down to the ground. Gun in hand, she made for the nearby jagged line of dark woods.

She ran.

When someone opened a window and took pot shots at her, she turned and fired back once, hoping to pin them down. With three rounds left in her cylinder, she reached the trees and melted into the forest.

Behind her, shouting and running footsteps.

Ahead of her, perhaps survival.

DiSanto

"We're cut off, I can't hear Lupo anymore." He was whispering in Colgrave's ear flesh to flesh—and it was a very *nice* ear, but he held his erotic thoughts at bay, or any jokes he might have based on them.

"Christ, now what?" Colgrave looked around as if she could spot the problem, her goggles making her resemble some kind of sensual android.

Earlier she'd pointed out an array of aerials and radio towers protruding from a corner of the building, and a radar dome. He didn't say so, but the thought hit him that maybe their comm units were being jammed.

"I dunno," DiSanto said, scraping his scalp beneath the itchy black watch cap that helped make him nearly invisible in the intense Minnesota night. There was no moon and it was cloudy, and they were far from city lights in any direction.

Thanks to Google Earth, their approach had been easy enough, on ATVs to a distance of two miles away, and then they'd packed in the rest of the way, through the thick woods. They had taken their time, had spotted and avoided dozens of cameras, but God only knew how many they hadn't seen at all. Thing was, the cameras they did see had appeared dead.

How likely was that? They'd looked at each other and shrugged.

Plus Nick had reiterated that if these guys were all werewolves, they might look upon an attempted raid as a training exercise. *Release the hounds.* He'd explained how the Wolfpaw compound in Georgia had been a training ground and they'd specifically released prisoners just to hunt them down. The thought would have given DiSanto shivers, except he was beyond that point because on the way in they'd come across remains that bore witness to the likelihood that the same practice applied here.

More than once.

Colgrave had been horrified at the first grouping of remains, but by the third pile of gnawed bones a grim look had washed over her face, making it seem rock-hard in the gloom. Whatever had happened to *her* in life had already turned her to stone.

DiSanto couldn't help wondering about her. What made her so willing to go off the books?

He could barely believe all Lupo had had to do was ask, and she'd willingly risked her career for somebody she didn't even know. On the other hand, she seemed to relish the commando stuff and he wondered again what else she'd been involved in that made this little foray into illegal demolition seem not so much strange as eccentric.

DiSanto patted the sheathed Vatican dagger on his belt strap. Colgrave had eyed it uncertainly, and DiSanto hadn't offered an explanation. She also hadn't been told they had filled her MP5 and Glock magazines with silver-loaded ammo. Better to protect her without risking her faith in them.

DiSanto wished they'd opted for more body armor, but they were wearing the latest Dragon Skin thanks to a CIA connection of hers. She'd borrowed one for Lupo, too, but DiSanto would have bet his partner wasn't wearing it. Being a werewolf was like wearing "Kevlar from God," Lupo had once told him, back when Kevlar was *the* thing.

The composition of the woods surrounding the high-tech cantilever house was an almost identical twin to that near Eagle River, with a high concentration of conifers interspersed with elm, ash, and poplar, most still winter-bare. The Superior National Forest was next door, but this property wasn't on any detailed map. Only the satellite view proved it existed at all, and then only if you knew where to look.

"Maybe some kind of jamming device?" DiSanto ventured. Now that he thought about it, the quiet was downright eerie. He'd expected patrols made up of werewolves. He'd had waking nightmares about it.

"I thought the same thing. They sure seem to be set up for it, based on all that antenna crap." Colgrave idly scratched a nonexistent itch. "No fence or anything, though? Isn't that weird for people you'd think would want their privacy?"

DiSanto shrugged. How could you tell someone about werewolves and how they wouldn't be needing normal protection and expect her to believe it? Hell, *he* wouldn't have believed it. Not if he hadn't been shown. He was something of a Thomas, the disciple who'd had to stick his hands in Christ's wounds to believe. So the story went, anyway.

"Well…no guts, no glory," DiSanto muttered, not having to dig too deep into his bag of clichés.

"That's original." Colgrave grinned.

"Fuck off. Let's get closer—it's what we came for."

Colgrave patted her pack full of thermite and C4 charges. "I thought *this* was what we came for."

DiSanto had to grin again. He was carrying a similar load, along with doctored magazines for both his Glock and MP5. Never in a million years had he expected to be doing this kind of thing, not as a cop. But then, he wasn't really acting as a cop now, was he?

There went *his* career. His mother would be proud. She'd wanted a priest in the family.

Right now, he felt an underlying shame he could barely put into words. But he hoped helping kill the bad guys would reverse his negative karma, or give his soul a good wash and rinse.

Jesus, what the hell have I done?

Then he did what he'd been doing and put Heather Wilson out of his thoughts.

Carefully they wended their way closer to the house, which had started out appearing small and square, but suddenly it seemed to widen in their view, and its cantilever portion now hovered over them like the lower deck of an alien mothership. They were only yards from the rear of the house, where they could make out a door. They waited in the cover of the tree line and DiSanto tried again to make contact with Lupo.

He kept expecting the door to swing open downwards and a batch of alien grays to come storming out, looking for earthlings to probe.

Hell, was that any weirder than what was actually going on?

He rattled his comm gear again. They'd had good reason to try to synchronize their attacks.

Now what, Nick? What the fuck you want us to do?

Chapter Forty-One

Lupo

"What do you know about this Bastone asshole?"

Lupo shrugged. "Not a whole lot." He told Charlie most of it in about a minute. "He sounds like a joke, really, a guy who wants to live in his grandfather's time. Plus I think he has an addiction problem."

"Drugs?"

"Sex. So they say. He's a cartoon, maybe. It's his enforcer I'm most worried about, this Rabbioso. I had Colgrave use her contacts to look him up. He was a soldier—a good one—and then he became a security contractor—a bad one—and it almost seems like two different people. He's supposedly a likeable, good-looking guy who enjoys killing people in various not-funny ways. Bodies disappear."

"Let's get this over with," Charlie said, echoing Lupo's thoughts.

He checked his watch. He hoped DiSanto remembered to do the same.

The comm being down or jammed was not good, but they'd planned to base their actions on timing. They were ostensibly in position, so there was no turning back. They'd figured

Bastone hadn't had time to stock up with muscle, but they couldn't be sure.

Lupo had mumbled something about not taking any prisoners, and Charlie was fine with that.

Cold as it was, they had come in on two borrowed Bozeman single-seat hunter's pontoon boats, paddling quietly across the fortunately calm lake and finally beaching onto the comma-shaped sandy stretch that was separated from the rear of the house by the stand of bare woods. They'd avoided the single path that connected house to beach. Then they had watched at length and finally spotted a glow where one of Bastone's guards paced the rear deck, a two-tier affair that led to several sets of French doors set into the back of the house.

While they surveilled, Lupo turned his face to the darkening sky and looked up. Stars were becoming distinct, swirls of the Milky Way reminding him how far he was from city lights. He stared upward, until his neck hurt. He saw a few shooting stars zipping across the wide canvas of the sky.

He hoped he was right.

He had to be right.

Now they crept up to the deck stairs from the near side, knowing the smoking sentry was almost immediately above them, puffing in the dark.

Lupo unslung a cocked Stryker compound crossbow and nocked a hunting-tip bolt into the breech. There was no room for error, but he'd been practicing. Jessie had insisted—long ago she'd used her father's crossbow in a critical situation. Lupo had taken to it easily, especially after the Archer case.

He used the infrared telescopic sight to line up the smoker's silhouette. The guy was huddled in a medium-weight parka, leaning up against the railing and staring off into space.

Lupo repositioned his crosshairs so they met over the thug's enhanced shape, then gently squeezed the trigger.

The bolt shot out and buried itself in the guy's back, the missile's velocity just about flipping him over. He went down without a whimper, though the double *thump* of his boots hitting the deck sounded unnaturally loud.

Lupo grimaced, waiting.

Nothing but breeze through the trees.

He nodded at Charlie and reloaded using the bow's stirrup, then approached the bottom of the stairs under cover of Charlie's suppressed MP5. Even though the strong breeze broke the quiet, the submachine gun's suppressed reports would still be too loud. Hence the crossbow. They'd only break the rule when they had no choice.

Lupo crept up the steps, hugging one side to avoid creaking, checked the windows and doors with a glance, then leaned over the thug he'd harpooned and felt for a pulse. There was none. He put out the guy's smoldering cigarette before it sparked a fire, then hung his head over the railing and waved Charlie up.

Once they were both on the deck, they checked the doors but all were locked from the inside. The deck wrapped around to the side and front of the house, so they hugged the shadows and worked their way along the planks.

That was when Lupo heard a familiar high-pitched insect-like buzzing that appeared to be rising from beyond the tree line, over the beach.

He'd been expecting it.

Then there was single gunshot from inside the house, and moments later there were surprised shouts as well.

A few ticks later two more gunshots rang out, farther from the house but on the side opposite of them.

What the fuck?

Lupo only had time to think the words before all hell broke loose.

Jessie

She ran, her feet sure under her, slapping too noisily on the vegetation's winter debris that covered the ground.

She slipped from shadow pocket to pocket, knowing she could be picked out by the flash of her clothing, by the snapping of twigs, by the sound of her breath hitching in her throat.

She had three rounds left, and she could make them count.

The problem was that she'd lost track of where the hell she was, and the night's shadows hindered as well as helped. She could imagine smacking her face on a tree trunk. Her nose throbbed painfully where Bastone had struck her, and she tasted a tendril of blood. She prayed not to trip, and tried to keep the sky's last light on her same side so she wouldn't run in circles. The noise she made she couldn't help much.

Aiming for a pocket of darkness, she hit a bog or shallow creek and slid like a baseball player heading home, except she hadn't intended to slide and she felt something rip in her right leg.

Oh God, no!

She rolled over in the muddy patch and got to her knees, and when she stood she saw them, two of the thugs, converging on her from the very dark patch she had hoped would shelter her.

She raised her hand and brought the gun to bear and got off one shot, which might well have hit one of the thugs, but the next trigger pull produced nothing. Even in the dark she could see that its cylinder was fouled with mud and twigs.

Desperate, she ignored the danger and pulled the trigger again and again, but it was no good, the gun was useless. Or even dangerous to her.

She tried to throw it at them, but they were upon her. They grabbed her roughly between them and threw her against a pine, knocking the wind out of her with a *whoosh*.

"Fuck, Manny, the bitch shot me!"

"Ah, it's just a scratch."

"Fuck you, man."

Jessie leaned on the pine, winded, hurting. Her face, her leg, her lungs. She was done.

She'd been so busy running, she hadn't heard the insect-like buzzing sound that suddenly echoed all around the woods, like cicadas on steroids she thought now.

But she had bigger problems. The wounded thug wanted to drag her back to the house, but the other one made clear what he wanted when he put his gun to her head and started to rip open her shirt.

The annoying buzzing increased its volume and seemed to spread out overhead. Then it was as if a cloud of large insects were heading for the house.

Then a quiet, deep voice from nearby said, *"Let her go."*

Rabbioso

He had no idea what the damned insects were up to here in the woods. He knew what night sounds were like in the desert, but this was a new one to him. It sounded like an electric cicada convention. *But much louder.*

He'd tracked the good doctor and almost had her when those two idiots had somehow cut her off, and now they were about to finish what the fucking Don had started.

For whatever reason, he felt his duty was to stop them. There was something about her…

When he said, "Let her go," he was stripping off his safari shirt, loosening his trousers. His feet were already bare.

When they spotted him — in the twilight he'd been invisible while clothed until his lighter bare skin lit up like a lantern — they hesitated.

Not only was he Don Bastone's lieutenant and enforcer, but it looked as though he was standing in front of them now completely naked.

In fact, they had to see clearly—now that he stood only a few feet away from them (not quite in front of Dr. Hawkins)—that he was sporting the biggest boner either of them could have imagined.

"What the fuckin'—"

Moments later Rabbioso was gone and the oversize black wolf that had taken his place growled as he lunged at the two startled goons.

Chapter Forty-Two

Colgrave

She felt helpless, lost, and more than a little miffed at the ease with which she'd succumbed to their pitch. This fiasco could mean her career.

Again.

Hell, it could mean prison.

She'd done it before, she was a fool for lost causes, or maybe she could admit having developed a little thing for Nick Lupo. His partner was cute, all youthful puppy energy and good looks, but he was married and he seemed decidedly unhappy. Colgrave knew she was overly serious and couldn't see herself with anyone who was unhappy, but also unserious.

But at the heart of her involvement was the belief that something wrong was being done, some evil was being perpetrated. The evidence was convincing, and her quiet inquiries through her friend Brant had rung alarm bells. She wondered if she'd been marked, if a flag had been raised right over her. A flag with a target.

DiSanto was frustrated with the lack of comm. But they'd predicted the possibility. She checked her watch. They were five minutes out from what they'd agreed with Lupo they would do simultaneously.

"Forget the comm," she whispered. "We've got five to go. The place seems quiet, so they're not expecting us."

"That's what worries me," DiSanto said. "There should be all kinds of security. This looks like leaving the back door open intentionally."

"Just because they have a shitload of resources doesn't mean they're not also overconfident. In my experience, just when you think you've run into an intelligent criminal, he surprises the hell out of you with his stupidity."

"I've noticed the same about cops," he said, grinning.

She punched him.

"Seriously, let's get this over with. Or I'm gonna back out."

"No way, we promised Nick."

"Yeah."

She pulled one of the thermite charges out of her backpack. It paid to have connections. Lupo had said, *Jesus, we sure came to the right person!* when he'd seen what she'd provided them with, including the Dragon Skin. She'd been lucky, Brant was in town. And he owed her. He'd paid off on the debt gleefully, almost regretful he wasn't included. At his age, he should have been on a shuffleboard court.

Now they scuttled up to the rear wall and the ominous door, crouched out of sight of the blank-eyed windows, and she armed the detonator. She attached the charge to the door, directly over the plate where the lock would be.

Thermite doesn't explode, it burns. *Hot.*

They flattened themselves against the wall on either side of the door and when the charge ignited the intense heat, the pyrotechnic device burned through the metal like a huge Fourth of July sparkler.

Then DiSanto kicked in the door.

DiSanto

They burst in, guns waving, but the oversize mudroom they were in and the sterile hallways outside it were eerily empty.

Following the blueprints that Wineacre dude had managed to obtain and include in the flash drive, they made their way through the maze. It reminded DiSanto of the halls at *U.N.C.L.E.* headquarters in the old television spy show. Every corridor looked the same. Doors were set at various intervals, but no one seemed to be eager to investigate the noise of their dramatic entrance.

Both DiSanto and Colgrave had trained for armed raids, so they were able to work their way toward the center of the complex's main floor using the standard approach, covering each other as they leapfrogged past doorways.

What had happened? Was this a trap?

Occasionally DiSanto jiggled a doorknob, but they all seemed to be locked.

There was no one home.

They continued toward the large room Wineacre had identified as the control room, where apparently the remote pilots flew the killer drones that Wolfclaw had developed.

Every other corner, or wherever they spotted a structural pillar, one of them placed a C4 charge. They both carried burner phone detonators.

"Someone tipped them off," whispered Colgrave.

"Or they planned to evacuate anyway, for some reason."

"The control room should be ahead, not far."

Then they heard a whimpering that came from an open doorway ahead.

Heather

The healing was slow, but she could feel the regenerative properties of the werewolf gene rearranging DNA strands and doing their magic on her organs and body.

Pain still jabbed through her nervous system, short-circuiting her thought process, but she maintained her wolf form in order to continue healing.

Through the haze of her pain, she wondered why no one else had come to that monster's aid. What had happened? Were they alone here in the huge complex?

She continued to heal, but the pain was blinding and she continued to whimper.

When the door opened she tried to gather herself for one last leap, imagining that a hit squad or Alpha team had finally arrived to kill her. Her extremities were still regenerating, growing faster now. She'd always been a fast healer, and perhaps that genetic quality had attached itself to the werewolf mutation. She was still feeling excruciating pain all over her body, but her thoughts were clearing.

She prepared for one last stand, growling at her new attackers.

And when she spotted a body-armored DiSanto coming in low, a submachine gun in his hands, she thought she'd lost her mind.

Another armored cop or soldier followed, offering cover with another stubby machine gun, and this was a woman. Heather recognized her from the precinct.

Forgetting that forcing a change would both slow her healing and also spike the pain that would go shooting through her body, she visualized herself changing and made her DNA realign and in a moment she was staggering to her feet—her mutilated, bloody human feet—and approaching her rescuers like a battle-damaged naked Amazon. The excruciating pain forced her to change again.

The woman cop nearly fainted, lowering her gun at first then swinging it up again, sensing danger...and weirdness. Her finger tightened on the trigger.

DiSanto knocked her gun muzzle up. "She's with us!"

The woman's eyes widened.

Heather was a wolf again, but a wounded one. Panting, she rolled onto her side. Her tongue lolled between her fangs.

DiSanto understood. "She's healing," he said.

His perception surprised her.

And then he dragged the confused woman out of the room.

Colgrave

Her mind was a jumble of disjointed thoughts. One of them was that she'd been drugged and just didn't know it. Another was that she'd been conned.

But she'd smelled the blood and death in the room, the scorched skin, flesh, and fur.

She had to accept...

But I can't accept it...

DiSanto distracted her by waving a C4 charge in her face. "Find the control room," he mouthed. "Everything else later."

She nodded, got herself back together. Covered him as they headed back into the maze.

Chapter Forty-Three

Lupo

The deafening buzzing of insects suddenly resolved itself into the very same sound he'd heard when he and Heather had been attacked by the black drones near his apartment.

He and Charlie were still on the deck, trying to decide whether to enter the house or not, when the unseen drones apparently reached the structure and circled it. Lupo thought he'd spotted one, a sort of saucer-shaped craft with four helicopter rotors, but they were quick-moving, like weaponized hummingbirds.

Lupo could almost feel the targeting equipment, the software, comparing his infra-red sensed face with one on a file photo somewhere, computing the similarities and differences and mapping them out to obtain a probability percentage. The GPS coordinates of his location had come by way of a rogue spy satellite, he was sure of it. Heather had described Wineacre as a loser, but there was a lot of incredibly sensitive material buried in his stolen files. The guy could have been another Wikileaks gadfly, if he'd survived.

Lupo thought he felt the sensing equipment mapping his features, comparing, deciding. And then it would release its

Reaper missile, heat-linked to his target coordinates, even if he moved…for it would move with him, tracking him like a heat-seeker.

They were nearly impossible to see, however, in the dark.

At that moment, the nearby French doors burst open and gunfire erupted from inside, where a few thugs took cover and began to hose down the deck with flying lead. Lupo aimed his loaded crossbow and watched the bolt take one of the thugs in the side, flipping him around. The other guy did a double-take, then dropped an empty magazine and reloaded. In that time, Charlie Bear felled him with a burst from his MP5.

Lupo dropped the crossbow and switched to his own MP5 because the thug he'd wounded was firing now, too, taking chunks of railing out from behind them, his aim just slightly off.

If he gets it together, he's got us.

Lupo's first burst caught the thug in the chest and almost cut him in two. He looked like the guy Jessie had described as the slick-haired one she'd overheard.

Jessie!

Where the hell was she?

Jesus, had they killed her already?

More shooters had taken cover inside the house and were pouring out a withering handgun fire, but Charlie's and Lupo's MP5 controlled bursts ate into the drywall and bookcases, destroying cornices and moldings, shattering windows.

Charlie shouted once, "Shit!" and half-sat on the deck, his gun falling silent.

Lupo looked over. A round had taken him below the vest, mangling his thigh.

The stain below him was spreading fast.

Fuck, it had nicked his artery.

Charlie looked at Lupo and shrugged, smiling crookedly. "Gotta go sometime, man!" he shouted.

"No!" Lupo screamed, emptying his MP5's magazine with a long burst that kept the thugs' heads down.

But Charlie was still firing too, drawing their fire away from Lupo.

Lupo reloaded, but then his ears were filled with the renewed insect-like buzzing of the drones, which had circled the house as they hunted his face with their infrared sensors.

And now they'd found him.

The first Reaper missile missed Lupo because he flattened himself, still firing at Bastone's men, who were if nothing else obstinate. The missile may have missed its intended target, but it blew up just as well when it hit the wall inside the den.

Screams indicated what had happened to the gunmen.

A second missile was fired and missed a rolling Lupo, who was trying to get to Charlie so he could apply a tourniquet. Another explosion rocked the house, and flames started to lick upwards inside and out of the shattered windows.

"Hold on," Lupo shouted. "I'm coming!"

"Fuck it, Lupo, I gotta cover you so you can duck out before those fuckin' wasps catch up with you." He emptied another magazine at the house, where someone had started shooting again. He screamed, half-laughing, "This was some helluva plan, Lupo!"

Another missile zoomed past, this time barely missing its target but blasting open a crater between Charlie and Lupo. They could still return fire, but now they were separated. Lupo knew Charlie's life's blood was rapidly seeping out between the deck planks, but there was nothing he could do.

There was an eerie silence for a moment as the fire that was destroying the beautiful house was the only thing they could hear. No one was shooting anymore.

Lupo started to make his way around the jagged crater to aid Charlie, but then they heard growling and screams from the woods just out of sight to the rear of the house.

Jessie...

The only other thug Lupo knew about was that Rabbioso guy, so he had to be wherever Jessie was. *This was bad.* He'd figured on her being in the house.

Lupo looked back at his companion, the dilemma clear on his face.

"Go! Get her back!" Charlie called out, but his voice was weakening. The flames were drowning him out.

Suddenly there was more buzzing—a new wave of drones?

And more shooting. Someone had a shotgun in there. The *booms* echoed over the lake no one could see.

A new Reaper took out the corner of the house he'd almost reached , and Lupo saw Charlie and the thug shotgunner engulfed in a ball of flame.

Charlie kept his finger on the trigger to the end.

Lupo snorted, snot flinging from his nose, his eyes burning from more than just the smoke and cordite.

No time to grieve...

Leaping off the deck, he rolled once as he landed and came up running toward the woods, praying to a very indistinct God that what he'd heard was Jessie—and that he would be in time.

He thought he saw Ghost Sam pointing the way, so he followed the old man's directional and found Jessie besieged by a werewolf.

His instinct was to fight the demon as an equal.

He shucked his clothes as he ran.

Don't be too late, don't be too fucking late...

And then he was *Over.*

Jessie

He'd killed the two thugs who had been out to rape her, tearing out their throats with savage effectiveness.

Now he was standing in front of her, growling, his huge snout full of displayed fangs. He'd backed her into the pine trunk and, even though he had saved her life, she had no reason to think there was any sense of decency to override whatever loyalty her so-called *not-Bruce* might have had to Don Bastone.

She couldn't help remembering how gigantic his erect penis had been before he'd changed and gone after them, a frighteningly surreal image forever burned in her memory.

She wanted to talk him down, but he was close enough that he could almost just open his jaws and snap them over her hands.

His kaleidoscope eyes held hers with intelligent malevolence.

When he growled, his fur shivering, she felt his hot breath on her shaking hands.

Suddenly another black wolf came bounding into her view and leaped onto the lighter-hued wolf, his jaws biting and paws going for the rib-snapping landing that might slow down the other.

Nick!

She recognized Nick's own Creature, his *beast within*, also oversized and quite ferocious.

Oh, Nick…

The arriving black wolf took the other wolf by surprise, but the enemy was experienced and he twisted to take Lupo's lunge on his side, almost harmlessly. His flesh and muscles there were deeply scraped, but otherwise he was unhurt.

Now the two wolves went after each other like vintage Harryhausen stop-action dinosaurs, each taking the offense and winning the round for a few seconds, then relinquishing. Blood bloomed like grotesque flowers on both their bodies as they tortured each other with their vicious jaws and supernaturally sharp claws.

Jessie didn't know what to do.

No gun, no silver ammo, nothing.

She started to hobble away from the dueling wolves, desperate to find some way to help the wolf that had to be Nick.

But her eyes settled on Lupo's clothes, which he'd tossed in a half-pile, probably when he thought he'd be saving her from a human threat. She saw something peeking out from one of his abandoned boots.

One of the Vatican daggers.

She jumped for it, staggering due to the shooting pain in her right leg. She tried to avoid the snapping, growling wolves as they charged each other and tore flesh and fur. They were too busy to see her, but they were working their way back in her direction.

Then Jessie had the dagger firmly in her hand, but she hesitated.

Should she call out to Nick, or wade in?

She unsheathed the ancient weapon, with its uneven silver-coated blade and mysterious runes and symbols carved on the grip, and attempted to lunge in for a slash at Rabbioso. She missed when her leg almost gave out on her. But then she gritted her teeth and forced herself to ignore the pain of whatever had torn in her leg, and slashed again, this time connecting. The blade zipped through the monster's fur and skin. Then she regained her balance and repositioned herself for a thrust, which she executed flawlessly. This one went home, deep.

The wolf howled in extreme agony as Jessie began to needle him with repeated small but highly painful wounds.

Even a super-wolf couldn't easily survive the blade's mystical magic. Though Rabbioso had protected her from the others, he was now engaged in trying to kill her Nick, and she was damned if she'd let him.

Her Nick.

Meanwhile, Lupo forced a change back into his human form, and then—naked, muscles gleaming with sweat and blood—he swept in and plucked the dagger from Jessie's tenuous grip and in one graceful motion dug the blade deeply into the Rabbioso-wolf's side, cutting through bone and tissue and muscle...

The other wolf screamed in pure agony, its sides heaving and its blood running from dozens of burning wounds where silver had entered his system.

Nick too screamed, because the Vatican blade was now too close and out of its protective sheath, so it was also scorching *his* arm and hand, melting his skin like a torch.

The stench of burning human flesh permeated the air.

Behind them, Don Bastone's new house blew up in a series of huge fireballs that lit the night like the sun at noon.

The shockwave knocked them both violently to the ground. Debris rained around them.

When they were able to reopen their eyes painfully, Rabbioso was gone, having stumbled into the woods and disappeared in the shadows. The house was a blazing ruin.

The buzzing reached a peak level and they looked at each other, resigned.

Jessie stifled a groan as her very bones seemed to crack and all at once she collapsed into Nick's arms.

Sudden silence spread across the wooded lot, leaving a vacuum that made their ears pop painfully.

Then...

Together they watched as one by one the drones blew up in midair, their missiles exploding, until a dozen fires were raging on the grounds where the hot debris fell.

Rabbioso

Burning with the liquid fire of the magical silver weapon in his veins and throughout his body, he ran unsteadily on three legs and never looked back.

The explosions behind him were bound to occupy the humans, and this wolf had had it.

Rabbioso ventured more deeply into the woods and searched for a place he could curl up and either begin healing or die—and right then he didn't care which.

As far as he was concerned, he no longer worked for Don Gus.

The late Don Gus?

When he finally collapsed, he was miles away. He needed hours before he could get up again, and even then he staggered like a drunkard.

The fever tipped him over, and he rolled and screamed as the silver blazed through his veins.

He made a vow. *A solemn vow.*

Chapter Forty-Four

DiSanto

When they reached the control room, they didn't need the plans to be certain they'd found it. A row of screens flickered, with a remote pilot seated behind each one, a joystick in one hand and a row of articulated arms bearing tablet devices that provided read-outs and virtual keyboards.

Here there were sentries, several of them, and they opened up with pistols when the door burst open.

Colgrave and DiSanto returned fire with their MP5s, raking the room with bursts that took out pilots and their drone pods.

If any of them were werewolves, at least they were taking deadly silver loads. DiSanto felt no guilt, knowing what the pilots were doing. They went down bloody and didn't get up.

He hoped they were in time.

But several sentries dropped their guns and clothes and turned, lunging after the raiders in their wolf forms.

DiSanto glanced at Colgrave as he drove a new magazine home. Her eyes were wide and glazed, still in shock at what she had witnessed yet again—the whole lycanthropy magic, the DNA near-instant realignment that turned men and women into wolves with inhuman strength. Her gun had fallen silent as she stared at the incredible transformation.

But the wolves were attacking.

"Colgrave!" he shouted. "Shoot the fuckers!"

They stood side by side and provided such withering silver-bullet gunfire that most of the lunging wolves were shot to bits, chunks of flesh exploding off their bodies as the scorching silver slugs dug deeply into their vital organs.

When one wounded wolf reached DiSanto after his magazine had emptied, he calmly unsheathed his Vatican blade and proceeded to carve that remaining monster like a Thanksgiving turkey, slicing into its belly and disemboweling it until it burned from the inside out and flickered back to a scorched human form, the stench of cooked human flesh cloying in their nostrils.

Their guns fell silent and the ejected brass casings stopped rolling around their boots.

Within minutes they had made short work of the drone control center, and DiSanto hoped fervently that the timing had helped Lupo and Charlie—and Jessie, if they'd gotten to her in time.

They planted C4 charges, then backed out through the empty corridors and retrieved Heather Wilson, who had waited for them in the torture room but as a badly wounded human.

Colgrave snapped out of her daze, managed to conquer her shock, and rounded up a coat for Heather to wear. Then they planted the rest of their charges and covered each other's back until they were out of the mostly deserted house.

When they were far enough away, Colgrave took out one of the burner phones and texted the sequence that blew all the C4 charges simultaneously. The place went up in a series of fireballs hundreds of feet high. The shock wave tossed them aside like a hot wind.

"Like the end of a Bond movie," DiSanto muttered, as they watched burning debris fall back to earth like lava bricks in a volcanic eruption. Lupo's old pal Sam Waters would have loved it.

Colgrave went to punch him, but she had no strength left.

Soon they were driving the ATVs back toward the border, where they'd stashed their SUV. Heather groaned and cocooned in the coat.

When the comm units finally worked again, the two teams related their mostly happy outcomes. But it was DiSanto who asked the question they all thought.

"Nick, why were most of the Wolfclaw people out of here? Where did they go, and who tipped them off?"

Lupo growled. "Dee, if you get any fuckin' idea, let me know."

Jessie

After they crossed the water in the pontoon boats, they collapsed on a rocky beach and watched the bruised sky overhead. Far away a glow was visible against the dark purples and browns that swirled above. They hoped volunteers from the Eagle River and rez fire departments would get there before the forest went up, but they were too drained to do anything about it. Presently they dragged themselves up the beach and leaned against a tree trunk as they watched the fire raging across the channel.

"What happened, Nick? How...?"

"It's kind of a miracle it worked, Jess." He let out a half-sob. "I thought I was too late. That bastard was going to kill you."

Angry as she had been, she was once again reminded how he tried to take care of her.

She nodded. She wasn't going to tell him everything. She hated showing weakness, and this time it had been her turn.

Nick made a visible effort to let it go and instead explained concisely the desperate plan he'd concocted—to lead the killer drones to Bastone's compound, where they could rain death from above, theoretically while he himself avoided the crosshairs. He'd figured the technology was good enough to lock in on his satellite-spotted image, but like all technology it could still be out-thought by a human…a *desperate* human. The synchronized raids, he'd hoped, would allow him to use the drones as weapons and the others to destroy the drone command facility before they could reprogram themselves and hunt down their target again. All he had to do was try to avoid the missiles in the meantime. Wineacre had described the technology fairly well, and hidden the information deep in his stolen materials.

She shook her head at the foolhardy risk and the outsized level of optimism he'd had to juggle to even think it could work.

"Hey, I'm a positive kind of guy," he said, chuckling through his fatigue.

She would have laughed, but the shadows that passed over his features stopped her.

He took the call with a new look of unbelieving relief.

"Yeah?" Then he smiled a moment.

The restored communications helped ease the pain of Charlie's death. At least they knew immediately that DiSanto, Colgrave, and Heather had all made it out of the Wolfclaw house. Though they were told Heather was in bad shape. When Nick signed off, they grinned weakly at each other because he'd cut off one of DiSanto's clichés in midsentence.

They stared at each other in silence, a minute passing and then two.

Before they knew it they had melted into each other's arms and let their lips do all their talking for them, albeit silently. And for a while, there was no one else in the world besides them.

Some time later, Jessie raised her head from where she'd been resting it along the curve of his muscular neck. He gently traced the bruise on her face, obvious pain in his eyes.

She laid her hand on his.

"I love you Nick," she said. "Make me a werewolf too."

Chapter Forty-Five

Franco Lupo

December 1945

The Jesuit had managed to leave the ship and return within the hour with Corrado, who appeared to be as angry as he had been the last time Franco had run into him.

"Tranelli tells me you've fucked up one of our operations yet again. Congratulations, now we will not learn what we need to know about this most valuable escape route for the cursed Nazi wolves. *Che testa di cazzo!*"

"You can insult me as long as you want, but right now I am your only chance to get back on track."

"How's that? You don't look like the courier."

"I don't think it will matter, but I'm willing to take a chance. Tranelli tells me you won't risk anyone taking the courier's place."

"The priest had no right to tell you anything. I have a volunteer—me. I will take his place and make the delivery."

"Corrado, we need you here—"

"Shut up, Father."

The priest stomped away. He looked defeated, old, and perhaps a little drunk after all, now.

"Listen to me well, Corrado. I am going to seek out the captain and report my arrival with the package. I will follow his directions, and I will see where they take me. Then I'll get off the ship and report to you. You'll have lost nothing."

"Not true—you still will have cost us the operation."

"They are desperate to get their people out of Europe. Every seaport is bleeding ex-Nazi bastards. I hear things, so I know they're also funneling refugees out of Napoli and Venezia. Let me work on this route, and I'll give you the information as soon as I have it. If they kill me, you're no worse off than you are now."

"Thanks to you," Corrado muttered.

"That may be," Franco spoke patiently. He was used to having his way. By now he had become a wise manipulator of men.

"*Va bene!*" *All right!* "It's done. Wrap up your package and get up to the bridge, if you can find your way." He kicked the courier's remains. "The priest will help me with this garbage."

Franco climbed back up the stairs to the main corridor above, reasoning it led to the crew's quarters. They'd be returning any time now, so it was imperative he fool the captain and get the information he needed now. He found the crew's empty quarters, based on the number of bunks and naked pinups tacked to the bulkhead. Down the corridor was another staircase, which he climbed in order to find himself in a similar corridor above. These cabins were most likely officers and the few passengers that might occasionally travel from port to port in the relative anonymity of a small freighter. Quickly, he checked them. They were empty, but...

He stared at the small stack of valises and trunks in one cabin. Could the person who owned this luggage be the cargo? Could it be a Nazi werewolf? Perhaps the payment delivery was from a third party, an organization. Perhaps Corrado hadn't told him everything.

Since when had Corrado told him anything of importance?

He turned to leave the cabin, but the door opened and two men entered. They froze in their tracks, staring at their visitor.

Franco smiled. "I am the cabin boy," he said in Italian. "I have just brought your luggage. Need anything else?"

The two men stood, their stares turning to smiles.

Cold smiles.

"Franz, I think the captain has provided a snack."

"Indeed. Very thoughtful of him, I dare say."

They were speaking accented Italian so he could understand. Their accents sounded German or Austrian to Franco. He'd heard enough of them to know.

"Thank you, young sire. You didn't bring our bags, as we had them delivered earlier, but you'll provide enough sustenance for tonight."

Franz and his friend were unbuttoning their shirts, still smiling.

Franco smiled too, pretending stupidity. His hand held the Vatican blade behind his back. "Let me help you with that," he said, approaching the two. This confused them and they stopped, perhaps thinking he was about to offer a different kind of service.

By the time he reached them, their surprise had turned to suspicion. Their fingers became claws and their faces went through the loathsome transformation to long, savage snouts full of snapping fangs.

And by then he was drawing the glowing blade, parrying Franz's lunge with the silver edge even as the jaws reached out for him. The blade reached its target before the monster's gaping mouth could come close enough to bite him, and he was grateful for his coat sleeves protecting him from the first swipe of the claws.

The monster's scream cut through his hearing as the blade sliced through the side of its head like a cook's cleaver, turning the monster's flesh to charred gristle and piercing its skull. Franco knocked aside the mortally injured werewolf and pivoted to meet the other, whose jaws were now snapping near his face, its eyes rolling and changing colors like a child's kaleidoscopes.

Franco and the incensed werewolf danced around each other for a moment and then Franco feinted left and the wolf didn't buy the trick, its jaws barely missing snatching his arm. Only Franco's experience allowed him to evade the grip that would tear through his clothing and shred his skin and muscles. He shoved the off balance half-man, half-wolf aside and tried to leap onto its back, but the monster shook him off.

On the cabin floor, right next to where Franco landed, the other werewolf had stopped struggling, its skull sizzling where the magical blade had carved into its brain. It was blurring, its limbs and head returning to their human mask, but it was dead.

The surviving wolf continued its shapeshifting, and the remaining clothing split along its seams as his body altering left him a more lethal four-footed wolf. The animal's glowing red eyes focused on Franco and went right for his throat as he struggled to his knees.

Suddenly the beast's lunge was halted—it was shoved aside and into the bulkhead, its body vibrating as slugs pierced its fur in explosions of blood and bits of bone.

In the cabin doorway stood Corrado, his legs spread wide, a smoking Mauser *broomhandle* pistol gripped in one hand like a duelist, brass raining down around his feet and rattling on the metal floor.

Franco looked at him gratefully, but then made his way to the werewolf, whose shrieks were fading fast. He singed the monster's fur with the Vatican blade, then drew its length across the muscular neck, parting it like butter. Then he stabbed its belly and twisted the length of the blade and slit the beast open.

He turned away as the sizzling and burning of the organs began.

He'd seen enough of this kind of thing, and his nose was already filled with the terrible stench of corrupted flesh going back to hell.

"What the fuck are you doing here?" he growled at Corrado.

"Protecting my investment. Nice silver slugs, no?" After watching both wolves return to their shapes as gutted, ruined humans, Corrado pulled a stripper clip from his pocket and reloaded the open-bolt pistol, stripping a row of cartridges into the box magazine. "You're lucky I had not left yet."

Franco nodded grimly. "Fine! Now get out. I'm going to make the payment. If these two were the cargo, then your work is done."

"We still need to know what the rest of the transaction is."

"What? Somebody pays, the werewolves sail away. Well, not these two. But what else is there?"

Corrado tucked the pistol under his coat. "The courier gets a package back. We need to know what that package contains. Then we might be happy enough to leave you to your little crusade of hate."

"*Va bene!* I will bring you the package the captain gives to me." Franco pushed him toward the door.

"I will be waiting. Send the priest. He'll wait for you down here. He's outside."

"He has the other Vatican blade?"

"Indeed," said Corrado. "Since you left with one of them, we had to go through hell to reacquire the other, and he has guarded it well."

They collected the bodies and stuffed them with little ceremony into two steamer trunks they'd emptied of clothing and coats. Franco spit onto each mutilated corpse before closing and locking the lids.

Bastardi assassini!

After Corrado had left and the priest took up guard duty in the cabin, Franco finally made his way to the bridge. His stomach fluttered. He stood out on the upper deck a few minutes and let some of the sputtering rain wet him down. With his coat buttoned to the top and collar turned up, he appeared to have just arrived when he found the captain on the bridge, holding a hot mug and slurping some kind of dark, fragrant tea.

Franco wasn't sure what to do or say, but he was willing to bet the captain was more in it for the money and there wouldn't be much ceremony. Franco simply walked up, nodded, and handed over the package of cash.

The captain stared at him harshly. "Where is the other one?" he asked in poor Italian.

Franco shrugged. "Maybe dead. They don't tell me."

The captain reflected a few moments, an eyebrow raised in doubt.

Franco gripped his own pistol, a small Beretta M1934 in his coat pocket, in case the captain balked.

They both seemed to hold their breaths. Then the captain sighed, put down his mug and pulled a small packet out of a satchel on the chart table.

"It's nothing to me either," he said. He tossed Franco the packet and stashed the cash in its place.

Franco nodded and started turning away. "What time do you sail?" He had no reason to care, but the captain glanced at his watch and said, "In an hour."

Franco left the bridge without a look back. Down below in the corridor, he stripped open the package and poured out a stream of tiny uncut diamonds. Perhaps from Brazil, he wasn't sure, but he did know that a dozen such stones fetched a huge price on the European black market. There were at least a hundred in the bag.

In the cabin recently occupied by the two illegal *passengers*, Franco pulled out the bag of diamonds and tossed it on one of the bunks.

"What is it?" said Tranelli.

"Well, let's look."

When the priest hunched over the packet, Franco swiped the Beretta across the back of his head once, driving the old man to his knees with a groan.

Coldly, Franco pushed the half-conscious man over onto his side, then quickly pulled rope out of his pockets and bound him hand and foot, relieving him of the second Vatican blade. Then he stuffed a wad of ripped undergarment into his mouth as a gag while making sure he could still breathe.

"Sorry, old man," he muttered.

Later, when the ship's engines increased their thrumming vibration, and the harbor tugs nosed the hull away from the pier, Franco stood at the rail out of sight of the bridge, huddling in his coat.

He wondered about the last-minute passenger whose trunks had been wheeled aboard mere minutes before the gangplank was rolled up. A sullen crew member had trundled a cart to the cabin across from Franco's and a glimpse of pleated skirt and creamy-skin legs at the cabin door told him only part of what he wanted to know.

The priest had stopped struggling against his bonds. Franco now owned a wonderful new wardrobe thanks to the two fugitive Nazis. He was wearing a fancy parka he could never have afforded in his entire life.

The ship was bound for Buenos Aires. Franco wondered what he would find in Argentina, at the end of the journey.

He gripped one of the Vatican blades.

He was willing to bet he would find Nazi werewolves.

And when he did, he would execute them.

The closed door across the corridor called to him. The Vatican blade warmed his hand, and he wondered when he would meet the mysterious passenger.

He had time. The voyage would last three or four weeks.

And there were bound to be other werewolves aboard.

He smiled grimly.

He was just starting.

Aftermath

Lupo

Ryeland had aged a decade in days. He looked tired and rundown, and some of his great size seemed diminished. He had called in Lupo and DiSanto and ranted at them for fifteen minutes straight, mostly about how they'd wanted off the task force and then had also gone AWOL during the department-wide hunt for the bus shooter. Which was a dead end. No leads, hardly any evidence, no motive. Everyone was holding his breath until the next shooting.

"The DHS guys aren't happy with you," he said finally, running out of steam.

DHS hadn't pulled up stakes yet, so there was plenty of shit to look forward to.

"I'm not too fond of them myself," said Lupo. He was tired too, and hurting. "I still don't get what DHS has to do with our shooter. What do they know?"

Ryeland shrugged. "They don't explain themselves. Feds never do, and these are the worst."

DiSanto said nothing. His return from the Minnesota raid had been greeted with less than appreciation at home—his wife was furious and suspicious. Lupo wondered what else had happened out there. Colgrave stubbornly wasn't talking, and DiSanto seemed to have temporarily run out of clichés.

Ryeland said, "Yeah, well, I don't like my cops going off the reservation, I've told you that before. You work for me, for the city, for the people. You're not in business for yourselves. You don't run your own department. This isn't L.A. I need you to use your experience for everybody's benefit, not just your own."

Lupo wanted to nod and agree and step away to call Jessie to make sure she was still all right.

She'd just learned the tribal council wanted her to run in opposition to Treewalker in a special council election, and she was considering it. Lupo hoped she would do it, thinking it would refocus her life and kill her addiction, even if she did have to spend more time in the casino.

Thinking of Jessie made him smile inside.

He'd almost lost her, and he realized how much she meant to him. Losing her would have gutted him as much as one of those damned Vatican blades. Despite their troubles, their bonds were solid and for that he was grateful.

Ryeland's understanding of what had happened up north was primitive, but it would do—the Organized Crime ties had been vetted by Colgrave, and she'd taken responsibility (and some credit) for instigating the so-called probe, which had become an unintentional bloodbath. The cover-up extended to the tribe, who had been able to whitewash what had happened on their border due to some sophisticated crime scene interventions. Apparently a gas leak had destroyed the house and grounds.

Lot of gas leaks lately, Lupo thought.

Maybe now they could get back to policing. At least, he hoped so.

Now instead of insisting on the detectives' agreement and then banishing them to some backwater routine assignment, Ryeland stood and went to open his office door. He waved someone in from the shadows of the hallway.

The guy who stepped inside the cramped office was tall and emaciated thin, with an angular face bearing serious pockmarks and long hair swept back like the scraggly beginnings of a ponytail.

"Detectives, this is Lieutenant Roman, our new head of Internal Affairs."

As they shook hands, Lupo could have sworn he saw Roman's eyes change color. Roman smiled a shark-mouthed smile, showing too many teeth. "Detective, I've read about some of your cases."

Lupo shrugged elaborately.

Roman's smile disappeared. "I'm sure we'll have plenty to talk about."

Uncomfortable silence settled over them.

Lupo stifled a rising growl, hiding it within an answering grunt. Suddenly he felt sure Roman was like him. And just as suddenly he knew Ghost Sam would be warning him about coming trouble on the homicide squad.

Bring it on, he thought.

Shooter

He wore a hoodie that obscured the top half of his face and cast a shadow over the rest. He carried one bag by hand and a backpack slung on one shoulder. He boarded the Amtrak train amidst the bustle of the station and disappeared into the passenger car, just one of dozens who melted into the pre-departure crowd.

Anyone who might have seen his eyes would have been disturbed, so he kept his glance lowered and his shoulders slumped.

In less than a minute, he might as well not have been there at all.

Marla Anders

The messages were very disturbing today.

First she'd put together parts of sentences from several magazines that shouldn't have been spread open, but were. Then there were the library books and their sentence fragments. Last, the magnetic letters on her refrigerator—which she'd purchased to aid in the possible communication—had spelled out several cryptic but highly intriguing phrases.

The fact was, she was more convinced than ever that she needed to talk to Detective Lupo.

She thought she might have a message for him.

Lupo

He was sitting in the dark, feeling every ache in his body.

In his hands he held his MP5 submachine gun.

His elbows rested on the desk and he felt the blotter under them, wondering how recently his father had done the same, rested his arms on the desk.

Lupo had hoped Ghost Sam would keep him company, but the Indian was nowhere to be seen or heard.

Maybe he's had enough.

Lupo was grateful, more grateful than his generally unreligious attitude usually allowed.

He was grateful that Jessie was home safe.

The few mobsters who'd survived the hellfire raid— probably including both Don Bastone and his lieutenant

Rabbioso, if the DNA separation tests were accurate—were on the run, not interested in casino takeovers at the moment. *That* would have to be cleaned up. Time had been bought, but good people had paid the price.

Charlie Bear had paid the ultimate price. Lupo hoped there was something to that afterlife fantasy, because the big guy deserved to be at peace with his family in some version of paradise.

But he doubted it.

DiSanto was going to be fine, but once again knowing Lupo had cost him. And after what he'd told Lupo, there was some question about how fine, how soon.

Colgrave.

Lupo wasn't sure what to think about Colgrave. She hadn't spoken of her experience with the werewolves, whether she accepted what she'd seen. But he'd caught a strong vibe from her, and maybe there was something to worry about. She seemed to have taken to him. And she was magnificent...

But whatever trouble he and Jess might still face, he wasn't ready to give up. Not after everything they'd been through.

Heather? Heather was still Heather. She would land on her feet, like she always did. Once they finished regrowing the chewed-off portions. But he knew firsthand that they would.

And the worst part: Who had warned the occupants of the drone house, and where had they gone to ground? The thought that the group Wineacre had uncovered—the group that called itself *Wolfclaw*—was still out there, still active, and still seeking to fulfill its nefarious agenda...it was almost more than Lupo could handle.

The padlock rattled gently in its hasp. He'd had DiSanto lock him in and leave. *No questions, no lies.*

He stiffened, his heart suddenly pumping blood faster.

His muscles tensed and he grasped the MP5 more tightly, finger brushing the trigger inside its guard. Only a tiny amount of pressure needed. A full magazine. He aimed the bulbous suppressor directly at the sound's source.

Goddamn it, now he would learn who had been dusting — and using — his father's files. Who'd been pulling strings, making Lupo dance from afar.

The storage unit door opened on its oiled hinges. There was a square of light from the hallway, a dark figure standing in it momentarily. The door swung closed behind the figure, then Lupo heard the sound of fingers searching for the light switch.

There was the hiss of inhaled breath as the overhead light revealed Lupo and his submachine gun.

"Surprise," Lupo said. His finger was on the trigger.

An older man stood in the doorway, startled but not terribly surprised at all. He wore khaki pants and a heavy sweater under a blue North Face vest.

"I wondered when you would find me," the older man said.

Lupo detected a slight accent. He said nothing.

They stared at each other for an endless minute. Then the older man spoke again, quietly.

"My name is Corrado, and I knew your father and grandfather."

Lupo felt his head spin. The gun in his hands was suddenly beyond heavy. The muzzle sagged downward.

Besides the impossibility of the moment, something else flared in Lupo's head like a lightning migraine. The blade tucked in Lupo's boot seemed to grow hot next to his skin.

If this was indeed Corrado, he had to be ninety-one or ninety-two.

But he looked barely fifty-five or sixty.

Lupo gripped the MP5 harder and brought it to bear, but even as he did he knew it was the wrong choice.

The overhead light winked out, and Lupo squeezed the trigger.

Meet the Author

W.D. Gagliani is the author of the horror-thrillers *Wolf's Trap* (a finalist for the Bram Stoker Award in 2004), *Wolf's Gambit*, *Wolf's Bluff*, *Wolf's Edge*, *Wolf's Cut*, *Wolf's Blind*, and *Savage Nights*, plus the novellas *Wolf's Deal* and both the original "The Great Belzoni and the Gait of Anubis" and the upcoming Acheron Books version. He has published fiction and nonfiction in numerous anthologies and publications such as *Robert Bloch's Psychos*, *Fearful Fathoms*, *Undead Tales*, *More Monsters From Memphis*, *The Midnighters Club*, *Extremes 3: Terror On The High Seas*, *Extremes 4: Darkest Africa*, and others, and early e-zines such as *Wicked Karnival*, *Horrorfind*, *1000Delights*, *Dark Muse*, and *The Grimoire*. His fiction has garnered six Honorable Mentions in *The Year's Best Fantasy & Horror* (one of which, the story "Starbird," is also part of Amazon's Story Front program). His book reviews and nonfiction articles have been included in *The Milwaukee Journal Sentinel*, *Chizine*, *HorrorWorld*, *Cemetery Dance*, *CD Online*, *The Writer* magazine, *The Scream Factory*,

Science Fiction Chronicle, Flesh & Blood, BookPage, Hellnotes, and many others, plus the books *Thrillers: The 100 Must Reads, They Bite,* and *On Writing Horror.* He is a member of the Horror Writers Association (HWA), the International Thriller Writers (ITW), and the Authors Guild. Additionally, the creative team of **W.D. Gagliani & David Benton** has published fiction in anthologies such as *THE X-FILES: Trust No One, SNAFU: An Anthology of Military Horror, SNAFU: Wolves at the Door, Dark Passions: Hot Blood 13, Zippered Flesh 2, Malpractice, Masters of Unreality,* etc., online venues such as *The Horror Zine, DeadLines* and *SplatterpunkZine,* plus the Amazon Kindle Worlds *Vampire Diaries* tie-in "Voracious in Vegas." Some of their collaborations are available in the collection *Mysteries & Mayhem.*

Contact:

www.wdgagliani.com
www.facebook.com/wdgagliani
Twitter: @WDGagliani

Books and Novellas:

Wolf's Trap
Wolf's Gambit
Wolf's Bluff
Wolf's Edge
Wolf's Cut
Wolf's Blind
Wolf's Deal
Savage Nights
Shadowplays (Tarkus Press; story collection)
Mysteries & Mayhem (Tarkus Press; story collection, *with David Benton*)

I Was a Seventh Grade Monster Hunter (Tarkus Press; Middle Grade, *with David Benton,* as A.G. Kent)

"The Great Belzoni and the Gait of Anubis" (Tarkus Press; novella)

"Jack Daniels and Associates: Hair of the Dog" (Kindle Worlds Novella; A Jack Daniels / Nick Lupo Thriller)

Curious about other Crossroad Press books? Stop by our
website: http://crossroadpress.com
We offer quality writing
in digital, audio, and print formats.

Subscribe to our newsletter on the website homepage and
receive a free eBook.

www.ingramcontent.com/pod-product-compliance
Lightning Source LLC
Chambersburg PA
CBHW030809260626
47169CB00001B/251